Praise for Douglas Skelton's Rebecca Connolly Thriller Series and *A Rattle of Bones*

"If you don't know Skelton, now's the time."
—Ian Rankin

"A master of his craft."
—*Scots Whay Hae*

"Grittily authentic."
—*Sunday Times*

"Among Scotland's top cadre of crime writers."
—*Scotsman*

"A compelling thriller, laced with dark humour."
—*Sunday Post*

"An intriguing Highland mystery peopled with
quirky characters and peppered with wit."
—*Times* Crime Club, Pick of the Week

"A cracking good read."
—Crime Fiction Lover

Praise for *Thunder Bay*, the first Rebecca Connolly Thriller

"Exquisite language, credible characters, and unrelenting suspense—this crime novel has it all. . . . Powerful flashbacks help build to the spectacular conclusion."

—*Publishers Weekly*, starred review

"Imbued with the stark beauty of Scottish island life, this atmospheric mystery pulls us into an exploration of human frailty, family loyalty, and the destructive power of secrets. For readers of Denise Mina or anyone seeking a relatable protagonist and a well-told story."

—*Library Journal*

"A darkly claustrophobic tale set on a remote Scottish island, where secrets and lies and family feuds all lead to murderous consequences. Douglas Skelton's writing always delivers, nowhere more than with *Thunder Bay*."

—Craig Russell, author of *The Devil Aspect*

"The risks Skelton took in creating *Thunder Bay* have paid off in spades."

—*Scotsman*

"Immersive, compelling, and shot through with Skelton's pitch-black humour, *Thunder Bay* will reverberate like the last echoes of a storm long after you read the jaw-dropping climax."

—Neil Broadfoot, author of the MacGregor and Drummond thrillers

"Razor sharp . . . An outstanding piece of crime fiction. Not to be missed."

—Denzil Meyrick, author of the Detective Daley thrillers

"Skelton builds up the suspense before going in for the kill. A particularly gripping thriller."

—*Herald*

"'Skelton [is] a writer who you can't pidgeon-hole or pin down. I, for one, can't wait to see what he gives us next."

—*Scots Whay Hae*

"Digs deeply, focuses closely on the families at the heart of events. The novel follows Rebecca's attempts to understand what being an islander means and her own relationship with the island of Stoirm. I'd say it's [Skelton's] best yet, and I hope there are more to come in this vein."

—*iScot Magazine*

"An evocative, beautiful, and tense tapestry of a read."

— *Live and Deadly*

"Almost everyone on this island is hiding something terrible. . . . It's the type of crime fiction that Irish and Scottish writers do particularly well."

—*Inside Flap*

"A surprisingly gripping read. I had no idea where things were going to end up. . . . Readers looking for something out of the ordinary and atmospheric might like this one."

—*A Bookish Type*

Praise for *The Blood Is Still*, the second Rebecca Connolly Thriller

"Credible, multilayered characters enhance the intricate, high-tension plot. Skelton's growing legion of fans will avidly await brave, dogged Rebecca's next outing."

—*Publishers Weekly*, starred review

"An intricately plotted thriller . . . Lyrical and thoughtful."

—*Library Journal*

"It would be so easy to romp through *The Blood Is Still*—the plot is compelling and the characters are so darn realistic, but I advise you to hold fire and take time to savour some of the gorgeously lyrical prose that's sitting there in among all of the drama."

—*Crime Fiction Lover*

"A corking read."

—*The Scotsman*

"A stand-out thriller."

—Scots Magazine

"Douglas Skelton's writing always delivers."
—Craig Russell, author of The Devil Aspect

"Skelton's intriguing premise keeps you reading avidly to see how he's going to tie it all together and make it work."

—Herald

"Suspenseful . . . Skelton's years as the editor of a local newspaper make for an intrinsic, pitch-black depiction of the competition between the police, the press, and the powers-that-be in the scramble to construct and control narratives."

—Dundee Courier, Scottish Book of the Week

"Once again great characters, we hear more from reporter, Rebecca Connolly and the tension just keeps you on your toes all the way through. It's also full of Douglas Skelton humour too which just makes it a marvellous read!"

—Independent Book Reviews

A RATTLE OF BONES

Also by Douglas Skelton
in the Rebecca Connolly Thriller series

Thunder Bay

The Blood Is Still

A
RATTLE
OF BONES

A REBECCA CONNOLLY THRILLER

DOUGLAS
SKELTON

ARCADE
CRIMEWISE
An Arcade CrimeWise Book

First North American Edition 2022

This is a work of fiction. Names, places, characters, and incidents are either the products of the author's imagination or are used fictitiously.

Arcade Publishing books may be purchased in bulk at special discounts for sales promotion, corporate gifts, fund-raising, or educational purposes. Special editions can also be created to specifications. For details, contact the Special Sales Department, Arcade Publishing, 307 West 36th Street, 11th Floor, New York, NY 10018 or arcade@skyhorsepublishing.com.

Arcade Publishing® and CrimeWise® are registered trademarks of Skyhorse Publishing, Inc.®, a Delaware corporation.

Visit our website at www.arcadepub.com.
Visit the author's website at douglasskelton.com.

10 9 8 7 6 5 4 3 2 1

Library of Congress Cataloging-in-Publication Data is available on file.
Library of Congress Control Number: 2022937888

Cover design by Erin Seaward-Hiatt
Cover photograph: © George W. Johnson / Getty Images

ISBN: 978-1-956763-01-0
Ebook ISBN: 978-1-956763-25-6

Printed in the United States of America

A
RATTLE
OF BONES

1

Near Ballachulish, the Scottish Highlands, 1755

The red-coated soldier was a bloodstain against the dull sky and drab scrub on the hill.

It had a name, this desolate lump above the waters, a heathenish Scotch concoction of sounds, but he was damned if he could pronounce it. To him it was little more than a pox-ridden mound of dirt that drew the elements like a hedge whore did corny-faced beard-splitters.

The waters of the lake shivered as a chill breeze weaved its way up the hill to find his solitary figure standing post. Private Harry Greenway huddled deeper into his coat, watching the small ferry being rowed across the narrows. He wished he was in his billet, a cup of hot grog in one hand and a mutton pie, warm from the oven, in the other. This was a pointless duty, a punishment for not taking proper care of the Brown Bess he now crooked loosely in one arm. His sergeant would be displeased to see him cradle the gun so carelessly, except there was no one here to bear witness, except the blasted elements and the one he guarded, who was beyond caring, Greenway wagered. Why the musket required to be pristine was beyond him. They were not in a field of battle, for these heathens were a beaten people. Yet here he stood, on this God-rotting windswept hill overlooking two lakes—Private Greenway refused to think of them with the Scotch term *loch*, even if he could manage the necessary guttural rasp, which to his ear sounded like someone trying to hawk up a gob of phlegm.

The sunrise had barely lightened the grey skies, and despite the thickness of his coat he feared he was in very real danger of freezing off his tallywags. That would not do, as he had hopes of deploying them soon with young Eilidh, the daughter of an innkeeper near their barracks who was known to wag her tail in return for a penny or two. She was a pert little doxy and he fully expected to dance the goat's jig before the week was out.

He thrust the vision of her firm roundness from his mind and stamped on the hard ground to bring some sensation back to his feet, frozen in his square black boots, and also to somehow stem the burgeoning bulge under his breeches. The islands anchored in the water were but black lumps, the one they called the Isle of the Dead seemingly darker than the others. It also had a name in their guttural tongue but he remembered only the proper English version for where the heathens buried their clan chiefs. Seeing it rise from the waters, hump-backed and sinister, reminded him of that which stood behind. During the bleak hours of night it had been a simple task to avoid gazing upon it. He had paced to and fro in order to ward off the infernal, eternal cold that seemed the norm here in Itchland, as his comrades referred to Scotchland. He had also ensured his face was turned away lest the sight be suddenly illuminated by a stray beam of moonlight. Though there was little chance of that, for a shroud of clouds buried any heavenly glow. Now that the day had dawned, dull and lifeless as it was, he endeavoured to keep facing the waters below and the hills beyond. He had no need to cast eyes upon the object of his charge, for he—it—was not going anywhere.

It had been a man once, but it was a man no longer. The flesh was gone, picked clean by the hooded crows and the ravages of the Scotch weather. Now it was but a frame of weathered bone on which had once clung muscle and sinew, hanging on a gibbet these three years. It had slipped from its bonds at least once, he had been informed with some relish by a corporal who claimed to have been present, but it had been strung together and rehung. A warning, the corporal had said in his strong West Country accent, to them Scotch who might still fancy a bit of rebellion.

Greenway knew not what the man had done to deserve such a fate—apart from being a treasonous Jacobite, which Greenway supposed was enough—but he cared little. Standing sentinel over a dead man's bones was merely a duty, a reminder to take better care of his weapon in future. And yet, he was unnerved. His old mum back in Spitalfields had filled his head with tales of ghosts and revenge from beyond the grave, and in the black Highland night he had imagined he heard those bones clattering as they climbed from the gibbet to repay whatever wrong it believed had been done.

His thick coat notwithstanding, the breeze seemed to cut through him as if he was not there, then swirl around the wooden gibbet like an old friend come to pay its respects. The chain creaked against the post like a cry for attention and, despite himself, the young soldier turned, if only to ensure that his night terrors had not become real.

He saw the old woman for the first time.

She was standing at the foot of the gibbet, gazing up as if in supplication. He had not heard her ascend the hill, and thus startled he swung his Brown Bess to a more ready position.

'Step back there,' he commanded, putting as much authority into his voice as he could muster, despite the chill rippling his words. Nonetheless, they were weak and fearful, and they wilted in the waft of the breeze.

The old hag neither acknowledged his words nor in turn paid heed. She continued to stand at the foot of the skeleton, staring at it as if it were Christ on the Cross and not some filthy rebel who defied his king. The young private considered this. Did not their saviour defy authority in the Holy Land? Was he not himself a rebel? Such thoughts were for scholars, though, and not a conscript raised in the stews of London, so he thrust them from his mind. He took a few paces closer to the woman, endeavouring to avoid gazing upon the bones swaying in the breeze. His weapon was braced across his chest, ready to level should he feel the need, the very act stiffening his resolve and injecting steel into his voice.

'D'you hear me, woman? Step back there.'

Her head turned then and he saw how old she was. Her face, framed by the tattered woollen shawl, was criss-crossed by lines that cut deep into flesh made leather by the attentions of too many winters. As her eyes fell on the musket he held across his chest like a shield, she gave him a small smile that was little more than the gaping of a small black maw, yet when she spoke her voice was strong but as cracked as her face.

'Are you feart, brave soldier?'

'No, mother,' he said gently as he lowered the weapon, his own mother's constant admonishments to show all women respect having nestled deeply in his soul. Peggy Greenway had not enjoyed much respect in her life, having been turned out at fourteen by her mother to service the culls of Southwark. 'You just cannot stand too close,' he warned. 'It is not safe.'

She glanced back at the gibbet and her smile became sad. 'Seumas would never harm me. Not in life and never in death. We are bound by blood, him and I.'

Greenway had been in this wretched land long enough to know that Seumas was Scotch for James. The man who had once walked in those bones was named James Stewart, a traitorous murderer. He cared little about the man that was, but that much he knew.

'You are kin to this man?'

A gnarled hand, the joints bulging and distorted, tenderly caressed one bleached foot of the hanged man. 'Aye, I am kin, as many are here in Appin. Kin by blood and by marriage. But even if we were not we would still have loved him, for he was a good man. Unlike those who led him to this end—and those who left him here to rot.'

Greenway was ill-equipped to debate the justice of the matter.

'Even so, I cannot have you stand so close. The gibbet is not secure and I have orders that no one must approach the . . .' He paused, his mind reaching for the correct word. 'Remains.'

The woman's laugh was as sharp as the back of his mother's hand. 'Would that your people were so concerned for my kinsman's well-being when your kind treated him so cruelly.'

Greenway could not help himself from saying, 'Justice has been done.'

Her head whirled to face him with a speed he would never have thought possible from one so aged. 'Justice, you say? Justice?' She spat something thick and rheumy at the ground between them. 'I give that for your English justice.'

4

She made the word *English* seem like something she would not feed even to pigs.

'Mother, I must caution you.'

She waved her claw-like hand at him. 'Ach, away, my lad. I am too far gone for your words to have meaning. What punishment can they deliver to an old woman who speaks her mind? An old woman who saw her sons and grandsons dead in the Rising? And a daughter pining for her child, left to freeze on the road from England? A boy of sixteen summers, dead from a fever caught on a fool's errand for a drunkard and a wastrel who cared nought for the country from which he would flee like a scalded pup.'

Greenway had not borne arms for his king in the rebellion of 1745, but he knew of whom the old woman spoke. Prince Charles Edward Stuart. The Young Pretender, who had fomented revolt among the clans and had led his army south to seize the throne. They had reached Derby before they turned for home. It was only through sheer force of numbers, the cunning of His Royal Highness Prince William Augustus, the Duke of Cumberland, and the inbred cowardice of Charles Stuart that the insurrection died on moorland near Inverness. Greenway kept his tongue still, for he sensed silence was the most prudent path to take. His eyes, however, darted about the open hilltop to ensure no one in authority had arrived to overhear her—or to witness him not taking her to task for her treason.

Her gaze had returned to the skeleton and her hand once more stroked the foot with what was obvious affection. 'There was no justice in what occurred here,' she muttered, half to herself. 'Not man's nor God's. This was murder.'

Duty encouraged Greenway to remain still no longer.

'Mother, I must again caution you to—'

The cold, invisible hand of the wind once more gripped the bones and made them shiver. The backward step Greenway took was involuntary, the raising of his musket a reflex. The old woman saw the flash of fear on his face and smiled once more.

'That scares you, my lad,' she said. 'The sound. And well it should. For though the flesh is gone and only these bare bones remain, the spirit

5

lives yet. You are young. You know nothing of these matters. But mark me, English soldier, you will witness injustice and you will witness cruelty and perfidy from your betters. And when you do, you must stop and you must listen, for this sound—this rattle of bones—will echo through the years.'

2

Inverness, present day

The man's smile was both annoying and ultimately disturbing. It was barely there, a little half-hearted smirk, but it was reflected in his eyes. Heavy-lidded; some might say sleepy.

Rebecca Connolly was tired, however. She hadn't been sleeping well, which in itself was nothing new but it was Saturday, it had been a busy week, what with one thing and another, and by rights at this time of the morning she should have been lounging at home in her pyjamas, looking forward to recharging her batteries by eating junk food and binge-watching *The Marvelous Mrs. Maisel*. She should not have been in the news agency's small office in the Old Town face-to-face with a man making a complaint while at the same time apparently listening to a joke that only he could hear.

He had appeared at her back as she had unlocked the office door. It crossed her mind that he had been outside, watching for her to arrive. She had heard his footsteps behind her as she climbed the stairway, and he had appeared as she turned in the open doorway at the top.

'You Rebecca Connolly?' he asked, his tone conversational, but not waiting for a reply before he held up a copy of a tabloid from two days before. 'You write this?'

She leaned forward to peer at the page in the dim light of the landing, a waft of strong aftershave presenting itself to her like a calling card. The story the man was tapping with the forefinger of his other hand was a report on a hearing in the Inverness court concerning a riot in the Inchferry area of the city.

'Yes, I am,' she said. 'But no, I didn't write that story.'

'It came from your company, right?'

'Yes, it did,' she replied, wondering how he knew.

The hand holding the newspaper dropped, and he fixed those almost languid eyes on her. 'I'm not happy.'

Rebecca wasn't surprised. Complaints about court stories were a weekly occurrence, as common when she had been with the *Highland Chronicle* as they were now, with the news agency. She was used to this.

'In what way, Mr . . .'

'Martin Bailey,' he said. 'It's my boy you've named here.'

Rebecca hadn't written the story—she had actually been present during the incident when youths ran amok during a demonstration that went very wrong—but she recognised the name as one of the accused.

'Okay,' she said.

His eyes flicked to the office behind her, as if he expected to be invited in, but she was happier here in the corridor where the door to the tailor's opposite lay open, with Katy Perry blasting from the radio. As much as these complaints were common, there was something about this thin-faced man that slightly unnerved her. The secret amusement in his eyes and the way he spoke in a soft monotone made her feel uncomfortable.

'I'm not happy,' he said again. 'I don't like my name being dragged through the papers.'

'Well, it's your son.'

'He's Martin Bailey too,' he said. 'And you've printed my address. I don't think that's right.'

'Does your son live with you, Mr Bailey?'

'Yes.'

'Then we and the newspaper have every right to print the address. It's a matter of public record.'

He stared at her for a few moments, that smile still there. She got the impression that he'd known she was going to say that. 'My lawyer says different.'

This argument was also common. Rebecca had lost count of the number of times she had heard people say what their lawyer had told them, when in fact it was likely their lawyer had told them exactly what Rebecca had said. She didn't call Bailey a liar, though. It was always best to be business-like in these situations.

'I can't help what he said, Mr Bailey. The fact is, in a court report we can print the accused's name and address. It is a matter of record.'

'People in my community think it's me.'

'I doubt that, Mr Bailey. How old is your son?'

'Twenty-three.'

'And that is stated in the story. You're not twenty-three, are you?'

'No.'

'There you are. People won't think it's you.'

He half nodded and again she had the impression she wasn't saying anything he didn't already know. He ran a hand through his long hair, which was swept back almost into a mullet.

It was a warm early summer's day and he had his shirt sleeves rolled up. Through the dark hairs of his sinewy forearm Rebecca caught a glimpse of a tattoo that looked suspiciously like the number 88. Rebecca knew this was used by neo-Nazis to signify *Heil Hitler*, the letter H being the eighth in the alphabet, and given what he was at that moment complaining about she thought the likelihood of an innocent reason for the tattoo extremely unlikely.

Bailey's son had not been arrested for a few months after the riot at Inchferry, which kicked off when the mob turned ugly following a speech by Finbar Dalgliesh, the leader of Spirit of the Gael, now more commonly shortened to SG. They preferred the Gaelic *Spioraid nan Gael*, but Rebecca thought it a cultural insult. They showed little spirit of the Gael and plenty of right-wing bluster, while insisting that tomorrow belonged to them. Rebecca had ended up trampled underfoot after someone had knocked her to the ground. It had not been a pleasant experience.

Seeing that tattoo made her wonder if this man was an SG member, and that thought sent something fluttering in her stomach. He might even be part of New Dawn, the more extreme branch of the party which both Dalgliesh and the movement at large denied even existed. Hell, this guy might even have been there that night and be the bastard who sent her flying. These people were nutjobs.

Her gaze darted over his shoulder to the tailor's open door, while in her mind she ran through some of the moves her self-defence instructor had been teaching her. Eyes, nose, throat and groin. Hit them hard and hit them fast.

He caught her look and his smile twitched. She cursed herself for letting him know she was intimidated, even if only slightly.

'It's all lies,' he said. 'What they said in court. You never hear the truth there.'

Rebecca knew very well that courts deal with what can be proved, but even lies can have provenance. And the truth can often be in the eyes—and ears—of the beholder. She was not about to throw him that bone, though, or debate the point with him.

'I'm sorry, Mr Bailey, but I have an appointment, so . . .'

'You were there that night,' he said.

So, he *had* been in Inchferry after all. Once again, she had the impression that he was playing games with her.

'Yes,' she said.

'Aye, I saw you.' His eyes narrowed. 'You were with the *Chronicle* then.'

'I was, but—'

'Finbar said you were an enemy.'

Finbar. First-name terms. That in itself didn't mean he was bosom buddies with the SG leader, for Dalgliesh was the type to share a pint and fag and tell anyone who might support him to call him Finbar, but it did confirm Bailey was SG. And she was an enemy now: it wasn't just the press in general, but her personally. Part of her was pleased, but not enough to quell her nerves, so she fought to remain outwardly calm.

'You're just like the rest. All the mainstream media. The liberal elite. Wouldn't know the truth if it bit you on the arse.' His lip curled into a sneer as his eyes crawled over her from head to foot. 'But it's all changed now. You had best remember that.'

Here we go, she thought. He had all the right-wing buzzwords. Mainstream media. Liberal elite. Rebecca felt he was repeating phrases he had heard at an SG meeting, all half-truths, downright lies and confirmation bias. Dealing with complaints about court stories was always stressful, but when they come from a member of SG there was an added level of concern. Something about his words, the way he delivered them, the way he laid heavy emphasis on the word 'you', the way he allowed those half-shut, mocking eyes to bore into her finally got the better of her patience. *Do something they don't expect*, her father had told her once. *Instead of pulling back, move in closer. Some people are all talk.*

She took a half-step closer to him, fixing her stance in the way her self-defence teacher had taught her, and said, 'Mr Bailey, that sounds like a threat to me.'

He didn't move. His smile only broadened. 'No threat, darling. This country is changing and folk like you better change with it, is all I'm saying. If you know what's good for you.' He stepped away, turned to the stairs, then twisted to face her again. Still smiling, his mind telling himself that little joke, he looked her up and down, as if he had sensed she had tensed up, ready for fight or flight. 'Believe me, Rebecca Connolly, this doesn't end here.'

She tried to think of something smart to say but she couldn't. She let him go without a word, listened to his footsteps on the stairs, then heard the door at street level opening and closing. Only then did she take a deep breath and let it out slowly, annoyed by the slight hitch in the exhalation. Breathe, she told herself. In, out.

Her phone bleeped. She opened the text and looked at the image, a banner across a monument, the words 'JAMES STEWART IS INNOCENT' clear and proud.

Then the phone rang.

'You get the photo?' Tom Muir's voice was crackly, distant. She didn't know if he was in an area with bad reception or if it was because his mobile was so old it should have had a rotary dial. She pushed Martin Bailey from her mind.

'Yes, looking at it now.'

'I don't know how long it will stay there. Some bugger is sure to take it down. We've got them at Keil Chapel, too, where James of the Glens was buried, and at Lettermore, where Colin Campbell was murdered.'

All sites relating to the original case, almost 270 years earlier, when James Stewart was convicted of murdering a government official. She knew the tale well, for her father had told her about it many years before.

But the banners did not relate to any historical figure. This James Stewart was very much in the present.

'Okay, Chaz is waiting for me outside,' she said. 'We'll get there probably early afternoon. I'm going to see Mrs Stewart first.'

'Well, I've paved the way with Afua for you as much as I can,' said the voice on the line, 'but I hope to God you've taken your brave pills, love.'

'First thing in the morning, every day,' she said, her mind flitting back to Martin Bailey and his final statement. Something told her it was more than a threat.

It was a promise.

3

Rebecca grabbed a fresh notebook and some pens, locked up and followed the traces of Bailey's aftershave to street level, where the heat of the day was near searing compared to the cool of the dingy stairway. The lock of the entrance door had been failing to engage properly, so she pulled hard until she heard it click. She had meant to purchase some 3-in-1 oil, but it continually slipped her mind. She made a mental note to buy some next time she was in the supermarket.

Chaz Wymark was leaning against a patch of wall between the doorway and a coffee house, one leg folded at the knee and the foot placed against the brickwork, his face raised to the sun. He opened one eye and squinted in her direction.

'A fella could get used to this weather,' he said.

'It's Scotland,' she said, 'it won't last.'

He dropped the raised leg and stooped to heft his camera bag, which had been sitting at his feet like a patient dog. 'Jeezo, rain on my parade, why don't you?' He slung the strap of his bag over his shoulder. 'What kept you?'

'Sorry, I had to deal with something.'

She welcomed the sun's rays: it had been a long winter and early summer was proving to be a stunner. A few tourists were out already, even though it was only just after nine. A party of sightseers was being guided down the street towards Church Street, perhaps heading for the Old High Kirk. Rebecca wondered how they'd feel if they were greeted with the vision of a man dressed in the red coat of a government soldier from 1746, his throat cut and his corpse draped over a flat gravestone, as had happened the year before. She hadn't seen it herself but she had spoken to a police officer who had. It had not been a pretty sight and it would have been more than enough to have the visitors dropping their guidebooks. She let the group pass and one of their number, an elderly woman, smiled at her. Rebecca nodded and smiled back, but it slid away when she saw Martin Bailey watching her from across the road.

She felt a frown pucker, but she turned away so Bailey wouldn't see.

'What's up?' Chaz asked, seeing her expression.

'The guy over there.'

Chaz craned round her to look. 'What guy?'

'Don't make it so obvious you're looking, for Christ's sake,' she whispered.

'Sorry,' said Chaz, 'didn't know we were in cloak-and-dagger mode.'

'Did you see him?'

'Didn't get a chance before you told me my spycraft was somehow wanting.'

Despite her concern, she smiled. 'He's across the other side of the road. He's moaning about his son's court report being in the paper. That's what kept me back.'

'Okay,' said Chaz, this time being more circumspect as he glanced towards the far pavement.

'He's also a member of SG. I think he is, anyway. He just threatened me, in an offhand sort of way.'

Not so offhand, she thought as she recalled his final look.

'Did he?' Chaz's voice hardened and he dropped any pretence as he peered round her to give the man what was now a glare. Rebecca didn't chastise him this time. God bless him, but they both knew he was unlikely to go all medieval. 'Oh yeah, I saw him go in just after you.'

Without turning, she asked, 'What's he doing now?'

'Just standing there looking at us.' Chaz kept his face straight. 'Not sure my best Clint Eastwood glower is worrying him at all. What kind of threat?'

'Ach, just the usual sort of thing. A threat that's not really a threat. You lot will learn, it's our time now, this doesn't end here, blah blah blah. It's more the way he said it than what he said. Oh yeah—and I'm the enemy.'

Chaz kept staring at Martin Bailey. He may not have been Clint Eastwood, but he was gutsy. 'Whose enemy? His?'

'The SG. Finbar Dalgliesh.'

'Anyone with half a brain is their enemy. You think he's dangerous?'

Her rational mind told her that he was a bully, and bullies only function if they think they *can* bully. Chances were, that would be the last she heard of it.

'Leave it,' she said. 'Come on, forget him. He's nothing.'

They walked up the street towards the railway station. Chaz's limp, following an incident when the vehicle he was driving left the road, was less pronounced now and he had discarded the cane he had sported for a time. He had never actually needed it anyway. She looked over her shoulder once and saw Bailey was shadowing them on the opposite side. When they reached the end of the road and he was still there, Rebecca decided it was time to nip this in the bud.

'Wait here,' she said to Chaz and immediately crossed over to face the man. Amusement still danced in his eyes as he looked at her, that smug little smile tickling his lips.

'Do we have a problem, Mr Bailey?' She kept her voice low, so passers-by couldn't hear.

He didn't say anything at first, just looked at her with that maddening smirk. 'Just walking, that's all.'

'Uh-huh,' she said.

'A bloke can walk in the street, can he no'?'

She drew in a harsh breath. She really had no answer for him. He leaned in a little closer and said quietly, 'But I'll be in touch.'

'I don't think we have anything further to discuss, Mr Bailey.'

He took a half-step back, shrugged, then turned and walked in the opposite direction. Rebecca watched him for a moment, then rejoined Chaz.

'Trouble, you think?' he asked.

She looked back across the road but Bailey was out of sight. 'I've dealt with his sort before. Back at the paper I had one who called me every day—another court story—and called me for everything. But this? I don't know. Feels different.'

'If you're worried you should tell the police. Maybe give Val Roach a call.'

Val Roach was a police officer Rebecca had met during the investigation into the murder in the kirkyard and another on Culloden. The whole thing ended with Rebecca almost catching a bullet. It also led to her leaving the *Highland Chronicle* to work at the agency. Roach let her down during that investigation by telling a suspect that Rebecca had broken a confidence, which she had not. She also threatened to have Rebecca arrested for withholding information. That did not endear the police officer to her and they had not spoken since.

'And tell her what?' Rebecca said. 'Somebody made a complaint and gave me a stern look, and then he dared to walk in the street outside the office? No, as I said, forget it. Guys like him aren't worth the blood pressure. Come on, let's go see Afua Stewart.'

'You think she'll speak to you?'

Rebecca's sideways look was reproving. 'Have you ever known anyone to refuse me?'

He let her walk a few steps ahead before he said, 'Well . . . yes.'

4

Mo Burke had her own table in Barney's, which was only fitting as she owned the place. She spent more time these days in the dingy little bar, tucked away in an alleyway in the Old Town, than at her home in Inchferry. It was a throwback to when pubs sold beer and spirits, and wine was something for posh folk, and she watched the customers come and go while Midge, her West Highland terrier, lay on a large cushion at her feet. She loved that wee dog. He was all she had now until her husband was released. She'd had two sons but one was dead and another in the jail. As she watched she drank coffee, and occasionally gin, and she smoked, for there was no one who would dare throw anti-smoking legislation in her face lest they wound up having something a lot more painful thrown in theirs. Any of her team who needed her knew where to find her, and so there was a steady flow of men back and forth, each of them feeling the need to buy something at the bar, so that helped profits. Not that Mo cared too much about that. Barney's was a front only, a way of cleaning up the dirty money she made elsewhere. The pub was haunted mostly by regulars, but that didn't mean a whisper couldn't be passed along to the law, so the sizeable cellar was handy if the subject under discussion was in any way delicate. Mo Burke had not survived this long by being overly trusting.

Martin Bailey was not a regular, but he knew where to find her, so she was not surprised when he pushed the door open, made straight for her table in the far corner and sat down without an invitation or, she noted, putting his hand in his pocket on the way. Well, if he wanted her to buy a round he was on to plums. His aftershave reached across the table and stuck two fingers up her nostrils. Jesus, where did he find that stuff, she wondered. She wanted to tell him that the '70s had just called and they wanted it and his hairstyle back.

'Did you get what I wanted?' he asked, that half-smile on his face. Bastard always looked as if he was pleased with himself and that pissed her off. Under the table, Midge raised his head and sniffed the air. He was a friendly wee dog, and usually got up and greeted whoever came to speak to Mo, but he didn't make a move towards Bailey. Mo thought he showed good sense. She didn't like Bailey, didn't like the people he floated around with, but she swallowed her annoyance. She had a use for him.

She reached into the pocket of her coat—it was always too cold in the pub for her, during the day anyway—and found a slip of notepaper. She held it across the table with a gloved hand and he took it from her, unfolded it, and looked at it.

'You have any trouble getting this?' he asked.

She shook her head. Mo Burke knew a lot of people; getting information was child's play. If he suspected it wasn't Mo's handwriting, he didn't show it. She would never give him anything that could be easily linked back to her.

'Copy it down,' she said, pushing a pencil towards him. 'There's space at the bottom. Then tear it off and give me the original back.'

He looked up, that glint mocking her. 'You serious?'

'I'm serious.'

He looked as if he was going to argue the point but he grunted a half-laugh, took the pencil and copied Rebecca Connolly's address and phone number. Mo was not taking any chances of him being caught with the original in his pocket, even if it wasn't in her handwriting. Precautions. Levels of security. Survival of the smartest.

'I saw her a wee while ago,' he said, as he carefully ripped the paper in half and handed her copy back. 'Sheer bloody luck. I was scoping out her office and she turned up, so I got the ball rolling.'

'You could have done it there and then.'

He shook his head. 'No, not my way. Too soon. I told you, I do this my way.'

She knew what his way entailed and, while she didn't approve, she didn't really care. There wasn't much Mo Burke didn't hear about, especially in Inchferry. She wasn't a native but she had lived there since she'd married her husband, Tony, and her family was part of the fabric. Like dry rot, as a police officer once said. What family she had left, at least.

Bailey also had a reputation in the Ferry. He didn't like women and he particularly didn't like women who he believed had done him a bad turn. He would, however, take a woman's money when it was offered. But he had other reasons for going after Rebecca Connolly. Bailey was SG and they really didn't like the reporter. Even though she was no fan of Finbar Dalgliesh and his cronies, Mo was happy to use that to her advantage. This was the real heart of Bailey's hatred. He didn't give two tosses for his boy, but she'd used it as a way in, whispering to him that it was time Connolly was taught a lesson. Men were so easy to manipulate sometimes. He hadn't needed much persuading. Rebecca Connolly had written about SG and had a habit of getting under Finbar's skin. For someone like Bailey, that was unacceptable. Especially from a woman.

'She's a cocky wee cow,' he said.

'Just make sure you do what you said. I want her to pay for what she did.'

His smirk intensified. 'Oh, she'll pay, don't you worry. We've felt that bitch has had it coming. Now's the time.'

Mo Burke put a flame to another cigarette and thought of her sons. Of the one doing time and the one lying in a grave.

And Rebecca Connolly was responsible for both.

5

The couch looked and felt expensive and its undoubtedly hefty price tag was reflected in its comfort quotient. Rebecca felt herself sinking into it as if it were a heavenly cloud. Would the owner mind if she curled up, drew one of those incredibly soft-looking throws around her—no five-quid jobs out of Tesco for this lady—and caught up on some sleep? She didn't ask. There was an air of chilly hostility in this tastefully furnished room that was almost tangible.

They had been welcomed with a frosty nod and a brief gesture to come in. That was something, at least. Now the woman sat very straight in a chair opposite them, her long legs together and slightly to the side, her hands clasped in her lap. It was a fine chair, pale green with a high back and winged headrest. It was old and probably cost more than Rebecca's three-piece suite. And her TV. Probably even the carpets, too. The entire room was a set designer's idea of good taste and refinement.

Afua Stewart was a beautiful woman and would look superb in the photographs Rebecca hoped they would get before they left. Optics, always the optics. She must have been over sixty, Rebecca estimated, and would bet she still had a smile that would have men's hearts fluttering. Her son, James, was thirty-one now; he had been twenty-one when he was convicted. Afua Stewart had been a model for ten years before she married and walked away from it all to be a wife and mother. Her skin was flawless and her cheekbones high, the jawline still firm, her black hair cut short. Her eyes were a pale blue, though, heightening the cold disdain with which she regarded Rebecca and Chaz. Mostly Rebecca, though. Maybe they were always like that. Or maybe it was a look reserved for Rebecca, because she had let her down before.

The house was large, situated on a quiet street in the Crown area of Inverness. The street outside, with its detached villas and carefully tended gardens and hedges and late-model cars gleaming in driveways, was quiet, with only the barking of a dog somewhere breaking the Saturday morning stillness. The dog was probably in the park at the end of the road, Rebecca thought, chasing a ball. Or a stick. Or just barking for the sheer hell of it.

'You have drifted off somewhere, Ms Connolly,' Afua Stewart said, her Scottish accent cultured, with even a faint transatlantic twang. Her roots were in the Ashanti region of Ghana, but Rebecca knew she had been born and brought up in Edinburgh, while her modelling had taken her to London and Paris. She'd never made it to the supermodel stage but she was successful enough.

'I'm sorry, Mrs Stewart. Something else came to mind. And please, call me Rebecca.' She hated being labelled a Ms or a Miss, even though she studiously ensured she used the appropriate honorific when addressing others.

The woman acknowledged the request with a twitch of one eyebrow. Rebecca couldn't tell if it signified she was annoyed, had accepted her momentary lack of attention or meant she was agreeing to be less formal. She did not return the favour by suggesting Rebecca call her by her first name, though. She was pissed off and was not hiding it.

'I asked why you are suddenly interested in my son's case when you weren't before?'

And there it was.

'I was always interested in the case, Mrs Stewart. Ever since Tom Muir told me about it.'

Rebecca had met Tom during the riot in Inchferry—which had resulted in skinned knees and palms for Rebecca and jailtime for young Martin Bailey—and he had brought the story to her on the very day she had decided to leave the *Chronicle*. The fact that she had been forced to leave James Stewart's story for so long did not sit well with his mother. Campaigns are only news when there is something to report, and financial reality meant that she had to move on to work that paid the rent. She had tried to get other editors interested—at newspapers, magazines, even TV and radio—but they had refused to bite.

The cool eyes softened. 'Tom has been a rock.'

That was Tom, rock solid. He had been a union man, town councillor and social activist. He was of the people and for the people, and he had fought injustice all his adult life. He himself admitted he wasn't always right, but he tried not to do wrong. He believed James Stewart was not guilty and that was that. It was good enough to pique Rebecca's news sense, but she required more than blind faith.

'The problem was, I couldn't get the media interested. I did explain that to you,' Rebecca said. 'As far as they were concerned, James was guilty. Miscarriage of justice cases take up a great deal of time and there is very little appetite for anything that might be a long haul, unless a TV documentary strand takes an interest. With no new evidence, nothing fresh, the story was dead.'

'But that has changed.'

It was a statement, not a question.

'Yes,' said Rebecca. 'The banners that Tom put up are a story, or at least enough to get some initial interest.'

Rebecca indicated Chaz at her side. 'We're going to head there today to have a look for ourselves, although there is always the possibility they will have been removed. Tom sent me some shots, though. As I said, they should be enough to generate some heat.' She paused. 'But Tom tells me you have made another breakthrough. He didn't tell me what it was. He said it wasn't his place.'

Rebecca left that to dangle, hoping the woman would pick it up and run with it, but Afua Stewart merely shifted her position, swinging her legs round and unclasping her hands as she sat back to rest them along the arms of the chair, her long fingers tapering to carefully manicured nails painted a soft silver. Her every movement was graceful, easy, showing evidence of her days on the catwalk. It may have been over thirty years since she had strutted and posed before the chatter of photographers' shutters but she still carried herself well. She waited for Rebecca to keep talking, obviously not in any mood to make this easy for her. But then, why should she? The woman did not trust the press, thanks to too many promises and not enough action.

The banners should be enough to get something started, but Rebecca really wanted—needed—to know what the new information was. Could it really kickstart an investigation? Would it be sufficient to either merit a new appeal or, at the very least, entice the Scottish Criminal Cases Review Commission on board?

However, as she studied Afua Stewart's impassive face, Rebecca sensed further information would not be volunteered. Her eyes were like a cold night in the Arctic Circle without a vest on. Yup, she was going to be awkward.

'Mrs Stewart,' Rebecca said, leaning forwards as well as she could, given the soft, dreamy grip this couch had on her. If she was to crack the ice between them, she needed to reduce the physical gap without penetrating the woman's personal space. Getting to her feet was going to be undignified, so she settled for perching on the edge of the cushion. 'I'm here to help, if I can.'

A flash then, some fire in the permafrost of those blue eyes. 'You're here because you smell a story.'

'That's how I can help.'

'You don't care about my James.'

'I don't know him. But I do care about justice.'

As soon as the words drew breath Rebecca knew they sounded pompous and self-serving. They didn't sit too well with Afua Stewart either.

'Justice?' Rebecca felt the woman would have snorted if it wasn't so unbecoming. If there was one thing she knew about Afua Stewart, it was that she had poise. It wasn't just the modelling background, it was her upbringing and perhaps something in her DNA stretching back to her Ashanti ancestors. Proud. Tough. Determined. A snort was not something she would ever do. 'Where was justice when my James was being railroaded ten years ago, aided and abetted by you people? No one believed his side of the story. He was found guilty by the press before the jury even retired.'

Rebecca had read the press coverage, or at least as much of it as she could. James Stewart had been found guilty of murdering Murdo Maxwell, a lawyer and environmental activist who advised—and confronted—both the Scottish and Westminster governments. He was found beaten to death in his country home, Kirkbrig House, in Appin, where the land shoulders into Loch Linnhe and heads south, hugging the water to Oban. James Stewart had been found naked and unconscious in the master bedroom, blood on his hands and on the bedsheets, the heavy poker used to murder Maxwell on the floor beside him. He and the fifty-five-year-old dead man had been lovers. Maxwell's sexuality was hardly under the radar, for he often campaigned regarding gay rights, but the tabloid press had a field day with the revelation of his affair with a much younger man.

'I realise that,' said Rebecca, 'and to an extent it's true . . .'

'To an extent? They crucified my boy! He was gay, he was sleeping with an older man, and to make matters worse he was not white. That outraged their sensibilities. As far as they were concerned, he was guilty and that was that.'

The woman was angry, but she was being unfair. Yes, certain titles had pursed their lips, but the quality press had reported the case evenly and without judgement. Naturally, no report covered everything said in court. It was the quick hit, the headline grab, these days the click-bait line, but always being careful to be balanced by presenting the cases for the prosecution and defence, to an extent, while still not reporting every hiccough and burp. As for his colour, Rebecca had seen no overt mention of it but had to admit she had detected a certain tone in some reports.

'I understand what you're saying, Mrs Stewart, but I'm sure Tom has told you that I'm not like that.'

Afua's clenched jaw loosened, but only slightly. 'Yes, he speaks highly of you. He said he thought you were different from the others. But what can you do to help us?'

'We're a small agency, certainly, but my boss, Elspeth McTaggart, has a great many contacts.'

'Tom said she had retired, left you to run the business.'

'She has stepped back, that's true, but she's still pretty hands-on. Basically I do the work, she takes the profits.' Rebecca flickered a smile. It wasn't returned. 'She's writing a book now, with my help, about the bodies found in Culloden and in the Old High Kirk. Do you remember?'

Afua's face did not reveal whether she remembered or not. The case had not been exactly low profile, so she had to know about it. 'And is that why you're here? You want another book?'

'I won't lie, Mrs Stewart, that is possible. But first, let's get the ball rolling legally. To do that, you're going to need the media. I agree that they didn't really help ten years ago, but they can help now. All they need is the story. And you need someone who can help steer that story to them.'

'Control it?'

Rebecca shook her head. 'No, I won't control the facts, Mrs Stewart. I will follow this as much as I can, but I won't manipulate and I won't suppress anything. To put it bluntly, if I find anything that doesn't help your son's case then I'm not going to ignore it. All I want is the truth, or as close to it as I can get.'

'And do you think you will know the truth when you see it?'

Rebecca paused, dredging up words she had once read in a book. 'Let me tell you about the truth, Mrs Stewart. Remember the Rubik's Cube?' The woman nodded. 'Well, the truth is like a Rubik's Cube. When you see it at first, everything seems right and proper. Makes sense, everything in its place, all the colours match. Then someone comes along and gives it a twist and things don't look quite so neat and tidy. The colours are still there but they're out of place. A few more twists and it's even worse. All the colours remain but they've been moved, displaced. There may still be a pattern, it may look okay in an abstract sense, but it's not the way it was. Unless you're an expert, or you really work at it, you may never get it back to the way it began.'

'So what are you saying?'

'That I may only manage to get one or two sides of the cube to its original state. The rest may still be in disarray.'

'In other words you feel we may never know the full truth?'

'In other words, Mrs Stewart, I'm willing to give it a try.'

Afua Stewart sat in silence for what seemed like an eternity, gazing at Rebecca with those cool blue eyes. 'Make sure you do, Ms Connolly.' She had thawed a little but not enough to call Rebecca by her first name. 'My son has been in prison long enough.'

25

6

I am writing this diary on the advice of a counsellor. She thinks if I get my thoughts down on paper that it might help me make sense of the jumble in my head. I hate it here. I hate what has happened to me. I hate the way time passes within these stone walls. I learned early on that in here time is both immaterial and important. In the macro sense the inexorable march of the hours beyond the bars and walls is abstract; its only impact on my life is that it slowly, minute by minute, hour by hour, day by day, week by week, year by never-ending year brings me closer to the end of my sentence. In the micro, my day is regimented, timetabled. When I get up, when I eat, when I work, where I work, when I walk, talk, piss, shit. All are dictated to me. Out of my control.

At first I wanted to fight back, the way I would have on the outside. I wanted to lash out. I wanted to rage and scream and snarl at everyone and everything.

But I knew I couldn't. All it would have brought me was solitary time in the digger. So I reined myself in. Now I sit here and let the written words say what my tongue cannot. Maybe it will help, after all.

Only the hours of sleeping are my domain, for when I am alone in my bunk, listening to the sounds of the prison around me—doors closing some-where, footsteps on the landing and stairs, men settling in and snoring and groaning and farting—only then am I the master of my own body, of my thoughts, of my fate. I can sleep or not sleep. It is my choice and no one can force me.

Curiously, the night-time symphony now gives me a sense of fellowship, a sense of belonging, as if we are all in this together. But we really aren't, not at all. For the other men here are guilty and I'm not.

7

Joseph McClymont hated being called Wee Joe. He didn't like being referred to in any way diminutive or by the diminutive, preferring to be called Joseph. No one actually called him Wee Joe to his face, of course; not even those who hated him. They knew better. He was five feet nine inches, he was slim and he was pale and he wore glasses, but he didn't think of himself as small. It didn't help that his father was known as Big Rab. All his life, his father had loomed large in his eyes, not simply because he had been a powerful figure but because he had achieved so much, and when people called him Wee Joe he felt it somehow belittled his own achievements. After all, it was he who had legitimised many of their enterprises, given them the kind of solid veneer of respectability that it would take an army of forensic account-ants to crack.

His father wasn't so big now, sitting in a chair and staring through the window to the garden at the rear of their large house. Age had withered him. The muscle had shrunk, the skin had tightened. Only the thick head of hair remained, once dark but now a dull grey. A stroke hadn't helped. He got around, but he was not the man he once was. His eyes were tired and haunted. He had nightmares most nights and Joseph heard him calling out the names of men now long dead.

The phone in Joseph's hand vibrated and he glanced at the screen. The caller usually kept strict office hours, so whatever it was that had led him to ring on a Saturday morning had to be important.

'Mr Williams,' he said. They kept their dealings business-like, this man and he. It was Mr Williams and Mr McClymont, as it should be between a man and his lawyer.

'I have heard something upon the grapevine,' said the lawyer, his voice as crisp and dry as a legal document. Joseph wondered if he wore his blue pinstripe suit at weekends, too. He had never seen him in anything else, his blue handkerchief in his breast pocket always carefully arranged to look as if it had somehow managed to land by accident and yet flower perfectly, the blue tie never loosened, his white shirt eye-wateringly brilliant, cufflinks ensuring a knife-like look to the sleeves at his wrists. Joseph pictured him at home, still in that suit and that tie and that shirt. Wherever home was, for Terence Williams always kept his private life separate from his work. Joseph knew Mr Williams was married but not his wife's name, and that he had two grown-up children, but nothing else.

'Is this line secure?'

'It is, Mr Williams.' Joseph changed mobiles every two weeks, none of them registered to him. New handset, new number, and that was given only to a select few. Anyone else wishing to communicate with him did so through his people, sometimes more than one, for when it came to degrees of separation there was safety in numbers. The legitimacy that he, Mr Williams and others had created was, after all, still only a veneer. 'What have you heard?'

'Of a matter once thought long buried now being resurrected,' said the lawyer. 'That of an old friend.'

'Which old friend?'

'Murdo Maxwell.'

Joseph closed his eyes at the name as if against an old pain. 'What about him?'

'A suggestion, a whisper, a mere breath of a rumour.'

Terence Williams always spoke as if he was about to deliver a soliloquy. Joseph wished he would get to the point but he knew from experience it was best to indulge the lawyer's speech patterns. Had it been anyone else he would have snapped at him to get on with it, but he needed that sharp legal mind on his side. Williams could hide money in ways that would make an accountant throw his calculator against the wall. He was also linked into a vast information network crossing Scotland and beyond, which more than once had proved fruitful. Joseph himself knew that it was very difficult to keep some things quiet, a thought which had long haunted him.

'Murdo Maxwell is dead, Mr Williams.'

'Dead but not forgotten, as we both know, Mr McClymont.'

He was right there. Murdo Maxwell was not forgotten, not by Joseph anyway. 'So what have you heard?'

'That there may be fresh eyes gazing upon the matter and manner of his death.'

'Someone is doing time for that. That young lover of his.'

'James Stewart, like the actor from the silver screen.'

Joseph knew who the actor was, for his father had been a fan of westerns and had tried to indoctrinate his son into the genre, but Joseph never took to it. He had little time for films, preferring books. The literary classics in particular. Give him Camus, Sartre and Tolstoy over men on horses any day. Still, the idea of Maxwell's death being examined again made him uneasy, for there were matters there that he did not wish to revisit.

He asked, 'So why are they going to look at the case again?'

'That old legal bête noire of the appeal courts. Fresh information.'

'What fresh information?'

'Alas, the details have as yet eluded me, but I have heard mention of a solicitor named Stephen Jordan being somehow involved.'

'Never heard of him.'

'No reason you should have. I have made enquiries, discreetly of course. He is a one-man operation, beavering away in the more squalid areas of my profession in Inverness.'

Squalid areas. Joseph McClymont knew some of his own people had used firms like that in the past, with varied results, but that was the way of it in the courts. Some you win, some you lose. Joseph himself had never seen the inside of the dock and that was the way he wanted to keep it. That's why he retained Terence Williams.

'I assumed you would want to know that, like the phoenix, old Murdo's spectre may rise from the ashes.'

Shit, thought Joseph, as he felt concern ripple through his frame, but he kept his voice steady. 'Why should it matter to me, Mr Williams?'

Something rasped that may have been a chuckle but sounded more like the scraping of parchment against stone. 'No reason, Mr McClymont, no reason at all. I thought merely you would wish to know, given your past—erm—connection to the deceased.'

Williams was only one of two people who knew about that connection, as far as Joseph was aware. The other was his father, at whom he now glanced. He hadn't moved, he was still looking at the garden as if he could see the ghosts of his past staring back at him. Joseph followed the gaze, but all he saw was grass and trees and a blackbird hopping about looking for food. No vaporous figures, no accusatory faces staring back from beyond the veil. If Big Rab was seeing spectres, none of them would be Murdo Maxwell. That ghost—and the shame he still carried—was confined to Joseph.

'Thank you, Mr Williams, but the matter holds little interest for me.'

His voice remained modulated, still no indication of the discomfort he felt by having the past stirred up. It was something he had learned as a child. The hard way. Keep your emotions in check. Never let anyone— not even Terence Williams—know what you are thinking. Call it what you will—emotion, passion, lust—he believed it dangerous but now that old need he had thought dead threatened him.

That little dry sound again rattled through the ether. Desiccated bones in the wind. 'As you say, Mr McClymont. If I hear anything further, do you wish me to keep you informed?'

Joseph thought about it. He didn't know how much the lawyer knew, or thought he knew, but it wouldn't do any harm to have him keep an ear open.

'Certainly, if you hear anything, but don't make a special effort to find out,' he said, keeping his voice light as air. 'I'm not that interested.'

'As you wish, Mr McClymont.' The lawyer didn't sound surprised but then he seemed never to be surprised by anything. A nuclear bomb going off nearby would elicit only a slightly raised eyebrow. That was one of the reasons Joseph found him useful. Imperturbable men were hard to come by in these days of conspicuous emotions. Williams cut the call without a goodbye, something else which no one else would dare do, but Joseph allowed it.

He stood for a while staring at his father, wondering if he should raise the matter with him, but decided against it. The whole thing with Maxwell all those years ago had only angered him, and Joseph did not want to rake all that up again. He didn't know, or really care, if it would upset the old man, he just didn't feel like facing it. Instead, he walked into the hall and punched a number into the phone. It was answered on the second ring.

'It's me,' he said, a redundancy if ever there was one, for Malky Reid would have known who was calling. Joseph didn't wait for a reply. 'Pack your bag—you're going to Inverness.'

8

Afua Stewart agreed to photographs. She even suggested that they take them in her son's old room, showing she still understood the impact of an image.

The room was tidy. The bed was neat and the linen, duvet cover and pillowcases fresh. A PC on the desk under the window was dark. Rebecca thought about how it might have looked had a young man been living in it for the past ten years. Clothes lying on the leather armchair in the corner, dirty socks on the floor, crumb-crusted plates left abandoned.

Chaz asked Afua to sit on the bed, look towards the window, where the light splashed on her face, and she did as she was asked easily, with no self-consciousness. Most people are awkward in front of a camera in such situations, even with someone as professional and likeable as Chaz, but she was relaxed and natural. She was used to life before the lens. Rebecca watched from the doorway, for this was Chaz's domain, but as he adjusted focus and changed lenses she asked questions about James. She needed some background to build on.

The words did not flow. They were halting, and not simply because Afua stopped regularly for Chaz to click off another few frames. For the first time, Rebecca saw a mother's sadness. Downstairs the woman had been both ice and fire, but here, in her son's room, unused for a decade but kept pristine, the weight of those years settled in her eyes. Shadows moaned in the darkness of her pupils, memories and regrets diluted the rage Rebecca had witnessed earlier.

She spoke of an intelligent, sensitive young boy who was bookish without being geeky, respectful without being obsequious, curious without being intrusive. As he grew he was neither a pack animal nor a loner.

He had friends but he also liked time alone. He wanted to be a writer and that was a solitary occupation.

'He loved to walk down the riverside,' Afua said, still staring at the light bouncing from the windowpane, as if she could see beyond it to the Ness curling through the city. 'He would go beyond the war memorial to the bridge that takes you to the islands. That was his favourite. I used to take him there when he was little and he would giggle when the bridge bounced as joggers went by.' What might have been a smile teased her lips but the sadness in her eyes scared it away. 'I loved to hear him laugh.'

She stopped, shifted her position a little at Chaz's request.

'He loves the islands, loves the tranquillity, loves to walk among the trees down there. Sometimes you catch a glimpse of a seal or an otter. I used to take him over to the other bank and we would walk back again. It was a long walk for a little man but he did it without complaint. That's my James. Never complains. Just accepts what he cannot change.'

'Does he accept his prison sentence?'

Afua's eyes snapped in Rebecca's direction. 'He will never accept that because he is innocent.'

Rebecca wondered if that really was the case. Perhaps it was Afua who could not accept it.

9

The two boys were at the wooden table: one, maybe ten, clutching a tablet, the other a couple of years younger, their smiles punctuated by chuckles as they stared at something on the screen. Occasionally, the younger reached out to take the device from his brother—the family resemblance was obvious—but the elder always turned away and deflected the attempt with a jerk of an elbow, a chronological accident of birth proving that possession is all tenths of the law. The adults beside them watched the children, the father smiling and every now and then saying something to his sons, even craning over to see what they were watching. The woman was on the opposite side, the forefinger of her right hand crooked in the handle of the coffee cup before her. She was older, so perhaps not the mother of the children. Grandmother, maybe. Despite the warm sunshine she was wearing what looked like a thick winter coat. Rebecca thought she must be sweating like a politician in a truth serum factory. The woman watched the children but her mind seemed to be elsewhere. Rebecca couldn't help but speculate where. There was sadness in the woman's slightly tilted head, a sigh in the eyes that stared without seeing across the courtyard. She had seen something like it in Afua Stewart, but in that instance she knew the cause. Rebecca wondered what this stranger was thinking about. Did she long to be somewhere else? Did she wish her life was different? Was she thinking about the past and wondering where it went wrong, thinking of a face she wished she could see one more time, a voice she was desperate to hear again? Then, in an instant, whatever it was that had darkened her mind was burned away by the sunshine of a child's laughter. Maybe Rebecca had imagined the wistfulness.

Looking around her, she wished the shadows that haunted her own mind could be chased away so easily. Though she knew they could not. A child's laughter could not erase her dark thoughts; it only intensified them. The light of a summer's day could not brighten them, for they were immune to it. They seemed to be with her more and more these days and she had to battle to keep them at bay.

Grief. Loss.

Guilt.

They came in snatches, darting like arrows to sting her when she didn't expect it. The Highlands were alive with the people and deeds of the past—they existed in the stone and the dirt and the trees—but her own history lived within her own mind, she had learned. It stalked the shadows of her room by night.

Her father, his body diminished by cancer, on a hospice bed. His eyes hollow but suddenly flaring as he sat upright, as if he had seen something terrifying in the room that others could not.

The sound of a baby crying softly. A child who had never drawn breath but who lived on in darkness. And whose cries only she could hear.

A gunshot on a wet night. A man dead by a bullet meant for her, his blood melding with the rainwater, his life washed away by the raindrops.

They were sounds and images that crept softly through the recesses of her mind in the dead hours, when the world outside slept and she did not. Eventually she would find rest, of a sort, but she knew the shadows were never far away. They walked with her even when the sun shone.

She coped, though, because she had to. She knew these memories were a part of her but she refused to let them define her. Life is both shade and light, and she had a great deal of the latter. She had good friends and she loved her job, even though it often introduced her to the sadness of others. A loved one had died. A relative was seriously ill. A son had been imprisoned for a murder he may not have committed.

They had left Afua Stewart alone in her comfortable, neat villa—alone apart from her memories and her rage. Before they drove off, Chaz had performed a quick digital edit on his shots and emailed them to Rebecca while she hammered out some words on the banners and the case and added some quotes from Afua. She then fired the story and the images off to her newspaper clients—mobile wi-fI being a wonderful thing. She checked BBC News and the local news websites; no one had an entry yet, which was good news.

They took the A82 south out of Inverness, hugging the banks of Loch Ness for a time. Tiny diamonds sparkled on the reflective blue ripples of the waters and the sunlight flickered between the trees. She had driven this road in all weather, not only on a bright summer's day like this but also as the weather closed around the hills on the opposite bank, shrouding them in a thick mist. The road here clung to the western edge of the loch and there was, as ever, a steady stream of traffic. It was not only a Saturday but the summer season as well, so this narrow road pulsed with private cars, commercial vehicles and coachloads of tourists heading to and from the Highland capital.

Even so, Rebecca still managed a glance now and then at the smooth blue waters of the loch in the hope that she might spot something large and mysterious breaking the surface. The dark days were the most atmospheric, when the water was grey and murky, kissed by mist, and you could believe that, somewhere in its depths, there lurked a creature cut off from time. She chose to believe the legend of the monster in the water—it was a matter of faith, she supposed, which was curious, given she had a hard time with religion. However, as usual, Nessie did not oblige—*someday, big girl, someday*—and soon the road left the loch and its tiny, gem-edged folds of water behind to head inland a short way to Drumnadrochit and the tearoom.

At the table, Chaz was on the phone to Alan, his partner, who was in Surrey visiting his parents for his father's birthday. Chaz had managed to avoid the chore because they'd known this trip to Appin was in the offing. He was relieved, as was Alan, not because his parents openly took a dim view of their sexuality but because there was an undercurrent of resentment, mainly from Alan's mother. She wanted her son to be happy, of course, and she was glad he was, but Alan always felt, although it was never expressed, that she wished he had found a nice girl with whom to settle down.

'Yeah, we're in Drumnadrochit now,' Chaz was saying. 'Then we'll go to Ballachulish and'—he glanced at Rebecca—'where after that?'

36

'Kilnacaple,' she said. 'It's in Appin.'

'Kilnacaple,' he repeated into his mobile. 'It's in Appin.' He listened. 'No, they don't skI there. That's Aspen and it's in Colorado, you Sassenach.'

Rebecca smiled. Chaz was also a Sassenach, born in England but raised in the Western Isles. She also knew that Alan was well aware where Aspen was.

'Who knows what we'll find,' Chaz said. 'We're interested in justice, apparently.'

Rebecca gave him a sideways look and saw he was grinning at her as he repeated the words she had used to Mrs Stewart.

'Oh yes, very impassioned,' he said, and even though she could not hear the other end of the conversation, she knew Alan would be lapping this up. Fun at her expense was what they both lived for. 'I expected her to get up and bang the table. It was all very Tom Cruise in *A Few Good Men.*' He paused again. 'Behave yourself, you couldn't handle a Tom Cruise. And you're almost a married man.'

That was the big news Alan was going to deliver to his parents and his brothers before he left. He and Chaz had decided to tie the knot. *It's time I made an honest man of him*, Alan had said, adding with a smirk, *All this illicit sex is not good for the soul.* They were friends, but that was too much information.

The tearoom-cum-bookshop was housed in a converted barn just beyond the village's hotel and monster exhibition centre. Elspeth McTaggart spent most of her time here with her partner, Julie, since relinquishing the majority of the agency work to Rebecca. They couldn't drive through the village on the way to Appin without calling in—and Rebecca knew Elspeth would want an update.

As they waited for her to return with coffee, Rebecca listened to the boys laugh as Chaz ended his call, told her Alan sent hugs and kisses, then set to first cleaning his camera lens and viewfinder, then reformatting his memory card, removing the images he had already stored on his PC and in the Cloud. Rebecca knew that the last thing a professional photographer wanted was to be on a job and find he only has enough memory for a shot or two.

She saw Elspeth's squat figure heading back now, a young woman in tow carrying a tray with a squat silver pot for tea and a taller one for coffee, three mugs, and plates with two bacon rolls each. Elspeth hadn't asked if she wanted anything to eat—her boss was well aware breakfast was not something Rebecca would have bothered with that morning. Rebecca had a mother at home in Glasgow, but to all intents and purposes Elspeth had taken on the role in the north. She always said Rebecca was too thin. Rebecca disagreed, but she had to admit she was hungry and could feel her mouth watering at the thought of food.

Elspeth sat down opposite them, propping her cane up in between the slats of the table top, and directed the waitress to place the tray in front of her. Rebecca saw the young woman sneaking appraising looks at Chaz and she smiled to herself. She had seen many like her eyeing up her friend. Blond of hair, manly of chin, broad of shoulder. Like an American college boy. Robert Redford in his twenties.

'Ah, this is the life,' Elspeth said after thanking the young waitress. She'd moved away, snatching one final glance at Chaz. 'Fabulous weather.'

'It won't last,' said Rebecca.

Elspeth's mouth straightened as she gave Rebecca a mild glare. 'You really need to stop being so optimistic, Rebecca.'

One of the boys began to laugh again, the sort of high-pitched ear-splitter to which overly excited children are prone, and it pierced the distance between them like a javelin. Elspeth shot him a look so sharp it could penetrate armour plating. Her boss's distaste for children was well known to Rebecca, but it still made her smile. The boys were too intent on their screen, and were too far away anyway, for it to have any effect. Elspeth sighed and began to pour her tea, Rebecca hiding her amusement by reaching for a bacon roll. She bit into it, tasted the tang of the brown sauce and was grateful for having two mothers.

As they ate, Elspeth told her how she was doing with the book, which was due to go to an agent—an old friend of Elspeth's—in two months. There had been interest from an Edinburgh publisher, Scotland's largest independent, but they wanted to see the full manuscript before committing. Even though they would share any proceeds, Rebecca had agreed that Elspeth would shoulder much of the actual writing, as she was not confident she could provide the kind of colour needed for the project. It left her free to do the bread-and-butter work at the agency. She was comfortable honing a useable news story, but the detail and depth of a book was something else, though she did enjoy reading over what Elspeth had written, making suggestions, adding detail. After all, she had lived through most of it.

'So,' said Elspeth, once she had completed her update on the book's progress, 'is Afua Stewart happy now for us to take up the story?'

Rebecca had started her second roll, so she nodded as she chewed and swallowed. 'Not sure "happy" is the word, but she's willing to let us become involved. I think Tom's word carries a great deal of weight. Got the impression she had already decided in our favour but was going to make it difficult for me.'

'Also,' Chaz piped up as he stretched for his roll, 'we are *in pursuit of justice*. Rebecca Connolly has got her cape on and is ready to seek the truth.'

Rebecca punched him on the arm. He yelped in mock hurt.

'What's this?' Elspeth asked.

Rebecca felt a burning at her cheeks. 'I said something kind of stupid to Afua Stewart. About justice. Chuckles McSarky here hasn't shut up about it since.'

Elspeth poured four sachets of sugars into her tea and stirred it with a wooden strip. Julie had been trying to entice her from the dark side towards a healthier lifestyle but it was proving to be an uphill task. Granted, she had managed to get Elspeth to give up cigarettes—at least, she thought she had—but she had never won regarding sugar. Elspeth argued that the sachets were not a full teaspoonful anyway.

'Hate these bloody things,' she said, stirring with enthusiasm, 'but Julie stopped using proper teaspoons because people kept stealing them. And she won't have plastic ones. It's like living with David bloody Attenborough.' Elspeth rolled her eyes at her partner's environmentally friendly leanings. 'She gave me a lecture the other night about the amount of plastic particles in our water.' She sighed. 'I'm really surprised I'm not shitting polythene.' She dropped the stirrer on the tray. 'Anyway, remember this is a story, Becks. Don't go on a crusade. These things have a way of drawing you in—like a black hole eating the light. Just stick to the story, don't let it eat you.'

Rebecca had no intention of letting that happen. 'Did you believe James Stewart was guilty?' she asked.

'At the time, yes.'

'Not now?'

Elspeth shrugged. 'Who the fu—' She stopped mid-swear and glanced at the far-off table, even though it was too distant for anyone to hear. That didn't stop her sighing theatrically, the need to temper her fondness for profanity yet another reason to despise children. 'Who the hell knows?'

'She said her son was convicted in the press before it got to trial.'

Elspeth plucked a roll from the plate. 'Aye, they always say that, don't they? Sometimes with good reason, right enough.'

'Did you believe it at the time?' Chaz asked.

Elspeth thought while she chewed. 'It seemed a slam dunk. Murdo Maxwell was found in Kirkbrig House, naked, battered to death, drugs in his bloodstream, young Stewart asleep in the bed upstairs, the weapon on the floor beside him, similarly bollock naked, blood on his hands and body, drugs in *his* bloodstream. Doors locked. The prosecution contended that there had been an argument and young Stewart picked up the nearest blunt instrument and went a-bludgeoning.'

'A brass poker,' said Rebecca.

'A brass poker, taken from the open fire in the master bedroom. There was evidence of rough or maybe angry sex—bruising round Stewart's throat and shoulders, as if he had been forced down—and the prosecution contended that afterwards Maxwell went downstairs, perhaps for something to drink or more drugs or just because he liked to parade around the house naked, who knows?'

Chaz said, 'Speculation, surely?'

'Of course, but that was the theory. Anyway, they believed James Stewart grabbed the weapon, went after him and caved his head in. There was a blood trail back upstairs as if it had dripped from the poker. He then passed out on the bed and stayed that way until Maxwell's sister found him. As I said, slam dunk.'

'Until now,' said Rebecca.

Elspeth raised her mug to her lips. 'Until now.' She sipped her tea. 'Maybe.'

Chaz asked, 'You're not convinced?'

'I don't need to be convinced. I just need to know there's a story we can punt.'

Rebecca thought about this. 'There is.'

'More than the banners, I hope. That's a one-day wonder. You're going to need something else.'

'There is more,' said Rebecca, 'but it's going to take digging.'

'How much digging?'

'I need to see Stephen Jordan.'

Elspeth's lips pursed. 'Oooh, that's not good. He is no lover of reporters. Especially those who once worked for the *Highland Chronicle*.'

'Don't I know it.' Rebecca hadn't had personal experience of dealing with the solicitor but others had and she knew he didn't like some of the coverage clients had experienced over the years.

Elspeth worked at her bacon roll again. 'So, what's his connection?'

'I don't know. Mrs Stewart wouldn't tell me. All she said was that I would have to speak to Stephen Jordan.'

Elspeth's eyes rolled slightly. 'Aye, Afua always was a stroppy cow. I suppose that's how she got through it all back then. And since.'

Rebecca felt it would take a strong personality to endure the stress of your only son being accused and convicted of murder, especially if it was a high-profile case. It took an even stronger personality to wage a continual, if largely unseen, war in the ten years since her son's conviction to clear his name.

'I think it's her way of ensuring I commit, somehow,' said Rebecca.

'I think it's her way of just being a stroppy cow,' said Elspeth. 'So, Stephen Jordan aside—what's your next step?'

'We're going down to Kilnacaple, have a poke around. Tom is already there, staying with his sister. He was the one who took the photographs this morning.'

Elspeth smiled. 'Aye, and probably hung the banners, too, if I know Tom.' Rebecca knew her boss had a soft spot for the former Labour activist. She didn't necessarily agree with him over everything—not all bosses were bastards, not all Tories were corrupt, not all forms of capitalism were designed to crush the working man—but right or wrong she believed he had always spoken from the heart and not because it suited his political career.

'You'll have to speak to Gregory Stewart, too.' Elspeth's grin took on a wicked look. 'The father. *Sir* Gregory Stewart now.'

'I asked Afua about him, but she blanked me.'

'I don't think they parted on the best of terms. But he's an affable sort, when he feels like it. He might talk, but with these guys it's not what they say, it's what they don't say and the way they don't say it.'

Rebecca knew that Gregory Stewart's father's family had owned a stable of successful magazines, which was how he met Afua in her modelling days. He and Afua divorced shortly after their son was convicted.

The children screamed at something on the screen and Elspeth's head turned sharply, her body language suggesting she felt the need to object. Rebecca decided to distract her. 'So, tell me about Murdo Maxwell.'

Elspeth said nothing for a beat, another, then returned her attention to Rebecca. 'Thought you'd done some reading?'

Rebecca had. She knew he had been a solicitor in Glasgow, had been a sheriff for a time, knew he was politically active and often advised the Scottish Government on legal matters, knew he believed in civil rights and gay rights and animal rights and environmental rights—if there was a right to be upheld, fought for, campaigned for, proclaimed, demanded and protected, he was the one to do it. She also knew it often got up the noses of the establishment, even those in the party he supported.

'Did you ever meet him?' Chaz asked Elspeth.

'A few times, at pressers, receptions, that sort of thing.'

'Did you like him?'

'He was an arrogant sod. Suppose he had to be in order to reach the position he did, to do the things he did. I got the impression he didn't like me one bit.'

'Why not?' Rebecca said, her eyes widening in innocence. 'You are such a delight.'

Elspeth's nose wrinkled. 'Up yours, darling. No, for all his supposed anti-establishment principles, he was still a part of it and he didn't like commoners like me sticking our noses into matters that were really the province of our betters.'

'So, was he some kind of hypocrite?'

Elspeth pursed her lips. 'No, I think he genuinely believed in the stances he took. But he was a snob. Such matters were for the great and the good to pursue, not the slime-dwellers in the press.'

'What about the causes he took up?'

Elspeth gathered her thoughts. 'Okay, the usual—nuclear waste, destruction of the environment for commercial gain, open-cast mining ripping up the land. There was something about a wind farm somehow polluting the water table of a nearby community. Gay rights, of course. He made no secret of his sexuality, which was pretty brave, even in these enlightened times. He was also heavily into the misuse of land owner-ship. Butted heads with a few of the estate owners. And he argued against the tolls on the Skye Bridge.'

'He was involved in campaigns?'

'"Involved" is perhaps overstating it. He provided soundbites, raised the issues in the corridors of power, advised the campaigns on the best way forward, that sort of thing.'

Chaz asked, 'So he didn't actually carry flags for them?'

'No. He said once that he felt he best served the causes by remaining separate, independent. Objective, I suppose.' Elspeth shrugged, as if unconvinced, then her attention reverted to the children, who were now running around the table and yelling.

'You think he was objective?' asked Rebecca.

'You know I don't trust anyone who takes up politics, Becks.' Elspeth's eyes shot flames at the children. 'As Mark Twain almost said, fleas can be taught everything a politician can. But I have to admit, when all was said and done, and bearing in mind my deep-rooted mistrust, he seemed to be kind of okay.'

'Oooh, high praise,' said Chaz with a grin.

Elspeth looked back at him and smiled, for she had developed a soft spot for him. Most women did. 'For a party political animal he did go against his own lot more than once, so maybe there was some integrity there. Well, as much as there can be in a system where compromise is the norm.'

'You can't get anywhere without compromise,' argued Chaz.

'Yes, but it's something that is reached; it shouldn't be a starting-off point.'

Rebecca realised she had to steer the conversation back to the matter in hand. 'I suppose I'd better speak to the sister.'

'You're in luck there,' said Elspeth. 'She inherited Kirkbrig House. Far as I know, she's still there.' She looked at Rebecca with the beginnings of a cheeky smile. 'You can door-step her. Won't that be fun?'

Door-stepping. Turning up unannounced at someone's door and trying to glean quotes and/or information from them. Rebecca had door-stepped many people in the few years she had been in journalism. The conversation usually started with the trite 'How do you feel about your son/daughter/husband/wife's death?' and the response—when not a door slammed in her face—was predictable. She didn't much like doing it, but she knew it had to be done. Sometimes. And occasionally it raised a bigger issue.

'And there's somebody else you might want to chat with,' Elspeth said, a playful look in her eyes. Rebecca had seen it before. *Something wicked this way comes*, she thought. 'This is the fun part,' said Elspeth, enjoying herself now, screaming brats or not. 'One of Murdo's bestest buds is someone you know.'

'Who?'

'You'll pee yourself when I tell you, because he's not the first person you might think would be the BFF of a gay civil-rights tub-thumper.'

'You going to tell me or do I have to take your stick and beat it out of you?'

Elspeth savoured the moment before her grin widened and she said, 'Murdo Maxwell's best friend, from university to his death—they were even partners in the law firm in Glasgow—was none other than your old chum Finbar Dalgliesh.'

There was silence between them as Elspeth let this sink in, her smile still flickering from lips to eyes. The boys continued their romp across the seating area, weaving between the tables and shouting to each other, almost colliding with the waitress who had carried the tray for Elspeth. Their father called out for them to be more careful.

Rebecca was aware of all this and yet it was as if it was happening very far away. All she could think of was the man Elspeth had named. He was already on her mind after her encounter with Martin Bailey.

It certainly was a small world. But, as someone sage had once said, she wouldn't want to paint it.

Finbar bloody Dalgliesh.

Shit.

10

You can't help but consider the nature of time when you're in here. It flows but it's slow, like a sluggish river. It's not one day at a time, or one hour at a time, or one minute at a time: it's one second at a time. You let each one come and go without thinking too much about it because to ponder the slow burn of time would drive you crazy. So you let each second tick by, becoming a minute, growing to an hour, stretching to a day.

And with every tick of the clock I remember what happened to me. It may be in my past but it is also my present and my future.

I cannot forget, but can I forgive? I have been wronged. I have been wounded. Will time heal all wounds?

I know the answer to that. It won't. The wound will scar. There will be a layer of flesh over it but it will be there. It will burn forever. For all time.

And, in time, I will have my revenge. It's that knowledge that sustains me.

11

The monument was simple. Erected in 1911, it had none of the Victorian ostentation of other such memorials. It was stark and it was grey and it was topped by a gnarled chunk of white granite. It stood in the centre of the trees and bushes bursting with summer promise like a fat, inverted exclamation mark emphasising a great wrong. This was Cnap a' Chaolais, the hillock by the narrows, and there was no way they could have driven past it without at least paying their respects.

They had made good time from Drumnadrochit, despite the steady traffic, but it was still past one in the afternoon and Rebecca wanted to get to Kilnacaple to meet up with Tom. Before they'd parted, she had promised to keep Elspeth updated on their progress. As if that wouldn't happen anyway—Elspeth was her boss, even though she tended to leave Rebecca to her own way of working. That kind of mutual respect was something Rebecca had not experienced in the dying days of her old job at the newspaper. The company saw her as cannon fodder to be sacrificed whenever the fiscal assault threatened shareholder income. She, and her work, was no more vital to them than the technology on the desks and the pens and notebooks that became increasingly shoddy. The stories she found, researched and wrote were merely a means of filling white space and generating online clicks. The idea seemed lost on the multinational owners that a weekly newspaper was a vital component in local democracy, that its function was not merely to generate profits but also to hold power to account and to give a voice to those who had none, apart from every few years at the ballot box. Rebecca was honest enough to understand that there was a fine line between community journalism and economics. Without the strong bottom line of the latter, the former was often not possible. However, she did feel that space-filling and click-bait had become the norm, while time to dig deep into stories had been squeezed into non-existence. That was why she'd left a steady job and income behind to join forces with Elspeth, who saw her as an equal partner rather than merely a payroll number. It wasn't an easy gig, and she had to work long hours to make sure she got the story and deliver it to clients on time. Not having much of a social life helped, of course. She had dinners with Chaz and Alan. The occasional date, although there was no one special.

They had parked at the side of the road opposite the hotel and climbed the steps to the knoll. The banners were still there, draped around the metal railings surrounding the monument. Chaz snapped some images and Rebecca stood by the information board, scanning the words, then the plaque on the monument itself.

Erected 1911 to the memory of James Stewart of Acharn.
Executed on this spot, November 8th 1752,
for a crime of which he was not guilty.

As she read it, the story came back to her, as usual in her father's voice.

They had stood here on this very spot when she was barely in her teens and he had told her about the case, his words frosted with rage, his face, normally quick to smile and laugh, frozen, but his eyes, as they stared at the finger of granite pointing to heaven, were soft almost to the point of liquid. She had sensed his sadness at the wrong done here and she sensed it once more as the sunlight dappled the rough surface of the stone and the birds sang their songs of joy. The execution of James of the Glens may have taken place 270 years earlier, but John Connolly was a man who had hated injustice. It was not just because he was a police officer. It was something inside him, something she had never understood when he was alive but she now knew was built upon a secret he had discovered about his family. A dark secret that had forced him to leave the place of his birth and never return, never to speak of it at any length, no matter how much his young daughter probed.

As Chaz walked around the edifice, she heard her father's voice as if he was standing right beside her again. But he wasn't. And he never would again. Not in this world.

If the history of the Highlands was a song, he had said, *it would be a lament. A song of sorrow, of loss, of grieving. You hear it at Culloden and Glencoe and in the deserted villages cleared to make way for sheep. You hear it on the battlefields with names and those without. And if you listen carefully, you hear it in the wind . . .*

It was something he often told her to do: just listen. Sometimes impatiently in relation to whatever point he or her mother was trying to make—'Just LISTEN, Becks'—but on their many trips to the Highlands or the coast he would have her stand very still and close her eyes and focus her senses on the sounds around her. Now she did it again. She closed her eyes. His voice, the memory of it, stilled. She filtered out the roar of the traffic on the road and bridge below, zeroed in on the soft whisper of the breeze as it wafted through the branches.

And she could have sworn she heard it.

A song of mourning lifting from the grass beneath her and joining a chorus in the leaves. A keening for the dead. And she thought she heard something else, adding a rhythm to the gentle wind that carried up to this knoll from the water.

Something rattling.

She opened her eyes to see Chaz staring at her.

'Catching up on some shut-eye?' he asked. 'Falling asleep on your feet, like a horse?'

'You think I need it?'

He shrugged, fired off a shot of her as she stood beside the railings around the memorial. 'You're looking tired, Becks.'

She shook her head to clear it. 'It's been a tough year.'

He didn't need to ask her what she meant. Even so, he stared at her for a long moment, then asked, 'So, what were you doing?'

She shot him a slightly embarrassed smile. 'You'd laugh if I told you.'

'Try me.'

'Nah, you'll think I'm nuts.'

'I already think you're nuts, Becks. Can't see anything new making much difference.'

She told him what her father had said about the song carried on the wind's breath. Chaz took it in without laughing, then closed his eyes to listen for himself. She watched him, barely breathing herself in case it kept him from experiencing it. He looked so handsome in the dappled sunlight, his hair slightly ruffled as if there were fingers in that breeze just desperate to caress him, his eyes closed—how the hell did he get such long lashes? When she had first met him she had thought he was flirting with her, but she soon learned he wasn't. His heart belonged to Alan—waspish, funny, infuriating, generous Alan—who returned his love with such fervour Rebecca could often feel the heat herself. Chaz had seemed so young back then, so innocent, but occasionally she now saw dark shadows in his eyes. It had only been a couple of years but so much had happened. Rebecca wondered how different things would be had she not ignored her editor's orders to go to his island to follow a story. They had almost lost Chaz in the car crash there, caused by homophobic louts.

Chaz opened his eyes. 'Sorry, all I hear is the wind and the traffic.' He jerked his head to the road below and the vehicles crossing the bridge. 'Maybe you need Celtic or Viking blood in you.'

Perhaps it was something in her island blood that helped her tune into the song, or at least imagine it. Although he had been brought up in the Western Isles, where his father was one of the GPs, Chaz had been born in London.

He studied the information board. 'So, tell me about James of the Glens.'

She took a deep breath and shifted her attention. 'It's all there,' she said. 'And you know it all anyway. I know you do.' Chaz was fascinated by Scottish history, so it went without saying he'd have some knowledge of the case.

'Actually, only the bare bones,' he said. 'Tell me what your dad told you.'

Chaz was one of the few people she spoke to about her father, apart from her mother in Glasgow, so she recalled what her dad had told her about the heavy price the Highlands had paid after the rout at Culloden, of the often violent pacification, of the outlawing of virtually everything that made the people and their culture unique, of the torch still carried for James Stuart, the King Over the Water. Many Highlanders paid two rents—one to the factor, the other to the Jacobite cause.

She explained to Chaz about the death of Colin Campbell of Glenure, appointed government factor after Culloden to the estate of Ardsheal in Appin and Locheil across the water in Lochaber. He was gunned down in the Lettermore Woods just around the headland. Seumas a' Ghlinne—James of the Glens—was accused of the murder and convicted under perjured evidence by a kangaroo court by a jury stuffed with Campbells.

Allan Breck Stewart, not the romantic figure of Stevenson's *Kidnapped* but a braggart and a wastrel who failed to live up to the high honour of the man who had raised him—none other than James Stewart—was also a suspect in the murder of Colin Campbell, but he was never captured or tried.

Then there came the execution on this little hill where they stood. Back then it was just a mound of spare heather and grass overlooking the narrows, the bridge over two centuries away. It had been a blustery day in November, the clouds dark and glowering, making midday seem like dusk, and the wind threw itself at the men and women clustered on this exposed summit as if it was trying to pick them and the gallows up to hurl them into the water below. The rain stung at faces and hands as James Stewart was led to the noose, where he was allowed to speak before the final terrible injustice was enacted. He spoke calmly and clearly from the gallows. He denounced those who had accused him and declared his innocence. He wished that God would forgive those who had perjured themselves and he declared himself an honest man.

'So did Allan Breck Stewart do it?' Chaz asked.

'Who knows? He may have been involved,' Rebecca said. 'James wasn't convicted of the actual shooting, though. He had an alibI and the law firmly believed that it was Allan Breck Stewart who did it. James was found guilty of being "airt and pairt". In other words, he didn't pull the trigger but he was part of a conspiracy and may even have ordered it.'

'You think that likely?'

'At this stage, who can say? Maybe a scholar who has studied the case from beginning to end. Certainly not me. All I can say is that the trial was a travesty. As Dad said, there were more strokes pulled than in the Oxford and Cambridge boat race.'

Chaz propped one leg up on the low railing around the monument and studied the inscription on the stone.

'He recited the 35th Psalm,' said Rebecca, and she heard it now, a Highland voice, strong, firm, without fear, speaking the words in Gaelic. She knew some of them in English:

Plead my cause, o Lord, with them that strive with me: fight against
them that fight against me . . .
Let them be as chaff before the wind . . .
Let their way be dark and slippery . . .

'They called it the Psalm of James of the Glens after that,' Rebecca explained. 'And then he was hanged. It wasn't the quick and easy death of later executions; it was painful and extended, a long, slow strangulation that was hard to witness, even in those days when death was often harsh and brutal. They let the body hang on the rope for five hours before it was hung in chains. And that was where it stayed for three years, open to the elements and hungry wildlife.'

'They made an example of him,' said Chaz, softly.

Rebecca recited a phrase she had committed to memory. It had been coined by some official at the time and she had read it only the night before, while reading up on the case to remind herself of the details. 'Nothing could be more material to the future well-governing of these distant parts of Scotland than the exemplary punishment of so notorious a criminal.' Bureaucrats had a way of making cruelty mundane, she thought.

'Friends and relatives tried to care for the remains as best they could. They came and cleaned the dead face, scared off the birds that pecked at it. But even that stopped. The flesh fell away, the clothes rotted, until only bones were left. Even they fell apart, but the authorities ordered they be restrung and hung back up again as a stark reminder of the fate in store for any Scot who might still wish to defy the King's law.'

She stopped, listened on the wind. There were no ethereal voices joining in sorrow this time, merely the underscore of the breeze in the grass and the branches.

'Finally, they allowed a kinsman to take the bones away and bury them in the ground of Keil Chapel, down the road at Duror,' she said. 'He was laid to rest beside the body of his wife, Margaret. They say the gallow post was hauled from the earth and thrown down there into the water, a curse laid on anyone who touched it.'

'I do like me a curse.' Chaz laughed.

'Not sure anyone ever suffered anything, though. It was eventually used as a fence post, I think, and no one reported any ill effects. They say the Stewart clan know the true culprit but will never speak it. Allan Breck, maybe. Another theory is that it was a conspiracy of young bloods from Appin and Lochaber, a contest to see who was the best shot. There might have been two shooters.'

'Ah—a grassy knoll scenario?'

Rebbeca smiled. 'Something like that. It could also have been a family affair. Colin Campbell's own nephew wanted his job and his inheritance . . .'

Chaz breathed in deeply though his nose, then out again. He turned back to her. 'What about our James Stewart?'

She considered her reply. 'That remains to be seen. It's one thing believing a story of romance and betrayal two and a half centuries ago, quite another having blind faith in innocence today. I've got a job to do. I can't let what happened here hundreds of years ago cloud that.'

Chaz gave a small nod, and with a last glance at the memorial he hefted his camera bag. 'We done here?'

Rebecca took a final look around the glade. She nodded and followed Chaz back to the steps. But faintly, as they moved, she could have sworn she heard the rattling sound again. She stopped and scanned the trees and bushes for the source but saw nothing. She didn't know what lay beyond them but she had seen fences with old CDs strung up on them before, she assumed to scare away pests. Maybe that was what it was. The sound continued as she left the memorial, with the voices on the wind behind, little more than an echo, as if it was a memory being shared by the land.

12

The dead don't listen, no matter what the psychics would have people believe. That was why Joseph McClymont came to this hill overlooking Glasgow Cathedral and the Royal Infirmary whenever he had something to say that he didn't want overheard, especially by his father who, despite his failing body and mind, still had ears like a bat.

The city of the dead, they call it. The Necropolis. There are many ways to die and many ways to describe it, and this vast, labyrinthian monument to those who had shuffled this mortal coil, left this veil of tears, gone to glory, kicked the bucket, was testament to them all. The Victorians liked to honour their dead and they did it in style. For Joseph McClymont, when you're dead you're dead. No fancy monument could change that. Over the years he had become very well acquainted with death. As a child he had been forcibly introduced to its finality when he saw his mother and little sister die. He would have been taken too, but he had wanted to stay with his dad, so his mother got in the car with his sister. The explosion blew him and Rab off their feet, the Range Rover high into the air in a ball of flame.

It was not something easily forgotten.

He stood at the summit in front of the Doric column topped by a statue of John Knox. The fiery old preacher wasn't buried here, but he was memorialised nonetheless. From his vantage point, Old John was pretty much master of all he surveyed. Joseph felt that way too, as he looked eastward across the city. He had expanded the empire built by his father to encompass enterprises both criminal and legal, not just in Glasgow but beyond. However, the East End very much remained his family's domain. From here, he could see the deep canyon of Duke Street and, if he looked really hard, could probably identify the area where the Range Rover had exploded all those years before. He didn't look, though. While not easily forgotten, he didn't let it get in the way. He had business to do.

He checked that his two men were a sufficient distance from him before he hit the number pre-dialled on his phone. He didn't want anyone to hear him talking.

'What do you want?'

The man's voice was terse. Ordinarily Joseph would have objected to such a tone, but this was not an ordinary man. Joseph was wealthy, but this guy was off the scale. If there was one thing Joseph respected, it was money. In fact, the *only* thing he respected was money.

'Believe me, I wouldn't be calling if I didn't have to,' said Joseph. He might have been impressed by the man's bank balance and position, but that didn't mean he had to be overly civil.

'I told you years ago I didn't want to speak to you again.'

'I know.'

'We made a deal. That was it, as far as I was concerned.'

'I know, but we need to talk.'

'Why?'

'Murdo Maxwell.'

'Ancient history.'

'They're looking into his death.' The line fell silent and Joseph wondered if the guy had hung up. 'You still there?'

'Who exactly is looking into his death?'

'The press, at the moment.'

'How do you know?'

'You not seen today's news?'

'The only things I read are business reports.'

'It says online there are banners up, claiming it's a miscarriage of justice.'

There was a moment's silence again, then the man said, 'And is that it? Banners?'

'No, I've been told there'll be more. There's a solicitor up in Inverness, name of Jordan. You know him?'

'Why the hell would I know some cheap little ambulance chaser?'

'Anyway, it seems he has something.'

'Something like what?'

'I don't know.'

'You don't know?'

'No.'

'Then why the hell are you bothering me, Wee Joe?'

Joseph winced at the nickname, which he knew the man was using deliberately. 'I've got someone up there now, seeing what he can find out.'

'You have someone in Inverness nosing around? And how much does this someone who is nosing around know about our arrangement?'

'Only what everyone on the street knows. All he's doing is trying to find out what this solicitor knows. I want to know if anything will come back on me.'

'On us, you mean?'

'No,' said Joseph. 'Frankly, I don't give a single shit about you. What happened back then was regrettable, but it was taken too far.'

'And it would have gone further if Big Rab hadn't taken charge. You screwed up when you pissed me off, sonny, and Daddy had to take over. You screwed up and people died. What you did to my son . . .'

Joseph didn't want to go into that, so he cut him off. 'The point is, if this goes further we all stand to lose, so we have to be on our mettle.'

'On our mettle? Now, there's the benefits of a university education. You'll be quoting Greek and Latin next.'

'If I did, I'm sure you would understand.'

A short laugh at that, little more than a clearing of the throat. 'Yes, I would. So, speaking of your dad, does he know you're talking to me?'

'No. My dad isn't well. He doesn't need to know.'

'He wouldn't be happy this is all rising again, would he? After all, he had to bail you out last time.'

Joseph was tired of the exchange. 'Look, I'm giving you the heads-up as a matter of courtesy. It's what my dad would want.'

'If he knew about it.'

'Yes, if he knew about it.' Joseph could feel his temper beginning to stretch.

If he'd had his way ten years before, this man would have been dealt with permanently, but Big Rab vetoed it. He's too big to take out, he had said. There are other ways to deal with men like him. Joseph remembered his father looking at him over his spectacles, the ones like John Lennon used to wear. And anyway, he went on, you were in the wrong. Big Rab had been ashamed of him. Joseph had been ashamed of himself. There had been a lot of shame back then. Time had dulled it. It was a bruise that had faded but refused to go away. All it took was the slightest pressure and the pain returned.

His father had set about smoothing things over, which pissed Joseph off. There was a time when Big Rab would have pulled the trigger himself, but he had mellowed with age, had become more reasonable. He began to favour negotiation over retaliation. There had already been unpleasantness. Blood had been shed. Joseph knew too well that violence attracted attention, but in this instance, with this particular man, he would have happily broken that rule.

And some day he might just do that.

'What happened between us is in the past. Everyone agreed.' He was struggling to keep his voice under control. 'We all made mistakes and all lost in the end. If I hear anything I feel you should know, I will be back in touch.'

He cut the connection before the other man could say anything further to enrage him.

13

Rebecca stared at the heavy double wooden gates, her fingers drumming on the steering wheel. Chaz waited, silently for once, and for that she was grateful. He had worked with her long enough to know this did not come easily. Some reporters took door-stepping in their stride, but Rebecca always had trouble with it, even though she was as adept at getting over the threshold as the best of them. Compared to James of the Glens facing certain death on a storm-tossed hill this was nothing, but she still had to steel herself. This was not like visiting someone in Inverness, where you walk up to the front door and rattle the letterbox. She had already decided not to drive onto the property—that somehow being a worse breach of privacy than approaching on foot—so she would have to open those gates, which were designed to intimidate, and were doing a damn good job, and then walk the length of the gravel driveway they could see through the wooden spars.

She had no idea how long that walk would be, for she couldn't see Kirkbrig House from where she sat in the car. A high hedge towered beside them, with branches stretching over the top as if they were desperate to escape captivity. The car was parked in a slightly elevated position above the A828, the sliproad to the gates having eased away from the road, then doubled back and upwards. Loch Linnhe shone blue in the afternoon sun behind them, and on its western edge were the hills of Ardgour. She had never been to Ardgour. She had been to Ardnamurchan, and she wondered if the far-off hills she could see belonged there. She suddenly wanted to cross the clear, smooth water of the loch in a little boat and find somewhere sunny to lie down and let the day slip away. She did not want to face a woman who had found her brother's beaten body ten years before in the very house she now lived. But she knew she had to. She needed to get this over with.

They had decided not to stop at Lettermore, where Colin Campbell was killed, or the ruined chapel at Keil where James of the Glens' bones were interred. Instead they pushed on a few more miles, intending to reach the small village of Kilnacaple where Tom was waiting, but en route Rebecca had suddenly decided she would tackle Murdo Maxwell's sister right away. Another of her father's lessons. If you have an unpleasant job to do, get it done as soon as you can. The anticipation of it is often worse than the execution.

'You sure you want to do this?' Chaz asked, unable to remain silent any longer.

'Yes,' she said. 'But I'll do it alone.'

She knew he would understand. He had been on such jobs before with Rebecca and was aware she was better facing this by herself. One person turning up unannounced to reopen old wounds was bad enough; two strangers, especially when one is carrying a camera, can be counter-productive. If she needed him, she would call.

She took a deep breath and opened the door, the warmth of the sun coming as a shock after the air-conditioned coolness of the car. She stood for a moment, breathing in the air. She thought she could detect a whiff of honeysuckle, but couldn't see any. It was one of the few plants she could recognise. Her mother had planted it in their garden in Milngavie.

'If something comes, I'll move the car,' said Chaz, and she acknowledged him with a wave of her hand before unlatching the gate and heaving it open. The honeysuckle scent was stronger here and she saw it wrapped around a wooden pergola set against the high hedge, a bench placed underneath. She savoured the delicious bouquet, let it take her back to her mother's garden at home in Glasgow, just for an instant. They had planted it together, her mother and father, and the aroma always sparked memories of laughter and eating at the rickety picnic table her father had put together none-too-expertly. The bench shifted to one side whenever someone sat down, the entire construction always on the verge of collapse. It never did, though. It remained standing for years, weather-beaten, its green paint flaking away to reveal the bare wood beneath, until it finally succumbed to the elements and fell to pieces in a high wind.

It was the winter her father died.

She moved away from the pergola, pushed the pangs of homesickness and the stabbing grief from her mind. She had a job to do. Best get it done.

The driveway curved between two stretches of well-tended lawn peppered with trees and bushes. She could see the house now, grey sandstone, two stories, four sets of windows on each floor at the front, more on the gable she could see. It was large, with the kind of ostentation some Victorians liked—a squat turret topped by a weathervane, railings around a flattened area at the edge of the roof. It was obviously well cared for; the window sills looked freshly painted, the gutters seemed original but sturdy enough, the dark slate roof watertight as far as she could see. The gardens were well maintained and extensive, stretching beyond and behind the house to woods that climbed to a grassy slope topped by a ridge. The person who lived here had money and was happy to spend it. Her feet crunched loudly on the dry surface of the drive and she looked around for signs of life but saw no one. Belatedly she wondered if Mona Maxwell, the dead man's sister, had a dog. And if she did, was it running around freely in the grounds? And if it was, did it bite?

To the right of the house, partially obscured by trees, was an old bridge, humpbacked and wide enough only for two people to walk side-by-side. She couldn't see the stream it crossed but she could detect a gap in the undergrowth that showed it running from the woods at the foot of the slope in the direction of the road. Beyond the bridge, through another patch of trees, was the triangle of a church spire.

The front door swung open before she reached it and a woman stepped out under the small vaunted porchway and gave her a stern look. Rebecca presumed this was Mona Maxwell. Her angular shape underneath the white blouse was slim rather than thin, her legs encased in grey slacks were long, her grey hair cut close, her brown eyes steady as she stared at Rebecca. She stood tall and straight and she exuded an air of no-nonsense that, in Rebecca's experience, indicated she was going to have a hard time getting anywhere.

'Can I help you?' the woman asked.

'Ms Maxwell?' Rebecca asked, her voice lacking confidence, not as to whether she had identified the woman correctly but at standing here in front of this imposing Victorian house and wilting under the gaze of a woman who looked as if she thought hanging was too good for some people.

'*Miss* Maxwell,' the woman replied. 'And who are you?'

'My name is Rebecca Connolly, Ms . . . Miss Maxwell.' She paused, she didn't know why, but the slight hesitation caused Mona Maxwell's mouth to tighten with ill-concealed impatience. Rebecca pressed on. 'I'm from the Highland News Agency.'

The mouth tightened even further. The woman waited.

Rebecca's experience was proving correct. 'I'm sorry to trouble you . . .'

Mona Maxwell's words came out like a whip. 'Please get on with it, girl.'

Yes, definitely onto a loser here, but she had come this far and she might as well go for it. 'Well, I wanted to talk to you about your brother.'

No reaction. If her mouth tightened any further her teeth would be ground to dust, Rebecca thought.

'There have been developments.' Rebecca felt the need to keep talking. 'In the case.' She paused again. 'Your brother's case.'

A slight flaring of the nostrils was the only reply. The gaze did not flinch, the erect posture did not loosen.

'I wondered if I might talk to you about it. There may well be further news coverage and I thought it only fair that I—'

'What sort of developments?'

Rebecca hesitated again. This woman really was intimidating, like an old school headmistress with a quick-draw tawse. She knew Mona Maxwell had been a teacher and she would bet her degree that she would favour corporal punishment, even if only as a means of exercise.

'Speak, girl—out with it,' Mona Maxwell snapped. She didn't need a belt, actually, she had her voice, which slapped Rebecca's face like a gauntlet.

'There were banners put up at various sites relating to James of the Glens. As you know . . .'

'Yes, yes.' Very real irritation now. 'He shared a name with the James Stewart who was convicted of murdering my brother. So, banners. What else?'

'Other information has come to light which may call the conviction of today's James Stewart into question.'

There was silence then. Mona Maxwell's gaze did not wither one bit. Her mouth was still a wedge of disapproval between nose and chin, her body language that of someone who wished she had a shotgun she could use to ward off trespassers. Rebecca was more convinced than ever that she was about to be told in no uncertain terms to leave.

'Well,' said the woman, and then she took a deep breath. 'It's about bloody time.'

14

I watched a butterfly in my cell this morning. I don't know how it got in, but there it was, flitting around the wall near the small window, attracted by the grey dawn, I suppose. It was white, its body black, and its delicate wings seemed to beat feverishly as it weaved its erratic way against the whitewashed brickwork towards the square of light.

I wondered if it felt fear, being trapped inside. I wondered if, within that frail little body, it understood why it could not penetrate that barrier and reach the rising sun and the free air.

I found it hard inside at first. It took me some time to develop my philosophy. But then I was angry. Being accused of and convicted of something you did not do makes you angry. It makes you hate the world. It starts with the court system—judges, witnesses, lawyers, especially the lawyers—and then the hate consumes you and it extends to everyone you come into contact with. But that hate kept me going, otherwise I might have ended it all.

Yes, it has been difficult. I am young. I am good-looking. I am gay. Put all that together and it adds up to a tough time. Yes, there are other inmates who are gay, and those who are gay for the stay, but by and large the intimidation is more subtle than dropping the soap. I caught some distasteful looks from a couple of staff members, as well as inmates. They thought I would be easy to bully. And I had to take it for a while.

I learned, too, as the weeks became months and the months became years. Now I'm an experienced convict, an old lag. I know the tricks and the dodges. I know who to avoid and who to socialise with. I avoid drugs and debt and gambling. I rebuff any sexual advances. I know the screws who are decent and those who have themselves been brutalised by a system which often still prioritises punishment over rehabilitation. The fear remains, though, and sometimes I am like that butterfly, yearning to break through that glass to reach the light. The fear flutters inside me, like an itch I can't get at.

I've seen inmates come and go. Some released. Others have killed themselves because they can't take the confinement or because the demons in their minds finally got the upper hand. Because they come calling, those demons—not to everyone, but I've heard them. I heard them but I ignored them, and soon they moved on to someone else in the wing, niggled at them until they gave in, gave up, tuned out, turned off.

The butterfly got out when the screws opened the cell doors. I saw it dodge and weave around the hall. So did some of the other guys and they watched it. Faces that were more accustomed to scowls and curses and blows suddenly softening at the sight of a flying insect, its white wings ghostly in the light, flitting around the landings and staircases. Finally, exhausted, it landed and one of the screws trapped it in a glass, carried it away. I hope he let it go. I hope now it's out there, somewhere, floating, flying, fluttering.

Free.

It seems strange to think that it will be long dead before I am free. A butterfly lives for an average of a month, I read once. A few weeks to me is an entire lifetime to it. Each beat of its wings is like the ticking of a clock, taking it closer to eternity. Each life has its own rhythm.

I have eased into the rhythm of the prison. The fear, the hate, the rage still gnaw at me, but it's become little more than white noise.

15

The exterior of Kirkbrig House was from a time when men tipped their hats and women were little more than possessions, but the interior was smart and modern and the high-ceilinged sitting room into which Mona Maxwell led Rebecca made good use of the light streaming in through the large windows. The hardwood floors were stained and polished to mirror quality and a series of Oriental rugs in subdued colours provided walking areas free from any threat of slippage.

Rebecca sat in a cream-coloured couch facing the window, through which she could see the front garden and the gate at the end of the driveway. It had seemed such a long walk as she approached the front door but now she had—amazingly—been made to feel welcome, it did not seem so far. She wondered if she should mention she had a friend waiting beyond the gate, but decided not to push her luck. Chaz would be okay in the car. She had cracked a window.

Mona Maxwell seated herself in a winged armchair beside the open fireplace, the grate cold and dead and concealed behind a screen bearing Chinese characters. The dark wood of the high mantle was also buffed to within an inch of its grain and decorated by Chinese figurines. Someone had a thing about China, it seemed. Rebecca's eyes fell on the heavy iron fireplace tools on a rotating stand and wondered if the brass poker hanging on one of the hooks was the one used years before to murder Murdo Maxwell. Surely not.

'You have a lovely house,' said Rebecca.

'Thank you.' The woman acknowledged the compliment with a bob of her head, then looked around as if seeing it for the first time.

'My brother renovated it completely when he bought it, oh, must be twenty-five years ago now, perhaps more. It was in a bit of a state, so he got it for a song. He needed somewhere away from the city, somewhere he could go and breathe air that was untainted, he said.' She paused, a faint smile diluting the severity of her face but not by much. 'He worked very hard at it, or rather, the men he hired worked very hard at it, but he made sure he got what he wanted. There was wet rot and dry rot, it needed rewired, refloored, reroofed. It had been allowed to fall into quite a state over the years.'

'Victorian, isn't it?'

'Yes, it was built by an Edinburgh textile merchant who made his pile in Far East trade.'

'Is that why the Oriental pieces are so prominent?'

'No, they are mine. I like Chinese art and culture. I speak Mandarin. I taught English in Shanghai for many years.' She settled back in the chair and steepled her fingers. 'So, Miss Connolly, what is this other information of which you spoke?'

Rebecca knew she was on thin ice here. The woman seemed sympathetic, but when she found out how little Rebecca knew, that attitude could alter. However, her judgement told her that Mona Maxwell valued honesty and straight-speaking. 'I'll be frank with you. All I know is that a solicitor in Inverness knows something about your—' She stopped short, then ventured delicately, 'About what happened to your brother.'

'You mean my brother's murder?' Rebecca had been right: Mona Maxwell liked straight-speaking. 'You can say it, you know. I know what happened. I found him. So what exactly does this solicitor know?'

Here it comes. 'I don't know—yet. I only heard of this development this morning. I have still to talk to the solicitor in question.'

'Then why are you here?'

'I wanted to warn you that there may well be renewed interest in your brother's, erm, case.'

'His murder.'

'Yes, his murder. The banners proclaiming James Stewart's innocence will set things off. I've interviewed his mother.'

'I see.'

'I've already written that story and it should run in at least one of the Sundays tomorrow. It's already online. The information regarding the dead man's statement will follow later, once I track it down. But given there is new information . . .'

'Whatever it is.'

'Yes, whatever it is. As I said, I'll find that out on Monday.' Hopefully, Rebecca thought. 'Anyway, between the banners and the new information, it's highly likely this will kickstart some sort of campaign and I thought you should know.'

'I see.' Mona studied her for a moment. Rebecca had the impression she was being weighed and measured. 'You also wanted to talk to me about that day, too, though. And see the scene of the crime. Am I correct?'

She was no fool. Again, Rebecca decided honesty was what was needed. 'Yes.'

A satisfied nod. 'Then come with me,' Mona said. 'Let me give you the tour.'

She led Rebecca back into the wide hallway. 'I had been away overnight, staying in Inverness with a friend . . .'

She remembered the birdsong that pierced the still morning air. She remembered that somewhere a tractor sputtered like a series of coughs in a waiting room. She remembered that on the roadway beyond the long gravel drive and the expanse of lawn and the carefully cut high hedge a motorbike roared past.

But most of all she remembered the deep silence within the house.

Outside, the world sang, coughed, roared. Inside, it was still. Normally there would have been noise here, for her brother avoided silence, perhaps even found it pernicious, so he countered it with the babble of TV, the opinions of talk radio, the mindfulness of music, but more often than not he filled it with the echo chamber of his own voice, of which he was inordinately fond. Always had been, even as a child. Always talking, often laughing, for he was quick to smile and even quicker to pontificate, as to leave an opinion unshared was, to him, a waste. But that morning there was no blaring TV. No sonorous voices on the radio. No soothing music. Just a deep silence that seemed to permeate every corner, reach every cornice, probe every cupboard. It hung heavily on the wide stairway and clung to the hardwood of the floors.

Now, as she hesitated in the open doorway, the Yale key still in the lock, daylight refracting through the myriad colours of the stained-glass window above the staircase, casting rainbow pools of blues and orange and green and red, she knew something lurked in that silence. Something was hidden deep within its folds. Something awful.

The deep red she saw at the foot of the stairs wasn't caused by sunlight streaming through the window, though. The filtered light was natural, welcome, warm. The streaks on the wood were alien. They should not have been there. It looked as if someone had spilled sauce from a spoon between the kitchen at the rear of the house and the stairs. Streaks and spots, slicing across or dotting the gleaming floor and soaking into the cream runner in the centre of the stairway.

But it wasn't sauce; she knew that.

She pursed her lips, stepped fully into the vestibule, leaving the door behind her open. She was not a fanciful person, but the silence was getting to her. She paused at the foot of the stairs, cocked her head to listen for any sound from the floor above, but heard nothing. She placed one foot on the bottom step, changed her mind, retracted it and turned towards the kitchen door at the end of the passageway. It was an old house, and this hallway was narrow with little light penetrating its shadows, but she could see the trail easily, so she kept to the far wall so as not to step in it.

The birds still sang; the tractor still coughed.

She could feel uneasiness building within her. She knew what she was going to find, but she still felt she had to reach that heavy wooden door and see it for herself. The passage from the vestibule to the door was long, but it seemed endless this morning, as step by step she moved towards it, her shoulder brushing the carefully painted walls, hitting the corner of the painting, a Landseer, which her brother had hated but it had been a gift from a former lover and he was sentimental. Murdo was like that. Verbose, opinionated, but generous and often warm-hearted. Not perfect, though. No, not perfect at all.

She reached the partially open door. Finally. She spread her hand on the wooden panels. Gently. She pushed. Slowly.

The door swung open with ease.

Light flooded in from the kitchen window. She noted the scene outside absently: the garden with its mature trees and the stone pathway snaking round bushes to a pond with a little wooden bridge, like something from the Willow Pattern; on the ridge above the house the old tractor. Jess from the farm, dragging a trailer. Then her attention became fixed on the floor. And what was on the floor.

The quarry tiles were an oven-baked red, as was the liquid—static now, sticky—that had pooled around her brother's head. He was naked and lay face down, his head set slightly to the side, his blank eyes open as if staring back at her. Black-red blood stiffened his hair and crusted in lines from his nose and ears. She could see where the flesh had ruptured and the skull had shattered and the brain had erupted.

As she stared at the body the silence within the house wrapped itself around her.

On the ridge, the tractor puttered out of sight. In the garden, the birds still sang.

16

Rebecca listened as the woman spoke in a strong, clear voice. She might have been relating a story she had been told, had Rebecca not seen the pain in her eyes as she fixed them on the spot on the vestibule floor where she had first seen the blood. Mona Maxwell was strong, but no one is that strong. Rebecca knew that personally. Grief and sadness can be locked away, but they still leak through the eyes, sometimes as tears but more often as a faraway look, a misting of the pupils and iris, as if something other than what is before them is being seen. She had acknowledged it in Afua Stewart, and she saw it too in Mona Maxwell at that moment. The mind is a time traveller: while Mona's body was in the here and now, her mind had leaped back ten years and she was reliving that morning.

Her voice stopped suddenly, as if the words had simply dried. They stood in silence in the airy entrance hall, the sun's rays streaming through the stained glass that dominated the wall above the stairway, the light bending and transforming into a psychedelic kaleidoscope of colours and shapes on the dark wooden floors.

Rebecca felt she had to say something. 'And the front door was locked, you said?'

Mona nodded.

Rebecca looked past her to the door. Two locks—a Yale, a mortice and two bolts, one at the top, one at the bottom.

Rebecca asked, 'No key in the lock?'

'It was only on the latch, the Yale.'

'And was that common?'

'No. The mortice was unlocked, the key still there on the table beside the door. Murdo would have locked up for the night and removed the key so I could get in the next morning.'

'So what does that mean to you?'

'I really don't know. We don't get much housebreaking up here. Perhaps he simply forgot.'

Rebecca noticed she used the term 'housebreaking' and not 'burglaries'. The benefits of being the sister of a Scottish lawyer. She probably knew what 'hamesucken' was, too. In old Scots law it was an aggravated assault in a person's home. That was what had happened here, in Kirkbrig House, except it was murder.

'Was he in the habit of forgetting?'

Mona's gaze was steady again; the mists had cleared. 'No, my brother was not in the habit of forgetting things. That was what made him a superb lawyer.'

'So someone else could have been here and pulled the door to when they left?'

'Yes.'

'But you saw no one?'

'No, but Murdo had been dead for a number of hours before I returned home.'

Rebecca opened the front door and looked at the locks. She had no idea why. 'Are these the same locks?'

'No, I had them changed. Later, of course. It seemed wise, under the circumstances.'

Rebecca closed the door again and moved into the centre of the entrance hall to study the wide staircase. The wooden bannister was of the same dark wood as the floor and just as highly polished. 'It's an impressive staircase. Is it original?'

'Restored, as was the window. A staircase was a signifier to visitors of the owner's wealth and position, and this one positively screamed nouveau riche. The whole house, actually, with its turret and its external ornamentation, is an example of them showing just how *riche* they were. Apparently the original owner liked to think himself the lord of the manor. From what I gather he did not endear himself to the locals.' She moved suddenly to the right. 'The kitchen is down here.'

Mona led Rebecca down a narrow hallway—a lobby, her mother would have called it—which ran beside and under the staircase. She pushed open the door at the end and pointed at a spot on the floor beside a long counter.

'Murdo was lying there, face down, blood all around. He was naked.'

Rebecca stared at the ochre tiles as if the body was still there. She looked around the spacious kitchen. It was bright and spotlessly clean. Everywhere she had seen so far was pristine and she wondered if Mona did it all herself or if she had a cleaner. Rebecca thought of her own home, back in Inverness. She hadn't vacuumed for days, let alone dusted. She vowed to give the place a going-over when she got back. Deep down, she knew she would break that vow.

She became aware of a noise. A rattling, just as she had heard at the monument site. It was faint but it was definitely there.

'Murdo had the kitchen completely remodelled, of course,' said Mona. 'Two old pantries were taken out, the floor re-tiled, the ceiling lowered a little.' She stood a little further down from where the body had been found and that soft look returned. One hand reached out and caressed the solid wood surface of the counter. 'He so loved this kitchen.'

Rebecca moved across the room and peered through the window above the sink to a collection of outbuildings and a rear garden just as spacious as the one she had walked through from the gate. It extended to another high hedge, beyond which she could see the green ridge. A large bird, perhaps some sort of raptor, floated against the blue sky, its wings barely moving, nothing more than a dark slash of lethal efficiency searching for its prey.

Looking out to the garden, she watched the breeze ruffle the branches of the trees. A large wooden wind chime hung from one of them. It swayed, then the pieces clattered together like dry bones.

Looking back at Mona, still staring at the spot on the floor, Rebecca felt the stab of guilt she always felt when forcing people to relive something dreadful.

'Miss Maxwell . . .' she began.

'Mona, please,' the woman said, raising her eyes. Her smile seemed to hang on her face, as if she had found it in one of the sealed containers on the counter and tried it on. 'You are in my home and we are talking about the worst day of my life. I think you can call me by my first name.'

'Thank you,' said Rebecca. 'Mona, may I ask why you stay here?'

The question puzzled the other woman for a moment. 'Why would I not? This was my brother's home. He built it, more or less. I shared it with him on my return from China. There is a bit of him in every room, every doorway, in every bit of remodelling. Why would I want to leave all that behind?'

'Because of the memories? What happened was extraordinary, the way your brother was . . .' Rebecca hesitated.

'Murdered?' Mona jumped in. 'You think perhaps I fear ghosts? I am not a superstitious woman, Miss Connolly.'

'Rebecca.'

'Rebecca, I do not see ghosts. What's done is done, and the past does not exist in the present.'

'Except in memories.'

'Memories can only harm you if you allow them to harm you. Like everything else—emotions, finances, lusts—they must be kept under control. There is no profit in looking back, Rebecca. If you need a biblical precedent, think of Lot's wife. There are no ghosts, no spirits, no visitations from beyond the grave. What ghosts there are inhabit our minds. We only haunt ourselves.'

Yes, we do, Rebecca thought, as she moved to the sturdy back door beside the wide window. There was a hefty-looking key in the lock and, like the front door, two heavy, black iron sliding bolts. 'Was this locked?'

Mona nodded an affirmative. 'And bolted. And no windows were open, before you ask.'

Another door led away to the left. Rebecca made a quick mental recce and worked out it would run under the stairs. 'Where does that lead?'

'To a small room that used to be the maid's accommodation back in the day. It's just a storeroom now. I keep the vacuum cleaner and other household items in there. All kinds of junk, to be honest, including the original locks from the front door, incidentally. I'm afraid I am something of a hoarder. It has a small window looking out to the rear but no external exit.'

'And does that door lock?'

'Yes.'

'And was it locked that day?'

'It was, with the key on the outside.'

So no one could have hidden in there, then. Rebecca looked around the spacious kitchen again. She didn't know what good this would do, but at least she was getting a feel for the locus. The locus, she thought. She had picked that up from her father long before she became a journalist. The work surfaces and cupboards looked as if they had all recently been fitted and never used. The whole place positively gleamed in the sunlight.

Mona's voice snapped her out of her thoughts. 'You will want to see my brother's bedroom, I suppose?'

'Do you mind?'

'That's why you're here, isn't it?'

Her words were not curt, merely a statement of fact, and she didn't wait for Rebecca to reply. She turned abruptly and walked down the passageway again. Rebecca knew it was one of the reasons she had forced herself to come to the house, but the bald statement still stung.

Mona remained silent as she led Rebecca up the magnificent stairway. There were two right turns before they reached a landing that ran the length of the house, above the vestibule, the sitting room in which they had sat and whatever function the other room to the right of the front door had. The stained-glass window looked even more impressive from here, the light slanting downwards, as if the colours were hanging above the stairway.

Mona opened the first of two doors.

'This is where James was found,' she said, and stepped back to let Rebecca enter. It was a massive bedroom with the now ubiquitous cream-coloured carpet and two bay windows looking down on the driveway. A desk made of heavy black wood faced the window, a leather office chair tucked neatly under it. The top of the desk was clear. An ornate fireplace dominated the wall to the left, the grate dark but not obscured like the one downstairs. A fireside set identical to the one Rebecca had seen in the sitting room stood on the tiled hearth. She wondered if it had a poker missing but didn't investigate.

Two mirrored wardrobes took up the walls on either side of the fireplace. A winged armchair was tucked in the corner. The bed was a huge four-poster that may have been mahogany and an antique, but, like everything else in the house, gleamed like new. It had a latticed canopy and the drapes were of heavy red velvet.

'The room has hardly been touched since Murdo died, apart from cleaning, of course.' Mona's voice was low now, its measured tone replaced by something else. Grief, perhaps. Loss. Sadness. Rebecca understood.

There was something about being in the room in which her brother had slept that seemed to have affected Mona more than the hallway or even the kitchen. Perhaps because this really was his personal space. Perhaps whatever ghosts flitted through her thoughts were stronger here.

'When I found Murdo downstairs I called the police immediately, then came up here and found James, still asleep. Or drugged, rather.'

Rebecca recalled Elspeth mentioning that traces of drugs were found in both the victim and James Stewart.

'Miss Maxwell . . .' she began. 'Mona.' She stopped. Shit, she thought, this wouldn't be an easy question. 'Was your brother in the habit of using drugs?'

Mona stared at her for what seemed like an eternity and Rebecca wondered if this had been the question that had broken the camel's back. It was, however, only a second or two before the woman took a breath. 'My brother was a man of strong conviction and stronger passions. He excelled in everything he did—his studies, his profession, his political achievements. The one area in which he never succeeded was his emotional life. That was always in a state of confusion, often high drama, and that saddened him. He took solace in substances. He was not an addict. He was not in the thrall of either alcohol or narcotics, but he took both.'

Mona turned to the door. Rebecca took one last look around before following her. In the hallway outside, Mona carefully, very carefully, made sure the door was tightly shut. The final, ever so light caress of the panel, like the similar gesture in the kitchen, was for her tantamount to a rending of garments.

There's a bit of him in every doorway . . .

As they made their way down the stairway again, Rebecca asked, 'Mona, can I ask why you said it was about time this was looked at again?'

Ahead of her, Mona stopped, looked back, one hand on the bannister as she thought for a moment. 'Because I was never convinced that James Stewart murdered my brother.'

'Why not?'

'He was too gentle a boy. And no matter what the newspapers said, or the prosecution inferred with not a shred of real proof, he and Murdo were very much in love. I'm sure that doesn't shock you, Miss Connolly.'

'Rebecca.'

'Rebecca, of course.' A thankful wave of the hand. 'Your generation is more open, more accepting, but back then there was a certain sanctimonious tone in the press regarding such matters. But I really believe that, finally, Murdo had found the one thing he had been looking for.'

'But James was found covered in blood, back there, in that room, in that bed, the poker lying on the floor beside him.'

'I know,' Mona said. 'But I still don't believe it. James would never have hurt Murdo, not even after an argument, which I'm not certain ever occurred. They were the only people here that night. How could the Crown Office say they had argued?'

'There was bruising around James's throat, as if they had been fighting.'

Mona started down the stairs again, her free hand waving the thought away. 'That means nothing. You have heard of erotic asphyxia, I suppose. When, during copulation, your partner restricts the oxygen to your brain to increase sexual arousal.' Her tone was clipped and matter-of-fact. She could have been introducing her students to the first person participle rather than discussing her brother's possible sexual predilections.

'And do you think that's what happened?'

'It's as plausible as the prosecution's case. James's defence put it forward but obviously the jury did not agree.'

'The blood and the fingerprints went against him.'

'Yes.'

'But you still disagree?'

'I do.'

They had reached the bottom of the stairs. 'So if not James Stewart,' said Rebecca, 'then who?'

Mona turned, the light from the stained glass painting her face with colourful fingers. 'I have no idea.'

'Your brother had no one who wished him harm?'

Mona allowed a short, sharp laugh to escape. 'Rebecca, my brother was involved not only in the law, but also in politics. There were countless numbers of people who wished him harm. The world has become a vastly polarised place, a lot worse now certainly, but there were strong feelings then too.'

'Had he received threats?'

She hesitated. 'Not threats, as such.'

'What then?'

Mona said nothing for a moment and Rebecca had the feeling she was debating whether or not to speak further. 'A few weeks before he died, Murdo told me that he thought he was under surveillance.'

'What kind of surveillance?'

'He thought he was being followed. He felt his phone calls were being intercepted somehow.'

'You mean tapped?'

'Yes.'

'By whom?'

She took a breath. The prism of her flesh seemed to ripple. 'He said the security services.'

17

The sign at the turn-off from the A828 told them that the Village Inn offered comfortable rooms, first-class seafood, bar meals, morning coffee and afternoon tea. The side road took Rebecca and Chaz downhill towards the edge of Loch Linnhe, where two peninsulas reached out like a thumb and forefinger to trap the water in a pincer movement. The tiny village of Kilnacaple nestled in the cleft, a row of brilliant white cottages and the two-storey Village Inn, while isolated cottages spread up the hill towards the road. At one time it had been a fishing village, but those days were long gone and now it was a stopping-off point for summer sailors drawn there by the small but sheltered harbour that jutted into the water from a shoreline made up of fine sand. The inn and its reputation for seafood were also an attraction to the yachting set, while the sign at the turn-off lured motorists from the road up above.

Rebecca parked in the small car park on the opposite side of the narrow road from the inn and stood for a moment taking in the view. All seemed still, the landscape hanging before her like a watercolour. Kilnacaple Bay was reasonably large and the blue water, untroubled by even a hint of a breeze, was speckled here and there by seabirds floating on the surface. She knew the coastline well enough to be aware that it would not always be so calm, for the gales could rage up the loch from the Atlantic to stir these tranquil waters into a seething mass, hence the need for the safe harbour. The small stone jetty seemed to point towards the distant splash of white set against the dark peaks of Mull that was the lighthouse at the far end of Lismore Island in the centre of the loch like a long streak of green paint floating on the water. Two yachts were moored to the stonework, while a handful of smaller boats sat comfortably on the tranquil water, riding any faint undulations easily. As views go, it was one to savour. She never tired of the splendours of her country, particularly where the water meets the land, for it offered up so many delights. And dangers, too.

She closed her eyes to let the sun's rays caress her face and the sounds soothe her: the faint lapping of the water on the arch of the shoreline that rocked the moored boats; the chatter of the birds in the trees lining the road that ended just beyond the village boundary. Somewhere, far off, she heard the muted growl of a quad bike, which was both alien and yet somehow part of this world. There was peace here and she needed it, even if only for a moment.

This story was becoming more complex by the minute. The possible miscarriage was a hard enough nut to crack, but she had a mother who was only grudgingly allowing her to follow up the case, the mysterious involvement of a solicitor not previously connected to the case, the fact that Finbar Dalgliesh knew the murder victim and now the suggestion that the security services had been keeping tabs on Murdo Maxwell. Then, of course, there was Martin Bailey, who had been filtered from her mind the further away from Inverness they got but who now oozed back.

She forced her lips into what she hoped was a bright grin as she saw Tom Muir striding towards them from the inn. She wasn't quite sure of his exact age, but as usual he looked far younger, despite his shaven head, which was now burnished brown. Tom kept himself fit, as was shown the first time she saw him, when he'd decked a much younger man with muscle where his brain should have been.

'Thought you pair were never getting here,' said Tom as he reached them. 'Mary's had the bloody kettle on for hours.'

Mary was now the sole owner of the inn after her husband had died the year before. Tom had been staying for a few months to help his sister prepare it for sale, but the market was sluggish.

'We stopped at Ballachulish,' said Chaz, as he slung his camera bag over his shoulder.

'And I spoke to Mona Maxwell,' added Rebecca.

Tom raised one eyebrow. 'Bugger me! Just jumped right in, eh?'

'Always best,' she said as they crossed the road towards the door of the inn. 'Get that plaster ripped off right away.'

'And did she speak to you?'

'Yes, surprisingly. She even let me call Chaz in for some pics. She's never believed James Stewart was guilty, it seems.'

Tom held the door open. 'And she told you that? The full Tommy Cooper, like? Just like that?'

'Just like that,' Rebecca repeated, as she stepped past Tom into the comparative gloom of the small reception area.

'Who is Tommy Cooper?' Chaz asked, his face a picture of innocence.

Tom gave him a reproving glare as he pointed them in the direction of the bar. 'He's from an age when comedians could be funny without swearing or talking about bodily functions.'

'Come on,' said Chaz, dropping his voice, 'you can't beat a good fart joke.'

Rebecca smiled. She only knew Tommy Cooper because her parents watched reruns of his old shows on satellite TV channels. As a child, she found him funny, but she wasn't so sure she would now. She was sophisticated these days. She drank wine and everything—and it sometimes cost more than a fiver. And Chaz was right: you can't beat a fart joke.

The bar was small, the ceiling low with dark beams decorated with framed images of the sea and fishing boats. The gantry, though, was well stocked with a variety of malts and blends, while on shelves below there were bottles of other spirits, including a number of gin brands. Rebecca was glad she had taken Mary up on her offer of rooms for the night because she felt she needed a drink. A gin and tonic would be most welcome.

Two men sat at the bar, probably locals, while a party of four with the kind of tan you couldn't buy out of a bottle, and sporting the carefully stylish casual wear that spoke of a buoyant bank account, had commandeered an alcove table at the far end of the narrow room. The men, forty-ish, coiffed and fit, were shaving-gel handsome, while the women, ages carefully indeterminate, blonde and tennis lean, had smiles straight out of a dentist's poster. Rebecca assumed they were the owners of one, or both, of the yachts at anchor by the jetty. Tom told Rebecca and Chaz to sit anywhere. She acknowledged with a nod his declaration to tell Mary they were here before vanishing through a narrow doorway to the right of the bar. They chose a table beside a small bay window so she could look out at the water.

She stared through the window. It really was beautiful here. Chaz had said at the monument that she looked tired and he was right. She hadn't had a break for over a year and even then it was just a trip home to her mother in Glasgow. The thought occurred to her that she should arrange for them to stay an extra night at the Village Inn. After all, she couldn't do much more until she spoke to the solicitor on Monday.

Tom appeared through the door again, this time carrying a wide tray with coffee and chocolate cake. The gin could wait, she decided—caffeine and a sugar hit would work for now. Tom's sister Mary, small, round, eternally cheerful, was at his heel and she had a plate piled high with sandwiches. Once again Rebecca realised how hungry she was. It was always that way with her, when she was focused on the job in hand she didn't feel hunger pangs until she was actually presented with food. The bacon rolls at Elspeth's place seemed such a long time ago.

'Thought you'd want something to eat. I'll show you to your rooms after,' said Mary with smile as she laid the plate of neatly triangled bread and various fillings in front of Rebecca. 'We were thinking you'd got lost.'

'No, had a few stops on the way,' she said, her eyes on the plate as her stomach sat up and took notice. 'No one else having any?'

Chaz reached over and grabbed a handful of food, placing his sandwiches on a napkin he had already removed from a holder on the table. 'In your dreams, Becks.'

Mary and Tom sat down at the table, and Mary began pouring coffee for everyone. 'Tom said you saw Mona Maxwell.'

'Yes, decided to get it over with right away. It's only fair she knew.'

Mary handed her a cup. 'She's a funny one, that Mona.'

'She seems very—erm—straight.'

'Oh, aye—any straighter and she'd snap in a high wind.'

'Some house, though. Have you ever been in?'

'No, love, never been inside. Me and my Harry . . .' She looked directly at Chaz. 'That's my late husband.'

'Sorry for your loss,' said Chaz, automatically.

Mary acknowledged with a tilt of her head and continued. 'Anyway, me and my Harry used to walk up that way now and then when it was empty, go over that old bridge to the new kirk.'

'The new kirk?' Chaz said. 'We drove past it on the way here and it looked old to me.'

'No, son, it's only about two hundred years old.'

Rebecca smiled. The new kirk. Only in the Highlands would something that had stood for two centuries be deemed new.

Chaz asked, 'So, is there an old kirk?'

'Aye, down by the shore there, beyond the village. It's a ruin now—no roof, open to the elements, the wee graveyard all weeds. That's how the village got its name—Kilnacaple means "church of the horses". They say the clans used to ride their horses, them that had them, along the beach to attend mass, leave them tethered outside. Sometimes, if there were too many, the priest would come outside and preach, so the horses were part of the congregation, if you like. That stopped with the Reformation. The wee kirk was allowed to fall into a ruin and eventually the new one was built up there beside the road.'

'And the merchant who built Kirkbrig House also built the bridge?'

'Aye. There wasn't a bridge there until he came and he decided to call the house Kirkbrig, which has a Lowland sound to it, but then he was an Edinburgh man. But by the time me and Harry would wander up there the house was boarded up and declared unsafe. Of course, that didn't stop some youngsters going in there with their drink and whatever.' She widened her eyes at the word 'whatever', a visual code for drugs. It was an issue, even here. 'As sad a place as you could think of then, that house,' Mary continued. 'That was before Murdo Maxwell bought it, of course. Right wreck of a place it was, but I hear he did wonders with it.'

'It's quite something,' said Rebecca. 'What about Murdo Maxwell? Did you know him?'

'He used to come down here for dinner, him and whatever young man he was with at the time.' There was no judgement in her tone that Rebecca could detect. She didn't know Mary well, had only met her once or twice before, but she understood her to be an easy-going woman, as fair-minded as her brother.

Chaz asked, 'He brought more than one lover up here, then?'

'Och, aye—he had a string of them, one after the other. All of a type, if you know what I mean.'

'What type?'

'Young, handsome, most of them looked like models or someone off the telly. I don't know what they saw in Murdo because he wasn't exactly God's gift. I mind one young lad, up from Glasgow he was, came down here one Saturday night on his own. I think Murdo was away somewhere. Anyway, this lad got himself drunk, fighting drunk. Ended up having to be thrown out by my Harry . . .'

She was in reception sorting out some receipts, she recalled, when the raised voices reached her. Harry had been in the kitchen, talking over the next day's menu with their chef and they both entered the bar at the same time but from opposite directions. The young man was standing in the middle of the room, a bar stool in his hands, waving it at the Gibson brothers, two men from the farm above Kirkbrig House. Mary could see there was colour on their cheeks and blood in their eyes. They had tempers and were known to cause trouble of a Saturday night, when they had filled up with beer and whisky and needed to let off some steam. Many a Sunday they woke up in a cell in Oban. But this was a Thursday and it was lambing season and Mary knew they would not drink on a work night, not to excess, because old Jess would have their guts for braces if they staggered home late, or not at all. They were in their forties but their father was tougher than both of them put together and even if he couldn't actually give them a leathering now, his tongue was sharp enough to strip paint off a barn door. However, she knew them, and whatever this was about she had no doubt it was they who had kicked it off.

The other patrons were watching, some shocked, some fearful, others enjoying it like it was a floor show for their benefit. No one moved to interfere, except her husband, who moved round the side of the bar, hands up, fingers splayed. A sign of peace.

'Right, boys,' said Harry, 'let's just cool down, eh?'

'Watch yourself, Harry,' said Connie, the barmaid.

She was in her thirties and more than capable of pulling a pint, but she was also decorous and greatly admired by the regulars. Well, the male ones. The women tended to view her platinum blonde hair and curves as if she was a siren out to steal their men. The truth was, she was devoted to her husband, who had been crippled in an accident while working on the rigs. Both of the Gibson boys, Mary knew for a fact, thought she had an eye for them, hence their presence on a night when they should have been at home in bed.

But the argument wouldn't be about her, not with this boy. She knew that.

Harry stepped forward and said, 'Okay, Evan.'

She had been trying to remember the young lad's name. Trust Harry to know. He was always good with names, was Harry. He positioned himself between the young man and the Gibson boys. They were big lads, both of them, big and weather-hardened. The boy was slim, soft and hadn't worked a day's graft in his life, she reckoned.

Harry kept his voice light and steady. Never get excited, he would say to her. If a situation is hot, then getting yourself excited can only bring it to the boil. 'Let's just put the stool down, eh?'

'I'll put it somewhere,' said Evan. He was usually soft-spoken, Mary recalled, when he had come down for dinner with Murdo Maxwell, but this night his tone was harsh, guttural and, although slurred with drink, it carried a knife-edge that she wouldn't have thought him capable. His hair was long and it fell over his face as he lowered his head and glared past Harry at the Gibsons. She knew her husband had dealt with many unruly customers over the years, but there was something about this lad that made her uneasy, always had. There was something unhinged about him, something in the way he stood, the way he talked, and now the way he wielded that stool.

He had done things like this before. She was certain of it.

'Harry,' she said, trying to inject a note of warning into simply saying his name, but all he did was nod to her. Evan half-turned at the sound of her voice, looked her up and down and decided she wasn't a threat, then whirled back again. Mary eased to the side in the hope that if he knew the exit was free he would take it.

'I think you'd best leave, son,' said Harry, nodding to her again, recognising why she had moved. They knew each other so well.

'I didn't do anything,' said Evan, swaying a little on his feet, the stool wavering in his hands.

'I don't care,' said Harry. 'I think you should go before this gets worse.'

Evan smiled. It wasn't a nice smile. 'Why? The fun's just beginning.'

'The fun's over.'

That smile again. Thin and without any humour. 'Not till I say it is.'

Harry sighed and threw a look over his shoulder to the brothers, who each stood ready to move, fingers like Cumberland sausages melded to giant meatballs. If they got those beefy hands on the young man, there would be blood on the carpet.

'What's all this about anyway?' Harry asked.

'Nothing,' said Brian, the eldest.

'We were talking to Connie, is all,' said his brother.

Evan's laugh barked around the room. 'You were getting nowhere with her and I said so.'

'He said they'd have more luck with a sheep, if they spoke to it nicely,' said Connie, a hint of a smile in her voice and eyes. The Gibsons gave each other a look and shifted their feet. She had found it funny and they didn't like that.

'Yeah, not so sure I was right about that, though,' sneered Evan. 'Even sheep have standards.'

Harry turned to face the brothers fully now. 'And that's it? You took exception to a bloody sheep joke? You kidding me? Christ, Connie's said worse to you!'

'Aye,' said Brian, 'but we're not taking it from his sort.'

'And there we have it,' said Evan, his voice raised to address the entire bar. 'My sort. A perv, wasn't that what you called me, big guy?' He shrugged that off. 'That's nothing, been called that and worse over the years. Then you asked what I would know about women?' His smile was thin and bitter. 'More than you, I'll bet. The pair of you are probably still virgins.'

Brian Gibson lunged forward, but Harry neatly shouldered him back. The brothers knew and respected Harry, everyone did, and they also knew that if they put a foot wrong their father would hear of it.

Harry turned back to Evan and forced his tone to reconciliation mode. 'Don't make it worse, son. Looks like there were faults on both sides here. Mr Maxwell wouldn't want this, would he? Take my advice, son, just go—now—no harm done.'

Evan seemed to flinch at the mention of Murdo's name. 'You know the problem with blokes like you?' He jabbed the stool in the direction of the brothers. 'You think that people like me are nothing. But just because I'm gay doesn't mean I'm helpless.'

He stared at the brothers as they bristled, Harry standing in front with his back to them, arms out like a barrier. Her husband had handled drunks all his working life and he knew the Gibsons were not the ones to watch. He told her later that he had seen something wild and unpredictable in that young man's eyes. For all his apparent softness, Evan was dangerous.

'And I'm not your son, old man. You're not my father.'

He lowered the stool then and turned abruptly, walking out and leaving silence and rage behind him. Nothing broke the stillness for a few moments, then finally Mary heard some people exhale and voices began to discuss what had happened in hushed tones.

Something slammed into the bay window and landed with a clatter on the concrete outside. Evan's voice, hoarse with defiance, could be heard shouting something indistinct. Mary stooped to look out and in the fading summer's light she saw him weaving away, heading for the hill road to take him back to Kirkbrig House.

18

'It was one of the big umbrellas he threw at the window,' said Mary, shaking her head. 'He probably tried to heft one of the tables too, but they're solid buggers. Anyway, didn't do any harm to the window. The umbrella was never the same again, though. Murdo came down the next day—we supposed Evan told him about it—and flashed some cash to smooth it all down. He even went up to old Jess's place, spoke to the brothers, apologised.'

Rebecca asked, 'What happened to Evan?'

'We never saw him after that—but the way he was? Wouldn't be surprised if he got himself into more trouble. Nothing more was said.'

Tom chimed in. 'Maxwell was bloody lucky it happened here—if that lad had pulled anything like that in Oban or Inverness or Glasgow, he could have been banged up and it would have hit the papers. Then where would old Murdo have been?'

'Maxwell didn't make a secret of being gay, though,' said Rebecca.

'No, but that sort of thing wouldn't look good in the tabloids, would it? Lover of political fixer arrested for affray. Or worse.'

'What was he like, Murdo Maxwell?' Chaz asked.

'He seemed okay,' Mary continued. 'A bit talky at times, but then he was a lawyer. You ever seen a letter from a lawyer? Sometimes I think they're paid by the word. Some of the bills I get make it look that way.'

Chaz asked, 'Tom, did you ever work with him on any of his issues?'

'Aye, once or twice—nothing big. Illegal scallop dredging on Loch Carron. We both campaigned against zero hours contracts, that sort of thing.'

'And what did you think of him?'

'Same as Mary. He was a talker.' He smiled. 'Don't say it—that's what people like me do. But sometimes that's all he did. Still, Murdo could focus attention like no other bugger.'

Rebecca said, 'He shared that with Finbar Dalgliesh then.'

Tom frowned. He had no love for Dalgliesh and his followers. 'What's he got to do with it?'

'It seems they were pals at unI and then business partners in Glasgow.' She saw this was news to Tom. 'You didn't know?'

'No, I knew he was a lawyer before he started up in politics, but that's all. And Finbar didn't come to the fore until a few years ago.' He cocked his head and smiled. 'Well, well—old Finbar, eh? The plot fair thickens.'

Yes, it does, Rebecca thought.

'What about James Stewart?' Chaz asked. 'Did he come here with Murdo Maxwell?'

'Oh, aye!' said Mary. 'Good-looking fella, that. But quiet, very quiet. Mind you, Murdo talked enough for both of them.'

Chaz asked, 'So what was the feeling in the village about the murder?'

While Mary answered, Rebecca stretched for a few sandwiches to satisfy her hunger pangs. 'Shock, of course. We've had our crime up here but nothing like that, not in modern times. Of course, historically it's another matter.'

'The Appin murder, you mean?'

'Aye, but it's the Highlands, love. You can't move without tripping over an old battleground or some atrocity or other.'

'It's one of the cornerstones of the tourist industry,' said Tom.

'So what happened around here?'

'Ach, the clans would forever be setting up a fuss over something,' said Mary. 'A slight, an insult, cattle lifting, an argument over land—the occasional abduction for ransom, that sort of thing. The next thing you know the fiery cross was going round the clachans and the men were drawing their claymores from the thatching of the black houses and going off for a scrap. That's what happened up where Kirkbrig House now stands.'

'There was a battle there?'

'Well, maybe battle is too big a word, but there was a scrap between the MacDougalls and the Stewarts. This would be hundreds of years ago. It was all about ownership of the land and the castle down below on the headland. You'll have seen that on the drive down the hill.'

They had. The fortification stood on a spit of land jutting into the loch that became an island at high tide, its ruined battlements slouched against the landscape like a tired old soldier.

'And who won?'

'The Stewarts claimed victory, but that was only because they had one man left standing. Anyway, the story goes there was so much killing that the ground was slick with blood. That's why it was called Raon Fala. Field of blood. Others know it as Achadh a' Mhallachd, the field of the curse.'

'Why?'

'The mother of four brothers who died that day laid a curse on the land, said that any crop planted would wither, that any beasts set to graze would sicken and die. As far as I know, no one has ever planted anything there, no animals were run in the field. When they were looking at where to build the new kirk, they avoided that parcel because superstitions die hard in the Highlands. So when the Edinburgh merchant came to build, he managed to get the land for a song. He wasn't too bothered about old Highland folklore, being a tough-minded big city businessman.'

Rebecca wasn't superstitious, but she had experienced things in the past that she could not explain—visions of her dead father, the baby who'd never breathed and yet cried in the night. Now this story had an ancient curse.

She asked, 'And did anything happen after he built the house?'

Mary sipped her coffee, glancing at her brother over the rim of her cup. Rebecca got the impression she did it for effect. 'Aye,' she said, finally, 'he died. There was them around here who said it was the curse, striking back at him for building his house on that land and, maybe worse, not giving it a more Highland name.' Another sip of coffee. 'Mind you, if it was the curse, the damn thing took its time because it was forty-odd years later and he died of natural causes in his bed.'

Mary's gaze drifted towards the bar, and the humour that had been there melted as she seemed to focus on something unseen. Was Harry there, smiling at Mary, just as Rebecca had seen her father so many times. 'But death itself is a curse, isn't it?' Mary said, softly.

19

Find something to look forward to.

One of the screws said that to me, early on. Find something, anything, that gives focus to time. Try not to think about life on the outside; focus on what is happening here and now. Find a food you like at mealtimes and look forward to it being served again. I've never been a fan of cheap TV, but I soon learned it broke the monotony.

So I put my name down for everything that made the seconds, minutes, hours, days more bearable. Work. Lessons. Visits by outsiders. Anything that offered a diversion. Anything that made the waters of time flow that bit faster.

Even watching a game of football became an event.

I've never liked football and still don't but whenever there is a match, whether between the inmates or against staff, I join the men to shout encouragement to guys I don't even know. There are limits, of course, to what we can shout, for we are in prison and there are still officers keeping a stern eye on us, lest anyone find a convenient hole in a fence and grab freedom. Swearing isn't allowed and neither is any kind of threat to the referee or the opposing players. After all, there are guys in here who are more than capable of carrying out such threats.

I don't even mind going out in the rain. The football matches are few and far between so I'm not going to let rain stop me from those precious moments of free air. It is all I have. But I especially like the days when the sky is blue and the air is clear—or as clear as it can be, given the prison isn't far from a busy road. The kind of cold, crisp days when frost bites at skin and tingles ears. The kind that reminds me of when I was a boy, living at home and I would go for walks, alone, because my memory of my teen-

age years is always of being alone. Up around the castle or down by the canal. I loved those days and those walks, the birds singing in the trees and the gurgle of the water beside me. Other people didn't exist on those days; there was just me and the crisp air and the water, always moving, like time. I remember thinking to myself that was the way I wanted to live my life. Like water. Always moving, never still. Movement was life, stagnation was death.

It was on the day of a match, on one of those wonderfully biting days, that the waters of time sent Gordie floating my way.

20

Rebecca lay in her room at the inn, listening to the faint, restful noises outside her window. In Inverness, when night stilled the sounds of day, she could hear the growl of vehicles on the A9, even though it was some distance from her rented home. Here, though, a gentle breeze stirred the bushes that lined the courtyard and, if she really listened, the water of the bay caressed the shore and kissed the stone of the small jetty. There was a full moon and its beams shone through the window, coating the bed on which she lay with soft silver.

After a superb dinner—steak pie, cheesy potatoes and roasted vegetables, which Rebecca wolfed down as if she hadn't eaten for a week—they sat outside and talked and laughed. Tom lit up a cigar, which she didn't mind as the smoke helped keep any midges at bay, and told stories about life in the pits of Ayrshire, about the miners' strike of 1984, about becoming a councillor when he returned home to Inverness. Some of it was serious, even libellous, most of it was funny. He was a born storyteller and he kept them entertained.

They purposely did not talk about the Maxwell case: Mary had said everything she could; Tom only knew what Mary had told him, what he had read at the time and what he had subsequently learned from Afua Stewart when he decided to help her. Rebecca had once asked him why he became involved and the only thing he said was that he had to. That was it. From what she knew of him, that was all that needed to be said. Tom Muir had fought injustice all his life, as a trade unionist and as a local councillor. He stood up for those who could not stand up themselves. He must have been over seventy now, she thought, and he showed no sign of slowing down.

He believed there was an injustice here and that was that. He needed no further reason. Rebecca could dress up her own involvement any way she liked—that she was doing it to right a wrong, or because she was moved by Afua Stewart's obvious pain over her son's plight, or that old journalistic stalwart, the public's right to know—but deep down she knew she was motivated by the need to make money and her own desire to break the story. Tom Muir had no such motivations. He wasn't looking for glory.

'It's no about me,' he had said before. 'It's about that lad in the jail and his poor mother.'

He also refused to tell Rebecca what the new information was, even though Rebecca asked him again after dinner, as they sat outside at one of the tables, the sun dying in the west, its spirit lingering in a golden spray in the air that gilded the water of the sea loch. A pair of oyster-catchers darted overhead, their call a staccato series of whistles, like a breathless football referee.

'Can't tell you, love. You know that,' he said, shaking his head. 'This is the way Afua wants it. She felt let down by you.'

'But, I didn't—' she began, then stopped when he held up a hand.

'I know, I know. There was nothing you could do. I know you tried to get interest in the story. But the way she sees it, you just walked away, like every other reporter over the years. Remember, her boy was not treated very well by the press. She doesn't trust you lot.'

'What were they supposed to think back then, Tom?' she argued. 'James Stewart was found literally red-handed.'

'Aye, true. But you have to admit the reporting was piss poor.'

'Not all of it. People have a habit of selecting only the reports that fit their biased view of journalism. It's like saying you don't like all tins of beans because the sauce in one brand isn't as good.'

He smiled. 'Maybe so, but I've got to abide by her wishes.'

'She wants to put me through my paces.'

'She does that. She won't hand it to you on a plate and I don't think that's a bad thing. Sure, she could tell you what Stephen Jordan has to say, but isn't it better that you talk to him yourself, make your own judgements about it?'

'Knowing in advance what he has to say won't stop me doing that.'

'She needs to see commitment, is all it is, Rebecca. Speak to the guy, hear what he has to say. There's a story in it, believe me.'

She grunted. 'That's if he'll even tell me.'

Tom smiled again as he watched a heron, huge and prehistoric, glide over the water, its vast curved wings beginning to brake as it came in for a landing. 'Rebecca, if anyone can get him to talk, it's you. I know that. And Afua needs to see that for herself.'

'So this is a test?'

'Of course it is,' he said, surprised that she even had to ask. 'Life's a bloody test, don't you know that yet?'

Now, as she watched the quicksilver square from the window ease ever so slowly up the bedspread, she thought about what she knew. Murdo Maxwell was found dead in his home, his lover asleep and bloody upstairs, the murder weapon beside the bed. The body was found by his sister, Mona. The front door was only on the snib, so someone else could have pulled it shut as they left. Maxwell generally locked the mortice too. So, if someone else was responsible, how did they get in? Did they have keys? Did Maxwell forget to lock the mortice? Did they force the Yale somehow? Was that credit card thing even possible? She suspected not. Locksmiths have a mica card, she knew from a story she did while at the *Highland Chronicle*, which was longer and far less brittle than a credit card so it could bend round the frame more easily without breaking. So, unless this third man was a professional housebreaker and could pick a lock—again, not as easy as the movies make it seem—he must have been allowed in. So who would Murdo let in?

Then there was his suspicion he was being followed and his communications monitored. What was that about? Was it the security services, as he had suggested to his sister? That brought a different complexion to everything. But why would he be under surveillance?

'If he knew they were following him, then the chances are they either wanted him to know or he was imagining it,' Tom had said when she'd asked him. 'These guys are very, very good. MI5, the Branch, they've had well over a century to perfect surveillance. Back in '84, they were all over us during the strike, the spooks and the police—Maggie's private army, we called them. Phones were tapped but more often than not we sussed it because it was an unofficial tap. There would be clicks on the lines, sometimes calls would end abruptly, that sort of thing. Remember, this was near forty years ago and though they had technology we didn't know they had, or could even imagine, it was nowhere near the sophisticated stuff they have today. Even ten years ago, if the spooks were keeping tabs on Maxwell the chances are he wouldn't know it. No, love, if he had come to suspect that they were on him, then he was either imagining it or they wanted him to know.'

All the same, Rebecca wanted to know who and what Murdo Maxwell was involved with at the time of his death. From what Mona could tell her, there seemed nothing particularly sensitive, but then if he was involved in something that pricked the ears of the security services, was he likely to say, even to his sister?

What it boiled down to was that she knew very little more than was out there already and not enough yet to punt a story. The banners were a preview, at best. Mona had decided to wait until after they knew what Stephen Jordan had to say before she would agree to stating her belief in James Stewart's innocence on the record. Whatever the lawyer told her, if he told her, might prove to be the touchpaper that could properly set off media interest once again.

But that would have to wait until Monday. She had decided against staying another night, but she and Chaz would spend most of Sunday here, relaxing for a while. He was right, she needed a break. It was only a short one, but it would have to be enough.

She rolled over. It had been a long day. She hoped she would sleep. She hoped her mind, and the restless ghosts that lived within it, would allow her to drift off. She closed her eyes and let the lullaby of the natural world outside ease her away.

The night passed with the creep of the moonbeams and she slept soundly. That night, her dead father did not speak, the baby did not cry from the dark, and there was no gunshot in the rain. For the first time in many months, Rebecca Connolly did not haunt herself.

21

Malky Reid thought pubs like this had died out with dial-up internet, VHS tapes and decent pop music. Sure there were dives like this in Glasgow, if you knew where to look, but he didn't expect to find one in Inverness. He thought all the pubs up here had accordion music piped into speakers and there was free shortbread with every half. But sitting in Barney's in the centre of town was like being transported back in time. It was small and it was dingy and it was situated up a lane narrow enough to accommodate only two people walking side by side if they stayed off the spuds. He would lay odds that the guys delivering the beer kegs cursed the day they had to come here.

It was quiet, but then it was just before lunchtime on a Sunday. The puggy flashing away in the corner was the only sign of life in the place. Even the telly above the bar was dark. The barman looked so bored he may have been contemplating washing the beer mugs.

Like the pub, the woman sitting opposite him was a throwback. She was blonde and she was good-looking, even though her features could slice bread, but there was a sadness in her eyes that touched Malky, hard Glasgow man that he was. She had known heartache and it all lived right there in her eyes as she squinted at him through the smoke that drifted up from the smouldering fag wedged between her fingers. The smoking ban meant nothing to Mo Burke, it seemed.

'So why you up here, Malky?' she asked, tapping the gold lighter in her other hand and revolving it in her fingers.

''Cos I was told to,' he replied.

'By Wee Joe?'

'By Mr McClymont, yes.' Malky made it a habit of never referring to his employer publicly as Wee Joe, for that way can lie a sore face. Privately it was another matter.

She glanced down at the copy of a tabloid Sunday paper lying on the scarred table top. 'And it's about this story?'

'Aye.'

She scanned the few paragraphs of text again, then studied the photograph of the monument and its banner. 'So what's his interest in this?'

Malky held up both hands. 'Mine is not to reason why.'

She raised the filter tip to her lips, inhaled some carcinogens, then blew some in his direction. 'And what makes you think I can help?'

'I wondered if you knew anything about this,' he replied, resisting the urge to wave the smoke away. He had the fervent evangelism of the converted smoker but he didn't say anything to her. This was her turf and it would be bad form to bitch about it, but he did wish he had sat at the next table.

The truth was, he had no idea what the hell he was doing up here. Wee Joe had not expanded on his reasons for wanting to know about a ten-year-old murder, even if it was Murdo Maxwell. Malky well remembered the guy because Maxwell had defended him once twenty years before, on an assault charge, back when Malky was straight out the schemes, a ned on the make. Got him off, too.

'How the hell should I know about an old murder?' said Mo, smoke belching from her mouth like steam from a boiling pot. 'And away the hell over there in Appin? Never even been over there.'

Malky understood, for he had been forced to look at a map to find out where it was. He had visited Inverness a few times over the years, the last time to forge an uneasy peace with this very woman. Until then, the Burkes had resisted the McClymont clan's overtures of a partnership but the heart seemed to have gone out of the woman following the death of one son and the jailing of another. God knows what would happen when her man got out of prison, but that was a problem for another day.

'I know you, Mo. Nothing happens up here without you getting wind of it, so if there was anything being muttered about this then you would hear about it,' he said. She was Glasgow-born but she had lived here for years and her family had fingers in more pies than a careless baker.

'I know bugger-all about this, Malky,' she said, pushing the paper away with one finger of the hand holding the lighter.

'Can you do me a favour, then? Put the word out with your people. On the off-chance they clock something.'

A brief jerk of the head told him she would do as asked. They'd had their differences over the years, and it had turned bloody and painful for some, but that was in the past for now. He knew he could trust her to do as she said. Mo Burke was straight-up that way.

He asked, 'What about the reporter, what you know about her?'

Another quick darting glance at the page. 'There's no name on the story.'

Malky, you idiot, he thought. As soon as he'd seen the story that morning he'd phoned a contact on the newsdesk, someone to whom he had steered a few stories when Wee Joe needed them steered. He told him the story came from a news agency right here in Inverness. 'You're right, sorry, Mo. It's someone up here called Rebecca Connolly.'

When she heard the name, Mo's head snapped up so sharply Malky was sure he heard the bones in her neck crack like a whip. The lighter twirling in her hand stilled. Her eyes narrowed, her lips flattened out. 'Aye, I know her.'

'What's she like? Will she play ball, talk to me?'

'She's bad news, that one. She's like the fuckin' plague.'

He was taken aback by the vehemence in her tone and Malky Reid had faced many a hard man in his day. Whatever this Rebecca Connolly had done, she had made a bad enemy in Mo Burke. 'I may need to have a word, though,' he said.

'Up to you, Malky, but she'll use you for what she wants and then she'll let you die in the street.'

22

When her boss phoned, Detective Chief Inspector Val Roach was curled up on the settee, enjoying her Sunday morning, reading a Hillary Mantel novel. Sibelius's *Symphony No.2* was playing on the iPod. She was fond of his dark, frosty Scandinavian romanticism. Her coffee, her third so far, was from Ethiopia and was also dark but rich and hot. There were three things that made her perfect Sunday morning: good reading, good listening and, all importantly, good coffee. She was content.

She turned the page, found she had reached the end of a chapter and laid the book down beside her on the couch. She sipped her coffee, savoured its aromatic, fruity taste, then laid her head back and listened to the music as it swelled. Outside the sun shone on her small garden and she could hear the birds twitter and whistle as they fluttered around the seed and nut feeders. Yes, everything in that garden was rosy right now. No actual roses, however, and just as she was wondering if she should plant some, the phone rang.

She glanced at the caller ID and might not have answered had it been anyone other than Superintendent Harry McIntyre. It might have been Sunday, but he believed senior officers were always on shift.

'Boss,' she said as she put the phone to her ear.

'Val, sorry to disturb your Sunday.' He didn't sound sorry at all.

'That's okay.' It really wasn't okay.

'I'm heading down to Gartcosh first thing tomorrow for a management meeting.'

'Yes, sir,' she said, wondering why he was telling her, sensing something was coming.

'So I thought I'd call you now. Have you seen the newspapers today?'

She shot a guilty glance at the broadsheet still folded neatly on the table. She should keep herself up to date with current affairs but, frankly, she had grown tired of lies, spin and prevarication. She got enough of that from the Sneck's merry band of miscreants.

'Not yet, sir,' she said.

'Right,' he said, and she couldn't tell if he was disappointed or satisfied. 'There's a story we should keep an eye on. Do you remember the Murdo Maxwell case?'

She searched her memory, came up with the bare bones. 'Lawyer, murdered somewhere out west, right? Must be—what? A good few years ago?'

'Ten. It was before my time here, but there's been whispers for a few days that it may become an issue. He was shacked up with his young lover in his country home in Appin. The young man beat him to death and is now doing time. It was your actual open-and-shut.'

'If that's so, sir, who has a feeling it may become an issue?'

'People who can call me up on a Sunday and tell me to have someone look into it.'

Roach hated it when those people picked up the phone because it usually ended up on her desk. This being a case in point. She dragged the newspaper towards her, flipped it open and began to thumb through the pages. 'So what's happened to prompt the call, sir?'

'Banners have appeared at historical sites relating to the execution of James Stewart over two hundred years ago. It was a political case and a miscarriage of justice.'

Roach could not find anything in her newspaper and she had no idea who this James Stewart was. 'And that relates to the Maxwell case how, sir?'

'The young man convicted was also called James Stewart.'

The penny dropped. 'Ah . . .'

'His mother has tried and failed to have the conviction overturned for years. She's a very tenacious woman, Val, lives here in Inverness.'

'And the father?'

'Sir Gregory Stewart, something of a big deal. Rich as sin and well connected. They're divorced and he has kept out of any campaigning his ex organised. Not that there has been that much. As I said, it was an open-and-shut case, and even though there have been some nibbles by the press over the years nothing really concrete has emerged.'

'So what's the issue, sir? Banners at historical sites will get attention for a day or so, but then the media will move on.'

'There may be a further complication.'

Of course there may, she thought. 'What kind of further complication, sir?'

'Do you know Stephen Jordan?'

'The solicitor?'

'Yes.'

'I've had a couple of encounters. Generally it's jotters down the trousers time when you face him in court.'

'Yes,' said McIntyre, the single word as dry as a prune. Jordan was predisposed to giving police officers verbal spankings in court. Even during solemn procedures when the High Court sits, during which as a mere solicitor he is not permitted to speak, officers often found themselves being questioned more rigorously by advocates retained by him on behalf of his client. Roach knew McIntyre to be a fair man, he was all for justice being seen to be done, but many of the neds defended by Jordan were as guilty as Judas and the divisional commander took attacks on his people personally. 'Word is, Mr Jordan has information concerning the murder that was not available at the time.'

'What sort of information?'

'I don't know,' he said. 'Yet.'

Roach knew she had a part to play in that 'yet'. 'And this information has not been made public?'

'No.'

'Then how do we know about it?'

'People talk, you know that, Val. Even within Police Scotland. And most definitely in the meaner streets of our fair city. It may not be public but the fact that it exists is known.'

'And both you and your mysterious callers want me to find out what it is?'

'Discreetly, Val, if you can, although I suspect it will be in the public domain soon enough. But what I really want to know is the level of Police Scotland's exposure on this. Neither of us were here at the time so we're ideally placed to be objective.'

'I don't think Jordan will see it that way, sir.'

'No, but it's either that or we bring someone in from outside the division, which may happen anyway if there is a suggestion of wrongdoing back then. But right now I'd rather be as forewarned and forearmed as I can.'

'I understand, sir.'

'Good. Nose around, Val. On the QT. The SIO of the original case died a couple of years ago, I'm afraid, but there are still a couple of officers around who worked on it. As I said, it all seemed pretty cut and dried, but . . .'

He left the sentence hanging.

'Sir, do you think there was something dodgy about the initial investigation?'

'I don't know, Val, but someone up the food chain wants us to look into it. As I said, it all seemed cut and dried—the boy was found at the locus, traces of the victim's blood on his person, the weapon by his side. But these things have a habit of turning rancid very quickly, especially if someone like Stephen Jordan is involved. He has no love for police.'

'Does anyone, sir?'

'My wife is rather fond of me personally.'

Lucky you, Roach thought.

23

Rebecca started the morning with a fine breakfast, then sat in the courtyard with a coffee and stared across the bay towards Lismore. She had slept well, she had eaten well and she felt better than she had for a long time. This was the life. She could get used to this kind of peace. If one night like that could have this effect, maybe she really did need a long break.

Chaz and Tom were down at the stone jetty, Chaz snapping shots as usual. He really couldn't help himself. Mary was busy in the inn. Business may not have been too brisk but there were always things to do. It was the same with Rebecca and she felt a ripple of guilt as she thought about the work piling up on her desk. The agency wasn't exactly giving the shareholders of Reuters and PA sleepless nights, but it was paying its way. Court cases had to be covered, stories sourced and sold to newspapers, magazines, even TV and radio. But here, in this quiet little village nestling on the cusp of a bay that opened out into the blue waters of a loch, listening to the insistent cry of the oystercatchers as they flew overhead and the whisper of the waves on the sand, it all seemed so far away.

She opened the contacts on her phone and hit Elspeth's number. 'Hi, thought I'd check in.'

'Good,' said Elspeth. 'I'm glad of the diversion. Julie is giving me GBH of the earhole because she caught me smoking. I felt like I was back at school, being caught behind the bike sheds by a teacher.'

Rebecca smiled. 'She has your best interests at heart.'

'Aye, aye,' said Elspeth dismissively, but Rebecca knew she agreed with her. 'So what's the story, morning glory?'

'An Oasis reference, Elspeth? I'm impressed.'

'Hey, I'm down with the kids, you know me.' Rebecca doubted whether quoting a song that was a quarter century old signified being down with the kids, but she let her boss have her illusions. She told her about the interview with Mona Maxwell and Mary's story about the angry young man, Evan.

'So, Mona Maxwell turned out to be easy,' said Elspeth. 'Never mind, you've still got Gregory Stewart and old Finbar to tackle.'

'Yeah,' said Rebecca, 'thanks for that.'

She made a vow to herself that she would try placing calls to both Sir Gregory Stewart and Dalgliesh that day. She didn't expect to get them but it would at least set those particular balls rolling.

'Listen, can you nip into the office when you get back?' Elspeth asked. 'There's a small notebook in the second drawer of the filing cabinet, I think. I jotted some thoughts down in it, forgot to bring it with me.'

'Is this for the Culloden case?'

'Yes.'

The Culloden case.

Two murders.

No, three.

He died, his head cradled on her lap . . .

And a fourth death, the killer, who swam into the cold waters of the Beauly Firth and never came back.

So much death.

She closed her eyes against the memories. It was too beautiful a day to think of such things and she had other matters to deal with. This was the way she had learned to cope with whatever life threw at her. Put it in the past, think of the present and look to the future. It wasn't easy, but she was managing to keep the darkness at bay, more or less.

Her phone pinged a text alert. She asked Elspeth to hold on and looked to see who it was from. No number. She opened it to find a photograph of a rat. She frowned. Why was someone sending her a picture of a rat? Was it sent to her in error maybe?

Then another message dropped in and it was as if a cloud had suddenly crossed the sun.

There was one word, seemingly innocuous, even with its lack of context, but Rebecca felt a scratching in her gut that it wasn't so innocent. *Soon.*

She frowned and stared at the screen. It could still be a wrong number, of course, but Rebecca had the feeling it wasn't. It was from Bailey. Obviously, the creepy shit really was going to be a problem.

She heard Elspeth's voice asking her if she was still there.

'Sorry,' she said, 'just had a text that's kind of worrying.'

'Who from?'

'I'm not sure, could be a mistake, but have you ever run into a guy called Martin Bailey?'

If there was anyone who would know about him, it was Elspeth. As the former editor of the *Highland Chronicle* and then managing the agency, she had run into most of the miscreants in Inverness.

'Aye, I know about him. Scumbag. What does the text say?'

'Just a word: "Soon". And a photo of a rat.'

'You certain it's from him?'

'No.'

'So what makes you think it is?'

'His son has been jailed for the riot in the Ferry. We provided the court report.'

'And daddy dearest is hyper unchuffed, I'll bet.'

'Yes.'

'Threatening legal action, the report was wrong, his boy was innocent, blah blah blah?'

'All of the above. And threatening me.'

Another short silence. 'He actually threatened you personally?'

'Well, he didn't come right out with it, it was more an inference.'

'Aye, that's his way.'

'And you think maybe you're the rat and he's going to do something soon, right?'

'Well, it's crossed my mind.' Rebecca laughed, but even she heard the nerves vibrating. 'Is he a blowhard?'

A sharp exhalation from Elspeth. 'No, Becks, he's not. He's a thoroughly bad bastard. He used to go with this woman from over Nairn way, nice girl, don't know what she saw in him. Anyway, she decided to end it and he didn't take it well. I think his masculine pride was hurt or something. He tormented her for weeks. Played with her, like a cat does with a mouse.'

'In what way?'

'Wee things. Phoned her but didn't say anything. She'd see him hanging around, watching her. He kept a key to her house and he would go in and move things around. It was all like a game or a show of power or whatever; I'm no psychologist. She spoke to him, told him to stop it and he seemed to get off on that. Loved the idea he was scaring her, spurred him on.'

'Did she tell the police?'

'Yes, and they took it seriously. They spoke to him but nothing could be traced back to him. Finally, she ended up in hospital when someone jumped her and knocked the living daylights out of her.'

'Was he charged?'

'No evidence, no witnesses. He even had an alibi. He's a clever bastard.' She paused before she amended her words. 'No, maybe not clever. But cunning. Sly.'

Rebecca felt that tingle in her stomach again. 'I don't think the court report is what he's annoyed about, not really. I think this is all because he's a member of SG. I've been named as an enemy, apparently.'

'Well, there's a badge of honour. I'd report all this to the police—get him told.'

'That didn't help his ex, did it?'

'No, it didn't,' said Elspeth reluctantly.

'So, what can they do? He can deny he said anything yesterday—actually, there was nothing that tangible in his words anyway, just a feeling I got. This text will be from a pay-as-you-go not linked to him, I'll bet. And if the police even do speak to him, then he'll just get his jollies knowing that he's got me spooked. I won't give him that satisfaction, Elspeth. This happened before, remember? Back with the paper? That guy who texted me and phoned me constantly when I named him. Nothing came of that.'

She heard her boss blow out some smoke. 'Maybe you're right, Becks. Maybe if you don't react he'll get bored. But my advice is watch your back.'

They set off for Inverness late afternoon. They could have stayed a couple of hours longer but Rebecca wanted to visit Keil Chapel, where James of the Glens was finally laid to rest. The ancient grey stones were ruined now, the roof gone, the interior overgrown, with gravestones thrusting through the long grass where once people had prayed. Further stones, more ancient, erupted from the ground outside as if in a bid to reach the light but were held back by the grass and the weeds and the moss. She tried to read some of the inscriptions but they were so weathered the letters were mere ghosts in the stone.

Chaz wandered through the graves, snapping away, while she stood in front of the small plaque set in the chapel wall. It was a simple memorial, with no poetic verse, no sense of the history, of the tragedy, of the man.

Here lie the remains of
James Stewart
"Seumas a'Glinnhe"
Who died 8th November 1752

She laid her hand on the chapel wall and closed her eyes, trying to feel her way through history to that day when his kinfolk carried his bones from Ballachulish to this old kirkyard. It had fallen into disrepair even then, but they still laid local people to rest. And James was local, for he farmed with his family in Glen Duror.

They would have mourned certainly. They would have been respect-ful. But there would also be rage. Their kinsman had been convicted and judicially murdered by a rigged system determined only to see someone hang for an attack against the state. *Pour encourager les autres*, Voltaire had once written. To encourage the others. He was talking about a Brit-ish admiral who had failed to relieve a siege; he was executed to encour-age others to do their duty. James of the Glens died to warn any Jacobites of dire consequences should they rise again, as if the bloody backlash after Culloden hadn't been enough of a red flag. Rebecca was certain the courts didn't care if they had the right man or not. James had been a Jacobite and that was enough. The fact that he was respected made him an even better candidate.

The sense of injustice seeped from the rough stone into her body. James of the Glens had been innocent, of that she had no doubt. Could his modern namesake be equally as innocent? Perhaps he did not murder Murdo Maxwell. There was no political motive, no suggestion of official malfeasance, but was it a miscarriage of justice all the same? She knew she should not think like that, knew the evidence all led to him having killed his lover, but she also felt something in her blood cry out against the wrong that had been done.

She would stick with this story this time. If interest waned, she would find some other way to keep it alive. She regretted allowing economics to force her to step away before. That would not happen again. There would be other stories that would pay the rent.

The sun was down by the time she dropped Chaz off in Inverness, but there was still a faint golden glow in the sky. The house he shared with Alan wasn't far from her own flat in Miller Road, but she didn't want to drag him into the town centre while she searched for Elspeth's notebook.

'When's Alan back?' she asked, as he hefted his camera bag from the rear seat.

'Tomorrow,' he said.

'Did he say how it went with his family?'

'He's breaking the news tonight. He says that way he only has to face one night of cold silence and funny looks from his brothers.'

'But they already know he's gay.'

'Yes, but there's knowing it and accepting it, and then him actually getting married to another man. It's all a matter of degrees of acceptance, he says.'

'Even now?'

Chaz looked at her. 'Even now, Becks. Not everyone accepts, you know.'

'So he doesn't think his family will accept it?'

'To be honest, he doesn't care. That's all BC.'

It was something Alan often said about his upbringing. BC. Before Chaz. His previous life. He kept in touch with his family, he cared for them in his way, but he no longer factored in their views on his lifestyle. The visit was both tradition and courtesy. He made the birthday trip because it was something that was done; informing them of his impending marriage to Chaz was merely a bulletin, not a request for blessing.

'Well,' said Rebecca, 'perhaps they'll surprise him.'

'Stranger things have happened,' he said, closing the car door. He leaned in through the open window on the passenger side. 'You've had a touch of the sun.'

She flipped the sun visor down to look at her face in the mirror. Her cheeks and nose looked somewhat florid, how badly she could not tell in the rosy hue of the setting sun. Nevertheless, she would slap on some moisturiser when she got home.

'You're looking better already,' said Chaz. 'So take my advice—have a proper break, Becks.'

He was right. While a single day at Kilnacaple was far from a break, she had felt the benefits. She had slept well, for the first time in a long time. She had felt whatever it was that ate at her constantly—anxiety, stress, grief, guilt—fade away, even if only for the few hours she was there. She had a friend who had inherited a bar on a Spanish coastal resort and perhaps she could go there for a week or two. A complete change of scene. Even though the weather was wonderful at present, she knew Scottish seasons to be fickle. It wouldn't last.

She resolved to have a real holiday when she could, but the vow she had made herself at Keil Chapel would stand. She would stick with this story no matter what.

She drove into the city centre, miraculously finding a space in Station Square. It was growing dark now, the streets quiet. She liked city streets like this. The shops closed. The only sound the faint rumble of traffic on another road or a drift of music from a pub. The town was not deserted, people still walked, but often it was more languid than during daylight. There was not such a sense of purpose. Couples walked slowly, hand in hand, or arm in arm, or with arms wrapped around waists. Groups of people headed to or from a pub, their voices often raised and shattering the peace. When the bars emptied later, the noise level would increase, but for now it was relatively peaceful and her footsteps sounded like drumbeats as she headed for the entrance to the offices above the coffee house.

The door lay slightly open, which meant someone had not ensured the lock had clicked. It had happened before—she had even done it herself. Once again, she made a mental note to get some oil to see if that would do the trick. It was dark in the entranceway and she reached out to turn on the light in the stairway. She flipped the switch but nothing happened. She sighed heavily. Damn it, bloody bulb had gone again. She fumbled in her pocket for her phone, found the torch app and swung the bright beam ahead of her on the stairs. She felt weariness pull at her legs as her steps reverberated up the stairwell. Relaxing though it was, it had been a long day with the drive back from Appin, so she was desperate to get home and go to bed. However, she had promised Elspeth, so she forced herself to climb the steps, the torch bleaching the way ahead.

She was turning towards the second flight to reach the first floor when she thought she heard a noise above. Soft, like someone scraping a shoe on the stone floor. She stopped. Listened. Heard nothing further. There were three floors and it was possible someone was working late. But on a Sunday? She thought about calling out, but dismissed it. It was probably nothing. Then she realised the light on the first-floor landing was also out.

She hesitated. She could normally depend on this lightbulb, if not the entrance one. From where she stood she could see the door to the tailor's workshop, but not the door to the agency, which was obscured by the solid wall of the stairwell. She listened again, not sure what she was trying to listen out for, but heard nothing anyway, apart from her own breathing and the thud of her heart.

But she could not help thinking about Martin Bailey, who had been nibbling away at her consciousness the closer she got to Inverness. Every nerve in her body told her to go back down those stairs, get outside, into the open, away from the dark stairwell. They screamed at her to get away, move, now, but all the while her legs refused to pay any attention. The part of her brain that was her father argued back at those nerves. No, it said. Do not let your imagination make you a victim.

She forced herself to climb the stairs.

Think, Rebecca, when was the last time that bulb was replaced?

She didn't know. She had certainly never replaced it, unlike the one at ground level.

Then isn't it conceivable that it just blew?

Yes. Bulbs blow. They just give up.

Halfway up now, half leaning against the wall, her legs sluggish, her phone held out before her like a shield as she neared the landing. She came to a halt on the step second from the top, swung the phone's beam towards the tailor's door. It was closed. She took the final step, edging round the wall, turning the light towards the agency door, one foot on the landing.

Something crunched under her foot.

She stopped, aimed the phone at the floor, saw a myriad of shining shards strewn across the stone and knew immediately what they were. The bulb's light hadn't just died. It had been killed.

She jerked the phone up again, whirled the light behind her, then bounced it around the narrow confines of the landing, flashing over the agency door, the walls, the ceiling even, her ears straining for the sound of feet rushing towards her, from either below or above, but there was nothing. She leaned back against the tailor's shop door, her breath ragged now, telling herself to calm down, forcing her lungs and heart into a steady rhythm.

But something jarred.

Something she had seen as she had jerked the phone this way and that in her sudden panic. Something that shouldn't have been there.

She raised her hand again and shone the beam across the landing . . .

24

It's a funny thing, fear.

It makes cowards of us all, really. I remember reading somewhere that there are no really brave men, there are only those who can overcome their terror. Many people live their entire lives in some sort of fear. Fear of oppression, fear of exposure, fear of heights, of insects, of germs, of flying, of enclosed spaces. Like prison cells. It's present, even omnipresent, and yet many overcome it. They refuse to let it rule their lives.

I know about fear now. I didn't really understand it until I came here, to this prison. On the outside I was protected, perhaps not loved, but my father's name alone was enough to insulate me from any such worries, even though my sexuality is an embarrassment to him. When I came here I learned what fear was, and even though I was not overly troubled by men who let their testosterone do their thinking, the idea of it—the fear of it—was still there. Yes, I learned who to stay away from and how to avoid the pitfalls of life inside but there was still something ever-present, like a noxious gas. It was the fear that no matter how careful I was, I could still—with a remark, a look or simply by breathing—annoy someone sufficiently to merit violence. I have had to defend myself in the past from morons but I learned that hit first, hit hard and flee was the best policy. That was not an approach available to me in here—where the hell would I flee to? So, even though I was mercifully spared any major confrontations—apart from a few moments of abject terror—and I was able to function normally, or as normally as I can, given I am in here, I knew that the invisible enemy, fear, lurked in my mind always.

It didn't leave me until I met Gordie.

The football match was prisoners against staff. I'm no judge of these things but it was a very dull game. The staff were winning, no real surprise frankly, and the prisoners had more or less given up. Even I could have done better. I was standing on the sidelines, trying to keep warm because it was cold, not the crisp cold I love but the dull, damp cold that comes with grey skies. Still, I was outside and that was the main thing. This guy came up to me and stood beside me for a while. I gave him a quick look. I hadn't seen him before. He wasn't big but he was powerfully built, a guy who worked out but not in a narcissistic way, like a lot of these guys do. I got the impression right away he wouldn't be admiring himself in mirrors and kissing his guns. He had a quiet way with his physicality, he knew what he could do and didn't need to prove it. He stood watching the game for a minute or two, didn't say anything. I had the feeling he hadn't found himself at my side by accident. He had placed himself there deliberately and I thought perhaps I was in for trouble, but he didn't say anything or even look at me for a few minutes. He just watched the game. I thought about moving but if he was trying to intimidate me for some reason I was not going to give him that satisfaction. Never back down. One of the few pieces of advice my father ever gave me.

I remember I was thinking about my father's words, passed on before he told me how disappointed he was in me, when the guy said, 'Your dad sent me.'

That surprised me, given how much my father seemed to despise me.

He said his name was Gordie. He said from now on he would have my back.

I told him I didn't need a babysitter and he just sort of smiled and said, 'Well, son, you've got one, whether you like it or not.'

Turns out he was doing time for an assault and when someone told my father he was being sent here, he had one of his contacts reach out to ask Gordie to keep an eye on me. Honestly, I was touched, because that was the first kind thing he had done for me since I was a kid. It was pure luck that the guy was being sent to this jail and this wing. Luck on my part because, even though I was wary of him at first, I found that knowing Gordie was there put the fears at rest.

We didn't share a cell, a 'Peter' he called it, but people got to know that Gordie had his eye on me. A lot of the guys in here knew him, so when word got round the few who would say things to me, give me the eye, they soon backed off. Gordie, it seemed, was not someone they wanted to mess with.

So the fear lessened.

The rage was still there, though.

25

'I wasn't the SIO,' Bill Sawyer said. 'I was just a DS on the case.'

'I know.' Val Roach nodded. 'But the SIO is dead.'

'Ted Wise. He was a good cop.'

Roach had not known the DCI in question, but she was willing to believe Sawyer's evaluation. 'You were around at the time,' she said, 'you worked on the inquiry. I just wanted to get your views.'

They were in the comfortable sitting room of Sawyer's bungalow in Holm, near a road leading to what was once a mill weaving tartan but was now a shopping village. Through his front window she looked out at an expanse of green grass. Beyond it, she knew but couldn't see, was the river and the canal, weaving side by side on this stretch before they parted to make way for the bulk of the city. She could see a rounded hill, shrouded by trees. She didn't know its name, though, or even if it had one.

Sawyer looked at her, not even bothering to hide his suspicion. 'Why me?'

She was puzzled by his reaction. 'Why not you?'

'There have to be other officers still around who can tell you about it.'

'I'm sure there are.'

'Then why me?'

Roach understood his suspicion. No officer wants an old case re-examined. It suggests they had somehow been derelict during the investigation; it also makes them fear being scapegoated if errors are found.

'You're retired, Bill,' she said. 'You won't tell me what I want to hear just to protect your job.'

'Everything I know will be in the case file.' He gave her a sideways glance. 'You think there's something about this case that the bosses don't want to hear?'

'I've no idea. I gave the records a quick scan earlier this morning.' She had gone into her office at Inshes very early to give her the time to read up on the case. 'It all seems kosher to me. Do you think there's something the bosses don't want to hear?'

He shook his head. 'It was as open and shut as I've ever worked. Bloke was found dead in the kitchen, the guy who did it was upstairs, the weapon beside him, his prints all over it.'

'But he never confessed.'

'Doesn't mean anything. He pleaded Not Guilty but they all do that. He did it, simple as.'

'What if he didn't?'

He laughed. 'Come on, give me a break.'

'There were no other suspects?'

'No.'

'No one who wished Maxwell harm?'

'That's a different question. But none of them were seen as viable suspects. I told you—the boy Stewart was found at the locus with the weapon practically in his paw.'

'Not much blood on his hand, though, and none on his body, which you would expect given the brutal nature of the attack. There were blood trails and cast-off all over the kitchen but not much on Stewart.'

Sawyer shrugged that away. 'We decided he'd washed himself—we found traces in the sink.'

'So why was there some still on his hand?'

'He must've touched the weapon again.'

'Nothing on a towel?'

'The towels were fresh. Unused.'

Roach didn't say anything; she didn't need to.

'Look,' said Sawyer, leaning forward. 'We had the boy, the body and the weapon. No one else in the house. Front door locked. Maybe he wiped his hands on something and got rid of it, or a paper towel and burnt it. We didn't find anything. What else were we supposed to think?'

117

Roach thought it was always possible and sometimes the most obvious solution is the correct one. However, she was here to ask questions.

'But there were other people who wished Maxwell harm?'

'Not physical harm. He had made a lot of people very unhappy.'

'In what way?'

'He'd been a defence lawyer, down in Glasgow, for starters. Got people off who shouldn't have been got off. So there's the PF there and the Crown Office for starters. And he was the solicitor for Andrew Guthrie.'

'Andrew Guthrie?'

'The Mad Bomber, they called him. Alt-right nutjob who planted bombs in Edinburgh and Glasgow. Supposed to be a founder member of New Dawn.'

New Dawn. Roach had been slightly involved in a probe into their activities before. She still did not fully believe they existed as an entity, more a wet dream of right-wing tosspots who drew the line at dressing up in sheets and hoods.

She asked, 'I thought they were Finbar Dalgliesh's attack dogs?'

'Aye, they are now—but this was when they were starting up, before Dalgliesh created SG and began noising up the SNP. He was Maxwell's partner, by the way.'

'Partner? Didn't know Dalgliesh was gay.'

'No, business partner.' He rolled his eyes. 'God, I wish we could just say girlfriend and boyfriend. I don't think Dalgliesh subscribes to the *Pink Times*. Well, not as far as I know. No, they were in practice together, down in Glasgow. Before Maxwell got environmental and political and all that shit.'

'Did Maxwell share Dalgliesh's views?'

Sawyer shook his head. 'Maxwell was mainstream political, but he still pissed a lot of people off, big style. He liked a cause, did Murdo. The higher the profile, the better. For him, anyway.'

'You don't think he was sincere?'

'I don't know, never really knew the man. But I think anyone political is a chancer. Goes with the territory. As for all that environment stuff, full of nutters, if you ask me. Anyway, Maxwell defended Guthrie and a few others like him, got himself a reputation. Some said he was too friendly with those guys.'

'But you really don't believe he was a member of SG?'

'Honestly? Nah. Maxwell was many things, but I don't believe he would have anything to do with New Dawn and SG, even if he was mates with Dalgliesh. He'd defend them on the basis that everyone has the right to a defence'—Sawyer rolled his eyes again—'but they are totally animal crackers, that lot. Call themselves nationalists but they're not. Just racists, is all.'

'So, apart from politics, who else did Maxwell piss off?'

'Who didn't he piss off? Central government. Local councillors up and down the country. Landowners. The gentry. Business people. Anyone he wanted to noise up.'

'Well, he was an environmental campaigner.'

'He was a troublemaker. Just wanted to get his face on the telly.'

She suppressed a smile. Sawyer was old-fashioned, dismissive of anyone who challenged the status quo. He had been a good cop, as far as she knew, although she had been told he was not averse to bending rules when he needed to. There had been one black mark—suspicions over a confession that seemed dubious—but that was water under the bridge now.

She thought for a moment before asking, 'So, who was he noising up at the time of his death?'

'Who wasn't he noising up, is closer to the truth. There was an American millionaire who wanted to build a resort near a site of Special Scientific Interest. The suggestion that the UK government was going to dump nuclear waste somewhere down in Galloway. Plans to build a new motorway near Glasgow that would cut through woodlands. Opencast mining, windfarms, game shooters threatening raptors, commercial fishing endangering fish stocks—you name it, he was against it. As long as it got his name in the papers.'

'And you looked into all this at the time?'

'Aye, we did our job. But as I said, we had our guy. It was a lovers' tiff that went bad was the way I saw it and so did the boss.'

She had read the notes and she had to agree. She couldn't see where there could be any blowback on this. Still, she had been given a job and she would do it.

'Was he pissing off anyone local?'

Sawyer paused. 'How closely did you read the file?'

'Skimmed,' she said, truthfully.

He studied her, trying to gauge if she was being honest. 'So you're not trying to trick me with anything?'

'Why the hell would I do that? I'm on a fishing expedition myself, not big game hunting. Why are you so worried?'

'Because I told the boss this after the murder, and if there's any shit attached to this I don't want it to land on him. Ted Wise was a good man and a bloody good cop. At the time he said it didn't matter, we had the boy bang to rights. He told me to write a report and we followed it up, but in the end it was decided that any argument Maxwell had wasn't important. I'm telling you right now I agreed with that then and I agree with it now.'

'Who was this argument with?'

'Sir Gregory Stewart. The boy's dad . . .'

Sawyer had never much liked black-tie affairs, but he had been asked by his boss to represent the police at this one. It was in aid of some charity or other, he forgot which one exactly, but it didn't matter because he wasn't going to stick his hand in his pocket. The civic reception took place in the Town House, the baronial building on the High Street, and the ladies and gentlemen in their finery mingled in the Main Hall, all ornate chandeliers dangling from the ceiling and banners hanging from walls. Waiters in white shirts carrying trays of drinks threaded through the various clusters of people talking and laughing in the large room. Sawyer had found himself part of a group surrounding the provost underneath the dark wooden platform of the Minstrel Gallery, in front of the Roll of Honour to those who had fallen in the two world wars. The provost was talking about plans to have the building renovated, saying that it would cost millions but it was worth it. He said the current colours of the wall would have to be returned to their original red hue. Sawyer thought the room looked okay, but he wasn't an interior decorator. He was a copper and he was out of place among the glitteratI of Inverness. He had recognised two MSPs, an MP, local councillors and business people. He'd even spotted an English actor he'd seen in *The Bill* and *Taggart* who was appearing at the Eden Court Theatre that week in a touring production of *Sleuth*. Sawyer's wife had dragged him along to see it the evening before and the guy was no Michael Caine.

Someone jogged his elbow, causing some of his drink to splash over his shoes. He turned to fire off a few choice words, but the man was already moving away from him, fairly unsteadily, it had to be said. Free wine had a lot to answer for. Sawyer had only sipped at the glass in his hand, trying not to grimace—he was a malt whisky man—but he had seen some of the rich and shameless around him knocking it back like it was mandatory. There was nothing those with money liked to do more than not spend it.

The man looked familiar, but Sawyer wasn't terribly sure from where. He looked a bit like that actor who used to be in *ER*. Sawyer didn't much like that guy, not least because his wife nearly wet herself whenever she saw him on screen. Okay, that was an exaggeration, he knew, but he had the feeling that if he hadn't been in the room she would have given the telly a right good lick. It wasn't Clooney, though he was certain he had seen him somewhere before. He met a lot of people in the course of his work—granted not a lot who would attend a function like this—but he couldn't quite place this one. He had never lifted him, of that he was certain. As he pondered this, only half listening to the provost talking about brickwork and woodwork and artwork, he watched the man make for three others on the opposite side of the room. Sawyer recognised them as an MSP and a local councillor, both from the same party; the third was well known to him but only because he was never off the telly spouting about some issue or another. Murdo Maxwell, as usual doing most of the talking, waved a hand holding a wine glass in what appeared to Sawyer to be a carefully cavalier manner, as if he was showing that he could do it without spilling any but really didn't care if he did. He was gesticulating towards the stained glass in the alcove behind him and Sawyer could hear his voice carrying across the room, although could not make out the words.

The man who had bumped into Sawyer was clearly drunk by the way he stood beside the trio, his body swaying in that ever-so-slight way, his back more erect than usual to compensate, his feet splayed. Something about the way he had made an unsteady bee-line for them resonated in Sawyer's copper's brain, so he left the provost's group—no one noticed him go, which showed how important he was—and edged closer so he could get a better look at what was going on. He kept his distance, skirting round the assembled dignitaries, catching snatches of chatter here, a bit of laughter there and generous amounts of toadying of the highest order, but never taking his eyes off the man, who had made no attempt to speak or interrupt Maxwell's flow. As Sawyer reached a point where he could see the man's face, he knew there was trouble ahead. He saw it in the expression, saw it in the eyes, in the tight set of the mouth, in the way he was focused on Maxwell.

Finally, Maxwell seemed to notice the newcomer to their little group and flashed a smile. Sawyer had never fully believed that smile when he'd seen it on the box—in his opinion, the bastard never seemed to be able to hide the self-interest that was ever-present in his eyes. As far as Sawyer was concerned, these do-gooders were all alike. It was all about making themselves look superior to everyone else. If you asked him, Maxwell was always on the lookout for whatever would benefit him. On the other hand, Sawyer was self-aware enough to know that, because he did not support the party of Maxwell's choice, he might be just a little prejudiced. What it came down to was that he did not like the man—and it was clear to him that neither did the newcomer.

'Sir Gregory,' Maxwell said. 'Nice to see you.'

Sawyer knew him now. Sir Gregory Stewart had lots of money and lots of influence. He had been in the news in connection with a wind-farm project. He was a big deal and this situation had to be treated carefully.

'I need a word, Maxwell,' the man said, the words slightly slurred, taking the edge off the apparent distaste reflected in his expression. His eyes were vague, unfocused, but there was a sneer picking away at the corner of his nose.

Maxwell dropped the smile and adopted a faint pucker. 'Seems serious. What can be so serious on a night like this?'

The glass was waved again. By the way Sir Gregory glared at it, he looked ready to slap it out of Maxwell's hand. Sawyer tensed. So far their conversation had been polite, but he was ready to move if it turned unpleasant.

'Not here,' said Sir Gregory, glancing at the MSP and councillor.

'You need a drink,' said Maxwell, raising his free hand to attract the attention of one of the waiters hovering with trays of champagne.

'I don't need a drink,' insisted Sir Gregory. 'I need you to come with me so we can talk.'

Maxwell seemed to be in no mood to go anywhere. Perhaps he sensed something more than words coming his way and felt safer in a crowd. The smile returned. 'Nonsense, my friend.'

'I'm not your friend, Maxwell.'

Maxwell's smile slipped a little and he glanced at his companions, who seemed embarrassed by the scene. The MSP looked away, the councillor at the floor. Sir Gregory obviously didn't give a damn.

'I think perhaps you should step away, Sir Gregory,' said Maxwell, his voice steelier than before. There was no noticeable fear there, but there was a rising anger.

'I think perhaps you should stay the fuck away from my son,' retorted Sir Gregory. 'You—' He stopped suddenly. Sawyer felt he hadn't meant to speak so loudly, or perhaps bluntly, but that was the way it came out. There's many a slip 'tween cup and lip, Sawyer's granny used to say. Sir Gregory was in his cups and his lips would have a mind of their own. His raised voice attracted attention and around them conversation hushed, eyes turned, all sycophancy was put on hold.

Maxwell's eyes flicked at the faces turned their way. 'This isn't the time or place, Sir Gregory.'

'The fuck it isn't!'

Time for Sawyer to move in. He took a couple of steps to place himself between them. 'Okay, Sir Gregory, I think perhaps we should get you some air.'

The man's eyes swivelled from Maxwell to centre on Sawyer. 'Who the fuck are you?'

'Detective Sergeant William Sawyer.'

Sir Gregory looked him up and down, as if checking for some visible proof. Handcuffs, a truncheon, flat feet perhaps. 'A police officer.'

'That's right, sir.'

The man tilted his head back to Maxwell. 'You need police protection now, that it? Can't say I'm surprised. You could piss off Mother Teresa.'

'Come on, sir. Don't embarrass yourself here.'

'I'm not embarrassed. It's this bastard who should be embarrassed. Ashamed.'

'I have nothing to be ashamed of,' said Maxwell, and Sawyer wished he hadn't. Sir Gregory moved, to get a better look beyond Sawyer or because he lost his footing. Either way, Sawyer wasn't taking any chances. He reached out to steady the man, but Sir Gregory brushed his hands away.

'You have nothing to be ashamed of? You have nothing?' He spread his arms, staggering a little once more as he raised his voice even louder to address the crowd. 'You hear that? He has nothing to be ashamed of!'

He reeled again and Sawyer grabbed his arm, but Sir Gregory snatched it away immediately. 'I won't be manhandled, thank you very much.'

'Sir, I think you should leave.'

'No, not until I've said what I have to say to this . . . this . . . *man*.' It came out like a snarl.

'As Mr Maxwell said, this is neither the time nor the place.'

'Oh, I disagree. This is the exactly the time and most decidedly the place.' He formed the words with difficulty and added a few more consonants than was necessary.

'It's all right, Detective Sergeant—Sawyer, was it?' Maxwell had laid a hand on Sawyer's shoulder. 'I think we should let Sir Gregory say his piece. But not here, in such a public forum. I think what he has to say to me is best aired in a more secluded setting.'

He didn't give Sir Gregory another look as he strode with purpose towards the doorway. Sir Gregory turned, tottered, but followed. Sawyer felt he had to go with them in case they needed a referee, or a minder. It would not do for a well-known face like Murdo Maxwell to end up rolling around the carpet of the Town House with a knight of the realm while he was swilling champagne with the beautiful people. Even though none of them appeared particularly beautiful to him.

In any case, his copper's nose was itching. He wanted to know what this was all about.

Maxwell led them into another sizeable room. The space was taken up by a horseshoe of tables and chairs beneath more ornate chandeliers and yet more stained-glass windows. This was the council chamber and, unlike the Main Hall, which they had just left, Sawyer had been in here before. The council had modern offices in Glenurquhart Road, but city committee meetings were still held here, the surroundings adding a touch of pomp. Not to mention pomposity, he thought.

Maxwell whirled as soon as Sawyer closed the door behind them. 'We don't need you, Detective Sergeant.'

'I think you do, sir,' Sawyer replied, and folded his arms to show that he wasn't budging. Maxwell stared at him for a second, saw that he wasn't going anywhere, then turned to Sir Gregory. His smile was gone—he had no audience to impress with his coolness—and his voice was hard and unyielding. 'What the hell was that all about?'

'I told you—stay away from my son.'

'That's none of your affair.'

'He is my son.'

'And he is an adult. He can make up his own mind over who he befriends. He doesn't need guidance from a father who has shown very little warmth to him for a number of years.'

That obviously stung. Sawyer had no idea what this was all about but he saw the man flinch as Maxwell's words hit home.

'You seduced him, Maxwell. You turned him away from what is—' He stopped suddenly, as if his drink-fogged mind had acknowledged that what he was about to say was no longer acceptable.

Maxwell seized on it, though. 'Turned him away from what?'

Sir Gregory swallowed, the muscles in his jaw tightening. 'Nothing,' he said.

'No, please—finish your sentence,' said Maxwell, his voice dripping with what Sawyer could only assume was irony. 'Enlighten us. Let us hear what the great Sir Gregory Stewart has to say. I turned him away from what?'

Sawyer cleared his throat. 'I think that perhaps this has gone far enough.'

'No, Sir Gregory here wants to get something off his chest. Please, Sir Gregory,' said Maxwell, his voice smooth, reasonable, but his hard eyes suggesting he already knew what the man had bitten back. 'I'm dying to know what you want to say.'

The effects of the drink had acted as both stimulant and armour to Sir Gregory, but now it sloughed away, leaving him exposed. Vulnerable, even. But the anger still simmered; Sawyer could see it bubbling just under the surface.

'Not willing to share?' said Maxwell. 'That's a shame.'

And then he reached out and patted the other man on the shoulder. It was nothing more than a quick tap, but even Sawyer felt the move was so patronising that it might as well have been an open-handed blow. There was a sting to it. I've won, it said. I've bested you. You have nothing, are nothing.

Sir Gregory's anger boiled over again. 'NORMAL!'

The word seemed to come out before he even knew he was going to say it. It cracked around the room like a slap and he was silent for a few beats afterwards. Sawyer knew what this was about now. Maxwell's homosexuality was no secret, he had spearheaded many gay causes. Sawyer had heard it was his openly gay lifestyle, and his tendency to get into people's faces for whatever reason, that had made him enemies and had prevented him from achieving public office. Sawyer had many prejudices—neds, politicians, reality TV—but he prided himself on his acceptance of sexual preferences. As far as he was concerned, how people got their jollies was nothing to do with him, as long as it didn't harm children or animals. It seemed Maxwell had been exercising his sexual preferences with Sir Gregory Stewart's son and that, in turn, had made him a new enemy. Sawyer knew a little about the drunk man swaying in front of him, trying hard to hold his face tight with rage but finding the drink had made his flesh prone to drooping. He was wealthy, he had varied business interests and there were rumours that some of them were not so much above board as board adjacent. Those rumours claimed he had friends you would not invite to a garden party. He had other friends who were so high up the ladder it would take magic beans to climb level with them.

Sir Gregory might have been having trouble standing still, his face turned to elastic, but his tongue still spat venom. 'You've taken him away from everything that is normal. You took a decent young man and you enticed him into your life of . . . of . . .'

'Perversion?' Maxwell offered, that smile still there but the sneer had returned.

'Yes, PERVERSION.'

'Well,' said Maxwell, his voice almost a purr, the cat who not only had the cream, but had locked away the cow. 'There we are.'

'He was perfectly normal until he met you!'

'There's that word again—"normal". The fact is, you ignored him and refused to accept his sexuality because it did not—does not—fit in with your life.'

Sir Gregory breathed heavily. Again, Sawyer felt Maxwell had hit home and the man did not wish to be drawn any further into that quagmire. 'All I'm saying is, stay away from him.'

'He will make his own mind up. You should respect that. And, frankly, it's a bit late for you to be worrying about his welfare. You've hardly been father of the century, have you?'

'What does that mean?'

'We've been through that. And anyway, I'm not sure this is just about James, is it?'

'What else could it be about?'

Maxwell gave it a beat, a lawyer's pause, Sawyer suspected for dramatic effect. 'The Craigdearg windfarm project.'

Sir Gregory's face dismissed the suggestion before his words came. 'Don't be ridiculous.'

'If the application is denied, you could lose a lot of money. You've put a lot of time and effort into that.'

'I told you, it's nothing to do with that.'

'Forgive me if I don't believe you. With your sort, it's always about the money.'

The two men stared at each other for a few moments. Sawyer sensed that, heated though the exchange was, there was no threat of any physical interaction. Name-calling was about as far as these gentlemen would go; the days of a skelp across the face with a glove and a date at dawn on the castle green were over.

'I think this has gone on long enough, gents,' Sawyer said. 'There has been an open and frank exchange of views, but perhaps you should leave, Sir Gregory. I'll have someone call a taxI for you.'

'Take a warning.' Sir Gregory didn't even acknowledge that Sawyer had spoken. 'Stay away from James.'

'And if I don't?'

Another long look from Sir Gregory, a glance at Sawyer, then back to Maxwell. He was still drunk but he knew better than to issue a verbal threat, especially with a police officer in the room. He turned and left the room without another word.

26

Rebecca missed Inverness's old court. It had been a ten-minute walk from the agency's office in the Old Town up the hill to the red-brick castle, but now she had to drive to the new Justice Centre, as it was called, on the Longman Industrial Estate. But ease of access was not the only reason she missed the old building. It overlooked the town like a stern but impartial guard. It was imposing, it was impressive, it oozed importance. The courtroom itself was all dark wood ambiance, its curved benches providing a theatre-in-the-round sense of grandeur. The new building, adjacent to the police station in Burnett Road near the harbour, looked like a shopping mall—all glass and columns—which she supposed was fitting because it was designed to be a one-stop shop for anything related to the justice service. Even the courtroom in which she was sitting, with its light wood and padded seating, looked like it had been outfitted by Ikea. She wondered if she should be worrying where the exit was. It was bright and clean and perhaps less threatening than the old building, but to her eye it lacked gravitas.

There wasn't much happening in the court that Monday morning. It was mostly custody cases in which people who had transgressed over the weekend and who had perhaps spent a couple of nights in the cells were either remanded or released pending their court date. She had already known there was nothing much of interest for her, and had not planned to attend, but she felt this was the best way to catch Stephen Jordan. She could have called his office on Castle Wynd to make an appointment but, given his antipathy towards the press, that would be too easy for him to refuse, or cancel if he chose to. No, it was best to catch him here in the court. He could still blank her, of course, but she felt it was worth a try.

She had tried to reach both Finbar Dalgliesh and Sir Gregory Stewart again. Their numbers had merely rung out the day before—given it was Sunday, it was not that much of a surprise—but this morning she'd been in luck. A man with a broad Glasgow accent had answered Dalgliesh's phone, not a surprise as the SG office was in the city. He said Finbar— was every member of SG on first-name terms with the guy?—was not there, but he would take a message. When she told him who she was, his voice became guarded. She was a representative of the hated liberal mainstream media, after all, and was probably out to stitch him and his messiah up somehow. She left the office landline number because she didn't relish the thought of anyone in SG being able to reach her 24/7. She could pick messages up remotely if she wanted.

The number she had for Sir Gregory was answered by a woman with a voice so toffee-nosed that Rebecca would bet Thornton's had the mineral rights. The woman was polite but aloof, and when Rebecca identified herself she thought she could hear a distinct note of distaste when the woman said that Sir Gregory was busy, could she take a message? This time Rebecca gave her the business mobile number.

She half-listened to the litany of misdemeanours being laid out before the sheriff in crisp, emotionless—even bored—tones. It was muted but still theatre. These were the little crimes, the little lives, the little tragedies that lack the fire and brimstone of the big budget, headline-grabbing melodramas. Public intoxication, brawling, petty theft, domestic strife all paraded before lawyers, court staff, police officers and sheriffs who often barely looked at the players on the stage, the climax often many months away. The accused were little more than bit parts in a never-ending saga being directed by blind justice. The stars of the show talked *about* them more often than they talked *to* them. They had no function in propelling the action here other than to stand there, extras in their own life story. But Rebecca knew they were people. Young, old, middle-aged. All genders, all religions, all ethnicities, all sexualities. The faces could be calm, scared, overawed, even bored. But they were people with lives and loves and ambitions, who found themselves in a spotlight because they were stupid, or drunk, or desperate, or simply bad.

The man hanging his head in the dock had been involved in a fight in Church Street on Saturday night. A woman sitting near to Rebecca in the public benches was sobbing softly, but no one paid her any heed. Rebecca assumed she was the man's wife, but she had no part to play here. She too was a mere extra, a face in the background.

Stephen Jordan delivered his soliloquy regarding his client clearly and concisely. His voice was the correct level of deep, just rough enough to make it interesting, and he commanded attention as he stood at the table, notepad in hand as a prompt. He struck a fine, tall figure in a three-piece blue suit, crisp white shirt, dark blue tie, his dark hair carefully cut, his face not astonishingly handsome but noticeable, a broken nose seemingly adding something to his otherwise even features. He at least glanced at his client occasionally as he addressed the sheriff, a balding man in his sixties with the florid face of someone who had perhaps enjoyed too many convivial sherries. That face was looking down from the slightly elevated bench with the expression of someone who had heard it all, seen it all and just wanted to get this particular scene over with, which he did by remanding the accused until trial. Another face for the vast crowd scene that was the prison service.

The woman was still sobbing as the man was led down to the cells below. Rebecca heard her say something, perhaps the man's name, as she watched him vanish into the system.

Ordinarily she would have been fascinated, but she was determined to keep whatever focus she had on why she was there. Her sleep had been fitful once more, any gains she had made with her single night's solid rest in Kilnacaple lost, because she now knew the significance of the rat photograph, which had probably been downloaded from the web. It was unlikely to be the actual rat she had found tied to the handle of her office door.

The stark shadows generated by her phone's beam had made it seem even more disgusting as it dangled, its little eyes open but blank, its mouth gaping, tiny little teeth seeming so white in the glare. She had dug a handful of paper tissues from her bag before she unwrapped the wire from the handle, bile rising in her throat, then gingerly carried the corpse downstairs at arm's length and through the rear door of the building where the various wheelie bins were kept. She dropped it in the nearest one, a shudder rippling through her body.

It had to be Bailey. He was doing what he did before to his old girl-friend. Teasing. Tormenting.

But she couldn't prove it.

Jordan was gathering his papers. He had represented four clients on the trot and it looked as if he was finished with the court for now. Rebecca began to edge along the rows of seats, keeping her eyes on the solicitor. He stopped for a word with a clerk, then he was out of the court with her a few feet behind him.

Jordan nodded to the staff member behind the glazed reception desk and pushed through the revolving door into the sunlight. Outside, the world continued on its merry way. Traffic slid past on the Longman Road dual carriageway. A woman stood at the pedestrian crossing wait-ing for the command to move, her hand leading a tartan shopping trol-ley like it was a child. A minibus stood at a pump on the petrol station forecourt opposite, the driver leaning against the side of the vehicle as he filled up with one hand. Beyond that lay a series of squat buildings: small businesses, larger concerns, local, national, thriving, struggling. Inside the court building it was easy to think that the judicial playhouse was a world apart. The days of life and death decisions, of black caps and pro-nouncements of doom were long gone, but what happened in those wood-panelled rooms, with their bright lights and TV screens and rou-tines and procedures, could still affect the lives of accused, witnesses and victims for many years to come. Cars and lorries and buses belched pol-lutants. People bought petrol or food from the shop. They went to work in the offices and workshops that sprawled around this island of legal arguments and precedents. The world spun, but in the cells it stood still, sometimes for years.

'Mr Jordan,' she shouted, halting him just before he reached the short flight of steps leading to street level. He said nothing as he looked back at her, but she thought she saw a flicker of recognition. She estimated he was in his early thirties, but there was something older in those brown eyes and she now saw lines of grey threading his dark hair. The suit, although three-piece, was not ostentatious; it was functional without being drab, and it hung well on his frame. He had the look of a man who kept himself fit.

'I'm Rebecca Connolly,' she said, as she moved across the paved courtyard. Behind him, the traffic lights beeped and the woman began to cross, the wheels of her trolley scraping on the tarmac. Somewhere seagulls screeched to each other.

'I know who you are,' he said, the words neither curt nor particularly welcoming. It was simply a statement of fact. 'You're with the *Chronicle*.'

'Not any more,' she said, and that made one eyebrow rise. 'I'm with the Highland News Agency now.'

For some reason that amused him. 'Ah, the redoubtable Ms McTaggart.'

Rebecca was used to that kind of reaction regarding her boss. The lawyer would have experienced the joys of dealing with Elspeth, as had just about every police officer, local councillor, MP, MSP and bin collector in the Highlands.

'I've been talking to Afua Stewart.'

He didn't say anything.

'About her son,' she continued.

He still didn't say anything.

'James Stewart,' she added, without actually knowing why. Something about the way he said nothing and waited for her to speak was irritating. She had seen him in court often and he had displayed that particular talent many times with sheriffs, which is not necessarily a good thing. He had also agitated police witnesses, depending on their level of experience, training or competence, or simply the shortness of their fuse, getting their goat so effectively that they said things they would rather they hadn't. It didn't necessarily mean that what they said was evidence of wrongdoing on their part, but he had a knack of taking their words and suggesting to the sheriff and, if there was one, the jury that they might well have been up to no good with regards to his client, who deserved the benefit of their reasonable doubt.

He still hadn't said anything in response to her, so she pressed on, trying to keep her own impatience under control. She was tired and stressed but she would not fall into the same trap as those police witnesses.

'Mrs Stewart tells me you have some information that might help her son's case?' She didn't mean it to sound like a question, more a statement, but the inflection crept in. She thought she'd broken herself of the habit, but it always seemed to come back when she was nervous.

Nerves were good, she convinced herself. They keep you alert—and she needed to be alert. Keep talking, Becks. 'I'm going to try to raise public awareness,' she said, 'so I thought perhaps we could have a chat, you and I.'

His eyes moved beyond her and fixed on something. She resisted the impulse to look. She had to keep her focus on him. His gaze rested on whatever it was very briefly, then returned to her. He pursed his lips, deciding, and gave her a brief nod.

'Not here,' he said. He looked at his watch. 'I have a consultation in my office in an hour. Meet me back there in fifteen minutes. We'll talk.'

He turned without waiting for her to reply and took the few steps up to Longman Road. Rebecca watched him stride in the direction of the town centre, his briefcase under his arm. If she'd known he was on foot, she would have offered him a lift. They could have spoken in the car.

She turned back to the court building and saw Val Roach standing in the shade of one of the columns, watching her.

27

The house used to be filled with noise. The boys pissing both her and each other off or simply having a laugh. Music playing, telly blaring. Mo and her man fighting or loving. Not now, though. There was no sound now, not in the Burke household. The air here was still. Tony was inside. The boys were gone too, one dead and one in the jail, both thanks to Rebecca Connolly. Mo was on her own and the house was silent. Even wee Midge didn't bark as much as he used to.

She sat in the armchair, a cigarette smouldering between her fingers, the only sound the faint whirr of the old electric clock on the mantelpiece. She should get rid of that bloody thing, get a real clock. One that ticked. If time had to pass, it should be marked properly, not with some electronic buzz that you only noticed because everything else in the house was hushed.

She sat in her armchair, longing to catch echoes of the past but hearing nothing. The smoke drifted up from her cigarette, writhing in the air before evaporating, Midge lay in his basket beside the radiator, his head between his paws, his eyes fixed on her, waiting for her to move. She gave him a little smile, that wee dog had kept her sane through the past few months, and raised the filter tip to her lips. She sucked in the sharp smoke, laid her head back on the chair and blew it at the ceiling.

She had made a mistake with Martin Bailey. She should have known he would piss around. He would do it his way, he had said. She had wanted that Connolly girl to feel some of her pain but Bailey was making a production number out of it. Typical man, she thought, making a mountain out of a molehill. She had thought he would be sufficiently motivated to do the job quickly, once she had whispered in his ear, of course. But no, he would pull a Sinatra and do it his way.

She ground the fag out in the ashtray perched on the arm of her chair. Bailey might still deliver but she was beginning to have her doubts. She didn't know what he was doing but she knew he was faffing about and Mo didn't like anyone faffing about. Get in, get the job done, get out: that was her working ethos. She needed a back-up plan.

As she sat there in the stillness of a house where time passed silently, while memories danced through rooms to songs that had long since ended, she thought of Malky Reid.

28

Jordan's office was small, an estate agent might say compact, but no matter which way you put it Rebecca was certain even the most professional of cat swingers would have a hard time. He had one employee, a perfectly coiffed red-haired woman in her forties who gave her the kind of no-nonsense look that could fell a man with a single glance. Rebecca wondered if she had inherited it from a very strict granny. It was the kind of easy glare Rebecca needed for many of the individuals she dealt with, Martin Bailey springing back into her mind like a particularly malodorous phantom, and it crossed her mind that the receptionist could give her lessons.

Thoughts of Bailey raised a question. Was Jordan the solicitor he had mentioned in her office on Saturday? She tried to recall the name of the lawyer who represented his son from the report but came up blank.

'Mr Jordan didn't mention you to me,' said the receptionist, bringing Rebecca's wandering thoughts back into focus.

'Is he back from court?'

'Yes, but, as I said, he didn't mention that he was expecting you.'

Rebecca had made good time, parking at the supermarket not far from the bottom of Castle Wynd, so Jordan must have flown back. He looked fit, but who'd have thought he was a superhero.

'Well, perhaps it slipped his mind. We only made the arrangement a few minutes ago and . . .'

'Mr Jordan is not in the habit of letting things slip his mind.'

Rebecca gave her what she hoped was her sweetest smile. 'I'm sure he's not, but if you could just let him know I'm here.'

The woman weighed this suggestion up, but her hand, with its carefully buffed fingernails, did not stray any closer to the phone.

'He's got a consultation with a client in a short while.'

'I know. In'—Rebecca glanced at the clock on the wall behind the receptionist—'thirty-five minutes, so time is getting on.'

The hand still did not move.

'Look,' said Rebecca, trying hard to keep the smile on her face and her patience in check, 'I'll make a deal with you. You phone through or buzz through or shout through or send up smoke signals, whatever you do to let your boss know there's someone here to see him. If he says he doesn't want to see me, then I'll go and never darken your office door again. How about it?'

A sigh and the hand at last rested on the phone. 'What was the name again?'

'Rebecca Connolly.'

'And what was it regarding?'

'Mr Jordan knows.'

'And you're not a client?'

Rebecca would bet this woman knew every client Stephen Jordan had. And possibly what they had for breakfast in the morning, even those who weren't doing porridge. 'No, I'm here on business.'

'And what company are you with?'

'The Highland News Agency.'

A flicker of an eyebrow. A flare of the nostrils. A twitch of the lips. She obviously shared her boss's suspicion for the workers at the coalface of Her Majesty's loyal press. Between the wariness of the guy in Dalgiesh's office and the haughty tone of the woman who answered Sir Gregory Stewart's phone, she was developing a complex. Nonetheless, the receptionist picked up the receiver and hit a button with a finger that had a manicurist somewhere puffed up with pride. Rebecca heard a corresponding buzz not far away and realised that modern technology was not needed here for communication; it could be possible just as easily with two tin cans and a length of string.

'There's a Rebecca . . .' The receptionist's voice trailed off and she looked at Rebecca quizzically.

'Connolly,' said Rebecca, still smiling but with more than a hint of teeth-gritting. She decided the woman was doing it on purpose in order to have some fun with a scumbag journalist.

'A Rebecca Connolly here to see you.' She listened, nodded as if Jordan could hear it. Perhaps he felt the draught. She hung up and aimed one delicate digit in the direction of a door to the left of her window. 'Through there, down the corridor and then turn left.' The door sprung open as if by magic, leading Rebecca to believe that, while she was transfixed by the pointing finger, the receptionist had sprung the lock with some sleight of hand.

'Thank you,' Rebecca said, her mother's advice ringing in her ears. Remain courteous at all times until the time comes not to be courteous. Nothing annoys people more than you remaining polite and pleasant when they are not.

The corridor was little more than an elongated entranceway. It only took three paces before she had to make the left turn and she was faced with an open door leading to Jordan's office, which was a cupboard with delusions of grandeur. He sat behind a desk, a filing cabinet on either side of his chair, over the back of which he had slung his suit jacket. A pile of folders sat in a tray on the desk and there were further files piled on the floor. There was only one other item of furniture, an uncomfortable-looking chair facing Jordan, and he waved her towards it.

'That receptionist is quite a front line of defence,' said Rebecca, sitting down.

There was a suggestion of a smile. 'Elaine is quite something. She's more a secretary, office manager and minder than a receptionist. Sometimes she scares even me.'

'I'm sure she comes in handy.'

'Worth her weight in gold. Couldn't run this place without her.' He made a pointed glance at his watch. 'Well, Ms Connolly, we're short of time.'

'Yes,' she said, while thinking we wouldn't have been quite so short of time if it hadn't been for the guardian at the gate. 'And it's Rebecca, please. As I said, I'm working with Afua Stewart on—'

'Yes, I spoke to her.'

'Good, so she tells me you have new information relating to her son's case.'

'I do.' There was a pause. 'But first I need to know what you plan to do with this information, if I share it with you.'

She was puzzled by the question. 'Plan to do? Write a story.'

'And that will help, will it?'

'It won't hurt.'

'But will it get Mr Stewart out of jail? I don't think so.'

'No, I can't promise that, but I believe it will get a conversation going.'

'A conversation.'

'Yes, questions raised. Doubts cast. Depending on what it is you have to say, of course.' It was her turn to pause, before adding, 'That is, if it's worth anything.'

She couldn't resist it. Sometimes being courteous isn't enough.

He stared at her. Glanced at his watch. Then he said, 'You used to go out with Simon Hughes.'

Ah, she should have known this would come up. The legal world, like the media, is a small one and he was bound to know her ex, who was a lawyer in Nairn.

'Yes,' she said, feeling a twinge of guilt. Simon had been somewhat clingy, which she hated, but she had still treated him badly. Following her miscarriage, she had felt she could not continue their relationship. She didn't blame him for what happened, and he didn't deserve the way she had treated him, but whatever feelings she had for him died along with their child.

'Is he a friend of yours?' she asked.

'No, we've met a few times, is all. I remember seeing you at a Bar Association function.'

So he didn't just know her from court. She fell silent, unsure what to say. He glanced at his watch, made no further comment.

'Time is getting on, Mr Jordan,' she said.

He didn't reply. She could tell he was considering whether or not to tell her anything, so she tried a gentle prod. 'You said you spoke to Mrs Stewart.'

'I did.'

'Then you know she wants me to have the information.' As she spoke, Rebecca had the worrying thought that Afua Stewart had said nothing of the sort.

Another look at his watch. That was growing annoying. If he would just bloody well tell her, she could be out of here.

'I don't take instructions from Mrs Stewart,' he said.

She decided to go on the offensive. 'Look, Mr Jordan, if you weren't going to tell me then why have me come here? You could have simply refused down at the court building.'

She let it hang between them. If he was offended or angry he didn't show it, but she had seen him in court. He was a cool customer. Quiet, reserved, his questioning of witnesses more a stiletto than a sabre. He was right—he was neither Afua Stewart's lawyer nor her son's. Whatever he had told her, he had done so for his own reasons. There was nothing she could do or say that would force him to talk, not to her anyway.

Her patience finally snapped and she stood up. She was too tired for this. The bastard was obviously playing some kind of game, deliberately wasting her time, perhaps punishing her for daring to report on his clients. 'Fine,' she said, her fingers already on the handle of the door, 'I did as Mrs Stewart wanted, I asked you, but if you won't tell me then I'll just have to go back to her and . . .'

'I take it you've never heard of a man named Roger Dodge?'

His voice was soft and she turned back to him. 'No, who is he?'

Jordan tilted his office chair back until it rested against the white wall behind him. 'He's a client of mine, or rather he *was* a client of mine, however briefly. Roger Dodge, known to the world and its mother as Dodger.'

'He's not a client now?'

Jordan stared off to the ceiling for a moment. 'No,' he said. 'He's dead now.'

It was a rainy autumn morning when Roger Dodge walked into the office. He told Elaine that he needed to speak to a lawyer and Mr Jordan had come highly recommended by some business acquaintances. Elaine did what Elaine did best and tried to get him to make an appointment for later in the week, but the man was quietly emphatic. If he didn't see Mr Jordan now, he would go elsewhere, simple as that. Elaine knew her boss had no appointments, so she buzzed through and asked him if he had a minute to see a walk-in.

Dodge was a big man and he filled Jordan's small office like a heavy piece of furniture. If he decided not to move, it would take three strong men with weight belts and a block and tackle to get him out of there. Large as he was, Rodger Dodge looked broken as he slumped in the chair. His squashed nose was threaded by blue and red veins like an AA road map, his cheeks were slightly sunken, emphasising a scar on the left side. His hair was thinning at the front but long and lank at the back in an emaciated mullet. The knuckles of his hands, which at one time had without doubt caused swelling in other people, were themselves disfigured by arthritis and he massaged them constantly while he talked, as if trying to rub away the pain. His eyes were showing signs of hollowing out and any light, any hope, that they may have once held had been washed away by years of bad choices, bad breaks and bad booze. His clothes were of decent quality but heading in the general direction of threadbare.

'How can I help you, Mr Dodge?' Jordan asked. Despite Elaine's probing, the man had resolutely refused to state his business.

'Call me Dodger, everybody else does.'

Jordan ignored the invitation. It would be Mr Dodge all the way.

'Need some advice, Mr Jordan, so I do.' The man's accent carried the hard edge of the Glasgow streets in which he was born, but there was a rasp to it, as if its concrete was beginning to crumble. 'I'll pay, so I will. No worries about that.'

He reached into the pocket of his coat and produced a clutch of crumpled banknotes, which he laid on the desk.

'There's a hunner quid there. Is that enough, for a consultation, like?'

Jordan let the money sit where it was. It was more than enough but he doubted he would take it. 'Mr Dodge, are you in trouble?'

Dodger's small laugh was like gravel being shaken in a bottle. 'Always, Mr Jordan. But maybe no' in the way you think.'

'So why do you need my help?' he asked.

Dodger sucked in a deep breath, which caught at something in his throat and rattled around for a while. 'I've no' got a charge hanging over me or nothing, like, Mr Jordan. Been keeping my nose clean the past year or so, trying to keep myself to myself, if you know what I'm saying. Wasn't always like that, as you can probably guess.'

Jordan listened without interruption as the man outlined his past as a fist for hire and a small-time reliever of other people's belongings. It was a story of violence, larceny and deceit, of a man from a decent family who took a wrong path, whether by accident or design or just plain bad-ness. Jordan did not judge because that was not his function and he had heard many like it before, for there were a thousand such tales in every city, town and village. So he listened and he digested and, even though he should have pushed the conversation along at a speedier pace, he waited for the point of the man's visit, for so far he had heard nothing that required his advice. At the time of some of the offences Dodge had sketched in a vague way, yes, but not now. Although he did not actually say it, Jordan had the feeling that this man had paid for some of his transgressions with loss of liberty. Some, not all.

'So then I ended up here, in Inverness, nine, ten years ago,' said the man, and then he paused. His story so far had flowed freely enough, even though some of the detail had been omitted, whether through self-preservation or shame Jordan could not tell. But whatever he now had to say, it was not proving as easy. Jordan saw genuine pain deepen the shadows in his eyes. And something else.

Something that might have been fear.

Finally, the man said, 'Mr Jordan, everything I tell you is confidential, right?'

'That's correct.'

'And you cannae tell nobody what I say?'

'I can't.'

'No matter what?'

'Not unless what you tell me means that someone will come to harm if I say nothing.'

Dodger nodded, happy with that answer. 'No one will come to harm. The harm's already been done, so it has.' He thought again. 'Well, I'll come to harm, but what I've got to say won't change that.'

'Someone will do you harm?'

'No, no, nothing like that.' Another deep breath. Whatever was lodged in his throat was slashing at it like a machete. 'I'm sick, Mr Jordan. They say I've no' got long. Pancreatic cancer.'

Jordan had already surmised the man was ill. From what he had heard, Roger Dodge was not what you would call a good man by any stretch of the imagination, but he still felt something like pity. 'I'm sorry to hear that, Mr Dodge.'

Dodger gave him a small smile, as if he was ashamed. 'Aye, well, my tea's oot and my pie's cauld, right enough,' he said. 'It's news like that makes a guy think, you know what I mean, Mr Jordan? When you know you're facing the end, you look at what you've done with your life and you think, was it wasted?'

Jordan sensed the man wanted to unburden himself, so he let him talk.

'I've no' been what you would call a model citizen, Mr Jordan, you know that now. In fact, I've been a right bastard.' He looked down at his hands, the fingers of his right still rubbing at the knuckles of his left, as if he was trying to clean away some blemish along with the arthritic pain. 'I've lied. I've stole. I've hurt people. If my auld ma knew half the things I've done she'd be birlin' in her grave. Probably claw her way back oot and give me a right skite over the back of the heid.'

'You've been punished for some of the things you've done, Mr Dodge,' Jordan said, gently.

'No' them all, Mr Jordan, no' them all.' Dodger's face was coloured with shame and Jordan felt it was sincere. 'And no' the one I want to talk to you about.'

'What one is that?'

'The one that brought me up here, from Glesga.' Dodger hesitated again, his fingers still working, first the right, then the left, back and forward. 'I killed a man, Mr Jordan. A man who had never done nothing to me, who I didnae even know, apart from when I saw him on the news.'

Jordan leaned forward, tried to keep his voice steady, business-like, but it's not every day someone confesses to murder. 'Mr Dodge, by telling me that, you cannot retain me as your solicitor if any charges are brought.'

'Nae charges will be brought, Mr Jordan, don't worry about that. This was years ago. No one knows I was involved. Well, no one that's gonnae say anything about it.'

'Who was the victim?'

Dodger paused, as if he was wondering how much he should say. Then he took a breath and said, 'A bloke called Murdo Maxwell, you remember him?'

Jordan sat back again. He had expected it to be some simple affair, like a fight that had gone wrong, nothing more complex than a low-level crook who had fallen foul of a bigger fish. He recalled the case. It had been big news. 'Someone was convicted for that,' he said.

'Aye.' There was so much sadness, so much regret in that single word it seemed to crush Dodger even further. 'That's why I'm telling you this. After I'm . . .' The fear that flared in his eyes forced him to pause. Dead. He was about to say *after I'm dead* but he couldn't. The word carried such a finality with it that Jordan felt Dodge could not utter it. Sick. Ill. Even the dread word *cancer* he could say, but dead, dying, death, he could not. 'After I'm gone, I want you to let people know that the boy in the jail didn't do it, that it was me. You need to help that boy, Mr Jordan. I need to help him. I'll sign anything you need.' He looked down at his rubbing fingers again, the friction growing as he became more and more troubled by what he was saying. 'It's the least I can do.'

Jordan knew it would take more than that to make the system examine itself but he kept that to himself for now.

He asked, 'Was it a robbery gone wrong?'

Rub.

'No.'

'Did you have something against Murdo Maxwell?'

Rub, rub.

'No.'

'Then what happened? Why did you kill him?'

145

Rub, rub, rub.

'I was hired to do it,' he said.

'Like a contract?' The use of that word seemed alien to Jordan, as if he was in a film. But this was real. This man was in his office, telling him that ten years ago he had committed a murder for hire.

'Aye, like a contract, that's what it was.'

'Who hired you, Mr Dodge?'

Dodger looked up then and Jordan saw the fear again. 'That I cannae say.'

'You've gone this far.'

'Naw, Mr Jordan, I cannae tell you who it was that hired me.'

'Why not?'

'I've been a bad bastard, Mr Jordan, I told you that, I recognise that myself. But what I did to that Maxwell fella and that young boy in the jail, well, it's no' right. Far from no' right. But see these guys? These guys are fuckin' scary.'

29

Rebecca walked through the sunshine with shoppers and tourists milling around and the faint notes of a piper busking in the pedestrianised area of Church Street. She heard voices, laughter, life. She thought about Dodger and she thought about death, not in a morbid way and not dispassionately—she had experienced death but not enough to make her cold and hard.

Dodger had been forced to stare into the dark abyss of his own mortality and his life had stared back at him. He did not like what he saw. He had been a man of blood, a man of pain, but while he had lived that life he had not been aware he was wasting what was, in fact, a gift. It was only as he realised that there were only so many breaths a man can take, so many steps, so many smiles to give, so many tears to shed, that he realised this and, like many people before him, wished he had done things differently. He was a hard man, so he was a realist. He could not change what had gone before. The only thing he could do was try somehow to make amends.

'I tried to get him to talk publicly about it,' Jordan had explained as he rose from his desk, the sign that her time was up, 'but he refused. Even then, when he knew that he didn't have long, he was terrified of whoever had hired him to do the job.'

'And he didn't give even a hint as to who it was?'

Jordan had opened the door for her and stepped back to let her pass. 'All he said was that if he talked, *they* would come after his family. Apparently he has a sister and a nephew here in Inverness and it seems *they*—whoever *they* are—knew that. He was adamant that he would not endanger his family. Whoever they were, they scared him even more than death itself.'

Rebecca's immediate thought was of the security services. Maxwell had believed they were keeping tabs on him. But why? And would they really kill a high-profile man such as he? That's conspiracy theory stuff. Wasn't it?

And even if it was some shadowy government agency, would they really hire a cheap thug to carry it out? They would have professionals on their team for jobs like that.

Wouldn't they?

'And is this affidavit enough to help James Stewart?' she asked.

'On its own, probably not. The Crown would dismiss it, saying they have no opportunity to cross-examine Mr Dodge and put his claim under legal scrutiny. I told him we would need some form of corroboration. I think he knew that—he'd been around the system all his adult life.'

'And what did he say?'

'That there was something, but it would be someone else's decision whether or not it should be taken forward.'

Rebecca was trying to imagine what this corroboration could possibly be, and who this someone else was, as she reached the door to her office. It swung open and Val Roach almost collided with her.

'DCI Roach,' said Rebecca, taken aback, but her tone pared of any warmth.

'Rebecca,' said the detective, her tone equally as clipped but, Rebecca hoped, through guilt. They had history and not all of it was good. However, the chances were Roach believed she had never been at fault and was simply being what she was—a ranking police officer with all the attitude that can bring.

'Someone has broken the bulb on your landing,' Roach observed.

'It was an accident,' she replied, keeping it vague. She knew in her heart Bailey was responsible but had no proof. Even if the police were to follow up on it, Bailey would no doubt get some perverted thrill out of knowing he had spooked her, and Rebecca still refused to allow that. 'What brings you here?'

'I wondered if you fancied a coffee.'

Rebecca could not hide her surprise. There was a time when she and the DCI might have had a working relationship, but that ended almost as soon as it began. Still, always be courteous.

'Sure, come on up to the office and I'll make us both one.'

Roach's face crinkled slightly. 'Does your coffee come out of a jar?'

Rebecca thought about the Kenco Smooth and nodded. 'But it's good,' she said, trying not to be defensive about her caffeine choices.

Roach was obviously both unimpressed and unconvinced. She jerked her head towards the door of the coffee house on the corner. 'Come on, my treat.'

Rebecca followed her, relieved and grateful that she had an excuse not to go up those stairs but that would not stop her from ordering something hideously expensive and a cake. She couldn't punish the police officer for what she did during the Culloden investigation, but she could cost her a little money.

In the coffee house, Roach did not react when she asked for a hot chocolate with cream, adding, just to see the look on her face, extra marshmallows. She decided against cake—frankly the drink was sweet enough to give the von Trapp family diabetes—but ordered a pork sausage on a sourdough roll instead. As usual, she hadn't eaten breakfast that morning and she didn't think she could last until lunchtime. Roach carefully studied the selection of coffees chalked up on the blackboard before selecting an Americano. No milk. They had been in this coffee house before and she had ordered the same. Rebecca guessed the reading of the menu was part of her ritual, as if she might discover something surprising there. Some new way to charge over the odds for coffee perhaps. Like adding marshmallows.

She led them to a table in the corner which looked out on both Union Street and Church Street. Roach didn't say anything. They sat opposite each other in silence, each watching the people striding, shuffling, easing past; the panoply of life in microcosm. Rebecca could still hear the faint strains of the lone piper and thought she recognised the tune as 'Flowers of the Forest'. The coffees arrived and Roach stirred hers idly, while Rebecca turned her attention to the heaped concoction before her and wondered how she was going to drink it and still retain her dignity.

The sun glinted through the window and caught Roach's face. She was a tough cop, but Rebecca was caught off guard by the elfin quality to her features. Roach always reminded her of Audrey Hepburn, her mother's favourite actress. The last time they had been in here she thought the woman had looked worn out, but she seemed fine and healthy today. Of course, last time she had been in the middle of a double murder investigation.

Rebecca dreaded to think how she looked. A quick glimpse in the mirror that morning of her pale face and panda eyes had been enough.

Roach decided it was up to her to break the ice and when she did she took the banal route. 'Beautiful weather we're having.'

Rebecca automatically looked outside again, as if checking it hadn't changed. 'It won't last.'

Roach's brief nod seemed to agree with her. Rebecca watched as she stared at her coffee cup, idly playing with a wooden stirrer.

'Did you come here to discuss the weather, DCI Roach?' Rebecca asked.

'Why don't you call me Val.'

Rebecca felt her lips slim into something that was not quite a grimace but nowhere near a smile. 'Yeah, we tried that once before—didn't work out so well.'

Roach had wanted information, a name, and Rebecca had refused to share it. She couldn't. Lawyers weren't the only people with codes.

'That was business,' said Roach, her tone dismissive but with something like regret rearing in her dark eyes.

Rebecca was glad to see the look, but it didn't make her feel any better about what had happened. 'You threatened to have me arrested.'

'I wouldn't have, though.'

'A threat is a threat,' said Rebecca, sipping her hot chocolate through the marshmallow layer. My God, it was sweet. Maybe it was what her body needed. 'And I thought we were pals.'

Roach stared down at her coffee. 'We could be.'

'Pals don't lie to people about each other.'

There was that little flash of pain in the detective's eyes again. She knew what Rebecca was referring to. Her telling a suspect that Rebecca had broken a confidence when she had not had led to tragedy. 'I was investigating two murders and I needed information,' said Roach, her voice firm. 'That was the only way I could get it. That's my job, Rebecca. Don't try to tell me that you've never misrepresented something to get a story.'

Rebecca did not answer at first. She didn't think she had ever told a blatant lie, but she had bent the truth a little in order to get someone to speak. 'Okay, apology accepted,' she said.

'I didn't apologise.'

'Let's agree to differ.'

Roach opened her mouth to argue the point, then a smile crept into her eyes and she ran her fingers through her short dark hair. 'You've grown up a lot since the last time. You're sharper.'

'Yes, I'm potty trained and everything now.'

The smile eased to her lips. 'You're tougher, too.'

Yeah, staring down the wrong end of a gun does that to a person, Rebecca thought. She didn't say it aloud, though. She felt she had been smart-mouthed enough for one conversation.

'So you've still not told me what I can do for you,' she said.

'What makes you think there's something you can do for me?'

'Because you're a DCI with Police Scotland and you're not in the habit of paying social calls to a journalist with a small news agency, no matter how scintillating that journalist's company is.'

The smile was real now. 'You're scintillating, are you?'

'I'm a bloody delight, DCI Roach.' Rebecca still wasn't ready to call her Val. Once bitten, as they say. 'And whatever this is, it's obviously off the record.'

Roach put her elbow on the table top and rested her chin on her hand. 'How do you work that out?'

'Because if it was official I would have been summoned to Inshes, where the full might of Police Scotland could be brought to bear to intimidate me.'

'We don't intimidate,' said Roach. 'We just tactfully advise that it's in someone's best interests to work with us.'

Rebecca made a *pfft* sound but Roach kept her face straight. They regarded each other for a moment in silence before the police officer laughed. Despite her lack of sleep and her deep suspicions over Roach's motives, Rebecca felt a smile tickle her lips and a laugh gathering momentum in her throat.

'And is that what this is?' Rebecca waved to the cups in front of them. 'Tactful advice?'

'Maybe.'

'So what is it you want?'

Roach drummed her fingers on her cheekbone, her eyes still dancing with good humour. 'You were speaking to Stephen Jordan.'

'I was.'

'May I ask what about?'

Rebecca peeled a marshmallow away and popped it in her mouth. This could only be about the Maxwell murder. 'You can ask.'

'Will you tell me?'

'I don't know—will you threaten to have me arrested if I don't?'

Roach sighed but the smile was still there. 'Okay, what if I ask you a straight question, will you give me a straight answer? Even if it's just yes or no?'

'Yes. Was that the question?'

'No.' Roach lowered her hand from her face, leaned forward and said softly, 'Were you talking to him about the Murdo Maxwell case?'

Even though forewarned, Rebecca was still slightly taken aback by the specificity of the question and she took a moment to form an answer. She thought about denying it but saw no real benefit in that. 'Yes,' she said.

Roach nodded. 'Are you willing to tell me what he said?'

'Are you willing to tell me why you're interested?'

There was a pause as Roach weighed up the pros and cons of being honest or spinning some communications department spin. Either way, Rebecca was confident that whatever the answer, she would recognise it for what it was. She now knew lies when she heard them. Another similarity between the legal profession and hers.

Roach finally reached a decision. 'This is off the record.'

Rebecca already knew that.

'The story in yesterday's paper about the banners—yours, I take it?' Roach asked.

Rebecca nodded.

'Well, it has, for some reason, set tongues wagging in pay grades above mine and the word is that Mr Jordan has information relating to the case. Information that has, as yet, not been made public. I've been asked, informally, to find out what that is.'

Rebecca took this in. 'Why are they so interested, those pay grades above yours?'

Roach spread her hands to show openness. 'I don't know, and that's the truth. Whatever it is, it was enough to have my boss send me out to investigate.'

'Unofficially.'

Roach inclined her head. 'Unofficially.'

Rebecca took a moment to study the detective's face. 'That bothers you, doesn't it?'

The corners of Roach's mouth turned down. 'Mine is not to reason why.'

Rebecca leaned forward. 'No, I can see it. You're wondering why the powers-that-be are so interested.'

Roach shrugged the observation away. 'It's quiet at the moment, not a lot happening. It keeps me on the streets.'

Rebecca wasn't buying that for an instant. 'Why don't you ask Stephen Jordan yourself?'

'He doesn't think much of police officers.'

'He doesn't think much of journalists.'

'But the difference is, you can help him.'

'Not sure he sees it that way.'

'So he told you whatever it is he knows?'

'Oh, he told me.'

'So will you tell me?'

It was Rebecca's turn to consider the options. She was going to write a story as soon as she got back to the office, so it would be online with the nationals within an hour or two, of that she had no doubt. What harm would it do to tell Roach ahead of time? On the other hand, she still didn't trust her.

'What's in it for me?' she asked.

Roach sat back as if she had been expecting the question. Rebecca hated herself for being predictable. 'I'm as interested in this as you are. I can help, perhaps.'

'Perhaps' was right. Rebecca had experienced Roach's help before and she wasn't sure she wanted a second dose. 'In what way? Access to official records?'

Roach dismissed the suggestion with a look. Rebecca was not disappointed. She hadn't expected anything of the sort. 'I told you, I've been asked to nose around. So, perhaps we could share information.'

'Unofficially.'

Roach sighed. 'Yes, unofficially.'

'Starting with me, of course.'

'Well, I have nothing to share.'

That figures.

Rebecca's phone bleeped and she saw she had a text from Jordan. He had refused to give her the address of Dodger's sister until he checked with her. The text told her it was a street in the Dalneigh district. She laid the phone down and looked back up to see Roach watching her with that half smile in her eyes. Rebecca had already decided to tell the police officer what Jordan had said, but she stretched the moment as long as she could. The story would be out there soon enough, but she would keep the bit about Dodger's sister to herself for now. She didn't want to seem a pushover.

She asked, 'Have you heard of a Roger Dodge, known as Dodger?'

'No.'

'Small-time crook and bone breaker, by the sounds of it.'

'Okay, what about him?'

Rebecca told her Jordan's story. Roach listened without interruption, occasionally sipping her coffee. At the end of the fairly short speech she stared out of the window again, where life walked by. Here they were, talking about death, and outside the sun shone and life went on. The world turned. People die, alone or in their thousands, and the world keeps turning. Grief and sorrow, pain and death, all are part of life and living, and the world turns. James Stewart was doing time for something he may not have done. Yet it turned. It kept turning when Rebecca's father died. It kept turning when she lost the baby. It kept turning when she almost lost Chaz. It kept turning as she sat on a wet pathway and the life oozed from the man she held. It turns, spins, revolves, never stops, never wavers.

'Of course, this can't be corroborated,' said Roach eventually.

Not yet, Rebecca thought, but she was keeping that to herself too. Whatever it was. 'Jordan had him provide a very detailed description of the interior of the house and also the murder itself. Where the poker came from, how it happened.'

'He could have learned that from news coverage at the time.'

'Not all of it. Not some of the detail. He signed an affidavit.'

A slight sneer. 'If we can believe any of this, of course. Could all be a tissue of lies.'

'Stephen Jordan is a respected solicitor.'

'He defends scumbags.'

'He does his job.'

'He profits from people's misery—and from the public purse.'

'Don't we all?'

Roach opened her mouth as if she was going to argue further but decided against it. 'Do you have this affidavit?'

Rebecca shook her head, sipped her hot chocolate, which was now tepid. She was regretting her childish attempt at point-scoring now. 'He's going to email me a copy.'

'Isn't that privileged in some way?'

'Not really. His client is dead and he had instructions to help James Stewart in any way he could. He's going to check with Dodge's sister first.'

'Will you forward it to me?'

'No.' Her answer came quick because she had expected the request.

'Why not?'

'It's not up to me to provide it.'

'I can't check its detail without it.'

That was true, Rebecca thought.

'Can you at least give me a precis of its contents?'

Rebecca felt a smile. 'A précis?'

'Yes, a summary.'

'Is that what it means?' Rebecca was enjoying the cut and thrust of their conversation. 'I'll think about it.'

Roach sipped her coffee. 'When my mother said that, it usually meant no.'

'Mine, too.'

Roach tilted her head. 'You still don't trust me, is that it?'

Rebecca had never been sure what a sardonic laugh was, but the sharp noise she emitted must have been pretty close to it. 'Okay, *Val*, as you've brought it up again, no, I don't. I don't like it when police officers come in heavy and threaten me. Whether you like it or not, whether you believe it or not, I have rules that I follow and you tried to force me to break one that is pretty damn basic in my game. So, no—I don't trust you. I've bought apples from your cart before—the friendly overture, the chat over coffee. I fell for it once but, let me tell you, it's going to take more than a fancy hot chocolate to win me over this time.'

Rebecca surprised herself with how much came out. She had not intended to be quite so blunt but she was tired and, if she was honest with herself, Bailey was getting to her. To her credit, Roach took the rant, hushed though it was in the confines of the coffee house. She pursed her lips slightly and nodded towards the half-finished hot chocolate. 'You didn't enjoy that, did you?'

Her suppressed anger still fizzing slightly, Rebecca found herself taken aback by the non sequitur. 'As it happens, no.'

'So why did you order it?'

'It seemed like a good idea at the time.' She nodded to the crumbs on the side plate. What the hell? When did she eat that roll? Did she simply inhale it? 'The roll and sausage was good, though.'

'I prefer square sausage,' said Roach.

'So do I, but any old pork in a storm,' said Rebecca.

Roach winced. 'You do know puns are the lowest form of wit.'

'Oh really? And I thought it was sarcasm. I can do that, too.'

They fell silent again and Rebecca wondered what the hell was going on between them. She had accused the woman of being totally untrustworthy, and she had sat there and taken it. Now she was chattering away as if nothing had been said. Rebecca had no regrets over what she said, unplanned and unnecessarily heated though it was. She'd had to get it out.

'So,' said Roach, eventually, 'now you've got all that off your chest, will you let me see that affidavit or what?'

This time Rebecca's laugh was genuine. 'We'll see.'

'Yeah, my mum used to say that, too.'

30

Malky Reid was beginning to think he was wasting his time in Inverness. He didn't know why he was even here, why Wee Joe had got his knickers in a twist over all this. Malky was not by nature a nosey man. He could be inquisitive if he was told to be—after all, Wee Joe and his dad before him paid the wages—but in general he let the world go on its merry way without him sticking his nose in. But he was as curious as a litter full of cats to know why some killing ten years ago was important enough to have him come north. Of course, it was useful to check all was hunky-bloody-dory on the final frontier, and it was important to reach out to Mo Burke now and again, make her feel important—part of the family, as it were. The lassie was on her own now. Until her man came out, anyway.

The thing was, Malky liked her. There had been friction in the past between the Burkes and the McClymonts. Wee Joe loved to find new income streams, even though Malky suspected he already had money he didn't know he had. Malky himself was reasonably comfortable. Okay, he didn't live in a villa decked out like a fortress in Mount Vernon like his boss. His own flat on Alexandra Parade was more modest. But it was still better than the council flat in which he grew up in Carntyne. He had money in the bank, he had a nice motor, he had no wife to piss him off since the divorce—and since she got hitched to a taxI driver from Riddrie, no alimony to pay—and no kids. Well, none that he knew of, because he hadn't been a monk, even when he was married. There were a couple of burds who threw him a shag every now and then but who weren't looking for anything permanent. One was also the bit on the side of a drug dealer from the Southside of Glasgow who, if he found out she was playing away from home, was capable of turning right nasty. That didn't worry Malky much because he was capable of turning nasty himself.

All in all, he was that rare breed, a man content with his lot.

Wee Joe, though, was a different matter. He never seemed happy, let alone satisfied. Always on the lookout for something and Malky would bet his last fiver the boy did not have a single clue what that something was. It was as if there was a shadow standing just behind the wee guy, something that hunted him. Or haunted maybe. Malky would have been like that too if he'd seen his mother and wee sister burn up in a car. Something like that was bound to scar a guy.

Mo Burke had been through a lot, too. He'd thought her a handsome woman when he'd met her for the first time the year before and he'd thought that again yesterday. Okay, she had a hard look around the eyes, but that was understandable, and she smoked like a bloody chimney. Malky had been off the coffin nails for five years and he felt all the better for it. He worked out, went to the gym at least three times a week, didn't drink much now. He was near fifty and there were those who said he looked fifteen years younger. He kept his hair short, dyed it brown regularly, made sure he remained clean-shaven because nothing ages a man more than long, grey hair and a beard.

Part of him was glad the aggro between the McClymonts and the Burkes was in the past, at least for now. He had helped broker the peace, which had not been easy, and he was well aware it might be temporary. But he hoped when her husband, Tony, came out he would see it as mutually beneficial. Wee Joe had an established supply chain for gear, initially set up by his dad but now a well-oiled machine. The stuff came from down south by car, passed through Glasgow and then carried on up north. Times and routes were staggered, but there was seldom a break in the supply. The Burkes had organised their own deliveries until Mo saw the sense of linking up with the McClymont clan and peace broke out. Better together, Malky had told her. He wasn't privy to the financial workings of the business—as long as he got his wedge he couldn't care less—but he was astute enough to know that Wee Joe made more out of the deal than Mo. Better together meant better for them.

He looked out of his open hotel window at a line of trees and thought about giving the woman a bell, maybe invite her out for a drink. He could hear traffic on the A96 and caught flashes of the vehicles heading to and from Inverness between the trunks and leaves. He was staying at a budget chain hotel because he liked the anonymity. Boarding houses and family-run hotels were fine but people asked questions, they couldn't help themselves. The big chains, less so. They just wheeled you in and wheeled you out and, apart from the occasional nod to the solo receptionist, he spoke to no one. From a professional point of view, given what his profession was, that was a good thing, but personally it was the opposite. Malky was the gregarious type. He liked to go out with mates and have a pint and see if he could pull. Up here he was on the job, so getting bladdered was not an option, certainly not on his own. Who knew what dumb-fuckery that could lead to. However, he still wasn't a monk, hence his thoughts of Mo Burke. He'd heard she was a one-guy gal, but that guy had been away for a couple of years now and gals had needs too, didn't they? Sure, she was still grieving the death of her boy, but he could help take her mind off her sorrow.

On the other hand, he was on the job. And talking to her was part of that job. Wee Joe would not like him mixing business with *the* business. Wee Joe was like one of those evangelists in that way. Malky had never seen him with a burd, never seen him look at one, never heard him talk about one. Whenever the boys discussed burds they'd shagged, usually in detail, for political correctness had as yet failed to penetrate the Life, they had to stop when he came in the room because he didn't like that kind of talk. He doubted if the wee guy had ever done the business. Fuck, *he* could be a monk. Brother Joe. He'd prefer that nickname, Malky would bet.

So, no. Best not try his arm with Mo. Stuff like that can backfire and that was the last thing he needed.

And that was when Mo Burke phoned him.

Malky stared at the phone on the table before him, wondering at the coincidence. He was from Glasgow and he didn't believe in coincidences, no matter how often they occurred. And yet, here he was, think-ing about someone and at that moment they call him. Downright spooky, so it was. In his mind he heard the tune to *The X-Files*.

'Mo,' he said, keeping his voice cool, even though in his head he was freaking out slightly.

'Got some news for you,' she said, and he heard the click of her gold lighter as she lit up a fag. Smoking again. Maybe he had made the right decision. Winching her would be like licking an ashtray.

'Knew I could rely on you.' It was true: if there was anyone up here in haggisland who would get him some gen, it was her.

'But there's a price.' He heard her exhale smoke. 'Aye, and it won't be cheap.'

She was going to haggle, for God's sake. 'All I want is a bit of info, I'm no' buying a used car, Mo.'

'Way of the world, son. Nothing is for nothing.' There was a slight pop as she sucked in more smoke and removed the filter tip from her lips. 'Call it a favour, then. A whatchamacallit—a quid pro quo.'

He mulled it over, then said, 'What do you need, Mo?'

'That reporter lassie, Rebecca Connolly.'

'What about her?'

'She's involved.'

'I know that, Mo—I told you!'

'Aye, I know.' Another drag on the cigarette. 'I want her hurt.'

'Wait a minute, Mo.'

'Naw, Malky, you wait a minute. That bitch caused the death of my boy and saw my other boy jailed and I owe her some hurt, so I do. I can't do it directly, too easily traced back to me. But you? You're no' a local face. You'll be away in a day or two.'

'Mo, I'm no' up here for anything like that. And it doesn't sit right with me, you know?'

'Don't give me that shite, Malky Reid. I know you, son.'

Son. She was younger than him.

'You've hurt people, a lot of people,' she went on, 'and for far less than what she's cost me.'

He couldn't deny it, he had hurt people, but he never liked hurting women, even though he had done it on occasion. Went against the grain. 'But that was business.'

'And so is this. You want my gen? You give me your word you'll do her a damage and you'll get it.'

'And you trust me to do it even after you tell me what it is?'

'As I said, son—I know you. You're a crook and you're a hard man, but when you give your word, you keep it. Am I wrong? 'Cos if I am, you get bugger-all out of me. So tell me, Malky Reid, am I wrong?'

He felt his heart sink. He generally did what he said he would do, that was why the McClymonts had trusted him all these years. 'Nah, you're no' wrong.'

'So you'll do it?'

'Aye.'

'I mean real damage, no' just a slap or two. I want her to suffer for what she did.'

Malky heard real hatred in Mo's voice and he wondered just what the hell this girl had done to her. She said she'd caused the death of her son, but how? Then he put it out of his mind. It didn't matter. He had been given a job to do by Wee Joe and he would do it. All part of keeping his word. If doing this favour for Mo Burke helped him, then he would do it too. The whys and wherefores mattered little to him.

'I want your promise, Malky,' she said, pressing him.

'I promise, Mo,' he said. 'Now, what have you got for me?'

Another drag on her cigarette, then, 'You need to talk to Mount Hector.'

31

At first Gordie didn't believe me when I said I was innocent. He just smiled and said we all were, but his tone told me that none of us were. I understood what he meant. In the year or two I'd been in here I'd heard so many men say they hadn't done what they had been accused of. Even when I was on remand, they said it. Of course, there were many who boasted about what they had done because that gave them some sort of position in the pecking order. Even given what had happened to me, I knew that what Gordie said was true. It was inconceivable that so many men had been wrongly convicted and I felt that, in some of them, it was a form of denial, that they could not face either what they had done or the fact that they had been caught doing it. But that didn't mean miscarriages didn't happen. After all, I am a case in point.

As time passed, the more I spoke to Gordie, the more he came to believe me and the angrier he became. He was a crook, he admitted it, was even proud of it. He had done things I didn't even want to think about, but he had a sense of justice, a sense of honour. That may seem perverted to some, but it was there. I know he was looking out for me because my father had asked him to, and it would bring him benefits when he got out; Gordie admitted this to me right off. So when he grew angry over what had been done to me, I knew it to be genuine. It was, as he said, a right fucking liberty. And something would have to be done about it.

32

The area known as Dalneigh is wedged between the River Ness to the east and the Caledonian Canal to the west, although neither body of water was visible from the street in which Dodger's sister lived. Rebecca walked up the path towards the well-tended mid-terrace house, skirting the edge of what would once have been a small garden but had been paved over to create a parking area for two vehicles, though only one car was there, a Honda Civic.

Eleanor Fraser herself was tall but almost painfully thin, the opposite of her late brother, based on Jordan's description. Her mid-length brown hair was pulled back from her face and held in place in a ponytail; her face was sharp and her eyes even sharper. She was wearing paint-speckled overalls and her hands and cheeks were also freckled with white.

She was not unfriendly when she opened the door but she wasn't overly welcoming either, even though she had agreed via Stephen Jordan to Rebecca's visit. She stepped back with a sigh and jerked her head down the hallway. 'We'll have to sit in the kitchen. I'm decorating the lounge,' she said.

The kitchen was at the back of the house and looked out onto a slightly larger garden than the one at the front. This one was grassy, with well-cultivated plants and shrubs lining the high wooden fence separating it from the neighbours on either side. The room itself was bright and clean, and again Rebecca felt shame at the state of her own small kitchen area.

Eleanor gestured towards a table and they sat facing each other. Tea was offered and declined. Rebecca laid her notepad out and checked it was permissible to record the conversation, which the woman accepted with a nod.

'Before we begin, Mrs Fraser,' said Rebecca, 'let me say I'm sorry for your loss.'

'Look,' said the woman, getting right down to it, 'you might as well know I didn't have much to do with Roger, not once we grew up. We were twins but not identical. We didn't have that connection I keep hearing about, you know, the telepathy and the bond that's supposed to exist. So, frankly, there's not been much mourning in this house. If you ask me, the cancer that took him was the badness in him eating him up.'

Her accent was recognisably Glaswegian, but it had been softened by her years of living in Inverness. Rebecca was surprised to hear the woman express herself in such stark terms. Mona Maxwell had been equally as blunt, but Rebecca had been aware of a level of grief even ten years after her brother's death. Eleanor Fraser's brother was only gone a matter of weeks and she didn't care.

Eleanor Fraser must have seen something in Rebecca's face because she looked slightly ashamed of herself. 'Sorry if I've shocked you.'

'No, it's all right.'

'It's just I don't believe in striking a pose, you know? What is it they call it these days—virtue signalling? I hate that.'

That is what they called it these days and Rebecca shared the woman's distaste.

'Roger and me were from a good family, a decent family,' Eleanor went on. 'Dad was a bus driver in Glasgow, Mum worked in BHS, in the restaurant, you know, up there in Sauchiehall Street? It's closed now. We used to go there for fish, chips and beans on a Saturday when Dad wasn't on shift. It said peas on the menu but if you asked they'd give you beans.'

The words came out in a rush, as if she wanted to get them out of her system. Perhaps because she knew Rebecca would be visiting, she had been thinking about it as she coated walls with paint, so now that the moment was here it had to be said before it was forgotten. Perhaps she had been desperate to say something like this for years. Rebecca had no idea. She was grateful she didn't have to ask questions.

'It was a good home, a nice home, our mum saw to that. And Dad was a good man. They're both gone now.' She paused, just a breath, but long enough for Rebecca to catch that familiar wistful look. Eleanor Fraser cared for her parents and she missed them. Rebecca wondered if her own eyes betrayed her feelings when she thought of her father.

'Anyway, Roger though, he was wayward. When we were young kids him and me were close, I suppose. In a way, anyway. We fought, I mean physical fights, rolling around the floor, but he was always bigger than me and he won.'

'What did you fight about?'

'What do kids always fight about? Nothing, really. Attention, maybe.' She stopped and remembered her childhood. 'There was a stuffed rabbit, just a wee thing.' She held her hands about six inches apart. 'We both claimed it as our own. We used to fight over that, I remember, even when we were too old to care about cuddly toys. It was a power thing, I suppose. Possession. First it was mine, then it was his. I'd take it back and he'd take it again and that's the way it went, back and forth. I grew out of it, the fighting; Roger didn't. He was always a big lad, a bit too quick with his fists, even in primary school. God knows how many kids he thumped and it just got worse as he went into secondary. He found other boys like him there and just went from bad to worse, did things he shouldn't. Dad used to say he just turned out wrong, but Mum said no, she said he had a bad seed in him.'

'I know he was a petty criminal, Mrs Fraser.'

Her face crumpled into something that was a slight sneer but mostly regret. 'Aye, some not so petty, it seems.'

'So you know what this is about?'

'Of course I do. That solicitor, Mr Jordan, he told me after Roger died what he'd said. Roger wanted it that way, apparently. He had to wait until after. He came here last week, brought me Roger's stuff in a big brown paper bag. It was all sealed, stapled, taped.' She blinked. 'I've never opened it. Threw it in a cupboard under the stairs. It's still there.'

The blinking increased. She swallowed. Was she feeling regret at dealing so dismissively with her brother's belongings?

Rebecca asked, 'And how did the news that Roger had killed someone make you feel?'

'How do you think it made me feel? I knew Roger was bad, but killing someone? For money?'

'I don't think it was just for money, Mrs Fraser. I think there were threats, too.'

'Aye, Mr Jordan said that he did it to protect me and mine. But I don't fully buy that.' The blinking stopped now and the hard, sharp look returned. She was back on firmer ground. 'Roger never gave a toss for me or my son. He never liked my husband—Pete works for the council, in the planning department. Roger never had any time for straight arrows, that's what him and his crooked pals called honest folk. Straight arrows.'

'So you never had any contact with him?'

'Aye, we'd keep in touch, mostly my doing, because my mum had asked me to keep an eye on him. I'd phone him now and then, birthdays, Christmas, that sort of thing.'

'But Roger didn't reciprocate?'

'No, never did.' She paused. 'Until that one time, he came to see me out the blue. Turned up on the doorstep one morning.'

'When was this?'

She thought about it. 'Oh, some months ago now. I hadn't seen him for ages. We'd spoken on the phone a couple of times, but there was no family reunion or anything. Then he just showed up that morning . . .'

He had aged.

They both had, she supposed, but her brother looked old and, well, weary. She hadn't seen him in five years, not since their mother's cremation. She had died almost two years to the day after her husband.

Their mother had left their father in his favourite chair in the living room, watching a film. He often did that, watched something late into the night while she went to bed. The following morning she woke up and he wasn't there beside her, which was unusual. She found him still in his chair. The TV had shut itself down. He looked as if he was sleeping, but of course he wasn't. It was a massive heart attack, they said. One minute he was there, the next he was gone, like he had switched himself off the way the TV had. She never recovered, their mother. It was as if something had switched off for her, too. She was there physically. She ate, she slept, she talked. But something about her had died with him and when she passed away it was like it was just the end of what had started the night their father died.

Anyway, Roger turned up for the funeral, which kind of surprised her because she really thought he wouldn't. Decent black coat on, but his shoes needed a polish. Used to drive their dad mad that, Roger's shoes always scuffed. Dad used to say the mark of a man was how well he polished his shoes, and maybe he was right. Roger was always a bit worn somehow. But he was there at the crematorium. Didn't shed a tear, but then Eleanor never knew him to cry, even as a child.

She didn't see him again until he showed up at her door that morning. Shoes still cracked, the leather turning white. Might even have been wearing the same black coat, although it had seen better days. He stood on the step, looking sheepish, she thought. He was never what you would call a good-looking man—she was no beauty herself, right enough—but he looked hellish that morning. His skin was waxy, he had dark circles under eyes that refused to connect with hers. Say what you wanted about her brother, but he always held your gaze—she knew that some people probably came to wish he hadn't. But this day he kept looking away from her.

'Hi, sis.' In those two words she heard weariness.

'This is a surprise,' she said.

He gave her a wee shrug. 'Aye, well.'

That was all he said: *Aye, well*. He'd said that since he was a wee boy when he had been caught at something and had nothing else to say. A shrug. A look at his scuffed shoes. *Aye, well*.

'What you doing up here?' she asked.

'Got some business to attend to.'

Business. She knew what that would be. Nothing honest, knowing Roger, and here he was standing at her door having probably just stolen something or hurt someone, or was on the way to steal or hurt. That was him all the way through. No thought as to what pain or suffering he might bring to others, even his own sister.

'You gonnae let me in, sis, or keep me waiting here like a milk bottle?'

She considered just closing the door in his face, but it was a fleeting thought. He was her brother, for all his faults, and that counted for something, didn't it? She stepped back to let him pass, her husband's possible reaction to the visit flitting through her mind. Pete had never liked Roger, never trusted him, never wanted him anywhere near their son, not that Roger showed any interest at all. As he passed, he gave her a small smile, grateful-like. She motioned him into the living room, where he took off his coat, dropped it on the settee, but didn't sit down.

He looked around. 'Nice place.'

'Needs decorating,' she said.

He studied the walls. 'Look all right to me.'

'Aye, well,' she said, 'you're more used to the inside of a cell than a decent home.'

He flinched, avoided her eyes, then caught sight of a framed photograph of her boy on the mantelpiece and picked it up. 'Darryl, right?' he said, staring at her son's features, a soft look in his eyes she had never seen before.

'Aye.'

'How's he doing?'

She didn't answer him as she took the picture from his hands and placed it back where it belonged. He had never shown any interest before, and the sight of him holding her son's image in those big gnarled paws of his, and looking at it with something akin to affection, annoyed her.

'What do you want, Rog?' she asked, her voice sharper than she intended, but there it was. She felt no filial connection to him at all. She only maintained some form of contact, sporadic as it was, out of loyalty to her dead parents, a loyalty he had never shared, given the heartache he had put them through over the years. Fights, police at the door, jail. His name in the papers. Nothing major, of course, but it was enough to shame them. Sometimes she wondered if that shame contributed to the death of her father and, by extension, that of her mother.

'Just thought I'd come by, say hello,' he said.

There was that little smile again, sort of shy. Might even have been appealing if it wasn't on that face.

'That's not like you,' she said.

He looked away again and she knew she had somehow wounded him. She didn't much care, though. He had done too much in the past to worry about his feelings. 'Why the sudden interest, Rog? What the hell are you up to?'

'Can a bloke no' come visit his sister?'

'Not you, Rog. You don't just come visit. What is it you want?'

He still didn't look at her. 'How about a cuppa tea, sis?'

She made no move. 'I'm no' having that, Rog. I'm no' having you coming here like it was a social call. How about you just answer my question? What do you want? If it's money, you can go whistle for it.'

'It's no' money.'

'And you're no' here to ask after my boy, either. So what gives?'

'I just thought...' He looked around him, as if searching for something but not finding it in her neat, clean living room with its three-piece suite, its widescreen telly mounted on the wall above the fake fireplace, its fitted carpet and its pictures of family. Her son, her parents, Pete's parents and sisters. None of Roger. Never Roger. To her eye the room needed touched up, but him standing there made it look untidy.

She folded her arms. 'You just thought what, Rog?'

His body seemed to wilt. He was a big man but he looked smaller somehow. 'I just wanted to say I'm sorry. For, you know . . . everything.'

She knew what he was talking about. He was apologising for his life, for being him, but she wasn't going to let him off the hook. 'Too late for that, isn't it?'

He stared at the carpet at his feet, suddenly looking like a little boy despite his size and his past and everything that came with both. The hurt. The hatred. 'Aye.' One word, filled with pain and exhaustion and full acceptance of the wrong he had done. 'But I just thought I'd come by and say it all the same.'

She felt something inside her begin to give. Her folded arms were now not so much a show of defiance as a way to restrain the pity that was rising in her breast.

'Well, okay,' she said, damning her voice for breaking slightly. He might take it as anger but she knew it was something softer and she was determined not to let it out.

'Okay,' he said. He looked as if he was going to say something more but thought better of it. She wondered if he had expected a warmer response from her but that was never going to happen. He had caused too much pain—to her parents, to her. He had done too much damage and some half-arsed apology out the blue was not going to make up for it all. He picked up his coat, folded it over his arm, but didn't put it on. He looked at her for a long moment then walked past her towards the hall. He stopped at the door and nothing more was said between them as he shrugged the coat over his big frame. She noticed then that he looked as if he had lost a little weight. He adjusted the collar and then reached out to rest his hand on the door knob. He stood still for a second, seemed to study the carpet. It crossed her mind that he was trying to estimate how much he would get for it, but she knew he was working up to saying something else. That was something else he'd done since he was a kid, looked down at the carpet before finally finding the words he needed to say.

'I just want you to know,' he began, then stopped. 'I just want you to know that in a wee while you'll hear some stuff about me.'

'What sort of stuff?'

'Bad stuff.'

'Is there any other kind when it comes to you, Rog?'

He winced slightly. 'No, I suppose you're right, sis. I've no' been a good brother, have I?'

'Or a son.'

He blinked. That hit home, for some reason. But it was too late, all too late. 'I just wanted you to know that, when you hear about it, that I'm sorry for what I did. I really am sorry and I'm trying to fix it, you've got to believe me. It's important that you believe me, sis.'

He looked at her as if he hoped she would finally salve him with a kind word, but she couldn't.

'Aye,' he said. That single word again, that same look of hope dying as quickly as it had been born.

She had no idea what he was talking about, of course, and he didn't say anything further. He opened the door then and walked down the path, pulling his coat around his neck against the soft rain. At the end of the path he turned and walked a few yards to a parked car. She saw the back of a man's head in the driver's seat, another big man like her brother. Roger walked round the passenger side and climbed in. The car pulled away immediately. At no time did he look back.

That was the last time she saw him.

33

Eleanor Fraser fell silent for a few moments after she told her story. Then she said, 'I haven't told anyone that before. Didn't tell Pete or Darryl. Kept his visit a secret.' She frowned. 'Don't know why.'

'He didn't tell you he'd been living up here for a while?' Rebecca asked.

'No, he didn't. I don't suppose I was that welcoming.'

'You can't blame yourself for that.'

Eleanor's gaze was steady and her voice was soft but firm. 'I don't.'

Rebecca didn't believe her. Eleanor Fraser did blame herself. The man was her brother, a twin no less. Despite what she said there had to be some connection. His blood was her blood. There had to be some kind of bond. That blinking earlier meant something.

'I didn't go to the funeral,' the woman went on. 'Mr Jordan contacted me when Rog died, but I didn't go to the funeral. I couldn't be that hypocritical, I told myself.'

'So who paid for it?'

'Rog took care of that before he died. Mr Jordan was there and only one other person, some guy Rog knew up here. Maybe the man I saw in the car.'

'Did he say who?'

'No, and I didn't ask. Some criminal, no doubt.'

'Do you regret not going?'

'No.'

That firm voice. That strong gaze. But it was a pose, a way of coping perhaps. People lie to themselves in some way or another to hold in check feelings that sometimes they don't even know they have. But they are still there, like shadows, like memories. Like ghosts.

Eleanor stood up suddenly and walked into the hall without a word, leaving Rebecca wondering if she should follow or if the interview was at an end. She stayed at the table, heard a door opening and closing, and then Eleanor returned carrying a brown paper bag with white plastic handles and a larger bulky package taped shut. In large black marker pen she saw the name Roger Dodge.

'This is what Mr Jordan brought me after the funeral,' said Eleanor, sitting back down and laying the bags on the table, then indicating the smaller bag. 'This is Roger. His ashes are in a box. A cardboard box.' She stared at it for a moment. She blinked. Once. Twice. Then she nodded to the other bag. 'And these are his possessions.' She raised the larger package on its edge and propped it up in both hands like it was an infant. 'Not much to show for an entire life, is it? Two brown paper bags. A cardboard box.' She stared at the package in front of her. 'I've never opened it.'

'Why not?'

She chewed the side of her mouth. 'I don't know.'

'What will you do with the ashes?'

A flick of the eyes to the smaller bag. More blinking. 'I should scatter them somewhere, don't you think? But when it comes down to it I didn't really know him. Was there somewhere he went when he was lonely or feeling sad? Was there somewhere that made him feel better? A beach, a forest, a view? Where? He was my brother but I didn't know him. I didn't know what he liked, what he did for fun, what made him happy. Did he laugh? Cry? Did he have dreams? Was he ever in love? All I knew was that he was a small-time crook who said he killed a man ten years ago and was never caught. And now everything he was fits into two brown bags. That's all. Two brown bags of rubbish.'

A sudden decision was made and she ripped at the tape on the larger bag and pulled it open. She tipped it towards her to look inside.

'Oh,' she said. That was all. One syllable and then the breath seemed to catch in her throat. She blinked a few more times and the tightness in her face sagged and her tongue darted out to moisten her lips.

She reached into the bag and slowly—gently—drew out a small toy rabbit, its fur threadbare where it had been rubbed away, one ear missing as if it had been wrenched off at some time. It had a scarf round its neck that was now a mere remembrance of red. Its arms were stretched high as if expecting someone to cuddle it. She held it in front of her, her eyes still shuttering, and she straightened the little scarf slightly.

'I can't believe he kept this,' she said, her tone hushed. 'Back and forward it went, him, me, back again. Sometimes it was at the centre of a tug of war. I'm surprised it survived.' She touched the head where the ear had once been. 'That's how this happened.' A little smile haunted her lips as her finger gently caressed the ragged wound. 'At some point I must have forgotten he was the last to have it. And he's kept it all these years.'

She clasped the child's toy to her chest and rocked slightly back and forward, her eyes now blinking furiously in a bid to prevent the tears from welling but it was too late, the dam had burst. Eleanor Fraser wept for the first time, as she thought of a little boy who had turned out wrong.

34

They called him Mount Hector for two reasons. One, Hector McNair was large. Malky thought anyone meeting him in the narrow lane leading to Barney's would have to meld their atoms with the brickwork to let him pass. Two, he had a temper that blew with such ease people thought he rehearsed it. He got his nickname after an acquaintance holidaying in Sicily saw the resemblance between Hector and an active Mount Etna.

Mo Burke had warned Malky of the man's tendency to blow his top, while at the same time holding to her side of the bargain.

'Word is that whatever this is all about, there's a bloke called Dodger involved,' she had told him on the phone. 'Roger Dodge was his real name, but most folk just called him Dodger. With good reason, 'cos he was as dodgy as fuck.'

She paused then. Malky assumed so she could take another drag.

'Anyway, Dodger is dead now—couldn't dodge that—but from what I hear he had been speaking to a solicitor called Stephen Jordan and the rumour is, it was something to do with the murder of your boy.'

It was vague, but Malky had expected nothing less. The thing about the Life is that it has a fine sense of rumour. Secrets are hard to keep. Someone drops a hint, someone else picks it up, throws it about. Sometimes the information is right on the money, other times it's little more than a whisper. A visit to that solicitor was not on the cards, though, and he knew Mo would understand that. She had to have something more for him, otherwise why extract the promise from him? So he did not interrupt and let her tell it her way.

'But Dodger was best buddies with Mount Hector,' Mo continued. 'I mean, *best* buddies. These guys were like a double act, know what

I mean? My thinking is that if Dodger told anyone other than Mr Jordan whatever the hell he knew, it would be Hector.'

And that was how things got around. This fella Dodger had whispered to a brief, but he also told his mate Mount Hector, who in turn mentioned it to someone else, who mentioned it to someone else, and so on and so forth until the whisper spread like a virus and landed in Mo's ear.

That was why Malky now sat outside a house in Inchferry. He had heard about this housing scheme, about how rough it was, but Malky had been brought up in the East End schemes of Glasgow in the 1990s and he knew what rough was. This place didn't look too bad really. Sure, the house—really a terrace of two buildings made up of four flats with the door to the upper levels at either side—looked a bit scabby, a bit worse for wear, and the patch of garden at the front was in dire need of a going-over with a Flymo, but Malky had seen worse. Hell, he had lived in worse. One flat his maw had rented, this was in Cambuslang, outside the city, was so rotten with damp they could grow mushrooms on the walls. They had been trying to get away from his dad, all four of them— Maw, Malky, his two sisters—but he found them, came in raging like a bear with a burnt arse, battered Maw and took them back to Carntyne. He'd hated his dad from that moment and he shed no tears when the old bastard popped his clogs. Good riddance.

He sat in his motor, Radio 2 on the speakers, a finger on the steering wheel tapping to an old Abba number. 'Does Your Mother Know'. He thought about his maw. She'd died two years ago. The flu. She survived years of abuse at the hands of the old fella only to be taken out by a serious dose of the bloody sniffles. That's what she called them, the bloody sniffles. He'd urged her to go get the flu jab every year, but she waved him away saying she didn't like bloody doctors, they were no good, and anyway it was only the flu. Aye, maw, he thought, only the flu. Killed you in the end.

The Swedes were still singing when he saw a big guy limp up the road carrying a Lidl bag that looked like a packet of crisps in his big mitt. Mo had not been exaggerating. This bloke really was big. Malky wasn't worried. He had dealt with big guys before and he was only here to talk.

Hector unlocked the door to the bottom flat and let himself in. Malky gave it a minute, then climbed out and walked up the path. The door hadn't seen the rough end of a paint brush in many a year and the opaque glass panes were caked with grime. He sighed. His own flat back in Glasgow was spotless, and he ensured the front door was always clean and painted. He abhorred slovenliness, perhaps because of some of the places they'd stayed when he was a boy. He rattled the letterbox and waited. A wide, filmy face loomed behind the glass and the door opened. Hector regarded him with suspicious eyes.

'Aye?' he said.

'Hector?' Malky knew he was Hector because there couldn't be two like him, but he asked all the same.

'Who's asking?'

Malky didn't want to answer that, not in the street. He lowered his voice. 'Mo Burke said I should come see you.'

'Mo Burke sent you?'

'No' so much sent as referred, know what I mean?'

The eyes narrowed to slits and the big man looked over Malky's head to scan the street. 'Referred? What for?'

'Need a wee word with you.' Malky gave him a smile. Hector didn't take it. 'If you've got a minute.'

'A word?'

'Aye.'

'What about?'

'There's no bother, big man. Just want to talk to you about a pal of yours, goes by the name Dodger.'

'Dodger?'

Malky kept his manner easy and polite. 'Aye.'

Hector blinked. 'Dodger's dead.'

'I know that, and please accept my condolences.'

'Your condolences?'

Malky's jaw tightened slightly. He was tiring of this guy's speech pattern. 'Aye.'

Hector's face told Malky he was in no mood to accept any condolences. 'Don't see what there is to talk about then.'

178

He started to close the door, but Malky put out a hand and held it open. 'Look, mate, I'm no' the law or nothing. I just need to ask you a—'

He didn't get to finish his sentence before a hand that could house a family of four reached out and grabbed him by the front of his jacket. Before he knew it, Malky was hauled off his feet, jerked into the flat and tossed with casual disdain the length of the hallway. He bounced off the wall and sprawled onto the bare floorboards. He propped himself up on his elbows and looked back at Hector, who blocked the light through the still-open doorway like a full eclipse. He lumbered stiff-legged down the hall and picked Malky up by the lapels again as if he was a bag of potatoes and carried him into the front room.

Malky was unhappy about being treated like tonight's chips and decided to do something about it. He lashed out with his left foot and connected with Hector's right knee. Malky was a street fighter and always wore a sturdy pair of working boots, their steel toecaps hidden under the leather. The man grunted and listed to one side. Malky did the same again to his other knee. Hector swore and let him go, his legs giving way. Malky didn't stop there. As the big man sank to the threadbare rug, he swung and buried his right boot deep into his groin. Hector squealed in a way at odds with his appearance and both hands shot to his crotch as if to protect himself, but it was too late for that. Malky raised his foot again and slammed the sole of his boot into the man's broad chest to send him flying backwards, his knees twisting under him, making him groan again. He landed on his side, his right arm outstretched to try to break his fall, and Malky ground the heel of his boot into the back of his hand with considerable force. Hector screamed again.

Malky stepped back and looked down at the big man as he rocked back and forward, moaning and swearing. He had spotted Hector limping and surmised that, like a lot of men his size, his joints were buggered, so he had targeted them first. Then, once he had him down, he had to ensure he got the message. There were twenty-seven bones in the hand and wrist and Malky was confident he had broken a few. That, along with his sore knees and throbbing gonads, would keep him at bay for a while. Malky had learned the hard way that when you start a fight you finish it as soon as you can. That means putting the other guy down and making sure he's hurt badly enough to make getting up again difficult.

He took a moment to look around. The blinds were drawn, but there was enough light for Malky to see that the room was sparsely furnished, just a settee with the stuffing bulging from the ripped material, a coffee table and a telly. Hector didn't live the life of a Highland gentleman, but then guys like him never did. They were walking muscle, that was all, a mixture of rage and physical strength that was exploited by people like Mo Burke when she needed him. People like Malky, too.

The big guy was out the game for a minute or two, not unconscious but he wouldn't be moving around, so Malky returned to the hallway to close the front door. He didn't know what the soundproofing was like in these flats—they were pretty solidly built by the looks of it, so shouldn't be too bad—but he didn't want anyone walking by hearing something they shouldn't.

'Let's try again, mate,' he said when he came back into the sitting room, his voice even despite what had happened. Hector had thrown him about a bit, but Malky had suffered worse. 'Let's chat about your pal Dodger.'

Hector rolled onto his back. He fixed Malky with a stare filled with hate and malevolence but watered down by pain. 'Fuck off,' he spat.

Malky tutted. 'So much for Highland hospitality.' He stamped again on Hector's right knee. Hector howled. 'See,' said Malky, leaning over him but ready to move if the guy was stupid enough to try anything. 'I can do this all day, know what I mean, big guy? I won't even break sweat. You know why? Because this is what I do. But you'll sweat buckets and probably even bleed more than a wee bit. You know why? Again, because this is what I do.' He stepped away. 'So, Dodger.'

Hector's eyes were squeezed tight against the agony. 'Dodger?'

'Aye, Dodger.'

'What about him?' Hector's voice was hoarse with rage and pain. 'I told you, he's dead.'

'I know.'

'Cancer.'

'That's sad.'

'He was my mate. He was a good guy.'

'My heart is warmed, but I'm not really here to eulogise him.'

Hector edged along the floor so he could prop himself up against the wall. Malky let him. 'To what him?'

'Eulogise. To praise his life and works.'

'What the fuck do you want to know then?' Hector was cradling his broken right hand with his left.

'Did he ever mention a guy called Murdo Maxwell?'

'Murdo Maxwell?'

Even with his knees buggered and his mitt shattered, this guy was pissing him off. But Malky just said, 'Aye.'

'No.'

'Take a minute to think. I want you to be sure.'

Hector winced as he bent his right leg slightly. 'I said no, didn't I?'

'You did, but you didn't think about it. I think you're letting your desire to get back at me overcome your common sense. And, Hector, if you even think about getting to your feet, I'll see it before you make a move and I give you my word I will fuck up your knees so much you'll never stand again without sticks.'

Hector's leg stopped moving. 'I'm telling you, I've never heard of the guy.'

'You sure?'

'Aye, I'm sure. What's he to Dodger?'

'That's what I want to know.'

Hector massaged his left knee with his good hand, his bad hand held across his chest as if it was in an invisible sling. 'Who is this Maxwell bloke anyhow?'

'You don't read the papers?'

'No. Too depressing.'

Malky almost laughed, but then, looking around again, life was depressing enough for Mount Hector. He lived in a shithole, his best friend was dead, and now a guy half his size had brought him down to earth.

'So you're certain he never mentioned Murdo Maxwell to you?'

'Positive.'

Malky stared at the prostrate giant and sighed. Mo had assured him that if Dodger had said anything about what he knew, it would have been to Hector here. But word had got out somehow and, as far as Malky knew, this was the most likely source. Also, he didn't believe the guy when he said he hadn't heard the name before.

He sighed and left the man lying against the wall to walk through an open doorway into a small kitchen. It was a surprise. Washed dishes were stacked neatly beside the metal sink, which itself shone like a TV commercial for bleach. The working surfaces were pristine, the cupboard units bright and clean, the lino freshly mopped. Even the window over the sink sparkled. The rest of the flat was like a slum but old Hector kept a gleaming kitchen. Malky was impressed.

He opened some drawers until he found something he could use. An old hammer, the head rusting, the claw end missing one tooth, but it was sturdy and he swung it at his side as he returned to Hector's side. The man stared at the tool being held easily in Malky's hand and tried to edge away. Malky let him twitch. He wasn't going anywhere.

'As you can probably tell from my accent, I'm from Glasgow. They used to say it was miles better, you heard that phrase? Glasgow's Miles Better?' Hector was watching the hammer swinging back and forward and didn't answer. 'Anyway, there was this guy I heard about, never met him but he was a legend, you know what I mean? And do you know what he was miles better at?' Hector still didn't reply. 'I'll tell you—hurting people. I mean, this bloke was a fucking expert at the pain game. One time, he took this bloke—a kiddy fiddler, he was—and he took a hammer like this one, and you know what he did?' Malky waited for a response, even though he didn't expect one. 'He broke every bone in that paedo bastard's hands, arms, feet, legs. He smashed elbows and he smashed knees. I mean, can you imagine that? You know how many bones there are in your extremities, Hector? Can you imagine how that must have felt? Okay, you're hurting now, but think about how that would feel.'

Malky squatted down beside the man, laid the flat of the hammer head on Hector's shin. He winced as if he had been struck.

'Hector, son, here's the thing. You're lying to me,' Malky said, his tone conversational. 'I don't want to spend any more time in this shithole than I have to—although congratulations on your kitchen area, big man. So I'll give you one more chance to tell me what your buddy told you about Murdo Maxwell before I go all DIY on your joints.' He ran the hammer head gently up the man's leg. 'What did Dodger tell you about Murdo Maxwell?'

Hector watched the hammer stroking his shin, his knee—jumped a little because they were still tender—then onto his thigh. He swallowed hard. Malky waited.

Finally, Hector spoke. 'He said he killed the guy.'

'Why?'

'Why?'

Malky sighed. 'Why did he kill him?'

'Someone paid him to do it.'

'Who?'

'Dodger wouldn't say.'

Malky let the hammer linger around the man's groin. 'Hector . . .' he warned.

Hector jerked. 'It's the truth, for fuck's sake. He said these guys were bad news.'

'Were they local?'

Hector's head shook. 'No, don't think so. Edinburgh, I think. Maybe Glasgow.'

Malky slid the hammer away and stood up. He knew the truth when he heard it. 'And he told this to the lawyer?'

Hector was surprised. 'The lawyer? You know about that?'

'No, son. I just made it up on the spur of the moment.' He let the hammer hang at his side as he looked down at the big man, who visibly relaxed. Only slightly, though. 'Did he have any other pals like you?'

'Pals like me?'

Malky felt irritation getting the better of him. 'Fuck's sake, do you really need to repeat everything?'

'Repeat everything? How do you mean?'

Malky put a lid on his exasperation. 'Never mind. Did Dodger have anyone else he might have confided in?'

'Confided in?' Hector fell silent, the pain and fear lining his face taking on a slightly reflective nature as he considered this. 'He wasn't the gregarious sort, was Dodger.'

Gregarious, thought Malky. He said gregarious. He didn't know the word eulogise but then he comes out with gregarious. People never ceased to amaze him.

'That's how we got on so well, him and me. We were good mates. Worked together, shared this place.'

Malky looked around once more. 'Be it ever so humble.'

Hector glared up at him, suddenly finding his balls. 'Aye, well, you can sneer as much as you like, but it was home, you know? Okay, so we're no' going to win any bloody awards for interior design, but who the fuck invited you in anyway?'

'Well, you kinda did, Hector, when you hauled me off the doorstep.'

Hector's brow worked as he thought about that. 'Aye, well. Dodger and me got on well, you know? We did jobs together, best locksman I'd ever seen. Could get into any place. Handy, too, when things got rough.'

Friendship, Malky thought, can be found in the most unlikely places. But right now he didn't much care about that. 'Hector, son, as much as I'm enjoying your wee trip down memory lane, can we get back on point? Was there anybody else Dodger might have spoken to?'

'Spoken to?'

Malky hefted the hammer again. 'Hector, son, don't make me hurt you again.'

'All right, all right.' Hector shrank away slightly. He took a breath, supported his broken hand, swallowed hard, weighing his loyalty to his dead friend against the certainty that Malky could and would deliver even more agony. He looked down at the floor and said, 'There was someone that no bugger knew about 'cept me. Dodger kept quiet about her, didn't want her associated with him. She's a straight arrow, he would say to me.' When he raised his eyes to Malky, there was self-revulsion there because he was about to break his only friend's confidence. 'He had a sister.'

'A sister?' Malky said. He couldn't resist.

35

Rebecca had told Roach that she had tried to get an appointment with Sir Gregory Stewart—he was not the kind of person you door-stepped—but had been unsuccessful. Roach knew she had the edge in this particular situation: a warrant card and the rank to use it. That would be enough to at least get her through the door; whether he would speak to her was another matter. This was not an official investigation, so there was very little she could do if he decided to tell her to take her warrant card and her rank and insert it somewhere extremely uncomfortable.

She thought about phoning ahead but it was her experience, as Rebecca also knew, that it is often better to turn up unannounced. The element of surprise is a powerful weapon, which is why police officers stage raids in the early hours. It's not because they like beautiful sunrises.

Roach turned off the A9 to go through the village of Daviot, a collection of houses about four miles south of Inverness. The satnav told her to drive past the white church on the left, ignore the turn-off to the school house and skirt around the edges of the tarmac quarry. Another three miles on, the satnav announced in clipped tones that Roach's destination was on the left. A pair of open white gates led to a long drive through mature trees, the sun slanting between the branches creating a zebra effect on the roadway. She could almost hear the crackle of Sir Gregory's banknotes as she rounded a bend and finally saw the three-storey building made of sturdy grey stone. The hard-top drive gave way to gravel and her tyres crunched as she spun the wheel to park beside a brand new Land Rover Discovery, with her bonnet pointing at an expanse of well-tended lawn leading to a walled garden among the trees.

As she climbed from the car she stopped for a moment to study the house. It was a converted farmhouse and it screamed affluence, with more money in the windowboxes than she had in her bank. She walked to the sturdy front door, each step sounding like a child eating cornflakes, and seized the weighty iron knocker. It was so heavy she wished she had done some stretches that morning, and the sound it made against the wood was like some sort of portent of doom. She fished her ID from her jacket pocket and waited. Once the echo of the knocking died, everything seemed so still. All she could hear were the birds singing in the trees and the sound of bees and other insects buzzing in the cotoneaster that grew up against the wall near to the door. If she closed her eyes, it was like being at a Formula 1 race. Not that she had ever actually been to a Formula 1 race, of course, but she knew the sound from the brief moments between switching the telly on and changing the channel.

She was beginning to wonder if there was no one at home—but if so, who owned the Discovery?—when the door opened and a fair-haired woman in her forties gave her the kind of look that was usually reserved for a door-to-door salesperson with the deeds to Nelson's Column in his pocket. She was very attractive in a healthy, haughty sort of way and Roach would bet those pale green eyes of hers would never date anyone without first doing a credit check. Roach guessed she had a name like Poppy or Penny or Primmy. Decided on Poppy.

'Yes?' the woman asked, both hands on the door jamb ready to close it again if she felt the need.

'DCI Val Roach,' she said, holding her card up so Poppy could see her photo. Then adding for no reason whatsoever, 'Police Scotland. I'd like to have a quick word with Sir Gregory Stewart, if I may.'

'What's this about?' The woman's accent was of the sort that looked down on posh and Roach could not tell from the few words if she was English or just Scottish with attitude.

'Routine inquiry,' she said. If in doubt, fall back on *routine inquiry*.

The woman seemed unimpressed. 'My husband is very busy.'

Ah, so this was the present Mrs Sir Gregory Stewart. 'I won't take up too much of his time, but I would appreciate it if I could see him.'

'Can't you make an appointment?'

Roach gave her what she hoped was her most charming smile. It felt fake from her side, God knows what it looked like from where Poppy stood. 'Well, I'm here now, so if you wouldn't mind letting him know. Seems such a shame to waste time and, as I said, it won't take long.'

A voice from behind the woman said, 'It's okay, Charmaine.'

Charmaine, not Poppy. Ah, well, can't win 'em all, Roach thought. She didn't think the present Mrs Sir Gregory looked like a Charmaine and it immediately brought an uncle to mind who, at family get-togethers, sang a song with the same name. A big hit in the early 1960s for The Bachelors, two Irish brothers and another fella, or so her uncle said. He was a big fan. Roach had never heard of them. She decided Mrs Sir Gregory would always be Poppy to her.

The woman stepped away and Sir Gregory stood there in all his Clooney-like glory. He had a tan that came neither from a bottle nor a sunbed, his iron-grey hair was carefully coiffed to within the millimetre and his brown eyes crinkled with what Roach took to be good humour but could easily have been disdain.

'DCI Roach,' she said, proffering her warrant card. He took it from her and scrutinised it, as if he was memorising the wording.

'I saw you from the window upstairs,' he said as he handed it back, apparently satisfied with her bona fides. 'I thought you were an estate agent coming to make an offer the way you looked at the place.'

So her quick look hadn't been as quick as she'd thought. She wasn't sure if she should be insulted that he thought she might be an estate agent. 'Do you get a lot of that?'

'On occasion.'

Roach took one pace back and surveyed the exterior again. 'It is quite a place.'

'Thank you. We've done a bit of work on it.'

I'll bet you barely made a dent in your bank book, she thought. 'Anyway, sorry to trouble you,' she said, even though she wasn't in the least bit sorry, 'but I wonder if I could have a few moments.'

'This will be about James,' he said.

'Yes.'

He nodded and moved over the threshold. 'I was just going to grab some air—do you mind?'

'Not at all,' she said, even though she had been hoping to have a look inside. She liked to see how the 1 per cent lived. Shit, maybe she *was* an estate agent at heart.

He gave his wife a kiss on the cheek and said, 'Won't be long, darling.' Charmaine accepted the kiss, but her eyes remained on Roach in case she decided to supplement her salary by stealing one of the ornamental flower pots.

'Don't be too long, darling,' the woman said. 'We have to be at the club for three. We tee off at three-fifteen.'

Golf. Roach liked a round or two herself when she could manage it and frankly would have preferred that to what she was doing. She found hitting that little white ball an enjoyable way to relieve tension. Sometimes she imagined it was a ned, or a lawyer. Or a fellow officer.

'Don't worry, darling,' said Sir Gregory as he joined Roach on the driveway. 'Plenty of time.'

He indicated they should head round the side of the house and with a final nod to Charmaine, the corners of whose mouth tightened slightly in return, Roach followed him. She resisted the urge to wiggle her fingers. *See you later, Poppy*.

'Thanks for giving me the time,' she said as their feet rasped on the gravel.

'I thought someone would come,' he said. 'Soon as I saw the stories in the press. The banners were one thing, but today's news about that criminal's confession really clinched it.'

So it was out there already, Roach thought. Rebecca didn't hang around.

'Some reporter has already tried to contact me, but I won't be speaking to her.'

'Well, thank you for speaking to me.'

His smile felt like a pat on the head. 'So how can I help, Detective Chief Inspector—can I call you Valerie? Detective Chief Inspector is something of a mouthful.'

'Val, please,' she said.

'So how can I help, Val?'

They had walked the length of the house and were heading into a courtyard at the rear with low buildings on three sides. At one time they would have been farm outhouses but now they had been converted into offices for Sir Gregory Stewart's various business interests. She had done a bit of homework before making the short drive down the A9 to Daviot. He had long ago sold his family's magazine business to a major publishing house but he was still involved in property development and landownership. She knew he had other sources of income, diversity being the secret of any good portfolio. Not that she had income other than her salary. She didn't even own shares, unlike some of her colleagues. She kept in mind Sawyer's suggestion that some of Sir Gregory's dealings weren't quite legal. The former Detective Sergeant had been vague about that, had stressed it was all rumour, so it could be little more than a bit of tax evasion. On the other hand, the man operated on a multinational scale so he could have brushed the shoulders, and even greased the palms, of some dodgy characters. And that was just in public school.

Then she thought about the pay grades above hers that had tapped McIntyre to have someone look into this matter. Was it possible Sir Gregory was behind that?

'This is simply a routine call, Sir Gregory,' she said, sticking to what she had said to Poppy as he led her beyond the courtyard to a gate beside a tall ash tree, its branches still carrying the bare look of winter, although as she grew nearer she could see dark buds beginning to sprout. It was only May and it might be a week or two yet before they opened. 'Naturally with a situation like this we are obliged to investigate.'

'Do you think there is anything in what this man, erm—'

'Dodge,' she said.

'Yes, Dodge.' He opened the gate and allowed her to go through first. Such a gentleman—but she wasn't fooled. Her homework told her he could be a ruthless bastard when he needed to be. 'Do you think there is something in it?'

'I don't know,' she said, truthfully. 'I'm simply dotting what i's and crossing what t's I can.'

They were on a dirt trail following the edge of a field, the ground packed hard by the on-going good weather. Sheep tugged at the green grass, some looking up to regard them with what might have been curiosity, while maturing lambs wandered between them. One stared at them from a few feet away, its legs splayed in that knock-kneed way of lambs as if resolute in its determination to stand its ground. Roach knew nothing about farm stock, so she could not tell if the look on its little black face was indeed curiosity or defiance. As they closed in on it, its natural mildness won over and it scampered away, bleating for its mother.

It seemed even warmer here and she took off her jacket and folded it over her arm. She was aware of him giving her shirt, or rather what was underneath it, a swift once-over. She felt a brief flare of annoyance—she always did when that happened because she didn't automatically check out a man's crotch—but she let it go.

His eyes flicked back ahead of them when he asked, 'So, how can I help?'

'What's your memory of what happened?'

He blew out his cheeks and studied the rutted path beneath them as they walked. 'I remember it well, Val. He was my son and he had been accused of murder.'

'Do you believe he killed Murdo Maxwell?'

'I found it hard to believe that James was capable of doing such a thing.'

'But you haven't been part of the campaign your wife has waged to clear his name.'

'My ex-wife. But no, I haven't.'

'May I ask why?'

He took a couple of paces before answering. 'Afua didn't want me involved. We did not part on the best of terms, her and I.'

'Did your marriage break down because of what happened with your son?'

'Partly, but there were issues before that. When I met Afua I thought she was the most beautiful thing I had ever seen. Don't tell Charmaine, but she still is, not that I see her much. Are you married, Val?'

190

She thought of Joe. Smiling. Then she thought of him with his new wife. 'No,' she said, not willing to expand on it.

'Have you ever been married?'

Joe again, laughing with her, holding her. Then her alone in the big house in Perth they had shared, the silence around her like a winding sheet. 'I was, but I'm divorced.'

'Ah,' he said, 'then you understand. Marriage isn't like dating. Dating is all promise and discovery, and marriage is work and compromise and often disappointment. Afua didn't understand that when we were merely going out. The courting ritual is very much fantasy, don't you find?'

'It's been a long time since I've been courted,' she said.

He seemed surprised. 'Really?'

She didn't know what he meant by that. Was he being ironic, or maybe she meant sarcastic? She never really knew. Or was he in the process of flirting with her? She was rooting for irony, or sarcasm, because if he was flirting—and that quick glance earlier, as if he was checking out the goods, suggested he might be—she thought it was too nice a day to have to slap a man down, even one who looked like George Clooney and who could pay her year's salary with what he found down the back of the sofa. As they say, a bat in the mouth often offends.

Thankfully, he didn't expand on his question. 'Anyway, you've been married, so you will know that marriage is the reality. She wanted the Hollywood rom-com version. She wanted a happy ending that I just couldn't provide.'

To his credit, there was a sadness in his voice that Roach recognised. She had heard it in her own thoughts when she considered what had happened in her own marriage. She had thought they were set to ride into the sunset together, but it wasn't to be. Life has a nasty habit of getting in the way of romance.

'But you married again,' she said.

'Yes, and I'm very happy. Who was it that said a second marriage is the triumph of hope over experience?' She didn't have a clue. 'Samuel Johnson, I think.' He smiled, as if he had formulated the line himself. 'Will you marry again?'

'Not if I can help it.'

'That sounds terribly final.'

'It is.' She eased him back on point. 'So you were on the way to a break-up before Murdo Maxwell was murdered?'

'Yes, and my inability to fully commit to James's innocence only accelerated the process.'

'So you do believe he is guilty?'

'I really don't want to, but he was the only other person in that house and his fingerprints were on the murder weapon. His DNA was all over the dead man.'

The dead man. Not Murdo Maxwell. To use his name makes him a real person.

'But it would be,' she said, 'given they were intimate.' She purposely made the comment to see how he reacted, but he didn't reply. 'Tell me about your son.'

'James?' He seemed taken aback by the question, for some reason. 'He was a quiet lad, not like his friends at all. And he had a lot of friends, he was popular, but he often preferred his own company. He would stay in his room, reading or watching TV, go on long walks along the river. He loved Ness Islands.'

'Okay. And how did you feel about his being gay?'

She stole another sideways glance at his face as they walked. His expression didn't change but when he answered she felt he was choosing his words carefully. Or maybe Sawyer's story was colouring her viewpoint.

'I respected his choices,' he said.

'Hardly a choice, is it? More a biological imperative.'

'Perhaps.'

So. Still not happy with his son being gay, then.

'And what about Mr Maxwell?'

'What about him?' Careful again.

'How did you get along with him?'

A silence, just for a moment. He was being forced to talk about a man he would far rather refer to only in the abstract. After what Sawyer had told her, Roach had good reason to guide him onto Maxwell. A walk in the sun was all very nice, but she was aware that she had been granted only a short window of opportunity here and it was time to get to the nub of the matter.

'I knew him,' he said and left it at that.

She wasn't about to let him leave it at that, though. 'How well did you know him?'

'Not well. He wasn't . . .' He paused again, trying to think of a way to explain. 'He wasn't my type.'

'Your type?'

'We were on opposite ends of the political spectrum, which I don't mind, but there was an insincerity about the fellow, a lack of any real conviction. He chose causes that would further his career and stroke his ego, nothing more. He was that worst of political creatures, the self-obsessed opportunist. He was the same when he practised law. As a defence counsel he had represented people I think should have been drowned at birth. Or at least executed.'

'You believe in capital punishment?'

'Does that shock you?'

'Even though your son would have been hanged?'

He didn't answer. She felt he had no answer to give but he used the opening of a second gate as a cover. They moved onto a shady pathway beside a tree-lined river. This would be the Nairn, she presumed. Good for salmon fishing, a sergeant once told her before treating her to what seemed like an interminable account of catching fish and releasing them. Playing the fish, he called it, and there followed mention of rod strength, leader visibility and current direction. All she had asked was how his weekend had gone.

Through the trees she could see the rear of the house and ahead she saw a third gate and yet another path taking them back towards it. This looked like it would be a very short walk indeed. Time to get to the point.

'Sir Gregory, tell me what happened in the Town House.'

His step didn't falter, but he didn't reply and she thought perhaps he had suddenly run out of patience. Bill Sawyer's words rang in her ears— *he can be a touchy bastard.* But then so could she.

'Sir Gregory?' she said again.

'Who told you about that?'

'It's in the record.'

The hiss of breath escaping through his nostrils was angry. 'That was all a misunderstanding. I had been drinking.'

'You threatened him.'

'I didn't threaten him.'

'Your behaviour was threatening.'

'I told you, I was drunk. Anyway, I explained all this afterwards, when I was asked about it. When James was arrested.'

Sawyer had told her he didn't report the incident until after the murder. Maxwell had not wanted to make it official in any way and there had been no real laws broken, except those of propriety. His death changed matters, though.

'Tell me about the wind farm development,' she said.

She had checked up before she drove down. The Craigdearg project would have seen one of the largest wind farms in the country, built on the slopes of a mountain in Sutherland. It had attracted the ire of environmentalists, walkers and elements of the tourist industry. Murdo Maxwell had spearheaded the campaign, citing the area's natural beauty and the damage the turbine construction would do to the local flora and fauna.

'I understand he had alleged that the project would lead to the destruction of the peatlands, releasing carbons that could contaminate streams, maybe even reach the water supply and result in E.colI contamination. And wasn't there something about a reaction with chlorine that would create a cancer-inducing chemical?'

Roach could neither pronounce nor spell the chemical so she was grateful when Sir Gregory said, 'Trihalomethane. And it was a lot of poorly researched nonsense. But that was what he specialised in. He knew all he needed to say was "cancer" and people would take notice. Anyway, my irritation that night had nothing to do with the development.'

He was growing testy; she could hear his tone sharpening. He practically threw the third gate open. This time he passed through first, no gentlemanly stepping back for her to go ahead of him. He even left her to latch it again. His pace quickened as they followed a line of birch trees back towards the house.

'Mr Maxwell seemed to think it was,' she said.

'Mr Maxwell was wrong.' There was a slight emphasis on the Mister. He couldn't help himself.

'It was eventually refused, just before he was murdered. Did you lose a lot of money?'

He stopped now and glared at her. The friendly Sir Gregory was gone. Was this, she wondered, the real one?

'What are you suggesting?'

'I'm not suggesting anything. I'm just asking, did you lose a lot of money?'

'I lose money all the time. I make it at other times. It evens out. But I don't like your inference.'

Can't help that, she thought, but didn't say it. Neither did she apologise. 'What am I inferring, Sir Gregory?'

'Don't play those games with me, Detective Chief Inspector.'

Uh-oh, she thought, he's not courting me now.

'What games?'

'Word games, mind games. Suggesting that I may have been involved in the man's murder, either because of my son or because of my business, without actually saying it out loud. Let me tell you right now, I had nothing to do with that man's death. It was cut and dried then, and it is just as cut and dried now. My son killed him. They fought, he picked up a poker and beat him to death. I don't take pleasure in that and I wish it was different, but no half-baked press report about some lowlife's confession will change that fact. Now, if you will excuse me, my wife is waiting. You can see yourself off the property.'

He turned away from her and stormed off down the pathway, perhaps to let Poppy stroke his fevered brow.

She saw herself off the property.

36

Malky could tell Wee Joe was far from happy with the news, even over the blower. He sat outside the neat row of terraces, thinking it was very like being back home in Glasgow. Why wouldn't it, right enough? Inverness wasn't a foreign country, even though he knew folk who had travelled abroad yet never been further north than Stirling.

Wee Joe's voice was subdued, but it throbbed with anger. 'Have you seen the story on the internet?'

Malky was scanning it now on the tablet he kept in the car, a red-top site with the headline 'DEAD NED CLAIMS MAXWELL MURDER WAS CONTRACT HIT'. He had wasted his time giving Hector a hiding because more or less everything was there: Dodger, the lawyer Jordan, the affidavit he had signed and a quick outline of the case itself. There was no byline but Malky would bet his bottom dollar it was written by that Connolly bird.

'So did this guy . . .' Wee Joe let it hang there, trying to recall the name.

'Hector. They call him Mount Hector.'

'Why?'

'Some play on Mount Etna, apparently.'

A pause. 'That doesn't even make sense.'

'Not everyone can be Billy Connolly.'

'So did this Dodger say who hired him?'

'Never breathed a word, refused to even drop a hint, and him and this Hector fella were good pals, as tight as blokes can get without exchanging saliva.'

There was another pause down the line. Once again Malky wondered why his boss was getting so hot under the collar about this. What the hell was his involvement here? Was it him who'd hired Dodger? And if he had, why?

Wee Joe asked, 'So what's your next step?'

'Dodger had a sister. I'm sitting outside her place now. Hector said that if he told anyone anything more it was her. Maybe.'

'Maybe?'

'They weren't close, but Hector said the past wee while Dodger was getting all misty-eyed about family. He came to see her a few months ago, first time in ages, same day as he saw that lawyer.'

'What about this lawyer? He straight?'

'I don't think I'll get anything out of him, if that's what you mean. No, best bet is the sister for now.'

'And if she doesn't know?'

'Then we're up against a brick wall.'

The long sigh told Malky that was not what Wee Joe wanted to hear. Fuck him, he couldn't work miracles.

'One other thing,' he said.

'What?'

'Mo Burke had a price for the steer to Hector.'

Another escape of breath, this time with a hint of exasperation. 'What does she want?'

'The reporter lassie, the one who probably wrote these stories, seems there's a history there. She wants her hurt a wee bit.'

'How much is a wee bit?'

'I got the impression in this case a wee bit is a lot.'

'And she wants you to do it, right?'

'Aye. I'm no' a face up here. Degrees of separation and all that.'

There was another silence.

'So?'

'So what?' Wee Joe asked.

'Do I do it?'

Even hundreds of miles away he could hear the cogs in his boss's head turning, working out the permutations, the advantages and disadvantages. 'I'll leave it to you, but if you do go for it, get it done just before you head back. I want to minimise your exposure. Hurting a

197

straight arrow is always a risky business, even if she is a slimeball journalist.'

'How long do you want me to stay up here?'

'See the sister, see where that takes you.'

Malky couldn't help himself from asking, 'Boss, what exactly am I looking for here?'

'Never you mind that. Just keep nosing around, report back everything and anything you find out.'

The line died. Malky frowned. He was wandering around in the dark here and he didn't like that. He was convinced he wouldn't find anything further, but he reasoned that if he was marching, he wasn't fighting. There were worse places than Inverness to spend a few days.

The door to the sister's house opened and a young woman appeared, auburn hair down to her shoulders, blue jacket, jeans. He recognised her immediately—he'd googled Rebecca Connolly after he'd left Mo Burke, found her photograph on a byline in one of the local rags. As he did with most women, he sized up her looks. She wasn't about to turn heads, but she wasn't bad-looking if you liked them pale and slim. The lassie had the kind of looks that creep up on a guy. It would be a shame if he had to spoil them.

So she was ahead of him here; he should have guessed. The woman she was saying goodbye to in the doorway was kind of plain; tall and thin enough to hold up a clothes line. She had what looked like a cuddly toy cradled against her chest. What the hell was that about? They exchanged a few words, and the reporter headed down the path and climbed into a blue Vauxhall Corsa with 2014 plates. It needed a wash. That grated with Malky because he always ensured his motor sparkled. No bugger was allowed to eat in it, he washed it every week, sometimes twice, hoovered it, polished it. To his mind, a man's motor and his home were reflections of the man himself.

He watched as she pulled away and passed him. He thought about following, but he would have to turn and by the time he did that she would be out the street and off. No, stick with his plan to chat to the sister first. He had found out where Connolly's' office was so he could always pick her up again when he needed to.

But almost immediately after she drove off another car pulled out further up. Black Ford Fiesta, 2016 plates—what, did no one buy new cars up here? Decent nick, though, certainly better cared for than the Connolly girl's car. Two blokes inside, their eyes fixed on the back of the Corsa.

The lassie had a tail.

And he couldn't be sure but he thought he knew one of them. He didn't know him well, but he had seen him a few times back home. A mate had told him the bloke's name. What was it? Paul something or other, he thought. He watched the car in his wing mirror until it turned out of sight, wondering why he was so interested in the reporter. Despite his best efforts, his curiosity was rising.

37

Rebecca normally didn't like music playing while she worked, but she switched on the DAB radio Chaz and Alan had bought her for Christmas. She needed some kind of noise in this small room. The sound of opera filled the small space—she thought it was something by Puccini, her mother's favourite, something lyrical and sad and heartfelt—and she didn't feel so alone. She clicked the kettle on, made a cup of coffee then sat down at the desk and concentrated on writing the piece on Eleanor Fraser. That would help keep the pot boiling, a nice human interest piece. She had even convinced Eleanor to let her take a shot of her holding the stuffed rabbit, which she took on her mobile, not wishing to delay things until Chaz could see her. Eleanor's agreement amazed her, but then she was constantly surprised by people. Those she believed would be easy to entice into pictures could prove elusive, others you think would run a mile before being photographed can readily agree. It's all about the right moment, she supposed. Eleanor had even given her a snapshot of her brother. It was a hard copy and it was about twenty years old, but it would have to do. It showed a broad face, a scar on one cheek, wispy hair and eyes that gazed at the camera with cold disinterest. She scanned it into her computer and attached it to the emails she sent out.

She flipped through the pages of her notebook, found the number for Mona Maxwell and was about to dial it on the landline, but her hand hovered over the receiver. That message was still there, like something malignant.

She used her personal mobile instead, leaving the agency mobile free for any queries from newsdesks, or a returned call from Sir Gregory. She

200

heard the phone in Kirkbrig House ring five times before it was picked up.

'Mona,' she said, pleased her voice was steady, 'Rebecca Connolly— we met on Saturday?'

'Yes, Rebecca, I remember you.' The woman's voice was dry. 'It was only two days ago. I see you have been busy regarding my brother's case.'

For some reason, Rebecca felt a twinge of guilt and she didn't know why. 'Yes, I hope it hasn't upset you in any way.'

'Why should it upset me? I want the truth to come out, whatever it may be. That's the way Murdo would have wanted it. This man Dodge I've been reading about on the internet—do you believe his story?'

'Who can say, Mona?'

'Of course, but that is not your concern, is it? Truth or lies, it's a story.'

Rebecca couldn't decide if she was having a go. The woman's delivery was always so crisp anyway. 'I much prefer truth. But in this case all I can say is that the truth of the matter is that he has made his claim and he has signed an affidavit.'

'Which cannot be tested in court, though, as he is dead.'

'True. But it's a start, Mona. You said yourself you couldn't believe that James Stewart was guilty.'

'Yes, I did.'

There was something in her voice that made Rebecca fear she was reconsidering her opinion. That could happen once people begin to see things in print. It takes on a different life, a different perspective, and what they were sure of, what they supported, can change.

Rebecca decided to press on. 'I wanted to ask you a question, Mona, if I may?' She waited for a response but there was silence down the line. She took that as a yes. 'Do you recall a young man named Evan?'

Silence again, broken only by a few faint clicks on the line. Rebecca wondered if the security services were tapping the phone again, if they ever had. If there had been interest in Maxwell ten years before, would they take an interest again? She thought about the people above Roach's pay grade who had ordered an unofficial investigation. Did whoever it was who had lifted the phone to Roach's boss have an office in Holyrood or Westminster?

'Mona?' Rebecca said when all she had heard were the clicks for a few seconds, fearing the woman had hung up.

'I never met him,' the woman said.

'But you know of him?'

'I was still in China at the time, and they were an item perhaps two years before I returned, so we are talking—oh—thirteen or fourteen years now.'

Mary had said the incident in the bar had taken place years ago.

'But your brother mentioned him?'

'Yes, we corresponded regularly while I was abroad and he always told me about his partners. There really weren't as many as the press suggested after his death. And they weren't all younger than he.'

'But Evan was?'

'Yes. I'm not sure what the exact age gap was, but Murdo was in his forties and I believe Evan was in his early twenties.'

'Like James.'

'Yes, like James.'

'Do you recall his surname?'

Silence again. More clicks and scrapes. 'Rose, if memory serves. Evan Rose.'

Rebecca scribbled the name down. Put a question mark after it for emphasis. 'And did your brother tell you anything about him?'

'Only that he was trouble.'

'What sort of trouble?'

'That was all he said. Evan was trouble and he had to end it. He had either already met James or he did so soon after.'

Rebecca underlined the name once, twice, three times. 'I don't suppose you have any idea where this Evan Rose might be now?'

'As a matter of fact, I do.'

'Where?'

A few clicks on the line. 'A graveyard in Edinburgh.'

38

Gordie will be getting out soon and he says he plans to talk to my father. He feels that the wrong done to me cannot go unpunished, that those who put me here must pay. To be honest, I'm not so sure any more. I don't know what has made me reconsider, whether it's recording my thoughts in this journal or the talks with Gordie over the past year or so. Whichever it is, I think it has helped, as if I have purged.

The fact is, my hatred of the people who put me in here has ebbed. That river of time again, I suppose. It has washed away at my rage. I don't know if I can ever forgive them, though. What they did was wrong and I didn't deserve it.

I've told Gordie all that, but he can't understand. To him, it is very simple. If he is wronged, he wants payback and he can't comprehend my change of heart. I can't even explain it to him because, to be honest, I don't understand it myself. The fact is I'm tired of hating, I'm tired of rage, I'm tired of blame. I'm just tired. No, I didn't deserve what was done to me. But will revenge on the outside make any difference?

39

Roach was in her office at Inshes when her boss called. Why Superintendent McIntyre was contacting her on her mobile and not via the office system briefly crossed her mind before the answer presented itself—she recalled he was still in Glasgow with other regional commanders, no doubt punching a hole in the ozone layer with their hot air.

'Sir,' she said.

'What the hell are you playing at, Val?'

His anger almost reached out and slapped her cheek. 'I'm sorry, sir?'

'You went to see Sir Gregory Stewart today.'

That news travelled quickly, she thought. The man must have phoned someone almost immediately. 'Yes, sir. I did.'

'Why?'

She was momentarily puzzled by the question. 'Why, sir?'

'Yes, Val—why?'

'You asked me to, sir.'

'I did not ask you to interview Sir Gregory Stewart.'

'You asked me to look into the investigation, sir.'

'Discreetly, Val. I said discreetly. Do you know what discreetly means?'

'Yes, sir.'

'Well, let me tell you, Detective Chief Inspector, that was far from discreet.'

'I believe it was necessary, sir. I learned that—'

'I don't care what you learned. I asked you to find out what that bastard Jordan had. Discreetly. Have you done that?'

Clearly he hadn't seen the news sites yet. 'Yes, sir.'

She gave him a quick rundown of the Dodger story. It didn't take long, and he let her talk without interruption, but she could still hear his harsh breathing down the line so his anger had not yet subsided. As she spoke, she wondered why he was so angry, who had Sir Gregory called and how far up the pay scale did his influence extend?

There was a short silence when she finished, then McIntyre said, 'And that's it?'

'Yes, sir.'

'Some small-time lowlife claims he was hired by some nameless individual or individuals to commit murder but he is conveniently dead so we have no opportunity to question him further?'

'It would seem so, sir.'

'And you haven't got a copy of this affidavit?'

'I do not, sir.'

'Can you get one?'

Roach thought about Rebecca. 'I'm working on it. But I would imagine it will be in our hands through the usual channels soon enough.'

The usual channels. In other words, whatever Jordan plans to do with it.

'Hmm,' he said. 'Very likely. It all seems somewhat thin, though. No corroboration, I take it?'

'Only some of the detail within the affidavit that was never in the public domain.'

'Not even during the trial?'

'Without going through the complete trial transcripts I really couldn't say. And I'm not likely to get access to the transcripts anytime soon.'

'No,' he agreed. 'So why did you bother Sir Gregory Stewart?'

'I didn't know he was out of bounds, sir, and I felt it necessary in the course of my inquiries.'

'Your unofficial and discreet inquiries.'

'Perhaps, but acting on information received I felt it necessary to ask him about an encounter he had with the victim a few weeks before his death.'

She had slipped into the rhythms and manner of giving evidence. She was, she felt, under cross-examination.

'How did you find out about this alleged encounter?'

'I did my job, sir. I spoke to someone who was there.'

'Who?'

Roach paused briefly, wondering whether to name Sawyer—she didn't think he would care. 'Former Sergeant Bill Sawyer. He reported it to his superior and was told, more or less, to forget it. I wonder why, sir?'

She heard his breathing at the other end. He didn't reply.

She added, 'I decided to follow it up in light of the fresh allegations.'

'So you suspect that it was Sir Gregory who hired this scrote Dodge? That's utter nonsense.'

'Yes, sir.' She wondered who Sir Gregory had called and who had in turn called her boss. Someone above their pay grade, no doubt.

'The man's a respected businessman, for God's sake.'

'He had reason to despise the dead man.'

'People like Sir Gregory Stewart do not have men killed just because they oppose a business deal.'

'He thought Murdo Maxwell had seduced his son, sir.'

'Even so, there's no way he entered into a conspiracy to murder. Drop it, Val.'

'By drop it, you mean—'

'The whole thing. Leave it. You've got me what I wanted, now let it go. As you say, if it goes any further, which I doubt given the weakness of this, erm, revelation, it will do so through the usual channels. No doubt lots of press coverage, they like any excuse to embarrass Police Scotland. But from what I hear, our guys did their job correctly at the time. That's all I wanted to know.'

'But are you certain that is all the people above my pay grade want to know, sir?'

'What does that mean?'

She regretted her words. 'Nothing, sir.'

'Hmm.'

He hung up without even so much as a cheerio, toodle-pip or see you later, alligator. Roach laid her phone back on her desktop and replayed the conversation. Sir Gregory certainly hadn't wasted any time contacting his pals. Was it because he had something to hide, or was it merely the act of an overly entitled twat who did not appreciate having to account for himself to a mere functionary? She had seen a lot of that in the news in the past year or so, men and women in public office who apparently resented the fact that they were accountable.

Now she had been told to drop it, even though she felt there were questions to be asked. She didn't like that. She would take a wild guess that Gregory Stewart had pulled some strings ten years ago to get the encounter in the Town House dismissed as unimportant. She couldn't say if he had called the same people he had called now or whether he was pally with the SIO then. Either way, Sawyer had been told to forget it. She didn't like that, either. Roach knew she was far from perfect, she could bend rules with the best of them, but she still believed in punishing the truly guilty and if there was even the slightest chance that the wrong man had been convicted for murder, they were duty-bound— legally and morally—to investigate it, no matter where it leads. However, she was also well aware that she had been given the order to stand down and if she continued looking into the matter she might find herself out of a job faster than you can say universal credit. She certainly didn't like that.

But she couldn't let it lie.

She picked up her phone, found Rebecca's number and hit the call button.

40

Alan said he was desperate for some convenience food after a weekend of home cooking—not by his mother, of course. His family was wealthy enough to ensure she had no need to sully her hands with anything more than clicking on the kettle if it was absolutely necessary. When Rebecca turned up at the flat he and Chaz shared, she saw Chinese takeaway already waiting.

'My body cries out for monosodium glutamate,' Alan said as he took her jacket and hung it on the coat stand behind the door.

She had texted her order before she left the office. Sweet and sour chicken. With chips. Alan was forever trying to get her to be more adventurous but she resisted. Call her boring—and he did—but she would have been just as happy with a fish supper.

While they ate, she asked Alan how news of his impending nuptials had gone down with his parents.

'Surprisingly well,' he said. 'There was no wailing and rending of garments. Mother dear was a bit reserved, but then she always is when it comes to my love life. Father shook my hand and said he hoped we would be very happy—not terribly original is Daddy, unless it's finding ways to make and hide money. He shows da Vinci—like creativity in that regard. The display of congratulatory enthusiasm from my brothers was distinctly underwhelming but they observed the proprieties. One even gave me a slap on the back, but I think perhaps he was trying to dislodge my very gayness as if it was something stuck in my throat. Overall, I think the family are finally coming round to the idea that I'm not a ladies' man. They don't much like it, but they've grown used to it. I think, to them, I am like something ugly that grows on your face. You either have it removed or you accept it, and they are all too family-orientated to cut me out completely.'

He gave Chaz a smile. It was his wicked smile and Rebecca knew there was something cheeky coming.

'I can't wait till we go down there as a couple,' said Alan. 'The idea of us sleeping together hundreds of miles away is one thing, they can ignore it, but under their roof in leafy Surrey? I mean, there might be spooning!'

Chaz's expression showed he was not as delighted with the prospect as Alan. He changed the subject, turning to Rebecca. 'How's the story coming along?'

Alan looked at her expectantly. 'Is this the miscarriage-of-justice thing?'

Most of the stories she covered failed to pique his interest but throw in a murder and a hint of mystery and he was all over it like Miss Marple's shawl. So she told him everything she had up to that point. Chaz knew most of it. About the murder in Kirkbrig House, James Stewart's conviction, even a bit of the historical detail. She told him about Murdo Maxwell and Dodger, and about Val Roach and the mysterious figures above her pay grade.

'So you told her about Dodger?' Alan asked, his eyes narrowing. He had become unwittingly involved in Roach's betrayal in the Culloden story and he shared Rebecca's mistrust.

'It was going to be public within hours anyway,' she explained. 'I didn't tell her anything she wouldn't read about soon.' She stopped to eat some chicken. 'And then there's Evan Rose,' she said.

'Ah yes, the previous lover,' said Alan.

'Mary had said there was something off about him, so I started to think, what if he was angry at being replaced? He might have had a key, could have got in, murdered Murdo, framed James. Easy peasy, lemon squeezy.' Rebecca stopped to chew some chicken.

'I sense a *but* hanging in the air,' said Alan.

'But,' she obliged, 'he died a year before the murder, in prison, it seems. Mary was wrong, the break-up wasn't just before Murdo took up with James Stewart, it was about three years before. The year after that,

Evan Rose was banged up for dealing in illegal weapons, providing guns for crooks in Glasgow.'

She had done an internet search and found the a newspaper report behind a paywall. Luckily, she subscribed.

'He was an armourer for the underworld?' Alan asked.

'An armourer for the underworld?' Chaz laughed. 'Where the hell do you pick this stuff up?'

'I know things. Now, shut your geggy and let me listen.'

Chaz laughed again. 'Shut my geggy? What? I mean—what?'

'It means shut your face. One of the lecturers used it last week. She's from Glasgow and I liked the sound of it.'

Rebecca had heard her own mother use the expression. This was why she loved these guys, for no matter how melancholy she could get—she fought it but it happened—they were always on hand to brighten her up.

'Evan was caught in a raid with an array of weapons under his floorboards,' she said. 'He claimed they had been planted there. Murdo actually helped defend him.'

'Old times' sake,' said Alan.

'Yes, but the jury didn't buy it and he was sent away for five years. He screamed from the dock that it was all a fit-up and that Murdo was part of it. He didn't complete the sentence—he collapsed in his cell one morning from a massive brain aneurysm. He never recovered, died in hospital.'

'How old was he?'

'Not sure exactly. Mona Maxwell didn't know, but she thought certainly early to mid-twenties.'

'Drug user?'

'Cocaine, apparently.'

Chaz asked, 'Even in prison?'

Rebecca shrugged. 'Who can say? They do get drugs in prison.'

'Cocaine abuse can cause artery walls to inflame and balloon,' said Alan. 'If he was an habitual user then that could have contributed to it.' He stopped when he caught Chaz's look. 'What?'

'How the hell do you know that?'

'I told you, I know all sorts of things. I'm a very knowledgeable person.'

'Unless it's football.'

'I mean about things that matter.'

Chaz studied him. 'You heard it on *House*, didn't you?'

'Don't be ridiculous. You know I read widely and I have an especially retentive brain.'

Chaz forked some food into his mouth but Rebecca could tell by the way he was looking at his partner that he remained unconvinced.

Alan looked back at Rebecca. 'I'll bet you thought you'd solved it, didn't you?'

'Not solved, but it was an angle.'

'An angle now closed.'

'It sure looks like that. But I learned something else today.'

Val Roach had been true to her word; she had supplied some information, albeit through a vague phone call, that suggested Rebecca give Bill Sawyer a call. She didn't amplify, but it was her way of keeping their bargain. For the moment, at least. She also said that she had been told to drop the matter by her boss. Rebecca wondered if those shadowy figures above Roach's pay grade had stepped in once again.

Rebecca knew Sawyer and after the usual awkward preamble—the former police officer made a point of never making it easy for her—he told her about the encounter between James Stewart's father and Murdo Maxwell. She repeated the story to Chaz and Alan.

'In-ter-esting,' said Alan.

Chaz said, 'You can't think Sir Gregory Stewart had someone killed and then framed his own son?'

'It's a stretch, certainly. But from the sounds of it there was no real warmth between them, not since the day James Stewart came out.'

'But really?' Chaz was insistent. 'Set his own son up for murder? Alan, back me up on this—your family haven't exactly accepted your sexuality, but do you think they would do you harm because of it?'

Alan blew out his cheeks. 'Got to say, Becks, I'm with the blond bombshell here. I don't buy it. I mean, hiring a hitman to bump off someone because he's sleeping with your son? It's a bit Channel 5 after-noon movie, isn't it?'

'Okay,' said Rebecca, 'so let's look at it this way. Sir Gregory stands to lose some money because Murdo Maxwell has gathered support against the windfarm plan. Maybe he thinks if he gets rid of the guy, that support will vanish.'

'But the fit-up of his son?'

'We don't know what was going through Dodger's mind. Perhaps that was something he improvised.'

'Assuming Dodger was telling the truth, of course.'

'This is all assumption, Alan. Dodger did say that whoever hired him was some sort of heavy mob, and to frighten someone like him I get the impression they would have to be very frightening indeed. Maybe Sir Gregory has some *really* dodgy connections.'

Alan had been listening to the exchange between Rebecca and Chaz, but he shook his head. 'It's too on-the-nose.'

'What do you mean?'

He wrinkled his face. 'Too obvious. It's never the obvious suspect.'

Rebecca rolled her eyes. 'Alan, this isn't *Midsomer Murders*. This is real.'

'I know that, darling, but would someone like Sir whatsisname—'

'Sir Gregory,' Chaz cut in. 'Are you even paying attention?'

'Mere details, my boy. Anyway, would someone like him really have a man murdered after he had threatened him just a week or two before in front of witnesses? And one of them a police officer?'

Rebecca had to agree it seemed unlikely, even if Alan's deductive powers did stem from an addiction to Agatha Christie. Nevertheless, he beamed. He loved being right.

Rebecca asked, 'But what if he is behind the order to have DCI Roach taken off the case?'

'You don't know that for certain. You're just pulling a Mulder.'

Pulling a Mulder. It was a phrase Alan, a big *X-Files* fan, had coined for making a mental leap.

'But let's say he did do that, just for the sake of argument,' Alan went on. 'Surely he would know it would lead to him eventually.'

'Arrogance?' said Rebecca. 'The arrogance of the very rich and the entitled. He hears there is something afoot, he talks to his buddies and they in turn talk to their buddies in the police and it lands on Roach's desk, unofficially. Then, when she turns up at his doorstep he doesn't like it one bit and calls the whole thing off.'

'It's also just as likely that her boss decided there were more important things for her to be doing,' argued Alan. 'But, okay, let's follow your thoughts, increasingly outlandish though they are. How would Sir Gregory know something was about to break?'

'I don't know. Perhaps Afua Stewart told him something was going to happen but didn't tell him what. That sounds like the sort of thing she would do. That's what she did to me.'

Alan nodded. 'There you are, then. Ipso facto, QED, Bob's your auntie's fancy man. Sir Gregory may have called in the rozzers but that doesn't mean he had Maxwell killed. In fact, I think it makes it even less likely.'

Rebecca had to admit it all made sense, but she did know that sometimes the obvious suspect is often the guilty party and also that people do stupid things.

Alan said, 'So is that our list of suspects? Evan . . .'

'But he died before the murder.'

'James's father.'

'Which I admit is a stretch.'

'The security services?'

'Another stretch, but I can't ignore it. It's too good a story.'

'But is it likely? Does the state really bump people off who are proving troublesome? If that was the case I can think of any number of public figures who piss the government off regularly and yet live to piss them off another day.'

'There is another possibility,' said Chaz.

'What's that?'

'James Stewart is guilty.' Chaz, forever the devil's advocate. 'That the prosecution case against him was sound.'

'Then why would someone like Dodger make up such a story? He was dying. What possible motive would he have to come up with it?'

They all fell silent. Rebecca was aware that Dodger's statement was problematic. Apart from some specialist knowledge—the fact that the door was not forced, small details concerning the layout of the house and the murder weapon—there was nothing of probative value. The claim that someone who scared him was at the back of it, using threats against his sister to ensure he kept his silence, was vague. However, as she had said to the boys, why would he come forward with it?

Then Chaz said, 'It was *Holby City*, wasn't it, where you got that stuff about aneurysms? Bloody *Holby City*!'

'Chaz, my love,' said Alan, 'why can't you accept that I am an intellectual giant? I read, I digest, I dispense knowledge when and where it is needed, like droplets from the heavens.'

'Intellectual giant, my arse. You picked it up from *Holby City*.'

'I did not pick it up from *Holby City*.'

'Then it was *Casualty*.'

Rebecca let them bicker. It was comforting. It was normal. Yet, she could not turn off completely and her mind continued to turn the story over and over. She had thought she was onto something regarding Evan, but that was now the deadest of dead ends. And she had Sir Gregory's threats against Murdo, even if only by look and suggestion. And Dodger's motivation was troubling. Why would he come forward? Was it simply guilt? Remorse? The need for some form of redemption? And if so, why not name names? He knew his days were numbered. He had ensured that it would not come out until after he was dead. The threat to his sister was only valid while he breathed, so why not tell Jordan who had hired him?

Unless he was put up to it somehow. But by whom? Who had anything to gain from getting a dying criminal to confess to a murder he may not have committed?

It was growing dark but the air was still warm as Chaz saw her to her car. Her own flat on Miller Road was only a few minutes' drive away—she could easily have gone home first and walked to their place—but she had decided to go straight there. It meant she couldn't have a glass of wine with her sweet and sour but that didn't bother her. She could have a nightcap before she went to bed.

'You still look tired, Becks,' he said.

'I am tired, Chaz.'

She considered telling him about Martin Bailey but decided against it. He was concerned enough about her already.

'Have you thought about what I said, about taking a break?'

She opened the car door. 'Can't, Chaz, not while all this is going on. And I have other work to do as well as the Stewart story.'

'You work too hard.' She didn't need to see his expression in the gathering gloom to know he was worried. She could hear it in his voice. 'Elspeth thinks so, too.'

That surprised her. 'You've talked to Elspeth about this?'

'She's concerned about you.'

'I'm fine,' she said, a little more emphatically than she had planned but she was trying to control her temper. She was angry that they had been discussing her behind her back. Chaz caught her tone, though, and said nothing further as she climbed in and pulled the door closed. He watched as she buckled up and turned the ignition before he rapped the window with his knuckle. She lowered the glass.

'You're pissed off,' he said.

'No,' she said, but it just made her sound even more pissed off.

'We're all worried about you, Becks. You've been through a lot these past few years.'

She took a breath, exhaled, felt the anger leave with it. They were her friends. They cared about her. She could not be angry with them. But, most of all, they were right. They knew it, she knew it. She wished she could shut off the baby crying in the night and memories of the man in her arms dying but she couldn't. Her mind had a mind of its own.

'Thanks, Chaz. I know you guys mean well, but I'm better off staying busy.'

'There's more to life than being busy.'

Not to my life, she wanted to say. Being busy is how I keep real life at bay. Real life is loss and death and sadness and I can't take any more of that.

Instead she gave him a smile that she hoped reassured him, then pulled away. In her rear-view mirror she saw him watching her drive off, the lights of another car pulling away briefly, haloing his body.

215

41

Malky hadn't learned anything from Dodger's sister. She didn't even let him over the door, which he had to admit was wise. If he'd turned up at his own door he wouldn't have let himself in, no matter how smooth his lies were. Malky knew what he was; he had no illusions and he didn't try to excuse it. He knew his childhood had been one of violence, of deprivation, that his father had been abusive and his mother victimised, as were he and his sisters. But he had made the choice to go into the Life. Nobody had forced him. He had seen that quick and easy money could be made if you were smart, didn't mind how it was made and were willing to hurt people in the making of it. He knew other guys who had shared the same upbringing and they were straight arrows. Okay, some of them could get a bit rambunctious when they had a drink in them, and at least one of them thought it was okay to slap his burd about. Malky didn't like that and one of these days he would make that bloke see the error of his ways.

That was why the idea of doing that Connolly lassie a damage was not something he relished. He had given his word, but if he could avoid it, he would. Violence was something to be used sparingly, and then only if necessary, although he had to admit he had quite enjoyed giving Hector a going-over. But hurting the lassie? He wasn't sure he would be able to do it.

Then there was that bloke Paul whatsisname to be considered. What was his interest? Why was he following the girl about? Malky was in the dark about everything and he didn't like that, so while he was waiting outside the Connolly's girl's flat he made some calls back home.

Mo Burke had provided the reporter's address, a detached property made up of four flats, but he avoided parking up in the small spaces in front. He planked himself in the roadway a bit away but close enough to keep an eye on her front door between two ornamental pillars. It was a quiet street of relatively new-built properties and the road kind of meandered here and there. So far the only people he had spotted on foot were two teenagers walking hand-in-hand and a blonde woman wearing a crop top and tight denims walking a West Highland terrier. She was in her fifties and shapely, and he wondered where she lived. He wondered if she was married. He wondered why he was so horny. First Mo Burke, now this woman he had only just set eyes on. What was it? The sun stimulating something?

He watched her walk the mutt on the grass between the blocks of flats and terraces, a black plastic bag over her hand in preparation for clean-up duties, while he chatted to a barman he knew in Glasgow, one of those guys who saw everything and nothing, when a movement drew his eyes back to the door and he spotted a squat-looking guy with forearms like Popeye's craning to see through the window. There was something about his body language—it was a definite lurk—that made Malky think the bloke was going to tan the place, but all he did was linger for a moment, look around him in a manner that was as furtive as shit, catch sight of the blonde dog walker and then turn away. He listened to his contact talking about his time a few years ago in a city centre pub as he watched the guy climb into an old Commer van and drive away.

Okay, who the fuck is this now?

42

The faint trace of aftershave hung in the air like a bad memory.

Soon, that text had said.

Soon.

Rebecca glanced around, at the car park, at the grass, at the squares of lights in the houses and flats. She saw no one lurking in any shadows. That didn't mean he wasn't out there somewhere, watching her, waiting. She stared at the few cars, trying to remember if she had seen them before but could not recall. Who remembers cars? She listened for sounds but only heard the faint rumble of traffic.

Phone the police right away, she told herself. But for what? A feeling? She unlocked her front door, pushed it wide open. She didn't step over the threshold but peered into the hallway, head cocked as she tried to catch any sound from within. She saw no lights, heard no stealthy footfalls.

She waited, but nothing happened. She looked over her shoulder again, half expecting to see him standing behind her. There was no one there, but she could feel something on the back of her neck, like a breath, even though there was no movement in the warm air. She shuddered, darted inside, closing, locking and bolting the door behind her. She dashed into the sitting room without switching on the light and peered from behind the curtain through the slats of the Venetian blind. Nothing had changed out there. No dark shapes detached themselves from dark corners. Nobody skulked.

Had she imagined it?

Maybe Chaz was right. She was so exhausted she was now jumping at shadows. Get a grip, Becks, she told herself. How would Bailey even know where she lived?

She slept fitfully that night, but she was used to that. Every creak had her eyes snapping open, ears straining to identify the source, every muffled bump had her convinced someone was in her flat. Houses make curious noises in the night: she had neighbours both above and through the wall and the sounds were them moving about, going to the toilet, perhaps making tea if they couldn't sleep. That was all.

She'd managed to sleep for two hours straight when she woke up. It wasn't enough, but it would have to do. No one had broken in, no one had threatened her, apart from in her own fertile imagination. If Chaz saw her today, she would get another lecture. She showered, made herself as presentable as possible, had coffee and toast, watched BBC *Breakfast*, looked out of the window and saw another beautiful day.

When she reached her car, she saw that all four tyres had been slashed.

43

Despite the two stories that had already appeared—the one on the banners and then the revelation of Dodger's affidavit—Rebecca still sensed suspicion from Afua Stewart. She had agreed to another interview, certainly, but that cool, distant look remained in her eyes. This time, though, she had offered coffee and cake, so perhaps that was some kind of breakthrough. Tom Muir was back in Inverness for a day or two and had agreed to meet to discuss the way forward. She hoped, with him present, this would be an easier conversation than the previous one, for she really didn't have the heart for it that morning. Finding all four tyres slashed had unnerved her. She had reported it to the police and, while she had waited for them to arrive, had banged on doors to see if anyone had seen anything, but even though she was certain she had heard neighbours up and about, it proved useless.

Two uniforms attended, both female, one fair-haired, the other dark, both around her age. They took a look at the damage and the blonde one asked her if there was anyone who had it in for her. She decided to tell them about Martin Bailey, but knew it wouldn't do any good. The police officers took note of his name and said they would look into it. Maybe they would, maybe they wouldn't. She left the car where it was and called a taxI to take her up to the Crown.

All the way she kept looking through the rear window to see if anyone was following.

'So we're getting some traction with the media,' Rebecca explained.

'Traction,' repeated Afua Stewart, as if she was studying the word. Rebecca wondered if she had taken offence somehow and she shot Tom a quick glance. A quick jerk of his head told her to keep going.

'Yes, but the question is, what now? We need to follow through, maintain momentum.'

'Maintain momentum,' intoned Afua, and Rebecca was now certain she was not winning her heart or mind. And no wonder—she was speaking like a bloody spin doctor.

She leaned forward, set her coffee cup on the table between her and the woman, who was sitting in the same chair as before. 'Look, Mrs Stewart, if we are to bring the public over to our side we need to keep the pot boiling. You have refused to speak to the media up until now and I think it's time to change that policy. I was called by BBC Scotland news this morning...'

'Yes, they contacted me yesterday. I turned them down.'

That explained why Lola McLeod, the reporter, had reached out to Rebecca. It had puzzled her, but she now knew that Lola, sharp as ever, had realised that as the originator of the stories she was a conduit to what she wanted, which was Afua Stewart.

'I think turning them down was a mistake, Mrs Stewart. I think we should put you front and centre with the media.'

'No.'

'Mrs Stewart...'

'I don't trust the media. They have not been fair to my son since the start.'

'I know, but we need them, Mrs Stewart,' insisted Rebecca, well aware that she was talking as if she herself was not part of the industry. 'And, like it or not, you—what you have gone through—is a story.'

'It's nothing to what my James has gone through.'

'Yes, but they can't speak to him, not yet. Perhaps if there is enough evidence gathered there can be a fresh appeal, and when he is released on interim liberation, with any luck, he will be able to tell his story.'

She didn't mention that she had no idea where that fresh evidence would come from. The affidavit alone was not enough.

'Becks is right,' said Tom. 'It's the court of public opinion, isn't it? You've tried appealing to the authorities every other way, it's time to get the masses behind you. You've been wanting this for ten years, Afua, and now here's your chance.'

Tom's opinion carried weight because Rebecca saw the thaw in the woman's eyes and the stiffness of her posture ease. Afua took a deep breath and said, 'Very well. I'll do it. But I have been down this road before. They lose interest very easily.' She looked directly at Rebecca, who felt her cheeks flush at what was a very clear accusation. 'Can you guarantee they will be sympathetic?'

'No, I can't,' said Rebecca, truthfully. 'Speaking to the media is always a gamble, Mrs Stewart. But I know Lola McLeod and she will be fair. She won't stitch you up.'

Afua said nothing, but Rebecca could tell she remained unconvinced. 'Okay,' she said, moving on slightly, 'I'm pretty confident I can get a piece in *Life Stories* magazine about you, too.'

'Is that one of those dreadful, cheap little things on sale in supermarkets?'

'Don't underestimate them. Yes, they are pretty direct—it's all first-person soap opera stuff—but it gets the message across. We have Chaz's shots and I can write it for you, but you will get full approval.'

'And you will be paid for this, of course.'

As usual, there was a critical icing over her words, as if Rebecca was profiteering. She wasn't doing this for altruistic reasons, but that didn't mean she didn't care. She tried to find the words to justify herself but Tom stepped in again.

'Afua, be reasonable here,' he said. 'Becks has a living to make. Sure, this is your life, and James's life, and you know I'm happy to help, but the agency is a business. She has to bring in the money otherwise she can't help us.'

'But is that all that motivates her?' Afua stared straight at Rebecca.

'No,' said Rebecca, matching her gaze. Time to hit this on the head. 'But it is a consideration. It has to be, otherwise I cannot function. To be honest, the amount I've made so far doesn't even begin to cover the time I've spent on it, but both myself and Elspeth feel it is necessary. I will do my best to keep the campaign in the public eye, but in order to do that you have to trust me, Mrs Stewart. I know I let you down before but, as I explained, I had nothing to work with. I do now. But we have to capitalise on it. We have to seek out different ways to get your story—James's story—out there. Yes, the public is fickle. The media is even worse. But I need your help to do that.'

She realised there had been a touch more anger in her tone than she had intended but the whole tyre incident had not been the best start to her day. Frankly, she was growing weary of the woman's attitude. Her words seemed to hit home, though, for Afua gave her a curt little nod.

Rebecca took that as both an apology and permission to proceed. 'Okay,' she said, feeling relieved and a little glad the air had been cleared. 'I'll write the piece for you, the magazine has very strict style guidelines and I've worked with them before so I know how to do it. I'll email it to you and you can let me know of any changes.' Rebecca looked at her notebook, ticked off the words TV and LIFE STORIES. She had only one other item to raise and it might prove to be the most difficult. She took a deep breath, held it for a second. 'Now I'd like to talk about your ex-husband.'

'What about him?'

'Did you know he had threatened Murdo Maxwell a short time before the murder, during an argument at a function in the Town House?'

Afua shrugged it away. 'Yes, he was drunk and he admitted he was out of control. He apologised to Mr Maxwell later.'

'This is something that needs to be followed up, you do realise that?'

'If you think it necessary, it makes no difference to me. I don't have much contact with Greg now. Our divorce wasn't exactly amicable.'

'Mrs Stewart, I have to ask—do you think it possible that your ex-husband would have hired someone to kill Murdo Maxwell?'

Afua thought about it for a few seconds before she replied. 'The Greg of that period in our marriage was not the Greg I fell in love with, Ms Connolly.'

'Rebecca, please.'

A slight inclination of the head acknowledged. 'He had become . . . consumed by making money. He was wealthy when I first met him, but sometimes profit becomes a sickness and that is all you think about.'

'What was he like when you met him?'

Her eyes drifted back in time. 'He was a lovely man—don't misunderstand, he can still be a lovely man. He's not a monster. He was never abusive, in case you think that.'

'I don't.'

That seemed to satisfy her. 'His family were unhappy when we started dating. They were—old-fashioned, shall we say? Having someone like me on the cover of their magazines was one thing, their only son and heir being seen in public with me—marrying me—was something else again.'

That explained her earlier comment about his new wife making his family happy. 'They were racist?'

'There is racism and there is racism, Rebecca. It was nothing overt. There was no name-calling, nothing offensive was said. It was all delivered by look and inflection, and I was left under no illusions that they were unhappy with his choice of wife. As I said, they were never open about it, but I knew that they would much rather have had someone marry their son with a little less melanin.'

'And how did your husband take that?'

'He didn't care. Ethnicity mattered nothing to him. He wasn't perfect, though. I knew that from the off. He had his prejudices, everyone does.'

Yeah, don't I know it, Rebecca thought. Some people don't like reporters.

'In his case, it was homosexuals. I was aware of it, of course, there were many people who were gay in the fashion world, in front and behind the camera. Greg kept it under control then, he had to because it was business, and he never said anything out loud. But I saw it in him. The same look, the same inflection, the same attitude that I had experienced in his family. I saw it in him. It was . . . discomfort, I suppose. That's what I sensed in his family and that's what I sensed in him. A feeling of unease. I had never heard the term homophobic then but I suppose that is exactly what Greg was.'

Rebecca had never met Alan's family, but this was exactly how he had described their reaction to him. She could not understand the attitude but could well believe it existed. She knew, though, that she could never fully grasp what it would be like to be on the receiving end of such treatment. What Afua and James and Alan and Chaz experienced was narrow-minded, bigoted and nasty. Rebecca was straight, white and middle-class—her father a ranking police officer, her mother a teacher. She had never—ever—experienced the kind of prejudice, whether open or casual, that Afua or Alan had experienced routinely in their lives. She never would.

She asked, 'So when James came out . . .'

'Greg couldn't handle it. It was like an overnight change. One day he was the son he loved, played with, went for walks with, helped with homework. The next he had become this . . . thing. This unspeakable creature that had inhabited his son.'

She stopped, a smile that was almost bashful rippled across her lips. It was the first time Rebecca had seen anything close to humour in the woman.

'I make it sound as if he believed James was possessed,' Afua said. 'It wasn't as bad as that. It was more subtle, like his family with me. But this sense of James being somehow lessened was there. I saw it. James saw it. And it broke his heart.'

'But given that your ex-husband attacked Murdo Maxwell over their relationship showed he still cared for James, don't you think?'

'Oh, he never stopped loving him. He was his son. James was part of him and me. But by that time Greg had begun to change. He was less interested in the magazines, more interested in property and investment. And he was mixing with people I would rather not have anything to do with. I'd seen them when I was modelling, these men on the fringes with their expensive suits and their jewellery and their money and their eyes on the girls—and the boys—as if they were cuts of meat for sale.'

'Who were these people?'

'Greg called them business associates, but I knew them. Gangsters. Russians. Chinese. Japanese. American. South American. All nationalities, all colours, all the same.'

'But why was your husband mixed up with them?'

'They had money and he wanted it. Don't get me wrong, I like having money, I wouldn't have all this'—she waved her arms around the

225

room—'without it. I was well paid when I was working. I was a commodity but I had a shelf life and I knew it, so if they wanted me they had to pay. But for me money is just a means to an end; Greg came to believe that it was the end itself.'

'The root of all evil,' said Rebecca.

'No, the Bible says *the love* of money is the root of all evil. That is the real sickness, that's what infected Greg, and it still does.'

44

Back at the office Rebecca tried to reach Sir Gregory Stewart once again. When you think you are being a real pain in the backside, you get a result, her father had said. Well, she was about to put that to the test.

The woman with the plummy voice answered with her now customary, 'Yes?'

'I'd like to speak to Sir Gregory Stewart, please.'

There was a pause on the line. 'You're the reporter?'

For a fleeting moment Rebecca debated denying it but decided it would be pointless. 'Yes. I am, and I really need to speak to him.'

'You are very persistent, aren't you?'

'I like to think so.'

A sigh. 'I passed on your messages and your number, so if Sir Gregory hasn't called you back I think you might take it as read that he has no wish to speak with you.'

'Even about his son?'

'I would hazard, given his lack of communication, that would be the case.'

Okay, Rebecca thought, time to fire a broadside. 'Would you mind passing on another message for me?'

Another sigh. 'Very well.'

'Tell him I would really like to discuss the conversation he had with Murdo Maxwell in the Town House.'

Rebecca had the impression the woman was writing it down. 'Very well.'

Footsteps on the stairs leading to the office made her look up and, as she thanked the woman and cut the call, a bulky shadow loomed at the frosted glass of the door. It opened and a man the size of a small elephant wearing jeans and a leather bomber jacket filled the doorway. Behind him she could just make out the shape of another similarly large individual. A thought that Martin Bailey had sent some friends filled her mind and she felt panic begin to well up. Then her rational mind kicked in. It was broad daylight and she could hear someone else passing by her door on their way to the upper levels. The tailor opposite was singing along to the radio as he worked. Rebecca decided it was unlikely these men, whoever they were, would try anything with witnesses around, so she relaxed a little.

Bomber Jacket's eyes flicked around the room briefly before settling on her. 'You Rebecca Connolly?' He sounded like Liam Gallagher. Maybe he had eaten him.

'I am,' she said, having to force her voice to remain steady despite her belief there was no immediate threat. 'How can I help?'

She hoped the other guy didn't try to come in. The office was not large and that might lead to them all getting up close and personal. She wasn't sure her self-defence skills were up to the job of tackling both of them.

'Mr Dalgliesh wants to see you.'

Okay, that surprised and worried her. She didn't even know the SG leader was in Inverness. However, just to be certain, she said, 'Finbar Dalgliesh?'

'That's right.'

She sat back in her chair to show no sign of going anywhere. She twirled the pencil in her hand to keep it from shaking. Bailey crept into her mind. Bailey was SG. Dalgliesh was the leader of SG. She had been trying to reach him but she hadn't expected two of his henchmen to show up. Despite her unease, she tried to remain calm. 'And I just drop my knitting and come away with you, is that the idea?'

He studied her, then scrutinised her desk. Probably looking for her knitting. 'He wants to see you,' he said again, as if that was sufficient explanation for any of the world's great mysteries.

There was no way in hell she was going anywhere with these men. She wanted to speak to Dalgliesh but it would be on her own terms. 'Where is he?'

'At his hotel.'

She knew which hotel he favoured and it wasn't far. 'I'll get there under my own steam, thanks. Tell him I'll be there in half an hour.'

'He wants to see you.'

'And he will, in half an hour.'

'He wants to see you now.'

She stared across the room at him, hoping her face showed steely determination. He looked confused as he tried to grasp the notion that someone would not jump when his boss snapped his fingers.

'He won't be happy,' he said.

'Bugger,' she said, 'that's me convinced then. You should have said that before because Finbar Dalgliesh's state of mind is important to me. I'll just get my coat, shall I?'

If he hadn't caught the sarcastic tone, he should have understood she was going nowhere by the way she remained fixed in her chair, still twirling her pencil like a baton. He didn't, though.

He asked, 'So, you coming then?'

He was either none too bright or he was also persistent. She might have admired him if it was the latter, but she had a sneaky suspicion it was the former. 'Half an hour,' she said again and picked up her phone to drive the point home. He watched as she made a show of thumbing a number. 'DCI Roach, please.'

The realisation spread across his wide face that not only was she not coming with him but she was also about to speak to a police officer. His expression had been impassive with a side order of confusion, but now his sleepy eyes darkened and when his massive brows creased she wondered if it caused a hurricane in New Zealand.

'Hi, Val, how are you doing?' she said, her voice warm and welcoming even though she was talking to dead air. 'Hang on, I've got someone with me from Finbar Dalgliesh's group . . . yes, *that* Finbar Dalgliesh . . . in Inverness apparently. I'm going to speak to him shortly.' She lowered the phone, placed her free hand over it and looked back at Bomber Jacket, who was still planted in front of her desk like a tree, and repeated with heavy emphasis, 'Half an hour.' She put the phone to her ear again. 'Sorry, I missed your call earlier, Val—and yes, would be great to meet up for a coffee.'

She rambled on for a while as he glared at her, then he turned, jerked his head to the other man mountain in the hallway, and they left. She listened to their heavy footfalls descending the stairs like an army on the march then dropped the phone on the desk and stood in order to peer out of the window towards the pavement below. She could just make out one bomber-jacketed shoulder heading up Union Street. She grabbed her phone, notebook and bag, and darted from the office.

She followed them to Station Square and into the hotel. It was a fine, old-fashioned place where her mother stayed when she came up to visit, there not being any space in Rebecca's small flat, so it was a shame the likes of Dalgliesh chose to sully it with his presence. The two men walked straight past reception and across the plaid carpet to where the man himself sat in a high-backed chair under the handsome, polished wooden staircase reading a daily newspaper not noted for its support of minority opinions. That figures, she thought. Bomber Jacket was explaining why they had returned empty-handed as she moved in behind them. Dalgliesh saw her first and smiled. It wasn't his 'I'm one of the lads, let's grab a pint and a fag' smile. He seemed genuinely amused by the fact that his man was explaining her reluctance to attend and yet here she was. That pleased Rebecca, because she never liked to be predictable.

'Ms Connolly,' Dalgliesh said. Bomber Jacket turned, his initial surprise giving way to irritation. 'You accepted my invitation, after all,' Dalgliesh continued.

'How could I resist?' She sat down opposite him across the table.

He gave the two men a nod and they moved a discreet distance from him, but she could still feel the heat of Bomber Jacket's stare.

'I see you still favour minders that buy their clothes from the extra large rack,' she said.

'They are good, loyal members.' He glanced over his shoulder at the two men. 'I think you have upset Ralph,' he said.

Ralph, that figured. He looked as if he really could wreck it. She thought about his Mancunian accent—did SG's reach extend across the border?

'My mum always told me never to go anywhere with strange men,' she said.

'I left a message on your phone saying I was in town and wanted to see you,' he said.

'I didn't get it,' she said.

'I left it on the agency landline service. I said I would send my lads for you.'

She cursed herself. She hadn't checked the messages on the office line that morning. But she would be damned if she apologised to him. 'Well, I'm here now. I've been trying to contact you.'

'I know, that's why I'm here.'

That made her think. 'You came to Inverness just to see me?'

'Ms Connolly, you are looking into the death of a man who was my dearest friend, not to mention partner. The least I could do is see you face to face. I had a meeting up here anyway, so I thought I'd kill two birds with one stone.'

She wondered what an SG meeting was like. Were there sheets and hoods and fiery crosses?

'So, Ms Connolly,' Finbar went on, his continual use of Ms beginning to vex her.

'Just call me Rebecca,' she said.

'Really? That's kind of you,' he said.

'It's not. I just don't like Ms or Miss.'

'You strike me as a Ms.'

She smiled sweetly. 'I haven't struck you at all but the day is young.'

His laugh, like his earlier smile, was genuine. 'You're quick and smart, Rebecca. I like that.'

'My heart is warmed.'

He raised a hand to Ralph, who immediately moved closer. 'Order us some coffee, will you, Ralph?' He looked at Rebecca. 'Or would you prefer tea?'

'Nothing for me, thanks,' she said. It was bad enough being seen with him without sipping coffee like it was a social occasion.

'Are you sure? The coffee here is wonderful.'

'Certain,' she said, then added, 'thanks.'

Always be polite until it's time not to be polite.

'Just for one then, Ralph, thank you.' He waved Ralph away. 'So, you want to talk to me about Murdo?'

'Yes.'

He saw her produce her notebook and digital recorder and he held up a hand. 'Please, just notes, if you have to. No recording.'

She had expected that but had chanced her arm anyway. If you don't try, you don't get. She put it back in her bag. 'I have to say that I find your friendship with Mr Maxwell a surprise.'

'Why?'

'Well,' she said, 'SG is not noted for its inclusiveness, is it? Mr Maxwell was openly gay.'

He winced at the abbreviation of his group's name. 'I hate that term, SG.'

That's tough, she thought. I hate the entire group, so we're even. If he expected her to give them their full name, he had better hunker down for a long wait. She would not demean the Gaelic language.

He realised she was not going to amend her wording because there was a slight clicking noise on his tongue before he said, almost wearily, 'Don't confuse the media's garbled version of our policies with what I truly believe, Rebecca.'

'So, are you saying that I didn't hear you speak out against gay people?'

'When was this?'

'At the protest in Inchferry, the night of the riot.'

That made her think about Martin Bailey again. She suppressed a shudder as she resolved to ask Dalgliesh about the man.

'I spoke out against the forcing of sexual and ethnic diversity on the public by the media and entertainment industries,' he said. 'I did not condemn homosexuality, only the normalisation of it.'

'It was in the subtext.'

'Ah, subtext. That can be very subjective, can't it? As authors say, sometimes a pair of curtains is just a pair of curtains.'

'So, Mr Maxwell's sexuality did not offend you?'

'Not at all. In fact, we had many debates about it. Murdo was always willing to discuss the matter. He knew my views and I knew his. It made for lively drinking sessions.'

'But you had other differences, didn't you? Your political views also diverged quite dramatically, I would imagine.'

'Again, it was no bar on our friendship. We had known each other since university and we went into business together. I think it was our differences that made our partnership work.' His voice turned sombre. 'His death affected me deeply. I miss him, Rebecca. I miss his humour and his laugh and his counsel. I miss the way he argued, passionately, vehemently, against everything I believed and yet we remained close friends. He was not a perfect man, none of us are. He could be petty and spiteful and blinkered, as we all can. He was no angel, he had done things in his life he regretted. He had taken stands that he shouldn't have taken. He had rubbed shoulders with people he should have avoided—and yes, in some people's eyes that may well have included me. But he was my friend, Rebecca, and he always will be.'

The dark hole in his voice seeped into his pupils as they flicked away from her, the careful, studied demeanour of the politician suddenly deserting him. Within it she sensed sincerity. To her, the man before her was hateful, his views and public utterances despicable, and yet he still mourned a close friend taken from him many years ago. As she scribbled his words down, something about them occurred to her.

'How much of what you just said relates to you, Mr Dalgliesh? How many shoulders have you rubbed that you shouldn't? How many stands have you adopted that you did not believe in solely for political gain? SG, for instance? And what about New Dawn and their bombing and vandalism and threats? How much do you regret?'

His eyes hardened again. 'New Dawn is nothing to do with my group,' he said.

He had claimed that once before. She hadn't believed him then and she didn't believe him now.

But then the flinty look vanished and he was Mr Reasonable once more. 'You don't like me, Rebecca,' he said. 'I understand that and I accept it. I'm used to being sneered at by the mainstream media, but, frankly, I'm not about to lose any sleep over it. But here, now, I don't want to argue with you about my politics or my organisation. I want to talk about my old friend.'

So did she, but her natural curiosity wondered about his motivation. 'Why?'

He leaned back in the chair, rested his head against the high back and propped his elbows up on the armrests, then tented his fingers in front of his face. He was carefully considering what he would say next. 'If there is something in these allegations, if someone did have him murdered, then I want to know. I do not believe the authorities will make any serious moves to reopen the case. There has been a conviction and they will resist any attempt to undermine that.'

'There is no suggestion of any wrongdoing on the part of any police officers or the prosecution,' she said. 'The evidence presented was, at the time, solid. They had no way of knowing that it may have been staged.'

'That may be so, but you are not taking into account the establishment's "if you're not for us, you're against us" mentality.'

'A mentality they share with you and your friends, I'd say.'

His hands lowered from his face and he closed his eyes briefly, as if he was counting to ten. Maybe he was. She was verbally flicking his ear for no good reason but she could not help herself.

His eyes opened again and she could tell from the forced evenness of his tone that he was trying hard to not argue back. 'The integrity of the system must be protected at all costs. The police and the legal profession are not fond of admitting error, Rebecca. Sometimes they have to be embarrassed into addressing their shortcomings and I think, perhaps, you and your colleagues in the media can help do that.'

'That will be the liberal mainstream media, won't it?'

She really couldn't help herself.

A tiny smile then. 'Yes, even the liberal elite has its uses.' He paused and studied her. 'You don't trust me, do you?'

'No,' she said. She wanted him to speak but she was not going to pander to him in any way. Despite that little glimpse of humanity earlier, she still despised him and everything he stood for.

He said, 'That works both ways, you understand that?'

She nodded.

'But there are times in life when you have to shake hands with the devil,' he went on. 'This is one of those times.'

'Yes, but which one of us is the devil?'

That smile again. 'There is a devil in all of us.'

'Some have more in them than most.'

'True, but one man's devil is another man's angel.'

He paused as a young waiter brought a tray with his coffee and a biscotti. Dalgliesh's eyes flicked over him, taking in his dark skin, then darted back to Rebecca. He knew she had seen the ripple of distaste but he was not ashamed. He did not thank the waiter as he stepped away again, so Rebecca did it for him. The young man nodded to her and briefly held her gaze as if to say, "What's a nice girl like you doing with a piece like this?" Of course he would recognise Dalgliesh. His face popped up on telly whenever they needed a soundbite and he was always happy to oblige. Brexit (which he supported), royal marriages (at least one of which he didn't), independence (which he supported but only if Scotland did a bit of ethnic and moral cleansing), law and order (which he supported as long as it was used against groups he didn't like).

A sneer crept into Ralph's lip as the waiter walked past him, while his partner grinned. The young man could not possibly have missed their obvious scorn; they made no attempt to hide it. He said nothing, but Rebecca thought she saw a tightening of his shoulders as if he really wanted to slam the metal tray in his hand into that smirk and that sneer. As he walked away, Ralph muttered something to his buddy that Rebecca did not catch but knew it would annoy her if she had. The waiter did hear it, though, and stopped, just briefly, to turn back to face them. There was no fear in his eyes. His face was taut and defiant. Ralph had been lounging against the reception desk and he straightened, his movement a throwing down of the gauntlet which the waiter was wise enough not to pick up. Nothing had been said, nothing had been done. If he accepted the challenge, he would come off worse, perhaps not physically if it went that far because Rebecca could see he had a powerful body beneath the white jacket, but there was a danger he would lose his job. He held the look long enough to let them know he was not intimidated by them and then turned away again. Ralph smirked and his friend laughed.

Was this the sort of thing Afua Stewart talked about? Those looks, the disdain. The remark—unheard but without a doubt distasteful—was a reminder to her that, despite Dalgliesh's reasonable demeanour, these people were scum. And then another thought struck her, one which gave her pause. In thinking that way, in viewing everything these people did or said with contempt, was she as bad as them? Was there such a thing as pious prejudice?

Dalgliesh sipped his coffee, laid the cup carefully back in its saucer. 'As I said before, but let me repeat it for emphasis, I have no agenda. I am here to talk about an old friend because I think he would wish me to. You and I have our differences of opinion, but at this table, for however long this takes, politics has no place. Agreed?'

She nodded and in that moment she knew she had figuratively made that deal with the devil.

'Good,' he said, and he sat back in the comfortable chair. 'So, ask your questions and I will answer them as best I can.'

She stared at her notebook for a moment. 'Did Murdo ever mention James Stewart to you?'

'Yes, many times. We spoke regularly, met when we could.'

'How did they meet?'

'I believe the young man was involved in a few environmental causes. Murdo, as you know, was active in that area.'

'And did he mention any friction between them?'

'Quite the contrary. I felt that they loved each other a great deal. I was delighted to see it.' He saw the quick look she gave him. 'You find that difficult to believe?'

'Frankly, yes. You're not too fond of mixed marriages either, if I recall from your speeches.'

'I thought we agreed we would not go down this road?'

'We did, but you have to agree that your concern in this case in particular is troubling, given your public pronouncements and SG's stance on anything that isn't white, Christian and male.'

'That is an incredible over-simplification of what we stand for. But for the record, and simply to clarify, I am a libertarian and I believe people should be free to do what they wish but not to force their ideals onto society as a whole.'

Every brain cell told her she should argue with him, but she had already needled him more than she should. She needed to get what she wanted and get away from him, perhaps grab a hot shower to sear away any contagion. 'James Stewart is the product of a mixed-race marriage.'

'I am aware of that and I liked the boy. He made Murdo happy and he was very personable, though with a tendency to be histrionic, like many of his kind.'

His kind. She felt her fingers tighten on her pen as she took notes.

'So that was enough for me. God knows, Murdo had chosen badly prior to him.'

'In what way chosen badly?'

'Love is a difficult concept, isn't it? We are attracted to someone by a look or a smile, or simply lust, and then they turn out to be not what we had hoped. Life and love are both great reservoirs of disappointment, don't you find?'

She wondered if he was talking from personal experience. She tried to recall if he was married, had children, but came up blank. She realised she knew nothing about this man apart from his public persona. As for life and love, that was not an area she wanted to consider, for there lay dragons.

'And Mr Maxwell had disappointments?' she asked.

'Haven't we all?'

Yes, we have. That was what she didn't want to consider.

She asked, 'Can you tell me about them?'

'Murdo had the annoying habit of falling in love with the wrong person. There are those who say he was promiscuous, and I suppose on some level he was, but I also saw it another way. He needed love and he loved too quickly. For such an astute man, both legally and politically— he could spot a good or bad witness with a glance, could tell who was trustworthy in Holyrood and who was not—he was capable of extremely poor judgement when it came to his emotions. He seemed to have an affinity for the lost and the broken, young men who had suffered, and he did not care from which walk of life they came. I warned him about it at least twice, when his poor choices led him into difficulties.'

'Was one of those young men Evan Rose?'

His eyebrows shot up. 'You have been working hard. You know about him?'

'Yes. He died, I understand.'

'Yes. A very disturbed young man, I have to say. But then, coming from such a father I'm not surprised.'

'Who was his father?'

'Ah, not dug that deeply then? His father was Arthur Rose. Have you heard of him?'

Something stirred in her memory, something from years ago, but she couldn't quite make it out. 'The name is familiar,' she said.

'His name is familiar to many people and most of them came to regret it. He was, probably still is, a serious player in the Edinburgh under-world, although he has risen above it all now. He's involved in all sorts of legitimate enterprises—finance, property, investments—but you know what they say about leopards and spots.'

Artie Rose, that's what she remembered. She had seen his name in the press on occasion and had a dim memory of overhearing her dad men-tioning him to her mum. Something about underworld violence.

'Murdo ended it with Evan, though,' she said.

'Yes, it was . . . messy.'

'Evan didn't take it well?'

'That is an understatement. There were scenes. Evan also enjoyed being overly dramatic and he turned up at Murdo's office, at his flat, even the house in Appin. Screaming threats.'

'What sort of threats?'

'Oh, just what you would expect—his father would wreak revenge, that sort of thing.'

'But Murdo defended him on the weapons charge.'

'Yes, I advised against it, but he felt he owed the young man some-thing. That was Murdo, loyal to a fault.'

'Evan claimed that he was fitted up.'

Dalgliesh grunted a laugh. 'Yes, the battle cry of felons everywhere.'

'You don't believe it?'

'I have no idea. I wasn't involved. Murdo dealt with it all himself.'

'I understand that he also alleged in court that Murdo was involved in the fit-up. Do you think it likely?'

He leaned forward, picked up his coffee cup, sipped, then settled back again, the cup still in his hand. 'I cannot believe the Murdo I know would have done such a thing, but if he did I wouldn't have blamed him. The boy Rose was proving troublesome in the extreme and getting him out of the way, even if for a limited period, would have been very tempting. I was in court on that last day and I saw the quite hysterical outburst from him when the jury returned their verdict. I must say it was quite typical of the boy. Very dramatic.'

'But he died in prison.'

'Yes,' Dalgliesh said, taking another sip of coffee. 'Very sad.'

Rebecca didn't believe for one minute he thought it sad. She was troubled by the way he kept saying 'the boy Rose'. There was disparagement there and it was nothing to do with the grief he caused his old friend.

'So if he was fitted up, who would have done it?' she asked.

'Oh, he was very clear on that, right from the start of the case. Murdo told me that the boy Rose told him who was behind it during his first interview while he was on remand. At that point I advised him once again to bow out of the defence, but he was adamant he would stay with it. He said he owed the boy that at least.'

'So who did he say was behind it?'

Another sip of coffee, then it was set down on the table again. 'You understand I am being forthright about this because I wish to see justice for my friend.'

'And James Stewart, if he wasn't guilty.'

'Of course.' There was a dismissive tone there, as if James Stewart was secondary. 'This is deep background—isn't that what you journalists call it?'

'Sometimes.'

'What I am about to say, you cannot possibly use in a story, or at least not attribute it to me, but it may help you.'

'Okay. So, why did you advise Murdo to pull out when you heard who was allegedly behind the fit-up?'

'Because the boy Rose claimed to have been sexually involved with this man.'

'And that was an issue why, exactly?'

A pause. 'Because I happened to know that Murdo had enjoyed sexual relations with him too.'

Dear God, she thought, how many lovers did this guy have? 'And who was he?'

Another pause. 'Have you heard the name Joseph McClymont?'

45

Roach heard the divisional commander before she saw him. His voice boomed through the CID office, asking if she was in, and she heard a mumbled reply from a DC. McIntyre did not knock because he did not need to, such were the privileges of rank. She had been struggling with some paperwork, so she was glad of the interruption until she detected tension in the way he stood just inside the doorway, his face tight and hard.

'I've just had a phone call from on high,' he said.

She waited for him to amplify. He must get lots of phone calls from on high but she didn't need to be a super sleuth to know why this particular one had caused such obvious annoyance. Or why that annoyance seemed to be, at this moment, directed at her. She shot a pointed look at the still open doorway and the faces of a couple of DCs watching them, having caught the big boss's tone and body language for themselves. He grunted and closed the door behind him.

'It seems they have had a very irate Sir Gregory Stewart on to them,' he said, turning back to her but not coming any nearer to her desk.

'Really, sir? He does seem to make a habit of being irate with senior officers.'

He gave her a glower. 'I thought I told you to drop it, DCI Roach.'

'You did, sir. And I did.'

He grunted. 'I will just ask you this straight out, DCI Roach. Did you pass information on to that reporter?'

'Which reporter, sir?'

'Don't give me the peaches-and-cream act, Roach, it doesn't suit you.'

She had no idea what he meant by that.

'That Connolly girl,' he said. 'Did you tell her about Sir Gregory?'

'I did not,' she lied. 'I take it she has been in touch with him?'

'He hasn't spoken to her, nor will he, it seems. But what I want to know is, how did she find out about that night in the Town House?'

'She's a good reporter, sir. She probably did her research.'

'So you didn't tell her?'

'No, sir.' She lied again. 'I don't know where she would have picked it up. Maybe she has spoken to other people—there were others there that night apart from Sir Gregory and Murdo Maxwell. As I said, she knows her job and she will be speaking to a lot of people. It wasn't exactly a secret, but the SIO, and even the PF, deemed it unimportant in light of the weight of evidence against James Stewart. The defence tried to make something of it, but it led nowhere.'

He stared at her, his eyes cold and hard. She could not tell if he believed her or not. He clicked his tongue, pursed his lips, breathed heavily through his nose, then sat down in the chair opposite her.

'Val,' he said, his voice now more exhausted than angry, 'how well do you know police history?'

'I know the basics, sir. What I need to know.'

'Does the name Oscar Slater mean anything?'

'Miscarriage of justice, sir. Glasgow, what, more than a hundred years ago?'

'Very good. He was convicted of the murder of a woman named Marion Gilchrist in 1908. Do you know the name Detective Lieutenant John Trench at all?'

She had heard the name but was wondering where this was all heading. 'It's familiar, sir.'

He folded his arms. 'John Trench was a Glasgow cop, Val, and a good one, it seems. He never believed Slater was the killer and he passed privileged information on to a lawyer. It didn't matter that he was right, it didn't matter that an innocent man spent years in jail. Trench was dismissed from the Force. He had disclosed official information to a third party. The Job took a dim view of it then and it still does.' He paused and tilted his head to one side as he stared at her. 'Do you catch my meaning, DCI Roach?'

242

He had lobbed his meaning with some force, so she had caught it very easily and the switch from Val to her rank put a hefty spin on it. 'Are you threatening me, sir?'

He breathed heavily again, then stood up. 'Just giving you a history lesson, is all. Things have not changed much in those hundred years, not really. We've gone from individual city forces to regional to national, but at our heart we remain the same. Officers do not convey privileged information to third parties, no matter who they are, no matter how effective an officer they are, and no matter how well intentioned they are. Period.'

Now that he had said what he had come to say, he had calmed down slightly, but she would not let it lie. Her own anger was rising, though she managed to keep her voice steady. 'It sounds very much like a threat to me, sir.'

He had the decency to look slightly ashamed. 'You have to take it whatever way you want. All I'm saying is, bear it in mind. If I find out you have spoken to this Connolly girl, I will not be pleased, do you understand?'

She understood he was the divisional commander and could not back down, but that didn't help assuage her anger any. She gave it a beat before she said, 'Yes, sir.'

If the conversation had been subtitled, it would have read, 'Fuck you, sir.'

He studied her and she wondered if he had caught the inflection but, finally, he nodded and left the room. He didn't close the door behind him and she watched his broad, straight back stride out of CID.

46

Rebecca didn't know how much use Dalgliesh's information was at this stage, wasn't sure how much she could use in a story, but she had the feeling there was something there she wasn't yet seeing. She was transcribing her notes when the agency mobile rang.

'Ms Connolly . . . Rebecca?' A man's voice, familiar. 'Stephen Jordan.'

'Hi,' she said. She was a little surprised to hear from him.

'I wonder if you're free just now for a chat?'

'Of course,' she said, wondering what it was. His voice seemed a little guarded, but perhaps that was the way he always spoke to reporters.

'Not on the phone,' he said. 'Can you come to the office?'

'Right now?'

'If you can. I have Mrs Fraser here.'

Her first thought was that Dodger's sister was making some sort of complaint against her and had consulted Jordan, but then she reasoned if that was the case he wouldn't phone her, he would send something by letter. Her second thought was, why would she have that thought in the first place? She had done nothing wrong.

'What's up?' she asked.

'She's found something in her brother's effects that she wants you to see.'

47

Malky was parked outside a budget hotel on the riverside, waiting for a bloke to come out. The water of the river was blue, the wispy clouds were white, the castle Malky could see on the hill was red. All in all, it was as patriotic as fuck, if that was the way you saluted.

He had phoned the guy from the car, told him he was waiting outside. It had taken all morning to get his phone number, and there was the chance he was already out and about, but no, he was still in his scratcher. He'd had a late night, right enough, but then so had Malky. But the guy was no spring chicken and he looked like someone who enjoyed a few shots of something before bed. Malky had cut back on the booze as well as stopping the fags and he was a good few years younger, so he was up and out, fresh as the proverbial daisy.

He had remembered Paul's second name the night before, while he was sitting outside the Connolly lassie's house making his calls. He had been right; he saw the same car he'd spotted at Dodger's sister's house turning into her street just as she was climbing out of her car. Malky had slid down in his seat but could still see over the steering wheel and the car pulled in a short distance ahead of him. It was dark by then, but he could see two heads, both watching her. The reporter hesitated at her front door, looked around, then finally went inside.

It was late and it was unlikely she would go anywhere else, so Malky decided to follow Paul. He knew he couldn't pull out behind him—he would be noticed—so he drove away and parked up again just around the corner, out of sight. There was only one way in and out of this estate, and he waited until they had passed him before making his move. There wasn't much traffic, so he kept his distance, almost lost him a couple of times on the way to the city centre, but Malky had done this sort of thing before. The car crossed the river and turned right, then stopped outside the budget hotel. Aye, that figured, Malky thought. The guy is a pro, like me. Paul got out, said something to the driver and then went inside.

Malky's various calls meant he was beginning to piece things together, but he wanted to have a sit-down with this guy. Another couple of calls had provided his mobile number, so he phoned him early in the morning, said they had some business to discuss. The guy was surprised; he remembered Malky from before, and turned cagey, but Malky said it was in their best interests to have a meet.

'Where?' the bloke asked.

Malky had already sussed that out. 'There's a place called Merkinch, down by the water, just beyond the harbour. There's a wee area near a nature reserve sort of thing, like a picnic spot. Meet me there at twelve. But on your tod, eh? We don't want nobody else earwigging.'

Then he hung up.

Now, as he waited outside the hotel, he saw the same car from before pull up and Paul emerge through the doors and walk down the ramp. So much for him coming alone, but that was okay, that was why Malky was here. The guy wasn't being cautious, wasn't paying attention to his surroundings, didn't know Malky was watching him. After all, he didn't know Malky knew where he was laying his head. He climbed in and the car pulled away.

Malky followed, even though he knew where they were going.

48

Elaine, Jordan's receptionist/secretary/office manager/Rottweiler, didn't give her anything like a welcoming smile, but she did buzz her through immediately with the words, 'Mr Jordan is waiting for you.'

It sounded like a reprimand, that somehow she was tardy, despite the fact it had only taken Rebecca ten minutes to lock up and walk from Union Street to the Castle Wynd.

'You know the way,' said Elaine, as if the office was somehow labyrinthian. His door was open and he nodded to her from behind his desk. To Rebecca's surprise, seated beside Eleanor Fraser was Afua Stewart, giving her the usual cold look. A third chair was waiting for her in the tiny space. Despite Afua's expression, things were going to get chummy.

Rebecca settled in as well as she could and gave them all an expectant look. Jordan said, 'Mrs Fraser, suppose you tell Ms Connolly what you found.'

Eleanor Fraser cleared her throat and held up an envelope. 'I found this letter in Rog's coat.'

It had been tucked away in an inside pocket, she explained, and at first she didn't know what to do with it, which was why she contacted Mr Jordan. She handed two sheets of paper to Rebecca bearing creases like slash wounds where they had been folded.

'Nice penmanship,' she observed with some surprise.

'That was mum's doing,' Eleanor Fraser explained. 'She made sure our handwriting was top notch, so she did. Always used to say the world judges you by your handwriting. For dad it was shoes, for her it was writing.'

Rebecca nodded and shot a glance at Afua's face. As usual, she gave very little away. Then Rebecca began to read.

Dear Sis,

I hope you find this and do something good with it. By now you will probably know what I did back then. I don't think you will be surprised to hear it, given the way I was. I was never any good, was I? You maybe never got the wee rabbit when we was kids, but you got all the decent genes, I think. I ended up with what was left. The dregs. The bad bits.

When I came to see you I tried to say I was sorry for all the pain I caused you and Mum and Dad. I don't think it came out right but I don't blame you for cutting me dead. I deserved it.

About that guy Maxwell and what I did. Back then I never thought about it, even though I'd never killed nobody before. But to tell you the truth it hit me hard. I never thought it would but it did. It changed me. Not enough to make me get out of the Life, right enough, I was too stuck in that rut, but I didn't want to hurt nobody any more.

I'm sick now, you'll know that too, and what I did has been really preying on my mind. I need to make amends somehow, to that boy in the jail, to his family. I explained to my lawyer that I kept quiet to protect you and your boy, cos the guys that hired me was right bad bastards. I kept my mouth shut. I didn't even tell Mr Jordan.

But I've been thinking about it, you know? And it's not right that they get away with it. You might say I got away with it but I didn't, not really. I've suffered, sis, I really have. Kept seeing that bloke's face, kept hearing the noise as the poker did his head in. Hellish noise. I never felt guilty over nothing I done but I felt guilty over that. Now I'm paying the ultimate price, you might say, because the way I see it my sickness is punishment for what I did.

If you don't find this letter, then, okay, things will go on as normal, but if you do and you do something with it, then maybe that's God's way of making things right. I'm leaving it up to you what you do with this—it has to be your decision.

Mr Jordan explained to me when I signed my affidavit that it would be of limited use without some kind of corroboration. I've been thinking about

*that, about corroboration, and what I could do to convince folk. And as
I was going through my stuff, playing keep or chuck—mind Mum used to
talk about that? Go through our stuff and keep it or chuck it? That's how
I found the rabbit. Anyway, I was getting rid of loads of shit and I found
the things I've enclosed in this letter.*

The writing came to a stop at the end of a page and Rebecca looked up
at Eleanor. 'Is there more? And what was it he had found?'

Eleanor glanced at Jordan, who held up another sheet. 'Before we give
you this—and I must stress that I'm not sure letting you see this is the
best course of action at this stage but Mrs Fraser seems to trust you and
Mrs Stewart has agreed.'

Rebecca gave them both a grateful nod and Eleanor's smile in return
was a little wan. She was out of her depth here. A letter from beyond the
grave was one thing, but to be put in this sort of position was not something a suburban mother expects to happen to her. As for Afua Stewart,
something gave the corners of her mouth a brief tug. She was a proud, if
stubborn, individual and changing her opinion did not come easily.

'First, this is what was enclosed,' said Jordan, as he slid something
across the desk. She couldn't see what it was at first but heard a metallic
scraping sound on the wood. He raised his hand to reveal two keys, a
Yale and a mortice.

Rebecca felt electricity surge through her bloodstream as she looked
at the slivers of shaped metal. These were the keys to Kirkbrig House,
she knew it.

'I believe you have made contact with Mr Maxwell's sister,' said Jordan. 'We thought you would be able to help me check if these were genuine.'

*I had the locks changed as soon as I could because you never know, do
you?*

But I still have the old ones somewhere.

Rebecca felt excitement build as she reached out to pick up the Yale
key and stared at it. There was nothing unusual about it. It was tarnished
with age but just an ordinary key, something you wouldn't give a second
glance, but if it fitted the lock Mona had put away somewhere—God,

she really hoped she did still have them, as she said—then this was new evidence, surely even in the restrictive eyes of the Scottish courts. These keys, and the details in Dodger's statement, should help them obtain leave to appeal James Stewart's conviction.

She looked back at Jordan, remembering the sheet of paper. 'What is in the rest of the letter?'

'The name of the man who hired him.'

She held her hand out so she could read for herself. Jordan passed it over and she scanned the few remaining lines.

The guy who approached me I knew from Edinburgh, a hard man. People think I'm hard but he was the real deal. Done time for armed robbery, assault, you name it. He could've done the business himself no bother but I knew they wanted distance. I knew I might have been setting myself up for a fall. But I sorted that.

I had been rooting around in this big sitting room in Maxwell's house, looking for anything I might lift, when I heard him coming downstairs and knew this was my chance. They told me about the poker, big heavy brass thing, but I lifted it and followed him into the kitchen. That's where I did him, sis. I didn't even think twice, God help me. The money was good, the bloke I was to kill meant nothing to me.

Afterwards I went upstairs to see if there was anything I could nick, make it look like a burglary or something. I realised I was covered in blood so I went into the bathroom and washed my face in the sink. I was wearing rubber gloves because I didn't want to accidentally leave any bloody prints. I didn't dry my face because there was no way I was leaving any DNA on a towel. My clothes were covered too but I had my suitcase in the motor. I changed later up a forestry road then burnt the clothes when I was away out on the wilds.

I pulled on a pair of new gloves and had a wee root around and I found the lad on the bed, out for the count. So it hit me then that I could give myself some insurance. I wrapped his fingers round the handle of the poker and let it drop on the floor beside him. There was another fireside set in that room, same as the one downstairs, so I took the poker from there and put it in that living room. I decided not to take anything from the place

because if I did the police would know there had been someone else there.
I was amazed I was thinking so clear.

Rebecca paused to look at Afua. She wondered if she had read this. Of course she had. Rebecca could tell by the way she held herself erect. That wasn't just a model's poise, it was something else. Tension. The need to stay in control. She was staring at something just above Jordan's head, her eyes fixed. Then her head slowly turned and Rebecca saw that the ice in her eyes had turned to water.

Rebecca stretched out a hand and gave her forearm a squeeze. Afua Stewart laid her other hand on top of it and left it there, then looked back at the spot on the white wall.

Rebecca returned to the letter.

Once they found out I'd fitted the boy up they needed another way to shut me up so that was when they mentioned you and your lad. If I breathed a word they knew where you lived.

So, the guy who hired me I've never named. Never told Mr Jordan. Never even told my mate Hector, who you maybe met at the funeral. Or maybe not, cos you might not have gone. I get that.

Paul Gordon was his name. His mates called him Gordie.

49

Gordie is still insistent that something must be done. He knows a lot of guilty people and he knows I'm not one of them. He's now more angry about what happened than me. Fit-ups are part of the Life, he told me today, police do it, even our own lot do it. There's no honour among thieves. The big guys in the Life have got where they are by grassing and violence, and when that wasn't possible or advisable then they would fit up a bloke, get him sent away. Out of sight, out of mind. And sometimes they never got out, jails being violent places for violent men. When I asked him why it had affected him so much, he just said because it always happened didn't mean he should like it.

It made me wonder about my father, had he ever fitted someone up just to get them out of his way? Has he made his way by being party to the very injustice that I have experienced?

It may be part of the Life, but Gordie has never wanted anything to do with it. It's dishonest, he said, and that made me laugh, given his record. But I know what he meant. Gordie is very direct. Someone gets in your way, you deal with it head-on. You don't manufacture a case against them, then grass them up to the law. He's a crook but an honest one, if you can believe that. He liked guys who were straight-up about their dishonesty and despised those who pretended to be upstanding but who were underneath just as venal and corrupt as the thief in the gutter. They just dressed better, he said. Crooked cops who claim to uphold the law while taking backhanders; crooked politicians who stand for decency and family values but who wet their snouts in the trough with the pigs.

He says when he gets out he wants to do something about it. I've tried to dissuade him, but he is a very determined individual. I like that in him,

252

but it scares me. The people he would go after are also very determined and I wouldn't want anything to happen to him. In the time I have known him he has been like a brother to me, a protective big brother. With him, my sexuality is not an issue. He has told me there were people he knew in his world who hid their true selves and it screws them up. I know all about that, for that's how I ended up here.

50

When she left Jordan's office, Rebecca turned right, to head up the Castle Wynd. What she had learned was exciting and the jigsaw in her brain was beginning to lock together. There were still pieces missing, but she thought a picture was emerging, slowly and a bit fuzzy, to be sure, but things were falling into place. She needed some space to breathe, to think, so she decided to sit on one of the benches in front of the castle, facing up-river towards the Great Glen.

As she trudged up the hill, realising how weary she felt and deciding she really needed to begin some kind of fitness regime, she called Mona Maxwell. She had no illusions—her contact with the dead man's sister was the real reason she had been called in to the little conclave in Jordan's office. She asked if she was certain she still had the old locks in what was once the maid's room off the kitchen.

'Why do you ask?'

'There have been developments, Mona. Can I come see you tomorrow? I would have a lawyer named Stephen Jordan with me, if that's okay?'

It was Jordan who had suggested it. He could easily have simply given her the keys, but he was not letting them out of his hands.

'Of course, but what developments?'

'We have the keys that might have been used that night and we need to see if they fit.'

'Keys to my door? But where did they come from?'

Clicks on the line made Rebecca more circumspect. It could simply be dodgy BT connections, but she wasn't going to take any chances.

254

'We'll explain tomorrow, if that's okay. We should be there mid-morning.'

Mona accepted it. 'Very well,' she said, but Rebecca could tell she was curious.

Rebecca added, 'One quick question, though.'

'Yes?'

'Remember we spoke about Evan?'

'Yes?'

'Would he have had keys to the house at all?'

There was a silence on the other end, apart from clicks and what sounded like wind down the line, even though Mona was indoors. 'I think he probably would have,' she said.

Another piece in the puzzle clicked into place. 'Okay, that's interesting. We'll see you tomorrow.'

51

Malky had waited until he saw Paul Gordon walk down the road towards the meeting spot. He was moving slowly, showing caution now. Gordie was a few years older than Malky and, like him, he kept himself fit, for he knew the day would come when he slowed down and in his business that could be lethal.

Malky assumed the man driving was local muscle, and it looked as if Gordie was honouring the agreement to meet with him alone because he had left the guy in the car. Malky wasn't going to take any chances, though. He sauntered up to the vehicle, making sure that Gordie wasn't looking back, and knuckled the window, which wound down. He saw a young bloke, mid-twenties maybe, trying to be hard and not quite making it. You're either hard or you're not, you don't try. Music blared out of the speakers. Some modern crap, all rhythm, no substance. Malky would bet his last fiver this boy was not allowed to listen to it while Gordie was in the motor.

'Sorry, mate,' said Malky, having a last check that no one was watching, 'you got a light?'

'Don't smoke,' said the boy.

'Neither do I,' said Malky, and he jabbed his fist through the open window into the boy's eye. He rocked back and Malky reached in with one hand, grabbed the back of his head and slammed his temple against the steering wheel. The boy grunted and struggled against his grip, so Malky gave his head another jerk. He heard something snap, but the boy was still writhing so Malky bounced him off the wheel a third and final time. He felt the tension leave the boy's body and he slumped to one side, blood streaming from the gash on his nose and his nostrils while a red welt blossomed on his forehead. Malky looked around again, then opened the door and clicked the button to slide the window back up. He made sure the boy was laid out across the front seats, head to the side—he didn't want to run the risk of him choking on anything—then switched off the racket from the radio. When he closed the car door, he satisfied himself that the unconscious driver wouldn't be noticed unless you peered right in, then he walked to the boot, clicked it open and laid the item he had hidden under his jacket beneath an old blanket. That would do it, he said to himself, before he walked after Gordie, peeling off the latex gloves he had been wearing and stuffing them in his pocket.

52

Rebecca had reached the plateau of the castle hill and was approaching the statue of Flora MacDonald, her right arm raised to her head as if she was shielding her eyes from the glare of the sun. The grass around the castle was redundant free of people, which was a redundant. There were a few, naturally, photographing the statue with the castle behind it, its red brick gleaming, while others leaned on the railings above the steep incline to the river taking in the view. It was one of her favourite spots, although she much preferred it when dark-tinged clouds glared from the heavens and you could feel the faint threat of rain on the breeze coming up from Loch Ness. Most people sought sun and blue skies, and although she appreciated them she had more of an affinity with the darkness. Maybe she should dye her auburn hair black, get some piercings and go full Goth.

Rebecca claimed one of the benches as her own, taking off her jacket and laying it and her bag beside her in a bid to ward off anyone who might wish to violate her personal space. She had completed the call to Mona, now she hit Elspeth's number. She told her about Dodger's letter and her interview with Dalgliesh.

'You know who McClymont is, Becks,' said Elspeth. 'He's the Glasgow gangster who was feuding with the Burke family until they reached détente.'

The Burke family.

'Yes,' said Rebecca, closing her eyes against the flash of memory. 'But I can't get all this straight in my head. Murdo Maxwell defended this Evan Rose character on a weapons charge. Rose insisted he was set up by McClymont. Maxwell had been in a relationship with both Rose and

McClymont. Rose later claimed that Maxwell purposely botched the defence to have him sent away.'

'Motive for revenge, you think?'

'Yes, but Rose died in prison before Murdo Maxwell died. And Dodger said he was hired by this Paul Gordon, but the suggestion is that there was someone else at his back.'

Elspeth thought about this. Rebecca thought she heard the flick of a lighter. 'Elspeth, are you smoking again?'

'Gimme a break. I have one vice.'

Rebecca laughed. '*One* vice?'

'Okay, it's one of my vices, but I get enough grief from Julie, so don't you start.' Rebecca heard her exhale smoke. 'I'll give an old pal a call. If there's a ned or crook in the Central Belt he doesn't know, then he's not a ned or a crook. Gimme ten minutes.'

Elspeth cut the call abruptly.

Gordie was sitting at a wooden picnic table on a stretch of grass beyond a horseshoe of parking spaces looking out over the water. The sky was wide here, and any cloud cover was so thin it was little more than a suggestion. To their right, a stone jetty jutted into the water, probably where a ferry used to dock, and beyond it, the bridge that had made it obsolete. There were a couple of cars parked in the spaces, and on the shore below the grassy area Malky saw a man with two children poking about among the rocks. Another table over to the left was taken up by a party of four, two young couples sharing a picnic from plastic containers.

He took a seat on the wooden bench on the other side of the green table from Gordie. There were no pleasantries.

'Why here?' Gordie asked, his east-coast accent pretty strong.

'Nice and open, nice and public.'

'You need witnesses?'

'Just to make sure there's no funny business.'

'Why would there be?'

'Shit happens, Gordie, you know that. And on that note, your lad back in the car won't be joining us.'

Gordie merely nodded, unsurprised. He knew the score. 'So what do you want—Malky, isn't it?'

'Aye.'

'I remember you, from before.'

'Then we remember each other, don't we?'

Another nod. In their business it pays to remember people. 'So, what's all this about?'

Malky got down to it. 'I think we're in Inverness for the same thing.'

'Holiday?'

Malky almost laughed. 'What kind of holiday sees you following a reporter around?'

Gordie frowned. 'Don't know what you're talking about.'

This time Malky did laugh. 'Gordie, mate, it's just you and me here, right? I think we've both been sent to do the same thing—find out what the hell is going on with the Murdo Maxwell thing.'

A slight flare in Gordie's eyes told Malky he was right. 'Wee Joe send you?'

'Aye—Artie send you?'

A nod.

'Okay,' said Malky, 'so here's the thing. I've kinda pieced some stuff together, but I'm still a wee bit puzzled, I don't mind admitting it.'

'So what do you want me to do about it?'

'Tell me what all this is about.'

Gordie stared across the water, at the tree-covered hill and the white dots that were houses. 'They call that the Black Isle.'

'I know.'

'Doesn't look very black to me.'

Malky knew the man was taking time to think, to weigh up the situation. 'It used to be covered in black moorland, way back when.'

Gordie's eyes returned to him. 'How do you know that?'

'Read it in the tourist book in my hotel room. So, how about it, Gordie? What can you tell me about all this?'

'Why should I?'

'Call it professional courtesy.' That made the man smile and Malky could see he wasn't biting. 'Okay, suppose I tell you what I know and what I think I know. We'll take it from there.'

Gordie shrugged. 'Go ahead. Tell me a story.'

Malky laid his forearms on the table and clasped his hands as he leaned in closer. 'Once upon a time, there was a handsome prince called Evan . . .'

53

Rebecca looked across the river at the kaleidoscope of greens, greys and blues of the trees, buildings and sky. A few frothy white clouds hung above the hill of Tomnahurich, lying like a beached whale covered in seaweed beyond the turret-like spires of the cathedral. She tilted her head back, the sun's rays resting on her cheeks while a warm breeze caressed her skin, as if trying to knead her temples. She was tired. Too little sleep, too much stress. Chaz was right, she needed a break. A real break, not just a day or two. Two weeks. She liked the clouds but she needed the sun. She would give her friend Daniella in Spain a call once this was over. Definitely.

She thought about the meeting in Jordan's office. Eleanor had told her an old friend of her brother's had visited just after Rebecca herself had left. He said he wanted to convey his condolences but had asked questions about Dodger—had he told her anything before he died, had he left her anything? He'd seemed very pleasant, but Eleanor had not let him in her house and had told him she had no contact with her brother at all.

So who was this guy? Was he connected to Paul Gordon or Joseph McClymont? And how much did he know?

At the picnic table beside the water, while the children on rocks called to each other, and the couples beside them laughed and chatted, Malky was outlining what he knew.

'Now, Evan was a very troubled prince and that upset his dad, King Arthur,' he said, 'for Prince Evan was not interested in any of the fair princesses in the land, he preferred the princes, if you know what I mean.

262

And one of them was the son of King Robert, who ruled a land in the west and was a rival of King Arthur.'

Malky had spent much of his time while sitting in the car, watching and waiting, making calls to anyone he thought might add a piece to the puzzle. Over the years he had built up a substantial database of informants. He may not have been a curious man, but he knew that while violence was a weapon, knowledge was power, and when necessary he used his army of crooks, reporters, lawyers, even police, to keep his power topped up. He had no ambitions to be in charge—he wasn't like Big Rab or even Wee Joe—but he did like to be ahead of the curve. Seeing Paul Gordon up here had made him realise there was a curve here he needed to be ahead of. One connection, a barman who Malky had helped out one night with some rowdy football fans, recalled seeing Wee Joe with Artie Rose's boy and they seemed friendly. They weren't doing anything to frighten the horses but there was a vibe, the barman said. A vibe. Put that together with Malky's existing questions about Wee Joe and he came up with *Brokeback Mountain*.

'Now, this other prince—let's call him Prince Joseph—wasn't as comfortable with his leisure activities as Prince Evan. He liked to keep it secret, while Prince Evan didn't give a tinker's who knew. How am I doing so far?'

Gordie pulled a face. 'It's your story.'

Rebecca was wondering how she would approach the story when Elspeth called back. It had taken her longer than ten minutes.

'Right,' she said. 'I had to be pretty cagey. That old pal of mine's an old-fashioned hack and sharp as a razor. If Pete got wind of a story, he'd scoop us.'

'So what did you say?'

'I kept it vague, just said it was something I was thinking about looking into when I finish this book.'

'Did he buy it?'

'I doubt it. So, Paul Gordon . . .' Rebecca had the feeling Elspeth was consulting her notes, probably scribbled on any clear space on a cigarette pack, a habit she picked up from an experienced Glasgow crime reporter when she was just starting out. Many a time Rebecca had seen her turn the pack this way and that, looking for a cohesive through line in her notes, which were merely words or phrases in shorthand to jog her memory.

'He's never actually offed someone, not that Pete knows of anyway, but he's done most everything else. Theft, extortion, robbery, GBH, serious assault.'

'Any connection to Murdo Maxwell?'

'Not directly, but Pete did a quick library search. This Paul Gordon fella was sent away for a serious assault just after Evan went down, so he was in the pokey at the same time.'

'I'm sure a lot of bad guys were.'

'Yes, but it's something to keep in mind. Could be a connection there, especially considering what I'm going to say next.' Elspeth paused and there was another click as a fresh cigarette was fired up. 'Don't say it,' warned Elspeth.

'Say what?' She hadn't been going to say anything at all. When Julie found out about it there would be things said a-plenty, perhaps not eloquently but certainly with passion. 'I've already said all I need to say.' At that moment, Rebecca was more interested in the information. 'Paul Gordon?' she prompted.

'Aye.' Smoke blowing out. 'Anyway, when he got out he went to work for Evan's dad.'

'Artie Rose,' said Rebecca.

There was a note of surprise in Elspeth's voice. 'You heard of him?'

'Dalgliesh mentioned him. My dad, too, years ago. He's a businessman now, apparently.'

'Aye, businessman in inverted commas. Big Pete says he's still up to his neck in all sorts of rackets but keeps them at arm's length now. Usually someone else's broken arm. It couldn't have been easy being his son, especially given Evan's sexual preferences. But Artie loved his son—didn't show it much, right enough—and tried to protect him at all times, although young Evan often made it difficult for him.'

Malky was enjoying telling his story. There were a lot of gaps in his knowledge but he filled them in with conjecture.

'See, Prince Evan is very fickle. In fact, he shags around and in the course of this shagging around he meets Count Murdo and he pals around with him while still seeing Prince Joseph. But Prince Joseph finds out about this palling around behind his back and it displeases him, especially as he had also once palled around with Count Murdo. This world of ours is kinda small, don't you think?'

Gordie didn't reply.

Malky continued. 'Anyway, Prince Joseph is a one-guy kind of guy and he breaks it off with Prince Evan. Pretty soon Count Murdo also ends things with Prince Evan because the boy is not what you might call stable.'

He saw something kindle in Gordie's eyes. Could have been anger, could have been pain, he really couldn't tell.

'Anyway, adrift with no one to pal around with, Prince Evan goes a bit haywire. He tries to get back with Prince Joseph but he won't have anything to do with him. Prince Joseph comes from a land where that sort of thing is kind of frowned upon and might be seen as weakness. But more importantly, Prince Joseph is himself ashamed of his sexual needs. He doesn't want them known far and wide because he hasn't come to terms with them himself and he fears Prince Evan will expose him, even if only to ridicule. Prince Joseph needs to do something. Now, normally he would just have the boy put to death, but he doesn't. Perhaps he had feelings for Prince Evan and couldn't bring himself to do it, even though Prince Evan was unfaithful. Instead he has him put away.'

This was a wild guess, based on what he had learned and what he knew of how Wee Joe worked, and Malky paused to let Gordie say something, but again the man made no move to speak. Malky had outlined most of his ideas to Wee Joe earlier but had skated over his boss's hang-ups about his own sexuality. Malky was gutsy but he wasn't stupid. Even so, it had not been an easy conversation.

Elspeth had paused and Rebecca, who had been mulling it all over as she gazed at the river below, took the opportunity to try some join-the-dots thinking.

'Right, we have Evan Rose, the son of a well-known Edinburgh gangster, involved with Murdo Maxwell, who is a lawyer and political fixer-cum-activist who really should have known better,' she said. 'He breaks it off but agrees to defend Evan on a weapons charge, which Evan claims was set up by this Joseph McClymont, who is also a wrong 'un but from Glasgow, and who Maxwell also had an affair with, according to Dalgliesh.'

'McClymont is gay? That's news. He would not have wanted that to get out. The Glasgow underworld was not known then for its enlightened attitude. Not sure it has moved on much either. And Murdo Maxwell was obviously not one for loving wisely, was he?'

'No, Dalgliesh thought it would bring him down eventually. He was open about his sexuality, defiant about it.'

'Why shouldn't he be?' Elspeth said.

Rebecca knew the question was rhetorical, so she continued her train of thought. 'Now, Evan was known to enjoy a bit of drama. He screams in court that he was being fitted up and that Maxwell was in on it.'

Malky was in full flow now. 'And so, Prince Evan is placed in the tower, thanks to Prince Joseph. Count Murdo tries to defend him, but he is unsuccessful. Prince Evan lies in his cell and he is well pissed off.'

'You're guessing all this, pal,' said Gordie.

'Educated guesses, aye,' said Malky. 'Have I got some bits wrong?'

Gordie sneered. 'I told you—it's your story.'

Malky leaned closer. 'It's no' really, though, is it, Gordie? My story. Okay, I might get some of it wrong, but I think this is broadly the way it happened.'

'Guesswork, son. Pure guesswork. You've got no evidence.'

'Evidence is for polis, Gordie, mate,' said Malky. 'Polis and lawyers. Anyway, in the tower the young prince meets up with another state prisoner. Oh, let's call him Sir Paul.'

Elspeth said, 'So you think it possible that Evan meets Paul Gordon in jail? We can't be certain—but Pete did tell me that when he got out he became a trusted lieutenant of Evan's dad.'

'That fits, and next thing you know Dodger is approached, by Gordon, to kill Maxwell.' Rebecca couldn't keep the excitement from her voice. 'Evan more than likely had keys to Kirkbrig House. After his death, Artie finds them among his stuff, gives them to Gordon, who gives them to Dodger.'

'So, was this Artie getting revenge for his son, blaming Maxwell?'

'Could be.'

'But why make it look like James Stewart did it?'

'That was Dodger's doing. He was canny enough to know he could have been set up himself so he made sure someone else took the blame. Gordon and Rose then used his sister to keep Dodger in line.'

She stopped speaking. Further information, further thought, might smooth off the edges of the theory which she had blurted out very much off the top of her head, but it all seemed to fit.

'Prince Evan dies in that lonely cell atop the tower,' Malky went on. 'Nobody knew he was sick, he didn't know he was sick, but his life and all that had happened took its toll on his poor, weak little brain and killed him. And King Arthur grieved. He was already angry over his son being fitted up by Prince Joseph and had lashed out, but the army of the west was strong and brave.'

Gordie laughed then. 'This *is* a fucking fairy story.'

'I have one question, though,' Rebecca said.

Elspeth laughed. 'Only one?'

'Why didn't Rose move against McClymont?'

'He did. My mate on the newsdesk told me that a few years back there was a wee war between them, west versus the east sort of thing. It ended when McClymont more or less signed over some of their business to Rose. Apparently, Big Rab, Joseph's father, came out of retirement to negotiate personally.'

That must have been what Rebecca's dad had referred to years ago. 'Bloody hell! McClymont senior bought Artie Rose off! Had to be. Is it possible neither father was happy about their boy's homosexuality? And this Big Rab would not have been pleased that he had to smooth everything over and lose territory or whatever.'

'But he still did it.'

'Because it's still his son. Blood being thicker and all that.'

A puff of the cigarette on the end of the line. 'Fathers and sons,' said Elspeth.

'Shame and regret,' said Rebecca. 'That's what this is all about.'

Elspeth added, 'And payback.'

'So business was one thing, but honour and blood dictated that someone had to pay with their life and the treaty meant there was only one person left,' Malky said. 'And so it came to pass that King Arthur ordered the execution of Count Murdo, who had failed to defend his son properly. It was left to Sir Paul to find them a mercenary, someone not connected with King Arthur's forces. The deed was done, the mercenary made it look like someone unconnected to the two kingdoms was responsible and they all lived unhappily ever after.'

Malky left it there. Behind him, on the rocks, he heard the children talking excitedly as they discovered something. At the other table, the couples were taking a group selfie, leaning over the table, the phone on a long stick, the water behind them. There was happiness in the air. Youthful promise, young love. For them, life was all ahead of them and it was something sunny and joyous.

He thought about Evan and Wee Joe. There wasn't much joy there.

Gordie was silent for a long time and Malky let him take it all in. When the man spoke, his voice was low. He stared at the top of the table. 'Artie wasn't ashamed of his boy, far from it. He loved him. But he didn't show it and Evan took that to mean he was disappointed in him because he was gay. He wasn't. What did disappoint him was the lad's drug use and the lack of control it caused.' He looked up and around before he continued, as if making sure no one was listening. 'Sell it, don't use it, you know? Rule number one. Evan never sold it but he used. Nothing heavy, no heroin or anything, but there was grass and there was coke. Made him . . . erratic.'

'Wild,' said Malky.

Gordie shrugged. 'Maybe. Big Rab was different, though. He didn't accept Wee Joe for what he was. Shit, you were right. Wee Joe couldn't accept himself for what he was. Still can't, from what I hear.'

It was Malky's turn to remain silent.

'You're right,' Gordie went on, 'when Evan died, Artie lost the place. He wanted blood and he got it. Big Rab protected his boy and gave up some territory and trade. Artie took it 'cos business is business, you know? That bastard Murdo Maxwell didn't do his job. He could have had Intentional? charges blown out the water, but he didn't. So he had to pay and someone saw to it.'

'You, right? Sir Paul.'

Gordie merely stared across the table at him. Malky hadn't expected him to implicate himself, but he knew he was right. Gordie had been loyal to Artie and to the boy Evan. It was touching in a way.

It wouldn't help him, though.

54

A breeze swung between the branches of the trees in the grounds of Kirkbrig House, finding the wooden chimes and making them clatter against each other as Mona produced the two locks. The Yale and the mortice. They were dark and dusty and Rebecca stared at them, willing them to fit the keys held in Stephen Jordan's hand. They had to fit.

They just had to.

Rebecca had collected her car from the garage—that was a hundred and fifty quid Martin Bailey owed her. It turned out Stephen Jordan couldn't drive, so she was behind the wheel. What man in his thirties, maybe forties, can't drive? she wondered. The answer sat beside her all the way to Appin.

She thought it would be an awkward journey, but it turned out the lawyer was very chatty. Very funny. Even charming. But then they did not speak of matters of great consequence. He asked about her family and she told him of her father and her mother. He told her about his parents, mum and dad still living, former solicitors but both retired now. He had taken over their practice. He was divorced. It didn't work out, was all he said.

A lot of that kind of thing about, she thought.

He didn't ask her about Simon and she wondered if he already knew, though he had said he didn't know Simon at all well. Perhaps he expected her to reciprocate when he told her about his failed marriage but she didn't.

Instead she asked, 'So why are you doing this?'

'What do you mean?'

'Why are you helping Mrs Stewart?'

'I'm following the instructions of my client.'

'But you're not getting paid.'

A tiny smile appeared. 'And we should only be motivated by money?'

She thought about her vow at Keil Chapel to see the story through this time, even if there was no paying customer. 'Okay, point taken.'

He was silent for a few moments. 'Sometimes you have to do something because it's the right thing to do. I do my job because I believe everyone has the right to a defence and a fair trial. That doesn't always happen. The scales of justice are often tipped towards the prosecution and I do what I can to redress the balance.'

'So your clients are all innocent?'

'Certainly not, but I don't think in terms of guilt or innocence. I only think in terms of what can be proved and what can't.'

'But don't you care what these people have done?'

'Of course I do. And I have lost sleep over it. But I go back to my belief that everyone deserves the best defence possible, even paid out of the public pocket. If the Crown brings charges and finances the prosecution, then it should also fund the defence.'

'Why?'

'Because the basic principle of innocent until proven guilty demands that. If someone with no money is charged with a crime and cannot afford a lawyer, then they will be put away without the evidence being properly explored. That's not justice. That's tyranny. In this case, I am doing this because I think it is the right thing to do.'

'So you believed Dodger?'

He thought about this. 'I hear a lot of lies in my job and not just from clients. I believe that what I heard from Mr Dodge was the truth.'

'Why?'

'Because he was dying. Because he needed to get it out there. Because he needed at the last gasp to do something good.'

It was Rebecca's turn to be silent. She drove for another mile before she asked, 'If the keys fit, what's the next step?'

'It's only the beginning, I'm afraid. I can lodge a petition for a further appeal based on the new evidence, basically the keys and Mr Dodge's declaration. I've also had a quick look at some of the details of the original trial and we may be able to put forward an Anderson appeal but that's always risky.'

'What's that?'

'That James had inadequate legal representation. His team didn't make enough of the lack of blood on his body, or even the argument his father had with Maxwell, so we may have wiggle room there.' He wrinkled his nose. 'But that's tenuous, to say the least. We also have the option of approaching the Scottish Criminal Case Review Commission to see if they will investigate and recommend an appeal.'

'Surely that's the best option—letting an official body look into it. Carries more weight, right?'

His short laugh was ironic. 'Yes, you would think so, but the Crown Office and the police can be just as awkward with them as they are with ordinary mortals. However, there is absolutely no suggestion of any official wrongdoing in this case—they did appear to do everything correctly—so perhaps they would be a little more sympathetic.'

Rebecca thought about Sawyer's story being conveniently filed away. In the end it had no bearing but it was still wrong.

'Either way,' Jordan went on, 'there's no guarantee the court will accept this new evidence, even if these keys do fit.'

'Why not?'

'Mr Dodge's statement could be viewed as a special knowledge confession—there are elements of it that might only be known to the real killer—if it had been made at the time. But time has passed. Details were released during the trial and then in the media. I'm sure the Crown will argue that Mr Dodge could have gleaned them that way.'

'But the keys? How would he have the keys?'

'It will help corroborate, I'm certain, but again the Crown might argue that we obtained them from Mona Maxwell.'

'What? They would say that Mona gave us the keys? Why would she do that?'

He smiled. 'I'm not saying they would, I'm just playing devil's advocate here. It's a court of law. Lawyers will say anything that helps their case or casts a doubt.'

'But the keys will help?'

'If they fit.'

Mona set the locks on the kitchen counter and the lawyer laid both keys beside them. All three stared at the items for a second before Jordan picked up the mortice first, inserted the key in the lock.

The moment of truth, Rebecca thought.

Jordan twisted the key.

It seemed to stick.

Shit, she thought.

He took it out, blew on it for some reason, tried again.

It went so far, then stopped.

Double shit.

Mona tutted and vanished into the storeroom again, then reappeared with a can of 3-in-1. Jordan tipped some of the lubricant inside, rotating the nozzle around the opening and then dribbled some on the key itself. He gave Rebecca a look that said *here goes nothing* and inserted the key again.

A pause.

He twisted.

The key turned.

Outside, the chimes gave the breeze a voice.

55

It had been a hard day. The drive to and from Appin had been long, and Rebecca had been tired before it began. She dropped Stephan Jordan off—she suspected he now saw that the media could offer assistance—and then returned to her office to type up the latest story. She didn't send it, she needed quotes from Afua Stewart and the lawyer, neither of which she had. Given she had spent the day with him, that was a serious oversight, but it did show how tired she was. She spoke to Elspeth and they agreed it would wait a day. The story wasn't going anywhere.

It was growing dark and all she wanted to do was to go home, get into bed with some kind of food that was fast and unhealthy, and finally catch up with Mrs Maisel.

As soon as she sniffed the air in her living room, she knew he was there.

Then she felt his hands around her, one around her waist and pinning both arms, the other clasped over her mouth while his aftershave gripped her throat in a stranglehold.

'Hello, bitch,' he breathed in her ear. 'You told the police about me.'

She tried to say something but his hand merely allowed a muffled protest. He didn't want to hear her.

'But you told Finbar, too. First you embarrass me to my neighbours, then you tell the law about me and now my friends.'

Dalgliesh had obviously tracked Bailey down. The notion flitted through her brain that the SG leader had encouraged the man to take this action. Or perhaps it was Ralph who dropped a word. But she couldn't think about that now. She had to quell the panic rising in her mind. She had to focus. She centred on the words of her self-defence instructor, her advice flicking through her mind at speed.

Don't panic. Breathe. Think. Weigh up your opponent.

Bailey wasn't a big man but he was strong. However, he didn't take care of himself. She was young, she was reasonably fit. And now she was angry. This bastard had messed with her, had terrorised her, now he had broken into her home. He was a useless piece of shit and she was done being intimidated by him. She felt the rage build up within her.

Use it. Use that rage. Streamline it. Channel it into your hands and your feet.

She relaxed into his grip and at the same time eased her hips to one side, the movement causing him to momentarily slacken his hold, allowing her to fix her footing, clench her fist and swing it as hard as she could into his groin. She felt his breath explode in her ear as his arms loosened even further, and she jerked her elbow free to jam it with considerable force into his nose. It would hurt, it had to hurt, and it did. He grunted, stepped back but recovered quickly, then roared and lunged at her with both hands. He didn't have a weapon, thankfully.

But she did.

She still had her house key in her hand and she slipped it between her fingers like a spike. He probably thought she would try to get away.

If you can, do the unexpected.

She ducked under his arms and darted the hand with the Yale key out in a slashing movement, jabbing the edge of the Yale under his eyes and scraping it down his cheek. He bellowed again but his hands instinctively went to his face. She danced away once more, saw she had drawn blood. It was little more than a scratch, but it would sting. She couldn't stop there, though. She took a moment to size up the position she was in. He was between her and both front and back doors. The surprise element was gone, he knew she was no pushover, now she had to do more.

She could feel the nerves rising again, making her hands tremble.

Don't let the fear rule you. You rule it. Use it. Use the adrenaline.

He crouched, the blood trickling down his cheek like runny paint, his eyes narrowed, a beast looking for an opening. He expected her to make a break for the door, to perhaps come at him.

Do the unexpected.

She waited. Hoped he couldn't see the quiver in her fingers. She distracted his attention, kept his gaze on her face.

She smiled.

It was a smile that said, 'Come on, scumbag, show me what you've got.' But it was a smile she hoped hid the gut-wrenching terror churning in her stomach and the voice that told her flight was better than fight: 'Get out, get past him, get out, get out, *get out*!'

She ignored the voice. She wouldn't try to escape. She needed him to come to her if this final move was to work. She needed to goad him further.

'That all you've got, Bailey?' she said, her breath stabbing at the words. She swallowed, forced her voice to steady. 'You all talk or what?'

She was pissing him off, she could see that, but he still didn't make any effort to move. Anger, that's what she wanted. She wanted to enrage him. Because when fury took over, he would be out of control. And if he was out of control he would make mistakes. And if he made mistakes, she would capitalise on them.

'God, what kind of man are you?' she goaded. 'Letting a wee lassie beat you, eh?'

His teeth clenched, his jaw tightened, his breathing increased. That's it, pal, let it come, let it take over. I have one move left. She wasn't sure she could pull it off, had only done it in class and even then not for real, but she couldn't let doubt paralyse her. If he attacked, she would have one chance to use it and she had to be ready.

'Come on,' she said, transferring the key from her right hand to her left in another tiny diversion. 'I thought you were going to teach me a lesson. I thought you were going to punish me.'

His rage was nearing boiling point; she felt it sear in the air between them. Any second now, she knew it. Dear Jesus, let this work. If she mistimed it, if she misplaced it, she was done. Any second now.

And then he leapt at her, and it was fast and it was sudden and he would have caught her by surprise if she wasn't ready for it, but she ducked under the right arm that swung her way and she straightened her knees while bringing her right hand—wrist hinged, fingers bent, palm uppermost—crashing into his nose again. He reeled backwards, more blood spraying, but she followed and she hit him again, elbow bending back, straightening, the heel of her hand smashing into flesh and gristle with all the power of her upper arm and her shoulder. All the frustration and fury that had been building within her for many months, all the grief and the heartache gave her strength, and when she connected she felt much of it release, as something inside his nose seemed to snap and his legs gave way and he was falling and whimpering.

Rebecca stood over him as he cursed at her, but there was no weight in his words. It ebbed away with the blood from his nose and the fluid that streamed from his eyes. Even so, she slammed the flat of her shoe into his groin. It was unnecessary but it felt good.

'Tell you one thing, hen,' said a voice, heavily Glaswegian, from the open doorway, 'I wouldn't like to bring you an open pay packet home on a Friday.'

Okay, who the hell was this guy? He was small, dark-haired, maybe in his forties but obviously in better condition than Bailey, who was currently rolling on the floor and groaning. She whirled, ready to defend herself, thinking he was a pal of Bailey's, but the man stepped back and held up his hands.

'Steady there, Buffy,' he said. 'I come in peace.'

'Who are you, then? And what do you want?'

The adrenaline still surged through her bloodstream and she felt invincible. Then she realised that this man was no Martin Bailey and might be harder to deal with.

'Never mind who I am,' he said. 'But I came here to see you.'

Who the hell was this guy? She remained alert. 'Why?'

'There was a bloke from Edinburgh arrested today, possession of heroin—half a kilo. He was in a car with a local boy and the police got a tip-off there was drugs in the boot. They popped him outside his hotel as he was leaving to head back home to Edinburgh. Thought you might want to know.'

'Why?'

'It's a story, isn't it?' He turned to leave. 'And you're a reporter, aren't you?'

'Yes, but why me?'

He stopped at the front door. 'You might be interested in the guy's name. Paul Gordon. Ring any bells?'

And then she found herself staring at the open doorway.

Who the hell was that guy?

Malky dropped his travel bag at his feet but didn't sit down opposite Mo Burke. He wouldn't be in the pub long. He was desperate to get on the road back to Glasgow. He'd had enough Highland air.

'Came to say *adios*,' he said.

She squinted at him through the smoke from the fag in her mouth. Jesus, did this woman ever not smoke?

She asked, 'Got what you came for?'

'More or less.'

'And what about our deal?'

He rested a hand on the back of the chair beside him. 'Been thinking about that. Decided no can do. Sorry.'

Her lips tightened. 'You're going back on your word.'

'Looks like it.'

She took the cigarette from her lips and stubbed it out with extreme prejudice in her ashtray. 'I thought Malky Reid always kept his promises.'

He smiled. 'I like to be unpredictable. Anyway, another guy had a go. Broke into her house through the back door, jumped her when she got home.' Malky saw triumph rise in the woman's eyes. He'd half suspected she had also sent whoever that amateur was and the look confirmed it. He suppressed his annoyance over being used as some sort of back-up. 'Didn't work out too well for him. He's even uglier now than he was before and he's been lifted by the police.'

'And that bitch?'

'Not a scratch. I'm telling you, she's got some moves on her, so she has.' He picked up his bag. 'The thing is, I think after that I would be plain daft to try anything, don't you?'

Mo Burke said nothing further, but the heat in her eyes told him that Rebecca Connolly still had an enemy.

56

I can't shake off this damned headache. It's been thundering away for a couple of days, like a storm in my brain. Gordie says I should go see the prison doctor, but the guys all say he's next to useless so I haven't bothered. Maybe if it keeps up I'll go.

Gordie gets out next week but I still have another year to go and maybe that's the reason for my headache. I'll miss him. He says I'll be okay on the wing, he's got it sorted, but I know that time will once again slow without him around, guiding me, advising me, protecting me. God knows, my own father never did much of that, even though he sent Gordie to me.

He's still talking about sorting Joe and Murdo when he gets out and I've urged him to forget it. I'm still bitter over what Joe did to me, and when I get out I plan to confront him. He feared I would reveal his secret, I understand that, but I would never do such a thing. He was furious with me for two-timing him with Murdo and I get that, too. Given he and Joe had been together, even if briefly, just rubbed salt in the wound. I was a fool. But I wouldn't tell anyone about who Joe really is. Coming out has to be the individual's decision, no one else's, and I suppose I understand the pressures he faces in the Life. No matter how angry at him I was, or am, I would never break that confidence. He has to realise, though, that times have changed, the world has changed. Thanks to his father he still thinks that being gay somehow makes you weak. The truth is it takes a strong person to be what they are.

Perhaps my time inside has been good for me. Time to think. Time to reflect. When I get out I will try to do better. I have had wrong done to me, but doing wrong to others is not the answer. I know that better than anyone. I'll try to build bridges with my father. I'll reach out to Joe, try to clear

279

the air between us. I hurt him and he hurt me back. I scared him and he terrified me. Even Murdo. I still believe he could have done better for me, and I cannot forget, but I will do what I can to forgive. I embarrassed him many times with my anger and I hear he has found someone else now. I wish him happiness.

I have been thinking about that butterfly I saw. It had to go through a lot in its short life. It had to survive as a caterpillar on the ground, then the time of darkness as a pupa before it emerged as a different creature. I wonder if I have experienced a similar metamorphosis. Perhaps this time in prison will allow me to put aside my early life. Maybe I can learn to fly.

I need to stop writing. This head is not letting up. Tomorrow I'll ask to see the doctor. I know the guys say he's only here because he couldn't make it in general practice but surely he can sort a headache.

Artie Rose closed the cheap little notebook and stared through the window as the car sped along the country road. Hedges flicked past in a green blur, now and then opened up for a glimpse of a field before another hedge zoomed in to obscure it.

He closed his eyes and thought about his son. He thought about how he had failed him. Evan was part of him, but he had more or less turned his back on him because he hadn't measured up to what he believed was the mark of a man. Then when he found out he had been having it away with—of all people—Rab McClymont's son, that had been too much to bear. He was not fond of Big Rab, but at least they were on the same wavelength. He hated dealing with Wee Joe, though. There was something creepy about that little shit.

Artie knew the weapons charge was a load of bollocks. Evan was many things—a bit wild, yes, even immoral—but he wasn't crooked. There was no way he was an underworld armourer, no way at all. Artie knew the boy had been fitted up and should have hit back harder, but in the end he had only used it to further business. Sure, there had been blood spilled on both sides but no one died. Big Rab was ashamed of his son. All he wanted was to paper everything over with a layer of money. And Artie was more than glad to oblige because profit was more important than family. At least that's what he thought. According to his diary Evan may have found some sort of peace, but Artie never had. He remained angry at what had occurred and in his world someone had to pay. The McClymonts paid with money, and Maxwell, who had seriously blown his defence as far as Artie was concerned, paid with blood.

Gordie had been trying to find out what exposure they had, but it turned out it really wasn't necessary because it was all hitting the bloody internet faster than he could uncover it. He phoned him from Inverness right after his sit-down with that Glasgow boy who had pieced a lot together, which was impressive. Bright guy, that Malky. Artie remembered him well. Tough cookie, too. Bright and tough was hard to come by.

Gordie getting himself arrested yesterday showed this wasn't over. No way was he carrying heroin, unless the boy they hired to drive him about was dealing, but Artie doubted that. That half-kilo had Wee Joe's fingerprints all over it, figuratively speaking. He would have to deal with that, once and for all. This time there was nothing Big Rab could do to smooth things over. It was time that wee bastard was seen to.

Artie knew there would be some hard questions coming his way, if the police followed up on the press reports. He hadn't been named, of course, but they had covered Dodger's confession. Artie wasn't too worried. No way could they connect Maxwell's murder to him, not enough to stand up in court, and Gordie was solid. He wouldn't grass, no matter what they offered him.

'Cop up ahead,' said Ray, his driver, and Artie craned past his head to see a uniform waving them down, another standing on the grass verge, his hands behind his back like he was in the chorus of *The Pirates of Penzance*. Artie liked a bit of Gilbert and Sullivan. The refrain from 'A Policeman's Lot Is Not A Happy One' ran through his head. The bumbling law in that story was just how Artie pictured real-life police. More than once they had screwed up cases against him, never seriously laid a glove on him. Because he was bright as well as tough. And he had money, which came in handy too. There was always someone whose greed was greater than his integrity.

'Better see what they want, Ray,' he said, laying his son's notebook on the seat beside him.

Ray slowed and the waving cop leaned in towards the driver's side window as it slid down. 'Sorry, gents, there's been an accident along the road there and it's completely blocked. You'd be best to go back unless you don't mind waiting.'

Shit, Artie thought. He had an appointment in quarter of an hour. 'How long do you think it will be?' he asked and the cop craned down to look at him.

'An eternity, mate,' he said.

Artie saw Ray's head erupt before he registered the sound of the gun and the glass smashing on the other side of the car. He saw the second officer, an automatic in his hand, already turning his way. So that was what he had behind his back, he realised, before he heard the first cop say, 'Wee Joe sends his regards.'

Artie Rose's blood sprayed across the brown cover of his son's note-book.

57

Six months later

The rain swept across Edinburgh's Parliament Square, but the photographers and reporters clustered in the car park didn't seem to care. They had a job to do and rain was not going to stop them. Rebecca stood under cover on the walkway that ran along the front of the dark stone buildings that housed the Court of Session. She had no need to form part of the crowd, no need to shout questions or call for faces to be turned this way or that. She had done her job. She had written her stories. Now she was only a witness.

On the west coast, 130 miles away, the wind swept in from the Atlantic, soared over and around Mull and Lismore, sailing on the surface of the loch, snatching moisture as it travelled towards land . . .

The actual hearing the week before had played out in the quiet, civilised manner of the British court. No histrionics, no drama, no tables pounded. The appeal stood or fell on Dodger's affidavit and the keys. In the end Jordan and the QC decided to soft pedal the inadequate legal representation angle. It would be a hard sell.

The Advocate Depute had mounted a spirited attack. As Rebecca sat in the hard benches that stretched back and up in the small courtroom she was reminded of Finbar Dalgliesh's belief that the system must not be undermined by any notion that it was fallible. The three red-robed Lordships sat above the lawyers and staff, the Scottish Coat of Arms behind them with its rampant unicorns and Latin admonishment that no one would provoke the nation with impunity. The judges gave nothing away as they listened and noted and queried.

The wind hit the front of the Village Inn in Kilnacaple, probed the open interior of the old kirk, swirled loose sand on the golden beach made drab by the dull light and rocked the boats moored in the small jetty, as if it was trying to set them free . . .

And all the while James Stewart sat in the dock, flanked by two prison officers. He looked older than his years but Rebecca assumed prison was no holiday camp, especially for someone who was not in any way a criminal. Even though he had been granted interim liberation four months before, pending his appeal, his complexion was sallow, for his time at home with his mother had not burnished his skin in any way. Free he had been, but Rebecca had spoken to him many times and the fear of returning to jail was a constant. He had been let down once by the legal system and it could happen again. He had no illusions.

It carried up the hill, following the road, diverting through the gorse and the grass and the trees, investigating the gardens of the cottages, enquiring at bins and garden furniture as if it was in search of something . . .

That morning he sat there again in his best suit. The prison officers on either side stared straight ahead as if they were wax dummies. The mace was hung in its bracket and the judges filed into their seats, their faces grave. The Advocate Depute and the QC representing James listened as they spoke, saying nothing, for their part in this drama was over. Now it was the judges' turn to take centre stage and to present their soliloquies to the audience. They gave nothing away. They went over what had been said in court. They outlined the cases for and against.

But then she heard the words 'I find there was a miscarriage of justice in this case.'

And a murmur grew in the court. She saw Afua's hand dart to her mouth. She saw Mona's mouth thin into her curious little smile.

Two out of the three appeal court judges had been sufficiently convinced by Dodger's confession—one even referred to it as very much a dying declaration—and so were persuaded there was sufficient doubt to set aside the conviction. Only one demurred and Rebecca wondered if he was doing it to protect a system that he felt must be deemed infallible, or if he truly felt the appeal had no grounds.

It didn't matter. After ten years, James Stewart was free.

The wind climbed the hill, whirled around the main road, buffeting the cars, forcing drivers to twitch and grip the steering wheels tighter . . .

And as she stood looking at the press scrum outside the building, the rain draping itself over the people, the cars, the statues, the daunting stone walls of St Giles' Cathedral, Rebecca felt something inside her uncoil. She had not been certain how it would go, neither had Stephen Jordan. But now, as she stood there in the damp Scottish weather, hoping it wouldn't wash off what was left of the tan she had gained after two weeks in the sun, she relaxed. It was over.

The wind shook the high hedge surrounding Kirkbrig House and bent the bare branches hanging over the top. It careered across the garden, disturbing fallen leaves, sending them fluttering in the air like startled birds, searching always searching, and slammed into the sturdy walls of the house itself.

As James spoke quietly to reporters, answering their questions politely but concisely, Afua Stewart stood by his side, her hand on his arm. She looked over her shoulder and found Rebecca. Afua was unsmiling—her opinion of the press hadn't changed, but she knew this circus was necessary. She stared at Rebecca for a few seconds then, slowly, she dipped her head. As a thanks it didn't seem much, but Rebecca knew it meant everything.

The wind veered, tested windows for weakness and picked at slates on the roof. It slid between the spare branches of the trees and blades of anaemic grass until, finally, it found what it was looking for.

The chimes.

It snatched at them, swinging them back and forth. To and fro. Here and there.

They clattered and jangled as if sounding an alarm and the wind attacked the tiles, surrounded them, attacked again, pulling and snatching and grasping and tugging at the thin wire that held them to the branch of the tree until at last it snapped and the chimes fell.

The pieces moved once more as the gale proclaimed its victory with a final gust, one final rattle, before they fell still forever.

And the wind moved on, its song at last one of triumph.

Author's Note and Acknowledgements

Please note that the village of Kilnacaple, Kirkbrig House and the part of Inverness I've called Inchferry are figments of my imagination, as are associated legends. All other places are real, as is the story of James of the Glens.

As usual, I have many people to thank for either reading the book during the writing process or offering information and/or advice. Author Denzil Meyrick provided a solution to an issue that arose during the editing process and also provided feedback on the entire book, as did Caro Ramsay, Michael J. Malone, Gordon Brown and Neil Broadfoot. I am hugely indebted to Jane Hamilton for her input, to Stephen Wilkie, Laura Thomson, Margaret Chrystall and David Kerr for some vital information, and Iain MacPherson for his help with the Gaelic phrases. Special thanks must go to Tanaka Natalie Musakambeva for her advice.

Once again, my gratitude goes to all the book bloggers, booksellers, book readers (in whatever format) and book festival organisers who have supported my work over the years. I've said it before and I'll say it again, I couldn't do it without you.

Thanks must also go to Polygon—Hugh Andrew, Alison Rae and all the staff—for all their hard work, as well as my editor, Debs Warner.

And a big hand goes to my agent, Jo Bell, who has kept me grounded.

About the Author

Douglas Skelton was born in Glasgow. He has been a bank clerk, tax officer, taxi driver (for two days), wine waiter (for two hours), journalist and investigator. He has written eleven true crime and Scottish criminal history books but now concentrates on fiction. *A Rattle of Bones* and *Thunder Bay*, the first Rebecca Connolly thriller, were longlisted for the McIlvanney Prize for best crime book of the year, as was his novel *Open Wounds*. He is now at work on the next Rebecca Connolly thriller and lives in southwest Scotland.